Praise for *Diamond in the Ruff*

"Carmichael is a master at delivering
fresh and funny books!" —*Romantic Times*

"Piggy's story is great fun." —*Booklist*

"Reading [Piggy's] combination of woman's sexy
wiles and canine instincts is hysterical, as is watching her
worry whenever her human mind is swamped beneath
doggy delights." —*Corgi Currents*

Praise for the work of
EMILY CARMICHAEL

"[*Finding Mr. Right*] has the irresistible warmth and
charm of a newborn puppy." —*Publishers Weekly*

"Fabulous . . . one of the most imaginative writers
working in historical romance." —*Affaire de Coeur*

"I howled with laughter. . . .
Emily Carmichael is a writer to savor!"
—Teresa Medeiros, bestselling author
of *A Kiss to Remember*

"Historical favorite Emily Carmichael expands into new
territory and quickly exposes her flair for both humor
and contemporary romance. . . . This delightful book
[has] a wickedly entertaining edge."
—*Romantic Times*

"Emily Carmichael's style is entertaining and her characters
are a delight. Fun and frolic! A nest full of laughs!"
—*The Literary Times*

THE GOOD, THE BAD, AND THE SEXY

Emily Carmichael

BANTAM BOOKS

New York   Toronto   London   Sydney   Auckland

The Good, the Bad, and the Sexy

A Bantam Book/June 2002

All rights reserved.
Copyright © 2002 by Emily Krokosz

No part of this book may be reproduced or transmitted in any form
or by any means, electronic or mechanical, including photocopying,
recording, or by any information storage and retrieval system,
without permission in writing from the publisher.
For information address: Bantam Books.

ISBN 0-553-58284-4

Published simultaneously in the United States and Canada

Bantam Books are published by Bantam Books, a division of Random
House, Inc. Its trademark, consisting of the words "Bantam Books" and the
portrayal of a rooster, is Registered in U.S. Patent and Trademark Office
and in other countries. Marca Registrada. Bantam Books, 1540 Broadway,
New York, New York 10036.

PRINTED IN THE UNITED STATES OF AMERICA

OPM   10   9   8   7   6   5   4   3   2

THE GOOD,
THE BAD,
AND THE SEXY

CHAPTER 1

⸻

♡

JACKSON STONE WAS a mess. Blood was everywhere. And the oozing wound on his leg wasn't exactly appetizing.

Maybe he should wash off the gore before lunch. But after a morning chasing drug runners through the southern Arizona desert, not to mention being beaten to a pulp by said drug runners, his tanks were on empty. If he took time to shower, all the salami sandwiches would be gone. He'd be stuck with ham, or worse, bologna. You would think a big film company working in the back of beyond would fly in enough salami so that everyone who wanted salami could have salami.

Right then the thought of any kind of a sandwich made his mouth water. For the fifth time in the last hour he lay down in the scorching sand, supposedly unconscious, while his partner awaited his cue to leap to the rescue. When this take was finally in the can, he decided, salami first, then a shower.

"Cut!" Dave Goldman yelled. "Dammit, Rick! You missed your goddamned cue again! What do you want? An engraved invitation?"

Jackson opened his eyes in time to see Rick Carroll step onto the set and pull a grimace.

"Sorry."

"Sorry," Goldman whined, dripping sarcasm. He was short, rotund, and resembled a bald teddy bear, but his unimpressive stature didn't keep him from being one of the most intimidating directors in the film industry. In his day he'd chewed up and spit out the likes of Harrison Ford and Clint Eastwood. A pipsqueak rock star turned movie actor didn't even make him blink. "He's sorry!" he snarled. "How many times do we have to shoot this scene to get a take? Goddamned amateurs!"

The female lead tossed her tousled blond hair and a sinister-looking drug lord leaned against a dusty Lincoln Navigator, watching with a smile as one of the "good guys" got his butt chewed. Reluctantly surrendering his visions of salami, Jackson sprang up, carefully preserving the fake blood splashed about his leg, chest, and shoulder. "How about some water over here? I've got enough dirt in my mouth to plant potatoes."

He and the director exchanged looks, and The Goldman reluctantly abandoned his tirade.

"Ten minute break, everybody, and then we're going to shoot this again. And I swear anyone who flubs a line or ruins this take is going to get his ass fired. That's a promise!" As a production assistant handed out cold bottles of Aquafina, he growled, "Water! Dammit, where's a bottle of whiskey when I need it?"

Jackson chuckled. "On the wagon again, Dave? That why you're such a bear?"

"Watch it, Stone. The mood I'm in, I might even fire *your* ass."

The production assistant looked horrified. Jackson smiled and gave her a good-natured wink. No film director, not even David Goldman, was going to fire Jackson Stone, and Jackson knew it.

"Take it easy on Carroll, Dave. This film's his big break. He's nervous."

"The kid's stupid."

"Rick Carroll has teenage hearts throbbing all over America and Europe. Do you know how much money teenagers spend on movies?"

"He's still stupid."

"I suppose you were never young and stupid?"

"Damned right I wasn't. Not that stupid."

Jackson smiled dryly. "Right. I wasn't, either."

Dave cast his eyes toward the sky, as if seeking help from on high. "Two more days of good shooting. Just give me two more days, and we'll wrap this puppy up on time and only slightly over budget. Is that so much to ask?" He looked sideways at Jackson and changed the subject abruptly. "The scuttlebutt is, your wife is going to get an Oscar for her Queen Elizabeth."

"*Ex-wife,* Dave. Very important. Ex-wife. Melanie was a natural for that part. QE I was one of her former lives, according to her."

"Whatever. It was a dynamite performance."

"I never said she doesn't have talent."

"So I would count it a favor if you'd put in a good word with her for the script Dreamworks just sent her. I'm directing."

"Mel doesn't listen to a thing I say, Dave."

"Ah, c'mon, Jackson. What about the rumor of you two getting back together after all this time? What's it been? Five years since the divorce?"

"Six. Been reading Josh Digby's column in the *Star,* have you? Don't you know that son of a bitch makes up stories out of thin air?"

Goldman grunted. "You and Mel are seen together a lot."

"We're friends. Sometimes. And sometimes we're not friends. Right now, Mel would rather annoy me than do me favors."

"Just employ a little of that famous Stone charm."

Jackson chuckled. "All right, Dave. For you, I'll try."

"That's my man. Now, you ready to get beat up again?"

"Bring it on."

Forty minutes later Dave had his take, and Jackson headed for a cold beer and air-conditioning in his trailer. Late July was hell in the southern Arizona desert.

His young co-star fell into step beside him. "Hey, Jackson. Thanks, man. I overhead what you said to Deadly Dave back there when I screwed up."

"Everyone screws up, Rick."

"Well, yeah, but I appreciate it, man. It was big of you. You know, some guys would've taken the chance to stab me in the back. Competition, you know. Not wanting to share the spotlight."

Jackson grinned. "Didn't think of that. Maybe I'll go back and tell Dave to toss you off the set."

Rick's baby blues widened for just a moment, then he grinned. "Right." He gave Jackson a manly punch on the shoulder and laughed. "I'm headed for the roach coach. Wanna come?"

Somehow, that salami sandwich just wouldn't have the same flavor eaten in Rick's company. "Not today. Got business."

"Yeah. I see you do."

A statuesque assistant to the assistant to the assistant producer intercepted them.

"Nice business," Rick gibed. "Hey, Carrie."

"Hey, Ricky." The twenty-something redhead gave the younger man a friendly smile, but when that smile settled on Jackson, it heated up. "I have a pitcher of margaritas in the motel freezer," she told Jackson. "Call me after shooting if you're interested."

She gave him a simmering smile as she left. Jackson and Rick both followed her retreating figure with appreciative eyes.

"Man, how do you do that?"

"Do what?" Jackson asked as they came up to his trailer.

"Handle babes like that? Every one of the hot ladies on this set has eyes for you, man. And not one of them seems to mind that you spread yourself around like butter on toast. They all know you're stepping out with everything female in a ten-mile radius."

Jackson raised a brow. "I'm not quite that active."

"Don't get me wrong, man. I'm in awe. Abject admiration."

Jackson resigned himself. If he wanted his beer and airconditioning, he was obviously going to have to invite the kid in for a few minutes. Rick accepted the invitation with alacrity. Jackson popped two cold ones and handed one to his guest.

"I wish I had your moves," Rick said. "You've got Carrie, Kendra, and Shirley all drooling over you. And didn't you take Sara Byron to the Golden Globe Awards? She is hot. Absolutely volcanic."

"From what I've seen, you don't do too bad yourself, Rick."

"Oh, yeah. No complaints. But last time I tried playing the field, I nearly got my eyes scratched out."

"There's a lesson there."

"What?"

"If you just want to have fun, go with women who want the same thing. Stay away from the ladies who want commitment until you're ready to commit. Simple as that. Be honest. Be direct. Don't promise what you're not going to deliver."

"Sounds right."

Jackson took a long pull on his Michelob. "The women I go out with are terrific. They're fun. They like good company and a good time but want to keep their independence. And they let me keep mine."

"And they stay friendly after you dump them."

"I've never dumped a woman."

"Well, for sure no woman is going to dump Jackson Stone."

"We reach a friendly mutual agreement." That was the way he and Mel had broken up—friendly mutual agreement. They agreed they weren't good for each other. Most of the time they managed to stay on friendly terms. The tabloids made a big deal of their occasionally going to dinner or showing up together at a party, but then, the tabloids tried to make a big deal of everything.

" 'Friendly mutual agreement,' " Rick echoed. "I like that. Maybe I should give it a try," Rick said. "It might limit the fireworks. But it seems like a dude your age would be looking for a permanent lady. You know"—his eyes crinkled puckishly—"someone to enjoy retirement with once I totally eclipse you on the big screen."

Jackson laughed. "Dream on, kid. You're not ready for my parts or my ladies. And you'll learn sooner or later that permanent relationships don't mix well with celebrity. It's one of the prices you pay. Most of us learn the hard way."

"That's a fact!" Rick grinned and tossed his beer bottle into the recycling can, a perfect shot. "Gotta go, man. Thanks for the beer."

"Anytime."

Alone at last, Jackson breathed in a welcome drag of air-conditioning and considered his options. Salami or shower?

Shower, he decided. Then sandwich. And another beer. He peeled off his shirt and tossed it in the laundry basket, but before he could turn on the shower, Harvey Mathias, his personal assistant, banged through the trailer door without knocking and slammed a newspaper down on the table.

Once a linebacker for the Nebraska Huskers, Harvey looked ready to tackle someone. "Did you read the garbage Helen Gordon wrote in the *Times* today?"

Helen Gordon was one of L.A.'s foremost critics. She criticized films, plays, actors, producers, directors, screenwriters, the mayor and city council, and just about anyone else who wandered within range. And all too frequently, The Powers That Be in the film industry listened to what she said.

"If it was about me," Jackson said, "I doubt it was anything good. She thinks I have about as much talent as a piece of white bread."

"Read!" Harvey invited.

Jackson picked up the paper, which was folded to Helen's column. He scanned through the paragraphs concerning other unfortunates who had merited the woman's attention and found the speculation that Touchstone was talking to him about taking the lead in a gritty, Steinbeck-like story set among struggling farm families in 1950s Kansas. Her speculation, as usual, was right on target. Touchstone was talking, and he was listening. The role would be a departure from his usual thrillers and gunpowder-stained westerns—a departure his career needed, if he was to keep making films once the public discovered a newer, younger action hero to root for.

He read:

> Touchstone will ensure the film's mediocrity if they cast Stone, whose box-office draw is considerably more substantial than his versatility. Despite Stone's nod from the Academy for *Second Sight*, this role

calls for someone with more grit than good looks, and if Stone has grit, he certainly hasn't shown it so far. I doubt the man has ever seen the business end of a shovel or has a pair of work gloves in his wardrobe. Director Howard doesn't need a manicured mannequin for this role; he needs someone who knows what it's like to get his hands dirty and blistered in the real world, where doubles don't stand in for the hard parts.

"The bitch," Harvey spat.

Jackson merely chuckled. "Don't worry about it. Helen thinks actors need to pay their dues by suffering through years of manual labor and poverty before getting a break. Teaching English Lit in community college doesn't qualify. Besides, she doesn't like me. Never has."

"Trouble is, Touchstone might listen."

"If they do, it's their loss. Don't lose sleep over it."

Harvey snorted. "Have you had lunch?"

"You just squashed my appetite. Why don't you get out of here? I'm going to take a shower."

Harvey got up.

"And take Ms. Gordon with you."

When the trailer door shut behind Harvey and the poison pen column, Jackson grimaced. "Damned old biddy," he grumbled. "I'd like to see Helen Gordon with a few well-placed blisters of her own."

Jackson had just stepped out of the shower when his cell phone tweedled. Dripping a puddle onto the tile, he sighed. "What now?"

The voice of his ex-wife crackled in his ear.

"Melanie, I can't understand a thing you're saying." *Not all that unusual,* he mused sourly. "Slow down."

"Jackson, darling, where are you? I called the beach house, and you weren't there. I was hoping you'd take me to the Queen Elizabeth opening."

So they could start yet another set of rumors, Jackson

thought. Mel did love publicity of any kind. "I'm still on location."

"Running late? Dave must be in a fit."

"Yeah. He's not real happy."

"I warned him that he started shooting on exactly the wrong date! Jupiter was in retrograde. Ignore the stars and you always end up sorry."

"Dave has a long history of ignoring stars, Mel. You and me included."

She missed a beat, then hmphed. "You are *so* not funny, as always, bonehead."

Jackson had to grin. Annoying Mel had once been a specialty of his.

"Anyway, Jackie, that's not why I called, exactly."

Jackie? Mel was good at annoyance also.

"All right, Mel, why did you call?"

"Well . . ."

Jackson suffered an evil premonition. "Well *what*?"

"It's Cherie."

His heart skipped a beat. "Is she all right?"

"Of course she's all right. I am her mother, Jackson. I'm a perfectly responsible parent on the rare occasions you allow her to visit me."

"Then, what?"

"You always jump to conclusions. That's so typical of you, Jackie. And that's why I called to warn you ahead of time, so you could center yourself and be cool when you see Cherie."

His eyes narrowed. "And why would I need to be cool?"

"Because when it comes to fatherhood you are so nineteenth century, truly you are. You would lock my child up and let her experience nothing and no one until she's thirty. I know how you are."

"This from the woman who'd wanted to take our daughter for training in spiritualism when she was five years old. Spit it out, Mel."

"Don't use that tone with me, Jackson."

"Now!"

"It's no huge deal, so don't get melodramatic. Cherie went shopping with her friends Deanna and Cyndie. Now I find out it was a prank, and the friends were in on it. She's gone on an adventure with Jimmy Toledo, that rocker from Boy Toys. He's the one—"

"I know who the hell he is. For crissakes, Melanie, how long have they been gone?"

"I'd say they've been on the road a couple of hours."

"Christ! Get the police on them. Cherie's only thirteen!"

"Jackson, that would make Cherie feel so . . . well, punished."

"Not half as punished as she's going to feel once I get her home!"

"Jackson, calm down. I knew you were going to react like this. It's not like Jimmy's an ax murderer or anything. He's not going to hurt her."

"I'm going to string Jimmy Toledo up by his nipple rings when I catch up to those two. And Cherie is spending the rest of her life grounded, in a locked cell."

"You're just contributing all sorts of negative energy to this—"

"You haven't seen negative energy yet, Mel. Where are they headed?"

"How should I know?"

"Did you ask Cherie's little co-conspirators?"

"They won't rat on her. They're very loyal to Cherie."

"They'll talk to me. I guarantee it."

"I'm feeling that negative energy again."

"I'm flying in, Melanie. Give me"—he glanced at his watch—"three hours, max. Have those featherbrained girls waiting and scared, and call the police."

"I'm not calling the police. This is just another one of Cherie's little escapades, and I won't see her humiliated and embarrassed. And one more little thing. The press seems to have gotten wind of this somehow. I think maybe one of the girls called the tabloids for kicks. I got a call from Josh Digby of the *National Star* an hour ago."

"Christ! Mel, you didn't say anything to him?"

"Well, no. Of course not."

That was all he needed—Josh Digby making a major story out of this. "I'm going to hang Josh Digby by his toes if he goes anywhere near Cherie!"

"Jackson, try to calm down. And don't you dare get all gruff with poor Cherie. She's experimenting with experience. I've met Jimmy a time or two. He's not that bad. I think what it is, Jackson, is that they have a karmic issue between them."

Jackson muttered a curse, then took a deep breath and tried to speak with patience into the phone. "Call the police, Melanie. I mean it!"

"If you insist on coming, Jackie, then I guess I'll see you in a few hours. Try to get a grip on the way here, won't you?"

Jackson resisted the impulse to throw the phone against the wall. Instead, he bellowed out the trailer door for Harvey. "Call the airport and tell them to fuel my plane. And tell Dave that I'm going to be out of pocket for a day or so. Personal emergency. He can shoot around me."

Harvey looked alarmed. "What's wrong?"

Jackson just shook his head in disgust. "If you ever have kids, don't let them grow up to be teenagers."

More than a hundred miles away and nearly a day later, Rachel Marsh squinted at the morning sun as it lifted over the pine-clad Arizona mountains. This was a daily ritual that she loved—watching the sun's first rays color the air with morning gold. Sunlight first touched a treeless expanse of pasture—known locally as a *cienega*—then the riding arena, the corrals, the smokehouse, and the two big barns. Next turned to gold was the bunkhouse, empty now of the crew, who started their day long before the sun got up, then the Chuckwagon dining hall, from which drifted the fragrance of bacon and cinnamon buns. Finally sunlight crept over the line of guest cabins at forest's edge, stretching to touch the big log ranch house, where Rachel sat rocking in the front-porch swing and smiling at the sight of morning stealing over her beloved home.

"Morning, Rachel!" Moira Keane greeted her cheerfully as she walked from the barn with a full pail of milk and a basket of fresh eggs. "Beautiful day, isn't it?"

"It is," Rachel called back. She sucked in a lungful of cool July air. How she loved these early mountain mornings. The deep, pure blue of the sky, the scent of pine-freshened air, the tranquil peace of a world just beginning to wake. Patches of ground fog cast the meadow in otherworldly mystery. A bird trilled a greeting to the new day.

The Lazy M Ranch had been home to the Marsh family for four generations, a matter of pride and heritage—or so said the splashy four-color brochure that lured city folk to the ranch for a few days of recreation and hospitality. For three years now, Rachel and her son, Sam, had been the only Marshes left. Rachel kept the Lazy M alive by catering to guests—city slickers, Sam called them—lodged in the neat small cabins that snuggled among the pines. Because vacationers would pay to indulge their fantasies of the west, the Lazy M survived in the face of falling beef prices and rising expenses. The guest fees maintained the ranch buildings, fed the livestock, and paid the ranch hands.

Every morning Rachel thanked heaven she no longer worked in Phoenix, where the air smelled of car exhaust, the ground sprouted asphalt and concrete instead of grass and trees, and a pale sky shimmered with dust and heat. She was done with that. Done with other things as well—climbing the corporate ladder, keeping up with the Joneses, worrying about bad hair days and projecting the right image.

Rachel got up, stretched mightily, and ambled over to the main barn, where seven horses stood tethered by their halter ropes to the corral. They fidgeted and snorted, stamping the dew-damp ground. Nearby stood seven expectant riders in brand-new cowboy boots and store-clean cowboy hats. They also fidgeted and stomped, trying to send blood through cold limbs and revive the feeling in their feet while the Lazy M wrangler and Sam saddled the horses.

Rachel couldn't suppress a smile at the sight of Sam working so diligently. The hands called him "Baby Face," much to the boy's embarrassment. At the advanced age of eleven, he wanted to both look and act the part of a man. He took his role of "cowboy" very seriously, and in truth, he was more responsible than some of the hands who lived in the bunkhouse. But Rachel was glad that he still looked like her baby. Cherubic curly blond hair was a gift from his father. The angelic blue eyes he'd inherited from Rachel.

At Sam's side, as always, was Chesterfield, his border collie. Chesty did more work around the Lazy M than most of the hands, and he was smarter than most of them, too.

Sam glanced Rachel's way and spared her a brief smile. Then he focused his attention on tightening the latigo strap of Daisy's saddle. A cowboy couldn't pay too much attention to his mom, after all. One of the city slickers might see and think he was a sissy.

Rachel shifted her gaze to the shivering guests. They hugged themselves, bounced up and down, and generally tried to generate body heat. "You folks look like someone stuck icicles up your jeans. We're going to have to toughen you up."

A chubby, fortyish schoolteacher slapped herself with her arms. "You know it's probably ninety-five degrees in Phoenix right now."

Rachel laughed. "That's why you're not in Phoenix, right?"

A middle-aged couple huddled with their teenage daughter. "I've lived in the desert forty years," the father said. "It's turned my blood thin."

"You'll warm up once you're on the trail, believe me! Paul's the best wrangler in Arizona, and Dennis is one of our best hands. They're going to make sure you have a great time today. You're going to love the picnic spot. It's the prettiest little lake in Arizona. More of the staff are going to meet you up there with steaks you can cut with a fork."

Louis, a stuffed-shirt from Albany, tried to achieve a cowboy drawl. "Hell, ma'am. We'll just cut ourselves out a steer and get our own steaks."

Rachel tried to picture dumpy Louis cutting out one of the ill-tempered range cows. She smiled at the picture. "You do that, Louis, and I'll hire you as a hand around here."

His wife, Cordelia, snickered "I doubt the wages would match his corporate salary."

Louis threw her a look. "No, but it would be a lot more fun."

"Okay, folks," wrangler Paul Brown called out in a good-natured voice. "Mount up. We're going to make cowboys out of you greenhorns yet."

The guests milled about like confused cattle, but Paul was accustomed to the herd mentality. So was young Sam and his canine pal, Chesty.

Paul pointed Louis toward a lanky bay mare. "You ride old Daisy today, Louis. Just watch her head when you mount. She sometimes likes to take a nip." Paul helped the man guide his left foot into the stirrup, then gave him a boost into the saddle.

Meanwhile, Sam guided Cordelia to a pretty chestnut. One horse over, Rachel assisted a hesitant teenage girl into the saddle. "The horse's left side," she instructed. "Always left. You'll confuse the horse if you mount on the right."

"No more confused than I am," the teenager muttered, rolling her eyes. "Left, right—why should the horse care, for crying out loud?" With the flexibility of youth she stepped in the stirrup, grabbed the saddle horn, and pulled herself up, only to narrowly miss going off the other side. The girl muttered a string of words that earned a glare from her father.

"Sit up straight," Rachel advised the girl. "This is a good little mare. She'll give you a great ride. Just try not to keep the reins so tight. It hurts her mouth."

Paying scant attention, the girl looked around the ranch yard, eyes searching. Rachel had a good idea whom she sought. Just the evening before she had called Toby Whitman, her youngest ranch hand, onto the carpet for flirting with their winsome little guest. The girl had certainly encouraged him, but the ranch hands were strictly forbidden to fraternize with the "greenhorns." Eighteen-year-old Toby fancied himself a ladies' man, though, and more often than not he thought the rules didn't apply to him. One more incident and that boy would find his duffle bag packed and on the front stoop of the bunkhouse.

She gave the long-suffering mare a pat and moved on to help the chubby schoolteacher, who clung to the saddle horn as if it were the only thing holding her on the horse.

"The saddle horn isn't going to hold you on, Susan. Your legs are. Sit up, heels down, toes slightly out, and keep your butt under you."

The schoolteacher laughed. "There's too much of it to keep under me, don'tcha know. Your cook here isn't helping. The food's too good."

"I'll tell Joanne you said so."

Rachel liked this batch of guests. They were good-natured, good-humored, and funny. She was glad they were staying for another week. Louis and Cordelia Armstrong were the only two she would be glad to see the back of when they left. The tension between them created sparks wherever they went, reminding Rachel that being alone had its advantages.

The only other trouble spot was the enticing teenager who was luring Toby into hot water. The girl was feeling her oats, and poor Toby had more hormones than sense. Rachel didn't want to see the kid get himself into trouble. She wasn't completely unsympathetic. Rachel could remember what it was like to have a crush, to suffer from a flood of hormones that washed all common sense from the brain. Not lately, she admitted, but there had been a time.

Finally all the guests were mounted, had both feet in the stirrups, and were upright, sort of. As Chesty paced officiously up and down the line of horses to make sure that everything was going along smoothly, Paul grinned and motioned them forward. "Head 'em up! Move 'em out!"

"Very funny," one of the guests groaned.

As they rode out, Paul pulled his chestnut gelding to a halt beside her.

"Quite a crew we have this weekend," the wrangler commented.

"Business is pretty good," Rachel agreed.

"I got in a new horse. Blood bay mare in stall six. Name's Sally. I'd appreciate your taking her out and working her a bit, decide if you want your people on her."

"I'll do that this afternoon. By then I'll need a break."

"Appreciate it. She's a good horse. A little frisky, is all. See what you think." With a wave, he was off to ride drag behind the slowest of the greenhorns. With the wrangler on station, Chesty gave a farewell bark to the departing group and ran across the meadow to rejoin Sam.

Rachel put a hand on her son's shoulder. "You want to ride with me this afternoon?"

"Yup." Cowboys didn't speak more words than necessary.

"If you ask Joanne to scare us up some lunch, we'll make a picnic of it."

"Sure thing, Ma. Right now me and Chesty's gonna go brand some horses."

Though Sam had his own flesh-and-blood horse, he also had a collection of stick horses he'd carved from small pine branches. Using a wood-burning set that had been a gift from his grandfather, he decorated his wooden horses with brands from everywhere in the West.

"Chesty and I are going to go brand horses," Rachel corrected automatically.

"Uh . . . yeah. That's it."

"Have fun."

Left alone in the ranch yard, Rachel stared after the mounted expedition riding off into the trees. Most of her guests resembled sacks of flour perched atop their mounts. Why was sitting atop a horse so hard for some people? Rachel wondered. When she had made her first visit to the Lazy M as Darin Marsh's bride, she'd been green and raw as a city girl could be. Her new father-in-law had taken her in hand, thrown her up on a big rawboned quarter horse gelding, and taken her on a full-day tour of the ranch, the herds, and the best trout streams in the area. Darin hadn't joined them. He'd been raised on the Lazy M, and he much preferred city life. But Rachel had loved the ranch, the horses, the chickens, the goats, and the cattle from day one. Going back to the city had always been a letdown.

She was grateful she could raise her son in such a place, even though keeping the Lazy M afloat took long days, hard work, and sacrifices. The place was worth it. The life was worth it. This was where she belonged.

All in all, Rachel figured she was lucky enough to live in heaven. And she intended to stay there.

On the same morning, the sun was rising over the desert mecca of Las Vegas, Nevada, just as a very tired, exceedingly cranky Jackson Stone dragged himself into the Desert Palace Hotel. Jackson didn't much care for Las Vegas. Outside the Palace, garish lights gave the newborn day a tired glitter. Inside, the lobby was bright and brassy. Slot machines ding-ding-dinged. The place reeked of money and cigarette smoke, and from the casino, voices of dealers, winners, losers, and good-time revelers combined in an annoying background drone.

The moment Jackson stepped into the lobby, heads turned in recognition. The registration clerk stared, then smiled an expansive welcome. An elderly lady regarded him with bright, curious eyes and whispered to the thin gray-haired man beside her. Two teenage boys poked each other, giggled, then tried to look nonchalant. A man in wrinkled evening attire raised a startled brow and turned away, refusing to be diverted from his plastic cup of liquor. The only people who didn't notice him sat at the lobby slots, and an H-bomb couldn't have pulled their attention from the machines.

"Mr. Stone!" gushed the desk clerk, a tall, sallow man with an abundance of dark frizzy hair. "Welcome to the Desert Palace! We are honored! Absolutely honored! What an unexpected pleasure! I am such a fan of yours!"

Jackson usually labored to be charming to the movie-going public, but right then he was too tired to bother with preliminaries. Since the previous afternoon he had flown his Cessna Baron from Arizona to Los Angeles, taken a half-dozen angry phone calls from Deadly Dave, grilled Deanna and Cyndie—defiant as only teenagers can be defiant—into revealing his daughter's whereabouts, then turned around and flew the Baron to Las Vegas. He was way beyond caring about PR. He needed his daughter. Then he needed a shower, a hot meal, and a comfortable bed, in that order.

Jackson skewered the clerk with his eyes. "You have Jimmy Toledo staying here. What room?"

The clerk's smile faded. He lowered his voice. "Mr Stone, I'm sure you of all people realize that celebrities value their privacy. I can't tell you where—"

"Look at me, Mr.—" He glanced at the gold name tag on the man's blue blazer. "—Mr. Sikes. Leon. Do I look as if I give a flying fig about Jimmy Toledo's precious privacy?"

Leon's eyes grew wide as he took in the scowl that had cowed Tommy Lee Jones in *Nights of New York.* "Uh . . . uh . . . well . . ."

Jackson shifted to a confidential tone. "Leon, Jimmy Toledo has an underage girl with him. Very underage. And she's my daughter. Now, I can either call the cops and make a big deal of this, focusing all sorts of negative publicity on the Desert Palace, or you can tell me Jimmy's room number and I take care of it privately. I prefer the second way, because it's faster and quieter. But the noisy way will do. Your choice."

The clerk paled and glanced desperately around the lobby, as if the answer to his problem were written somewhere on the walls. Their low-voiced confrontation at the desk had attracted attention. Even a couple of people at the lobby slots looked up curiously.

"I . . . I . . . Let me get the manager."

"Do it fast, Leon. I don't have all day."

Ten minutes later Jackson knocked on the door of a top-floor suite. Music blared inside the room. Jackson welcomed the noise. It might cover the sounds of him killing Jimmy Toledo if the punk had touched Cherie.

His first knock was ignored, so he pounded again. His daughter's voice called out, "Jimmy! Somebody's at the door. Go answer it."

"I told that fuckin' clerk we weren't supposed to be disturbed! I'll have his job, the fucker!"

The door jerked open and there stood the punk in all his skinny, bare-chested, nipple-ringed glory. Jimmy Toledo's black scowl became alarm. "It's you!"

Jackson pushed his way into the room. At four inches over six feet, he had both height and breadth on the Lean Mean Music Machine, as the rock singer billed himself. "That's right, Jimmy. And you're lucky there's a law against throwing people out of thirtieth-floor windows. Cherie! Get your things, kiddo. We're leaving."

"Daddy? Daddy! Oh, shit!"

Cherie jumped up from a leather love seat. She wore her Morticia Addams look—black jeans, black tee that sported a sequined likeness of Jimmy Toledo, dark-gray eye shadow, black lipstick and nail polish. Her hair was colored jet black to complete the image. Very goth. Very cool.

Jimmy Toledo made Cherie look like Mary Poppins, though. Tall and stringy, his every appendage and protuberance boasted a gold stud or hoop. Eyebrow, nose—in two places—both ears, and tongue. Jackson was grateful that he was covered from the waist down. At least whatever else was pierced remained hidden.

The rock star placed himself between Jackson and his daughter. "Hey, dude! Wait a minute. Cherie wants to be here."

"Like I care? Jimmy boy, you have broken the law in more ways than I care to name. And if that bag of white stuff on the dresser is what I think it is, there's another charge to add to the list."

"Fuck! Don't get uptight, Mr. Law and Order. Rules are the refuge of a weak mind, you know?"

"Is that what they are? Ever hear the one about statutory rape? Know how old my daughter is?"

"Don't even try to pin something like that on me, old man. I've got, like, a solid wall of lawyers around me. No one messes with Jimmy Toledo."

"Cherie, get your things." Jackson's voice was deadly.

Cherie was not impressed. "Dad, you're treating me like a child!"

"You are a child."

She flounced down upon the king-size bed that was, fortunately, still neatly made. "I'm not a child; I'm a slave! Do this! Do that! Go here! Go there! Don't go here! Don't talk to these people. Suck up to these other jerks."

"If you want your things, you'd better get them, because we're leaving."

She scorched him with a look.

"Or I could get the cops up here to haul away your friend. How do you think he'd like a few years in the slammer?"

"You wouldn't!"

"Hey, babe," Jimmy said. "Tell your old man to fuck off, or I'll get my bodyguard to show him some action."

"Jimmy!" To Cherie's credit, she sounded horrified.

The rocker gave her an assessing look. "How old are you, anyway?"

Cherie hesitated.

"She's thirteen, Jimmy boy."

"Fuck! Truth?"

Cherie grimaced.

"Babe, you sure as hell look hotter than thirteen. But it doesn't do my rep any good to be seen with a snot-nosed kid."

Jackson didn't wait for the conversation to play out. "Get your things, Morticia."

"Don't call me that!"

"I could call you a lot worse right now. Be grateful."

Jimmy Toledo did not bid them good-bye as Jackson dragged Cherie out the door, but he didn't object, either.

"Hey, man," Jimmy called after him. "I can do better than a thirteen-year-old."

Riding down the elevator, Cherie was sullen. "Dad! Nothing happened! Are you going to call the cops on him?"

"No." Jackson remained untouched by her sulky indignation. He was feeling a bit sullen himself. "I'm not going to call the cops, because I figure this is as much your fault as his. And I don't want your name splashed all over the papers. Not any more than it's going to be already. One of your pals called the *Star*."

"Sweet! Maybe I'll get my picture in the paper."

He refused to rise to the bait. His daughter thought herself an expert at annoyance, but she didn't hold a candle to the pros in the film industry.

"Tell me you weren't snorting that coke," he demanded.

"God, no! I'm not that stupid."

"Sometimes you act that stupid. You are not to say one word to the press. Understand? Not one word."

"Afraid that your rep as world's greatest dad might be damaged?"

"More like your rep as world's snottiest daughter will become legend. Cherie, you're a kid. You're thirteen measly years old. Why can't you act your age?"

"I am acting my age."

That was what he was afraid of.

They arrived in the lobby just in time to see Josh Digby walk through the front entrance, camera in hand. Jackson hastily pushed Cherie through the door of a handy ladies' room and followed her in.

"Dad! You can't come here!"

"If Digby sees us, he'll hound us until he has enough photos to fill a whole issue of the *Star*. We'll never shake him. He's like a bloodhound."

Cherie rolled her eyes. "Who cares?"

"You might care once he starts making up dirt to create a little excitement."

"Sheesh! You're just lucky there's no one in here. You can be soooo embarrassing!"

Fortunately, Digby disappeared into the elevator, giving them a chance to slip out of the hotel. Silence, a heavy, ominous, uncomfortable silence, reigned during the cab ride to the airport. As the minutes dragged on, Cherie squirmed a bit and darted surreptitious glances at her father. Whenever he glanced back, she stared out the window with studied nonchalance. Finally she broke down.

"Who was the turncoat who ratted me out? Deanna or Cyndie?"

Jackson grinned wickedly. "They both came to see the wisdom of cooperation."

"Hmmph! Traitors! See if I ever hang with them again!"

"See if you ever leave the house again, period."

"Oh! Like you're going to ground me till I'm thirty-five? I've heard that before."

"It's a thought. Then again, there's always military school. They take females these days."

"Dad, you are such a caveman!"

"A caveman that you should be sucking up to, kiddo, seeing that I hold your foreseeable future in my hands."

"Well, maybe I'll just go live with Mom. She's a lot cooler than you are."

"Granted, she is. But that's not an option."

Jackson directed the cabdriver to the general aviation terminal. Inside the terminal, he called flight service and filed a flight plan for the two-hour trip back to Los Angeles.

"City of Boredom!" Cherie dubbed it. "Hell with a beach."

Jackson smiled. In that they agreed.

She slumped into a plastic chair. Weariness had eroded her truculence, and tears appeared to be close to the surface. Jackson suffered a pang of compassion along with a stab of guilt. Cherie was a brat. No doubt about it. But she'd been pushed toward brathood by divorced parents, a father who was consumed by work, a mother who was in some ways less sensible than her daughter, and a community that worshiped youth, celebrity, and wealth above all things. How was a kid supposed to grow up normal with all that going against her?

"Why are you looking at me like that?" Cherie asked suspiciously.

"Like what?"

"Like I'm a bug under a microscope."

"I wasn't. I was just thinking that maybe you and I should spend some quality time together."

"You want to go to the mall? Maybe to a concert? Great."

"Not exactly." He thought a moment. "I was planning a hiking and fishing trip this fall. Why don't I move it up a bit? We're about finished shooting *Hell's Border,* so I can get away in a week or so. And you can come."

Cherie blanched. "Hiking? Fishing? Gross!"

"You've never gone with me on one of these trips. You'll like it."

"Oh, sure! I'll like it! Not! Dad, that's like sentencing me to hell!"

"Then consider yourself sentenced to two weeks in hell, and lucky you got off so lightly. It'll be good for your character."

Jackson sank wearily into a plastic chair and squinted out the window at the blazing sun climbing over the Nevada mountains. His heart could find scant welcome for the new day.

CHAPTER 2

♡

CHERIE HEFTED HER backpack experimentally. "You are *not* expecting me to carry this thing, are you?"

Jackson shrugged on his own pack and regarded his daughter patiently. "If you don't want your lunch, or water to drink, or a raincoat, or dry socks, then you don't have to carry a pack. But I warn you, August in these mountains brings rain almost every afternoon."

"Great! I wouldn't need any of those stupid things if I didn't have to go on this stupid hike. Why can't we just go back to the campground and watch some DVDs in the motor home?"

He gave her a look.

"Okay, better—you hike, I'll go back to the campground. I'll drive the Jeep back, then you can call on your cell phone when you're ready to come back and I'll pick you up."

"You don't have a driver's license, Cherie."

She rolled her eyes. "So? This isn't exactly the freeways in L.A."

"Give it up. You're hiking. Put on the pack."

"Man oh man! I haven't done anything to deserve *this*!"

He gave her a stern look.

"It's been two whole weeks since I went off with Jimmy!" she complained. "Don't you ever let anything go?"

At his silence, she sighed in resignation.

They walked. Jackson's step lifted with energy inspired by the pine-scented air, the fresh breeze, the sheer joy of being alone in a place so big, so quiet, so private. Cherie's feet dragged mopishly along the trail. Her father could literally hear her feet drag—a deliberate ploy on her part, he was sure. Sooner or later the beauty of this country would get under her skin. She wouldn't be human if she didn't appreciate these mountains.

And Cherie was human. He'd been told by those in the know that teenagers were experts at disguising their humanity, but the disguise wore off eventually.

The trail led through a grove of quaking aspen and on through a big open expanse where tough range grass competed with rocks and an occasional cow pie. Occasional cows as well. Soon the meadow narrowed, following the course of a creek with green, grassy banks and a pebbly bottom.

"Haven't we gone far enough?" Cherie asked with a martyred sigh.

"We've only been walking a little over an hour. Isn't this gorgeous country?"

Cherie snorted.

"Look at that sky! Have you ever seen anything so blue? And those clouds boiling up over the mountain, there. Like big puffs of cotton."

"Dad, this is, like, booorring."

He ignored her. "See that mountain where the clouds are building? That's Mount Baldy. Second-highest peak in Arizona. There's a trail to the top. Maybe tomorrow we should hike up there."

"Daaaad! That's got to be a million miles!"

"Only seven miles from where the trail starts."

"How do you know all this . . . this useless stuff?"

"I've come up here a time or two. It's one of my favorite fishing and hiking areas. It's a great place to get away from the crowds."

"I like crowds. There's nothing to do here. Jeez!" She stopped and bent over, propping her hands on her knees. "Can't we rest? I'm tired."

"Sure. This is a great place for lunch. Look over there. In that big open area ahead, the creek runs into a lake. We can sit on that log over there and watch the ducks."

"Oh, thrill. If you wanted to stare at water and birds, we could have stayed home at the beach house."

A log in the shade of the pines provided them with a great view. They dug out the lunches Jackson had prepared for them that morning—salami on rye with lots of Swiss cheese, two chocolate chip cookies each, and an apple. No tofu, bean sprouts, salad, soy, bottled water with added electrolytes, or anything else his fitness trainer at the gym might have recommended. His one concession to health was the apple.

As they ate, Jackson absorbed the scene spread out before them. The tableau inspired a sense of peace. He loved making films, being part of the helter-skelter world of the entertainment industry, but now and then the noise, bustle, and the essential loneliness of celebrity wore on him. Then he would take off for a place like this one.

Cherie had always found an excuse not to come. Like her mother, she wasn't into roughing it. But dammit, it was time the girl learned there was something more to the world than Hollywood weirdness. He hoped the grandeur spread before them, this awesome silence and serenity, would have the same effect on Cherie that it had on him.

Beside him, Cherie surveyed the lake, the stream, the meandering meadow, and in the distance, Mount Baldy with its crown of cottony clouds. Her mouth pinched in disdain. "It isn't exactly the Swiss Alps, is it? Pretty lame, if you ask me."

Jackson sighed.

"Speaking of Switzerland, do you know Deanna Cohen?"

"The girl you vowed never to speak to again because she blabbed about your plan with Jimmy Toledo?"

"Yeah, well, I've decided to forgive her. After all, you probably scared her into wetting her pants."

Jackson sighed again.

"Anyway, speaking of Switzerland, Deanna and her parents

are going to do kind of a grand tour, you know? They're starting in France, then going to Austria and Switzerland and Italy. And Deanna wants me to come along."

"When?"

"Late September. And most of October. Cool, huh? School would give us credit and let us make up the work we missed."

Right about then Jackson decided that the pitfalls of being a movie star didn't hold a candle to the pitfalls of being a father. He wanted to give Cherie an immediate no. In fact, he wanted to lock her in a room for the next ten years until she learned some sense.

Maybe if Cherie had a mother who didn't pay more attention to her past lives than her present one, maybe if she had a father who didn't work fifteen hours a day, and maybe if they weren't prime targets for all the paparazzi on the planet. Maybe if they lived in Omaha, Nebraska, instead of in a beach house in L.A., raising a daughter would be easier.

But then, Omaha probably had its problems, too. And Melanie Carr *was* Cherie's mother, Jackson Stone *was* her father, they *did* live in the most insane town in the most insane state in the union, and none of that was going to change. Cherie was just going to have to survive it.

"Do you think, considering the escapade with Jimmy Toledo, that you have enough maturity and responsibility to go traipsing around Europe for a month?"

"Well, yeah, Dad! Deanna's parents will be going along, you know!"

"I'll think about it."

"Think hard?"

"I said that I'd think about it."

She got up and hugged him with a rare show of affection. "I love you, Dad."

"I didn't say yes."

She grinned. "I still love you."

"Love you, too, kiddo. If you're finished eating, shall we hike on?"

A complaint crossed her face, but she didn't voice it. "If we have to."

They moved up the trail, which skirted the lake at the tree line, sometimes in the forest, sometimes in the meadow. Cattle grazed peacefully. Birds sang. White clouds floated across an unbelievably blue sky. A pleasant breeze whispered through the pines and rattled the aspen leaves.

Even Cherie seemed to cheer up, and as they hiked, Jackson felt a load of weariness lift from his shoulders—weariness bred from too many long hours on the set, too much time spent with people who wanted to be with him only because of his celebrity, his money, his power to make or break careers. Much as he enjoyed the Industry, it was a dog-eat-dog business where true friends were rare. Here, under a clean sky, with a fresh breeze caressing his face, he felt youthful, strong, carefree. He felt as if he could sprint up hills and fly over canyons.

In sheer exuberance, he vaulted over a little creek that crossed the trail.

"Hey, Dad! Watch it! You're not exactly young anymore, you know?"

That hurt. Just to prove that pushing forty was not yet old age, he jumped onto a boulder half buried in the soil beside the trail. From there he jumped to another rock, and another farther away, then to the lightning-seared trunk of a huge ponderosa pine.

"A man doesn't need to be in his twenties to—yikes!"

And so he fell, landing badly and proving that common sense doesn't always come with age.

Rachel didn't really need to ride up the mountain to check on the steer with the gashed leg. The men had kept an eye on him, and they'd have told her if the animal required a vet. But she would take any excuse to get away from her little cubbyhole office where she should have been balancing the books, answering inquiries from potential guests, or deciding if she could afford to give the staff a pay raise. August was a gorgeous month in the Arizona mountains, and she wished she could spend every day outdoors, preferably in the saddle.

She felt like a kid playing hooky, her face wearing a grin that just wouldn't go away. What made the escape even better was Sam riding along with her—and Chesty, too. Where boy went, dog went. He ran ten times the distance covered by the horses, dashing into thickets to investigate, running ahead, then circling back, ever alert for squirrels, rabbits, and birds.

For the past half hour they had been following a little-traveled trail that climbed through jack pine and ponderosa, detouring around fallen trees and scrambling up rocky ledges. Sam's horse, Thunder, a steady, sensible trail horse, took everything in stride. Paul's new mare, Sally, though, made Rachel work to stay in the saddle. The mare spooked at the sound of the wind, at fluttering birds, at rabbits, and any other excuse she could find. The spookiness was a game, a bit of mischief to test the person in the saddle, but Rachel knew the game well, and she had a few tricks of her own to teach Sally the error of her ways.

Finally they reached the top, where the going was easier. Sam twisted in his saddle to look back at her. "That mare seems real skittish, Ma."

"She is a bit. Paul asked me to work her down some." Rachel wished Sam would get over calling her "Ma"—a word he'd favored since watching a John Wayne marathon on one of the movie channels two months ago. Any "Ma" should have gray hair, wrinkled skin, and wear an apron smudged with flour. Rachel wasn't quite there yet, but if Sam kept calling her "Ma," she would be soon.

"She just about scraped you off under that tree branch," Sam noted solemnly. "And that rabbit nearly sent her off the edge of the trail back there on the ledge."

"We don't want Paul using her for the guests, that's for sure. But she's got potential. Really comfortable little jog trot. Nice fast walk. In good shape, too. That climb didn't even wind her. I'm thinking of buying her from Paul."

"Probably just what Paul wants," Sam said sagely.

The wrangler owned the string of horses he brought to the Lazy M every summer. During the winter he moved them to a desert resort near Scottsdale. Every once in a while Rachel would purchase a horse from his string to add to the Lazy M bunch. She didn't doubt Paul had brought the mare to the ranch hoping Rachel would buy her. The purchase would put a strain on her bank account, though. Despite needing some work, Sally was a very nice mare. Paul wouldn't take peanuts for her.

The trail wound through a narrow green meadow bordered on either side by a thick stand of aspen. Cattle grazed by a creek, too far away for Rachel to see their brands. They might have been Lazy M animals, or they might belong to one of the other outfits that grazed cattle on this range. In the distance was sparkling Butler Lake, one of her favorite places. When the meadow widened into a spacious, grassy basin, Chesty dashed up the trail at a gallop, detoured into the trees, and broke the peaceful silence with a barrage of barking.

"Hey, Ma! Look at Chesty! I think he's found something."

Rachel tried to spot what had alerted the dog. "Hikers. Just beyond the tree line."

One of the hikers waved a jacket in the air. "Help!" came a wavering feminine cry.

"Uh-oh," Sam said ominously.

Rachel reined her mare off the trail and nudged her into a canter up the hill. Sam was right behind her.

The couple was a man and young girl. The man sat on the ground, scratching Chesty's ears. He was very good-looking in a rugged way, with brown hair worn just long enough to be tousled by the wind. A slightly crooked nose gave him a rough-edged look, and his mouth, curled in a chagrined smile, was enough to set a woman's heart racing. Rachel looked away before she could be accused of staring. Yes, she did still notice the opposite sex. A woman would have to be dead not to notice this one.

The young girl with the man would have been cute without

the Halloween horror getup she affected—tight jeans, tube top, an overlarge man's shirt tied around her waist, all in black, including the details. Black lipstick, nail polish, eye shadow. But the packaging and the attitude—oh, yeah, she could sense the little princess had an attitude even before the girl opened her mouth—didn't hide the fact she was way young.

Rachel greeted them. "Is everything okay? I thought I heard someone yell for help."

"That would be me," the girl chimed in before the man could reply. She regarded Rachel and Sam with a certain degree of suspicion. "My dad fell. I think he broke his leg."

She gave the girl a smile. "Well, that's not good out here in the middle of nowhere, is it? Let me take a look." She dismounted, handed Sally's reins to Sam, and squatted down beside the man. "Which leg?"

"Left."

"Hm." Rachel was competent at first aid, but learning anything about a jeans-clad leg was fairly difficult. It was a nicely muscular leg that filled out the jeans in a quite attractive way. She did learn that.

"I tried using my cell phone to get help, but I couldn't get a signal."

"Yeah, cell phones aren't much use around here unless you're at the very top of the hill. I don't see any blood, and there's no bone sticking out where it shouldn't stick out."

"Oh, gag!" the girl commented.

"Perhaps we should take off your boot. No, sit still. I'll do it."

With the hiking boot off, Rachel could see that his ankle was plainly swollen. She ran her hand up his calf—a very attractive, muscular calf, she noted. At her touch, his eyes met hers, and for a moment, just a moment, her stomach turned to water. Then he flinched, and the moment was gone.

"Hurt?"

"Well, no. But I expected it to."

She smiled to herself. Why did big men who looked tough as nails so often turn out to be crybabies?

"I don't think it's broken." She poked gingerly at the swelling.

"Ow!"

"Sorry. A bit tender, are we?"

"Yes! We are."

Nice legs or not, he was an irritable crybaby.

She stood up and regarded him thoughtfully. "It doesn't seem to be broken, but I can't really be positive."

His eyes were a startling green, Rachel noticed. As a matter of fact, now that she looked at the fellow more closely, she could see he looked remarkably like Jackson Stone, action superstar. The same rugged, engaging face. The same broad shoulders. The same drop-dead gorgeous eyes and sensuous mouth. She decided not to comment. The poor man probably got razzed about the resemblance all the time.

"Have you tried to stand on it?"

"He did," the man's daughter told her. "You should have heard him bellow."

The man rolled his eyes, but he smiled. Oh, God, he had Stone's smile as well, the smile that had seduced countless leading ladies on-screen, and according to rumor, offscreen as well. The guy could work as Stone's double.

"Uh . . . I can splint it, just in case you did break something. Do you have a vehicle somewhere around here?"

"Our Jeep is at the trailhead. About four miles back." He sighed. "Uphill."

"Okay. Let me find something to splint your leg. Sam, tie the horses to a tree and find me some really straight, small branches."

"Yes'm." Sam looked toward the girl with obvious expectations of help in the chore, but she merely sniffed and sat down on a log.

While she waited, Rachel liberated her jacket of the cord that gathered the bottom hem. She felt the man's eyes upon her, his gaze resting like a silent weight. A sudden flush heated her cheeks, and her fingers fumbled in their task. Foolishly she wished she didn't look quite so drab. Makeup was only a special-occasion thing here, and her curling iron was beneath the bathroom sink gathering dust.

The man pinioned her with a smile. He had a really great smile. "It's awfully nice of you and your, uh—your son?—"

She nodded.

"—to come to our rescue."

"No trouble." That smile of his could make a woman positively dizzy, and Rachel suspected he knew it. She felt embarrassed for being so predictably susceptible. Usually she had more sense. "You fell?"

"Uh . . . yeah."

She looked around, perplexed. "What did you fall from?"

The smile skewed ruefully. "My backrest here."

"The log? That log?" She tried not to chortle.

His daughter elaborated with a spiteful giggle. She sat on the log in the pretzel-legged position that only the very young can assume. "He was fooling around, showing off."

He shrugged sheepishly.

Rachel didn't comment. The guy looked embarrassed enough as it was. "Ah. Here's Sam with our splint. Thanks, honey."

Sam dropped an armful of aspen sticks beside her, then he stood back and regarded the injured man with narrowed eyes. "Are you Jackson Stone?"

"Sam! Don't be silly."

With a chuckle, the man admitted it. "Well, actually, yes."

The girl grimaced. "They'll probably sell *The National Enquirer* a story about how they saved your life in the wilderness."

Rachel shot the black-clad teenager a look. She could get tired of Miss Goth America really fast.

Jackson Stone, movie star, the genuine McCoy, grimaced ruefully. "That's my daughter, Cherie."

A flood of resentment caught Rachel off guard. The guy could look like Jackson Stone all he wanted, but now he actually *was* Jackson Stone. Like shooting stars in the night sky, such creatures were supposed to stay in their own universe, not come down to earth to mix with ordinary people and complicate their ordinary lives.

Sam, however, was excited right out of his cowboy seriousness. "Wow, Jackson Stone in our own backyard. Cool!" Reacting to Sam's tone, Chesty barked and did a couple of enthusiastic spins.

"Yeah, cool." Rachel was tolerant only for Sam's sake. She, for one, wasn't keen on jet-setters cluttering up the Arizona countryside, bringing their self-indulgent lifestyles with them. No telling when they might decide to stay, buying up the best property and turning it into private retreats, forcing up land values until only the rich could afford to stay.

She gave him a sour look. "A bit out of your territory, aren't you, Mr. Stone?"

He grinned engagingly. "They do let us out of California now and again."

Which was a shame, Rachel thought.

"And you would be . . . ?"

"Rachel Marsh, owner of the Lazy M Ranch."

Sam had no shame. "I've seen a lot of your movies, Mr. Stone."

Stone grinned at the boy. "Thanks, Sam. If people didn't go to see my films, I'm afraid I'd be out on the street."

How munificent. How humble.

"Ma's a big fan, too."

Flinching at "Ma," Rachel demurred, "I'm afraid I don't have much time for movies."

"That's not true, Ma. Remember that great one about the space station?"

"Well—"

"And you went with me to see *Trueheart*."

Busted. "Uh . . . oh, yes. That was the one about the Cheyenne war chief, wasn't it? With Kevin Costner."

Cherie snorted with miffed pride. "Dad's part was the real lead. If Kevin Costner had known how to play an Indian, *Trueheart* would have gotten Best Picture that year."

"Cherie."

The girl merely sniffed at her father's quelling tone.

Obviously, the guy lacked authority with his kid. "I liked Costner in that one," Rachel said.

Sam wasn't through embarrassing her. "We saw *Second Sight,* too." He grinned and rolled his eyes. "The loooooovvve story. Mom used a whole box of tissues in that one."

Rachel concluded she could use a bit more authority with her own kid. "I had a cold," she said firmly. "And enough about the movies. We need to get Mr. Stone's leg splinted, so he can go home to California." *Where he belongs.*

Rachel was fairly sure that Jackson Stone's leg wasn't broken, but she couldn't take the chance on being wrong. After all, she didn't want to end his career of sprinting after bad guys and jumping from the top of a moving truck to tackle a fleeing terrorist. (The truck thing had been in *Thunder Passage.*)

"I'm going to splint you right over your jeans," she told him. "I'll just fold them tight to your leg like—"

"Ouch!"

She'd scarcely touched him. "You want a bullet to bite on?"

He unashamedly came right back at her. "Do you have one?"

"Didn't I see you endure torture in *Trueheart* without uttering a single cry?"

"I use up all my stoicism being brave in the movies."

"Ah."

"Besides, all that blood was fake."

"And the pain, too, I guess."

He grinned. "You got it. I don't do real pain. For that I use a double."

"In that case, just pretend I'm splinting your double's leg. He'll tell you it doesn't hurt that much."

"Ouch! Damn!"

"Now what did I do?"

"It just hurts!"

Rachel sighed.

Between them, she and Sam managed to put a makeshift splint on Mr. Macho's leg and ankle without too much trouble other than listening to the man's complaints. His daughter simply watched, a bored look on her face. When they were through, Cherie gloated. "I told you we should have stayed in camp and watched DVDs."

"Don't start," her father warned.

"Or better yet, we could have stayed home and I could have gone to the beach."

"Cherie . . ."

Rachel forestalled the blossoming wrangle by steering them back to practicalities. "Can you two do this later? We still have to get you back to civilization."

"That would be about an eight-hour drive," Cherie sniped.

Rachel ignored her. "I think it would be best if you ride double with Sam, Mr. Stone. His horse is steadier. Cherie can ride with me, and—"

"Call me Jackson. And I don't do horses." Now he was beginning to sound genuinely irritated.

"What do you mean, you don't do horses? Any idiot can sit behind a saddle and hold on."

"Nope. Horses don't like me."

"Horses seldom care one way or the other who is riding."

He looked stubborn in a way that only a man could look stubborn. Arrogant, too, Rachel decided.

"Well, I suppose you could walk," she offered facetiously. "Four miles. Uphill."

"Why don't you just ride to the nearest phone and call a helicopter to airlift him out?" Cherie suggested.

"Don't you think that's a little extravagant for what's probably only a sprained ankle?"

"Like we care what it costs?" Cherie sniped. "Do you know how much per movie my dad makes?"

"Cherie!" Jackson growled. "You're already grounded until you're thirty-five. Want to try for forty?"

The girl added an embarrassed flush to her black-on-gray color scheme, but she didn't fold. Since smirking at her father obviously would have consequences, she grimaced instead at Sam, who regarded her as if she had just landed from Mars. Rachel sighed. She was doing a lot of sighing this afternoon.

The star came up with a suggestion. "How about if I stay here and Cherie shows you where our Jeep is? It's a four-wheel drive. Do you think you could get it down here?"

"You really don't want to take the easy way out and ride to your Jeep? Sam's horse is well able to carry the both of you."

"Nope."

"How did you make all those westerns? No. Don't tell me. A double. Right?"

"When there's money in it, I can sit a saddle at a sedate walk. Anything faster than that . . ."

"We'll walk all the way. Promise."

He grinned wickedly. "Sure. But right now there's no money in it."

Jackson Stone was a man who enjoyed nettling people, Rachel decided. "Okay, Mr. Stone."

"Jackson."

She clenched her jaw. "Jackson. If you don't mind waiting here."

"Cherie's good on horses."

"Glad to hear your disability doesn't run in the family."

He merely grinned.

Cherie climbed aboard Thunder, showing a surprising degree of agility as she swung up behind Sam's saddle. She declined to steady herself by gripping the boy at the waist. The two kids avoided touching each other with theatrical exaggeration.

As they started up the trail, Rachel groused to herself. This would be so much easier if Mr. Pampered Hollywood would just make the effort to get on a horse. Give some people a little fame and money and suddenly they expected everyone to tiptoe around their idiot idiosyncrasies. In a sudden attack of pique, she called back to him. "Don't worry about that big black bear that's been cruising around here. He hasn't eaten anyone. Yet."

This day had turned out worse than Cherie had imagined it would, and she had imagined it would be pretty bad. First her father had insisted she get up for breakfast. And what a breakfast. Yuk. At least a pound of bacon fried in a cast-iron skillet over a campfire (as if they didn't have a perfectly good stove in the motor home, and nonstick cookware as well) and then eggs cooked in the bacon drippings. Gross! The meal had contained enough fat to kill an elephant, much less a human being.

The most Cherie usually ate in the morning was juice, or maybe a Diet Coke, depending on her mood. If her morning experience with the bathroom scale was a positive one, she might splurge and have a latte—if her dad wasn't home. He didn't like her drinking coffee. Of course, if he had his way she'd probably still be drinking milk from a baby bottle.

But this morning her dad wouldn't let leave until she ate enough to sink the *Titanic*. Blimphood was just around the corner. Melanie had once told her that camping trips turned her dad into a maniac, and in this case her mom had been telling the truth. Good thing her dad didn't eat like that every day. He would drop of a heart attack before he was forty, and then Cherie would be stuck living with her flaky mother.

After breakfast the day had gotten worse. Cherie didn't mind her dad getting off on dull, boring things like hiking and fishing, but why did he have to insist on her going with him? She could have just as easily stayed in the motor home and watched television or DVDs. What was the use of having a satellite dish on your RV if you didn't use it? What did he think she'd do if he let her out from under his thumb? Run off with some guy?

Well, maybe he did have reason to not trust her in that arena, but this place was so empty of interesting guys that it was like they were all sucked into a black hole or something. The campers at the RV park could have qualified for AARP group therapy.

And now, as if the day weren't a total disaster already, her klutzoid father had to prance around like Baryshnikov and take a Daffy Duck pratfall. Probably all those grams of breakfast fat had gone to his brain. Sheesh! Then a cowgirl in a ponytail and ball cap—how uncool was that?—rides to the rescue. What else could happen?

Suddenly, a terrible thought struck her. She frowned over at the woman riding beside her. "You were kidding about the bear, right?"

"I was kidding."

"Yeah. I knew that. Just checking. Everything else has gone wrong today. Dad might as well get eaten by a bear."

"Your dad will be fine. His leg isn't broken, I'm almost sure of it. And if your Jeep is only four miles up the trail, we'll be back in no time."

The cowgirl had to be almost as old as her dad—way too old to be not wearing makeup and letting her skin go like she did. If she didn't start protecting herself from the sun and getting major facials, she would look positively over the hill in no time.

"Like, I can't believe you didn't recognize my dad. He's, you know, the number one box-office draw in the country."

"I recognized him," the cowgirl admitted. "At least, I knew your dad looked a lot like Jackson Stone. But I didn't expect someone like him to be wandering around our mountains. I guess most people expect the jet set to stay in the jet lanes and leave the nice slow lanes to the rest of us."

Cherie sent her a narrow look. "Was that a slam?"

Cowgirl looked surprised. "A slam? Of course not. Why should I care where your father goes?"

"Well, most women would be thrilled to stumble across Jackson Stone in the middle of nowhere."

"Ma isn't most women," Sam interjected.

"Well, excuse me!"

"Samuel, mind your manners. Cherie, the trail forks up here. Which branch did you come down?"

Like she had been paying any attention? "I don't know."

"Well, look around. Do you recognize anything?"

Who was she supposed to be? Danielle Boone? Cherie sighed and pointed left. Everything looked different when you were coming from the other direction. "That way, I think."

They rode on in silence. Calamity Jane and her stupid son

were probably thinking how stupid she was. Like they knew anything. "Do you guys live around here someplace? Like in a log cabin or something?"

"We have a guest ranch down the valley a ways," the cowgirl said.

"A resort? That's sweet."

"It's a real ranch," the kid insisted. "Mom just takes in guests for a little extra cash."

"You have real cows?"

"Sure we do," the boy bragged. "Only it's cattle, not cows. Don't you know anything?"

"Sam," his mother chided.

Cherie was tolerant. From her position of superiority, she could afford to be. "I didn't know there were real ranches anymore."

"Where do you think hamburger comes from?" the kid asked.

Cherie had never thought about it before, to tell the truth. "That's gross. Now I see why my friend Deanna is a vegetarian."

When they met a rushing stream that crossed the trail, she called a halt. "Oops. Wrong fork. We never crossed this."

She heard the kid sigh in disgust. Like he could do better? Even the stupid dog gave her look. Like she was supposed to have a map imprinted on her brain?

By the time they backtracked and took the other fork, the afternoon was wearing on. And the tender parts where Cherie met the horse were hurting. She wasn't about to complain, though. Not with the stupid kid just waiting to laugh at her.

"Whoa! There's our Jeep, there in the trees. It's the toughest four-wheel drive on the market. That's what my dad says. He says it can go anywhere."

"We're about to find out, aren't we?" The cowgirl smiled a smile the Cherie didn't much like.

Jackson would have kicked himself, but his ankle hurt too much. And the pain made him want to kick himself even more. What had possessed him to bounce around like a teenager with rubber bones, paying no attention to what he did and where he stepped? Idiot. That's what he was—a twenty-four-carat idiot. Any thirty-eight-year-old man who acted like a fifteen-year-old deserved what he got.

And he had gotten it. Damned if he hadn't. There went his vacation. Even if his ankle was just sprained, he wouldn't be hiking around the mountains or bushwhacking along trout streams for a while. Cherie would be delighted, because all he could do now was vegetate in the motor home. They couldn't go home yet, not with Josh Digby and his paparazzi comrades still lurking in hopes of some tidbit of information about Cherie's escapade. A call from Harvey had warned him that the star-watcher press, in the absence of anything better to write about, had seized with relish onto Cherie's adventure with Jimmy Toledo. Digby had interviewed "eyewitnesses" in the Las Vegas hotel—or made them up, more likely—and had spun an exaggerated account that caught the imagination of tabloid readers. If Jackson went home, his daughter was going to be treated to a festival of photographers and rude questions, and then she would find herself splashed on the front page of every tabloid in the country. While Jackson himself was accustomed to media excess—they'd had an absolute heyday when he and Melanie had divorced—he'd be damned if he would let his daughter suffer the same kind of exposure. Knowing Cherie, she might think the attention was fun, but she would soon discover that notoriety can rob the unwary of their very soul.

He sighed, moved his foot experimentally, and winced. He foresaw a really bad mood in his near future, like in the next half hour if his rescuer and his daughter didn't show up with his goddamned Jeep.

Jackson frowned up the trail where Cherie had disappeared with the woman and her son. What had she said her name was? He might have been foolish to let Cherie go off alone with those two. They had seemed honest enough, in a salt-of-the-earth sort of way, but celebrity families were always vulnerable targets for the unscrupulous. Why had he been such an ass about getting on a damned horse? With his daughter's safety at stake, he should have been willing to climb aboard a giraffe if need be.

Rachel. Rachel Marsh. That was the woman's name. And her son was Samuel. Rachel and Sam were probably exactly what they seemed. Good people. The woman was pretty, too, though judging was difficult with her hair pulled into a curly ponytail and stuffed through the opening of a ball cap. Not exactly the height of fashion. An angular face. Blue eyes snapping at him from beneath the brim of her hat. A mouth that might have been lush if not constantly thinned in disapproval. Tanned, slender arms revealed by her sleeveless seersucker shirt. Did anyone on the face of the earth still wear seersucker?

This Rachel woman wasn't good-looking in the way that the Industry thought of good-looking. But there was something about her that knocked a man off balance, and getting knocked off balance was always intriguing. What exactly about the woman arrested the eye? Her hair, her interesting face, her mobile, expressive mouth, the way her jeans hugged her backside? They did hug her backside, he remembered fondly. Indeed they did.

Suddenly Jackson realized the most intriguing aspect of Rachel Marsh was that she didn't like him. He seemed to annoy her merely by breathing. Women usually fell all over themselves to get his attention. Young, not young—it didn't matter. His image on the silver screen drew women from preteens to grandmothers. Maybe that had gone to his head. Along came a woman who turned up her nose at his charm, and the turned-up nose bugged him. His larger-than-life ego went into shock. Very instructive, Jackson acknowledged. Could be that his ex-wife was right when she accused him of needing his chakras overhauled.

He leaned back against the log and sighed impatiently. All this pastoral quietude rasped on his nerves, goddammit! Paradise could be hell when a man was trapped there. Rachel Marsh was taking her own sweet time about fetching his Jeep. He stared up the trail. No sign of a Jeep, no sound of a Jeep, no Jeep. And what was that black hulking mass partly hidden by the trees? The dratted woman had been kidding about the bear, right? Of course she had. What he saw was nothing more than a big, dark tree stump. The movement was just an illusion.

Or was it? It did move. It definitely moved. Shit! That pony-tailed little wretch hadn't been kidding after all! In these peaceful-looking woods lurked a goddamned real, stinking, nonanimatronic bear. No special effects here, just real teeth and claws.

Jackson froze as the bear's head swung in his direction. An information tidbit from the past flashed into his brain—a conversation with a zookeeper when he'd taken Cherie to the zoo for her fourth birthday.

"It's a fact," the man had told him as Cherie had admired a huge grizzly. "The animal keepers least want to see escape a zoo is a bear. Fast, vicious, unpredictable—a bear is all of that. Lions and tigers are scary, but bears are just downright bad news."

Great! Just great! he thought as the bear got up and ambled in his direction. The country's hottest male box-office draw was about to become lunch for Ungentle Ben.

CHAPTER 3

♡

JACKSON'S EARS PERKED to the whine of a Jeep.

The woman had a knack of appearing just in the nick of time. Good thing, he thought. His masculine ego might be miffed at once again being rescued by a female, but his will to live was duly grateful.

The Jeep did not come along the trail, but blazed a careful path through the trees, rocks, and stumps on the mountainside behind him. The four-wheel drive whined in low gear, and above the whine came Cherie's voice.

"Yeow! I don't believe you did that! We went straight off the friggin' edge! Straight down!"

Jackson fidgeted as the Jeep drew closer. The woman was taking her own goddamned time! Didn't she see what watched from the edge of the trees?

"You didn't like my shortcut?" Rachel asked Cherie as the Jeep finally pulled up to where Jackson nervously balanced on one leg.

"It beat Space Mountain at Disneyland! You ought to be a stunt driver, you know?"

"Now, why would any sensible person want to do that?"

"*Mucho* bucks. Not as much as a star makes, but—"

"Mr. Stone, you shouldn't be hopping around like that. Just stay still and let me help."

"Call me Jackson," he reminded her tersely as he kept on hopping toward them. "The late, extinct Jackson if we don't get out of here. Don't you see what's over there in the trees? It's a goddamned bear!"

Both females looked in the direction of his pointing finger.

"Omigod!" Cherie shrieked. "You're right! We're going to get eaten!"

Rachel Marsh was a good deal calmer. "It is a bear. Fancy that."

"I thought you were kidding with the smart remark when you left."

"I was kidding."

"But there's a bear! A real goddamned bear!"

"Pretty funny coincidence."

"I don't think it's funny at all. Let's get out of here."

"Just take it easy, and stop that silly hopping."

Rachel jumped lithely out of the vehicle and came toward him with a jaunty, hip-swinging walk that he would have admired in other circumstances. Right then, however, his mind was focused on other things, such as the likelihood of that bear deciding that today's lunch came served in a Jeep.

Rachel took his arm and braced it across her own slender shoulders. The semi-embrace sent a ribbon of heat through his blood. He filed away the pleasant jolt to appreciate at another time, when he wasn't about to be dismembered and eaten.

"Come on now, and be careful," she said. "Don't destroy all my handiwork on that splint. Cherie, get in the backseat."

Cherie squealed. "Oh! Oh! The bear's going to attack! He's coming out of the trees! We're done for!"

"The bear isn't going to attack," Rachel said calmly. "Not unless he's as annoyed by your screaming as I am. Get in the backseat so your dad can stretch his leg out in the front."

"It's coming for us, I tell you!"

"He's just wanting to get a closer look."

"He's perusing the menu," Jackson said as Rachel lowered him onto the passenger seat.

"Really, Mr. Stone. You're just scaring her."

"Scaring her? I'm scaring me!"

"The bears we have around here don't bother people. This one has an eye for that runty calf down there. They don't often attack cattle, but that poor runt is a natural-born target."

"Oh, gross!" Cherie groaned.

"Not that bears are creatures to mess around with," Rachel said. "They can be bad-tempered and aggressive, and a bear can outrun a horse over a short distance."

"But not a Jeep," Jackson said hopefully.

"Not on the open highway. But in this kind of country, certainly."

Cherie moaned. "You're kidding. Please tell me you're kidding."

Jackson knew there was a reason he didn't like bears. "We're getting out of here, right?"

The woman gave him a wicked smile. "You'd leave that poor little calf to be mauled by a mean old bear? What kind of hero are you?"

"A fake one," he admitted readily.

She sighed dramatically. "There ends my hope that any of you movie supermen are the real thing."

"Sarcasm doesn't become you. Can we leave?"

"As soon as I send this fellow on his way."

"What are you going to do, walk up to him and ask him politely to find his lunch elsewhere?"

She chuckled.

The woman was having an annoyingly good time at his expense, Jackson sensed. And he didn't like it one bit.

"I'm really fond of that particular calf." She dug through a saddle pack on the backseat beside Cherie. "I delivered it from its mama's womb a couple of months ago. Horrible birth. We didn't expect the poor little guy to live, but he did. Ah! I knew I threw it in here this morning."

She pulled a holstered pistol from her pack, a big automatic .36 caliber that probably had a kick that would flatten a mule.

Jackson gaped. "You carry a gun?"

"Of course I carry a gun." She took in his surprise with a patient smile. "I never know what I'm going to meet out here in the wilderness, especially with all you tourists roaming around."

Feeling stupid, he simply continued to gape.

"Don't worry, Mr. Stone. The gun is perfectly legal, and I know how to use it."

"Jackson," he reminded her automatically. And he didn't doubt for a moment that she knew how to use that howitzer. "You're not going to shoot that bear, are you?"

"Of course not. That would really make him mad, wouldn't it?"

Cherie looked on the verge of tearing out her hair, which might have improved the style a bit. "Man oh man! We're all going to die. I'm too young to die!"

Rachel rolled her eyes. "I'm just going to fire in the air to scare off Smokey there. Likely he won't come back till long after the calf and his mama have moved on." She pointed the pistol toward the sky and fired twice. Jackson and Cherie both clapped hands over their ears. The startled bear rose briefly to his hind legs, sent them a disgusted look, then turned and disappeared into the trees. The knot of grazing cattle jerked up their heads and also took flight.

Their ponytailed Annie Oakley blew a wisp of gun smoke from the barrel of the gun and gave them a smile as they gingerly uncovered their ears.

"I think my eardrums are busted," Cherie complained.

"No kidding!" Jackson had to agree with his daughter.

"Haven't you ever heard a real gun fired?" Rachel stashed the pistol and climbed into the Jeep. "I suppose you use doubles for all your gunplay scenes, hm?"

"We use blanks. They're not that loud."

"Well, I don't. There's no sense in carrying a gun if you can't defend yourself with it."

"Remind me not to make you mad," Jackson told her with a grin.

Her answering smile brought out dimples he hadn't noticed before. "Believe me, Mr. Stone—"

"Jackson."

"I am the least dangerous thing you might encounter in these mountains."

He didn't believe that for one moment.

She pointed the Jeep up the mountainside in the same direction she had come down.

"Man oh man!" Cherie had recovered her spirits now that the bear was gone. "We're going back up this way? Dad, you should have seen us come down! We were following this road, then just made a left turn into nowhere, you know? Straight down the mountain, between the trees, over rocks. Absolutely sweet! I told Rachel she should be a stunt driver and make a wad of money."

"Don't you have roads around here?" Jackson clung for dear life to the roll bar of the open Jeep.

"Of course we have roads. This is the shortest route to get to the road."

He grimaced as they nearly scraped a big pine. "All in all, I suppose it's no scarier than driving L.A.'s freeways."

"So I've heard. Try to keep your leg still, Mr. . . . uh . . . Jackson."

"Try to find a flat surface to drive on."

She chuckled. "This is a nice Jeep. I like the gear ratio. Did you rent it?"

"M-mine." His teeth clicked together as they bounced over a rock. "Cherie, do you have your seat belt on?"

"Oh, Dad!"

"Fasten it, young lady!"

A tortured sigh accompanied the metallic click of the buckle.

They detoured around a windfall of downed pines, the Jeep tilting sideways precariously. Cherie was right, Jackson thought as he held on for dear life. The woman really ought to be a stunt driver. He tried to pretend unconcern, but he thought it likely that they were about to put the roll bar to use. He could see the headline in the *L.A. Times* entertainment section: JACKSON STONE SQUASHED FLAT IN JEEP ROLLOVER! In smaller print beneath the headline: *Cherie Stone thrown clear. Says of dad, "He shouldn't have been wearing his stupid seat belt."*

"Speaking of children," he said through a clenched jaw, "what happened to yours?"

"Sam is taking the horses back to the ranch."

"Alone?"

"He has Chesty with him."

"Chesty's just a dog."

"Don't let Chesty hear you say that. Besides, Sam is very competent."

"I suppose he carries a gun, too?"

She gave him a look. "Of course not. He's only eleven. Ah, look. Here's the road. You can release that death grip on the roll bar now."

The road was hardly a highway, being dirt, gravel, and washboards that made the Jeep take to the air like a hydroplane.

"I think the campground is thataway." Jackson pointed in a direction opposite to the one they were traveling.

"Your leg needs to be treated. I don't mind driving you to the hospital in Springerville."

"No hospital."

"What?"

"I said, no hospital. Stop the Jeep."

She pulled over and stopped. "Listen, I don't think you should trust my diagnostic abilities, Mr. Stone. What if your ankle is broken? If you don't get it set, you could end up hopping one-legged through your next action thriller. How is that going to look?"

"Yeah, Dad." Cherie leaned over between the front seats. "How would that look? Besides, where there's a hospital, there's civilization, right? I could find a video store, maybe."

"We have a satellite dish and DVDs at the motor home. We don't need civilization, because with civilization comes reporters and newspapers, even in a small town like Springerville." He explained to Rachel. "Right at the moment I'd just as soon stay away from the press—a little incident with Cherie that will be forgotten faster if she isn't in sight."

Cherie collapsed into the backseat in disgust. "It was no big deal. Let 'em talk."

"Don't you have a doctor who might pay a house call?"

Rachel didn't look sympathetic. "You really do live in a different world." She considered a moment, as he impatiently tapped a finger against the Jeep. "I suppose there's one thing we could do. I could take you down to Molly Satler. She's the postmistress in Greer, and she's seen enough broken legs, arms, and fingers to know if your ankle is busted or just sprained."

"A postmistress?"

"Molly and her family had the big Satler Ranch before the Forest Service turned part of it into campgrounds and private developers put up resorts on the rest. The woman's at least eighty-five. She used to patch up the hands back when there wasn't a doctor within a hundred miles. Working cattle breeds a lot of sprains, bruises, and breaks."

"Is she the kind to call *The National Enquirer*?" Cherie asked half hopefully.

"I doubt Molly even knows what *The National Enquirer* is. And I can guarantee if you ask her to keep quiet, that's what she'll do. I'll drop you off there, and if the bone needs setting, she can probably do a good job of it. Just don't come whining to me if you end up a cripple."

"My father doesn't whine," Cherie insisted.

"Yeah," Rachel said with a cynical laugh. "Right."

Jackson didn't like her tone one bit.

Rachel hung her ball cap on a peg inside the back door and threw her riding gloves on the kitchen table.

"Ah-ah! Not there." Joanne, the cook and head housekeeper and a lady of intimidating proportions, was very particular about items of clothing being draped over chairs or tossed onto tables. "You have a dresser drawer. Use it."

"Yes, Mother." Rachel picked up the gloves and stuffed them into her jeans pocket.

Joanne didn't miss a beat in kneading the mass of bread dough on the kitchen counter while she skewered Rachel with sharp brown eyes. "Don't get cheeky with me, Miss Smarty Pants. Wonderland Lodge made me a very attractive offer to come and work for them. And *they* have a swimming pool."

"That they can use two whole weeks during the summer. Besides, dear heart, you wouldn't want to go somewhere that would pay you what you're worth. Then what would you complain about?"

"I would find something."

Rachel smiled. "I'm sure you would."

This was a daily conversation. Joanne had been at the Lazy M for at least thirty-five years. She'd seen Rachel's husband, Darin, grow from a boy to a man and had been there to welcome Rachel to the family on her first visit to the ranch. When Darin had died and Rachel had decided to keep the place running as a guest ranch, Joanne had stayed on to make sure, in her words, that the Lazy M didn't suffer from all the tourists trooping through her house. She hadn't been ready to hit the retirement trail, even though the Marsh family had set aside a good pension for her. Rachel thanked heaven every day that Joanne had stayed. She had hired a couple of girls to help her—Terri Schaefer and Moira Keane—because a herd of guests on top of a troop of hungry cowboys was more than any sixty-something woman should be asked to handle. Joanne ruled all of them, including Rachel, with an iron hand. She knew more about running a household than Rachel would learn in her entire life, and she let Rachel know that several times a day.

"Sam trailed in a while back leading that mare Sally. We all thought you'd been dumped, but he said you'd rescued some greenhorn and a kid up top."

"Yeah. I drove them into Greer in their Jeep." She collapsed into a kitchen chair and propped her elbows on the table. "I don't suppose we have any iced tea."

"We do. I just put it in the fridge, so it's still warm. The *turistas* guzzled down the first batch when they got back from the lunch ride."

"We've got ice, don't we?"

"Help yourself."

Rachel got up and filled a tumbler with ice from the freezer, then poured herself tea warm enough to make most of the cubes melt. "At least they left me some lemon," she said, digging through the refrigerator. The guests ate in the Chuck-wagon, a separate building with an industrial-size kitchen, but they had free roam of the house, the family kitchen, and the refrigerator. Sometimes Rachel regretted that policy.

"That's about all they left. I had to send Moira into Springerville to do an extra grocery shopping."

"Do you know where Sam took himself to?"

"He and that dog of his are out helping Paul shoe a couple of horses. He said to tell you he'd eat dinner with the hands. Who were these people you got outta trouble? Sam said the kid has more lip than brains."

Rachel sighed and shook her head. "You wouldn't believe."

"Yes I would. I was a pretty cheeky youngster myself at one time, though you'd hardly believe it to see me now. The other one her dad?"

Rachel smiled, picturing Jackson Stone when she and Sam had first ridden up. "An exasperated, frustrated, at his wits' end dad, if you ask me. And real embarrassed at what a klutz he'd been."

Joanne sent her a speculative look. "Nice guy?"

"A real city slicker. Too much money and too little sense."

"Good-looking?"

Rachel shrugged. "Oh, yeah. Good-looking and knows it."

"Single?" asked the hopeful housekeeper.

"So I understand. Not that it matters. No interest here."

She sat down at the table with her iced tea and stretched out long legs to relieve the kinks brought on by the cramped Jeep. She would rather spend all day in a saddle than an hour in that thing. Anyone with half a brain would prefer a horse.

God! Listen to her, Rachel thought. She was as bad as some of the old mountain rats around here, complaining about everything and everyone that wasn't from the nineteenth century. Still, even though Jackson Stone seemed okay, the world he represented rubbed her wrong. It was a world where looks and charm reaped outlandish rewards, while an old-fashioned honest work ethic earned only contempt.

On the other hand, not reacting to all that, well, downright masculinity—she might as well admit it—was pretty much impossible.

You should have higher standards, she told herself. She did have higher standards. But sometimes her hormones didn't listen.

Sometimes Joanne didn't listen, either.

"Don't get your hopes up, Joanne. Likely I won't see the guy again. I drove him into Greer so Aunt Molly could look at his ankle. Karen gave me a ride back. Besides, I don't think this guy is my type."

"Girl, you gotta get back on that horse sometime. Just because your husband went and had himself an early heart attack doesn't mean you have to make widowhood a profession. A young woman like you withering on the vine—it's a crime."

"I'm hardly withering, dear heart. And believe it or not, every single guy who comes along is not necessarily husband material. Besides, I'm quite content as I am. Why complicate a nearly perfect life with something difficult like a husband?"

Joanne shook her head. "It's a woman's lot, honey."

Rachel responded with an impolite sound. "I have some book work to do. If you need help with dinner, let me know. I'll be in the office." She took her tea and fled the looming lecture before Joanne could get her engines revved.

In the safety of her office, Rachel switched on her computer and tapped fingers on the desk while it booted. The moment she sat in her chair, a gray-and-white cat jumped onto her lap.

"You should have met this guy, Fang. He's almost as handsome as you are."

Fang looked put out, but being a cat, Fang usually looked put out.

"Good thing Joanne didn't see him. She would never give me any peace."

Rachel knew Joanne's exhortations by heart. The housekeeper hailed from a generation that believed a woman's highest calling was at the side of a man. Joanne herself had never married, but her excuse was the Marsh family, who she claimed couldn't manage without her. But Rachel neglected her duty, the housekeeper kept telling her, in refusing to look for a good father for Sam and a caring husband for Sam's mother.

Rachel didn't mind the idea of remarriage. She'd had a good marriage with Darin Marsh. She was willing to try again. But husband material didn't amble along every day, especially in the Arizona mountains. And Rachel had no intention of leaving these mountains. She fit here, like a round peg slipping smoothly into its hole.

Besides, even Joanne would admit that a pampered Hollywood icon was a poor match for a plain-living woman, a woman whose entire wardrobe consisted of blue jeans and cowboy boots, whose idea of high living was downing more than one beer at the monthly barn dance.

The computer finally beeped alive. She clicked on her reservation book to enter some phone reservations from yesterday. Davidsons, two adults, two children, four days, mid-September—the last week of the season. No doubt hoping to see the aspen change color. She was generally full when the aspen put on their show. Henry Markam and Jeanne Tilburg, two adults, August 15–23. A whole week. Romancing, no doubt. This was a good place to do it.

Romancing Katie. The movie popped into Rachel's mind. It was one of Jackson Stone's rare departures into romantic comedy—a chick flick, Sam would say with a groan. Stone was one of the few Hollywood actors who fit well in any role. She'd both laughed and cried while watching *Romancing Katie*. His comedic timing was flawless. And his screen lovemaking was enough to make any woman break a fevered sweat. Rachel kicked herself under the desk for thinking about his lovemaking at all. "Quit that, you moron. Honestly!"

The cat looked up with a glare.

"Go back to sleep," Rachel advised crossly.

She entered the data on the reservations and looked at the list for the next two weeks. They still had a few vacancies. Two of the six cabins were available, except for two days, when three were vacant. Only one of the two ranch house rooms was booked for the following week. After that both were open. Not great for August, which was generally their biggest month. Late summer, when the monsoon rains settled the dust and turned the cienegas lush green, was always popular. Oh well, maybe she would get some last-minute reservations. If she didn't, it was going to be a tight winter.

She closed the reservation book and clicked on the Lazy M accounts. Here she had a solid hour's work trying to juggle funds to find money for a plumbing upgrade in the cabins and a new roof for the ranch house. It seemed that every time she thought they might be ahead financially, something came up to set them back.

She and Darin had inherited a truckload of debt along with the Lazy M, and when he had died and she'd converted the ranch to a guest resort, the necessary upgrades made the situation even worse. For three years she'd been trying to climb out of that hole, but even when business was good, something always came up to dig the hole deeper. The reduced beef market, increased energy costs, vet bills, storm damage, Sam's bout with appendicitis the year before—everything from A to Z cost money. The wolves weren't exactly howling at the Lazy M's door, but they certainly circled at a distance.

Being in constant debt drove Rachel crazy, a holdover from her days as a bank VP. No matter, she would still rather be struggling with finances at the Lazy M than suffering the traffic and heat in Phoenix, not to mention dying of boredom. If she never again had to wear stockings and heels it would be too soon.

The door opened and Joanne stuck in her head. "Miss Skin-and-bones, are you going to eat dinner or go hungry?"

"Is it dinnertime already?"

"Past dinnertime. The guests have eaten already. Sam is listening to tall tales in the bunkhouse. The Richardsons are reading in the rec room. The Boones are fighting in their cabin. Mary Hansen is pestering Paul about giving her riding lessons tomorrow, and that fellow with the hairpiece is wandering around hoping to catch a glimpse of Mary Hansen."

Rachel laughed. "What a nosy old biddy you are."

"It's part of the job. Are you going to eat? I have salad, beef stew, and fresh-made biscuits with homemade strawberry jam."

Rachel sighed and stretched. She didn't really want to wrestle with the accounts this evening. "I think I'll just take a bowl of that stew of yours to my room and enjoy some quiet time. I'm beat."

"Well, I don't wonder. Chatting up the guests all day, riding all over these mountains, pulling some greenhorn tourist outta trouble, taking care of that bear—Sam had to tell me about that. Who do you think you are, Davy Crockett?"

"That bear wasn't out to hurt anyone except my poor little calf. It's been kind of lean for the bears this season. Too dry."

"Hmmph! Lucky you didn't run into that bear while you were riding that green mare of Paul's. Give that fool horse a whiff of bear scent and she'd throw you tail over teacup. You woulda' ended up with something broke or bent, just like that tourist fella."

"Yes, Joanne." Rachel decided to agree before Joanne got more deeply into lecture mode. "I'll be by directly to get some dinner. You can just leave it on the stove if you want to go relax. I'll clean up. And Joanne?"

"Hm?"

"Enjoy your Sunday off tomorrow. I don't want to see you hanging around here working."

Joanne grinned. "Not me. I'm going into Springerville with Mr. Perkins to see a movie."

"Good for you."

Rachel took one more look at the account summary, decided that she really did need to put the job off, and shut down the computer.

While Rachel was dishing out her stew, Sam banged through the back door and tossed his hat onto a peg. A real cowboy, he'd once told her, didn't go without his hat even if the sun was down.

"Howdy, Ma!"

"Howdy, pardner."

Chesty bounced in behind his boy and came sniffing toward the stew pot.

"I guess I'd better feed him," Sam said.

"I guess you'd better."

"Can I have some ice cream?"

"Help yourself."

"You know that girl Donna?"

The Richardsons' fifteen-year-old daughter, Rachel remembered.

"She wants to see my new video game on the rec room computer. Is that okay?"

"If it's okay with you."

"Can I get her some ice cream, too?"

"Sure thing."

"Donna's a lot nicer than that creepy Cherie up on the mountain today. Girls must get nicer as they get older."

"Then I must be about as nice as a girl can get, eh?"

"Oh, Ma!"

"I'll be in my room if you need me."

Rachel's bedroom was the only truly private retreat she possessed. The Marshes' master bedroom was more a suite than a mere bedroom, plenty big enough for her to hang out in when she felt the need to be alone. A king-size bed dominated the space, but there was room for a sofa, coffee table, and entertainment center besides the usual chest of drawers and dressing table. She had her own bathroom, which was truly a godsend, and a spacious walk-in closet as well. The ranch house was old, but the Marsh who had built it four generations earlier hadn't stinted on space.

Rachel put her stew and iced tea on the coffee table and pried off her boots. Coming into this room after a long day felt like retreating to her own personal haven. All she needed to kick back was some light entertainment.

With that in mind, she sifted through the movies on the shelf of the entertainment center. When *Second Sight* appeared out of the pile, she warned herself away. She would not, absolutely not, slide a Jackson Stone movie into the DVD player. Not! No way!

She turned on the television and slid the Jackson Stone movie into the DVD player. Feeling guilty as well as silly, she settled onto the sofa. How many times had she seen this movie? At least three. Once in the theater, twice sitting curled up on her bedroom sofa. Ridiculous.

All her protestations didn't stop her from being absorbed as the opening credits rolled past and the story started. Jackson Stone on the screen, she mused, was okay. Better than okay, really. No denying that. Jackson Stone in the flesh wasn't much like his screen persona. The character he played in *Second Sight* was vulnerable, but it was a Greek tragedy, heroic, larger-than-life sort of Hollywood vulnerability. He was blind and bitter, waiting for true love to bring him out of his shell and back to life.

The Jackson Stone Rachel had met on the mountain was vulnerable with no heroism or larger-than-life trappings. Painfully human. Almost comically human. One didn't expect a Hollywood idol to be cursed with a sullen teenage daughter, a fear of horses, or something as mundane as an inconveniently sprained ankle. And who would have guessed the man who walked among lions in *Dawn in Africa* would have an anxiety attack over a silly little bear? Of course, she hadn't helped much with that story about the bear outrunning a Jeep. Not that it couldn't happen, but that bear wasn't interested in chasing them. Sometimes a little imp sat on her shoulder and tempted her to be wicked. She shouldn't have needled the poor man, but with his "I don't do horses" attitude, he had it coming.

Rachel put aside her empty stew bowl, settled more deeply into the sofa, and grabbed a cushion to hug. Hugging something was a requirement when watching a romantic movie. Here came the heroine with bouncy, tousled honey-blond curls framing an impossibly piquant face. Her perfectly ordinary sweater and jeans looked somehow extraordinary on that perfectly toned, perfectly proportioned, perfectly skinny body. Too bad Stone's tragically blind character couldn't see her to appreciate all the work the woman had put in with her fitness trainer.

Rachel wound a strand of her own dark brown badly-in-need-of-a-trim hair around one finger. "In my next life," she comforted herself, "I'm going to look like her. And have a hot romance with a guy who looks like him."

And in the looks department, Rachel mused, the real Jackson Stone did very well even without makeup and flattering camera angles. The rugged face might appear just a bit more rugged than on the screen, but those famous green eyes were positively alive. They animated his whole face. The slightly crooked nose, supposedly broken in a college boxing match, and the tiny scar cutting his left eyebrow made him look more real than Hollywood. And the smile—*megawatt* was the only adjective that came close. That somewhat skewed, heart-meltingly boyish, ever so slightly cocky smile was one of his trademarks. It melted the hearts of women everywhere and made men want to clap him on the shoulder and be his best friend. It was a total put-on, of course. No man could be that charming without working at it.

"Disgusting," Rachel complained to the man on the screen. "Next thing you know, I'll be writing you fan letters." But she kept watching the screen and hugging her cushion.

The blind guy and his annoyingly lovely savior had just indulged in their first kiss—big buildup, swelling music, wonderful close-up—when Sam's voice blasted up the stairs to break the mood.

"Hey, Ma! Ma! Guess who's here?"

CHAPTER 4

♡

RACHEL RAN DOWN the stairs to find herself confronted by the same brilliant green eyes that had looked out from her television screen. Startled, she blurted out, "What are you doing here?"

Jackson Stone's left brow—the one with the tiny scar—rose ever so slightly.

She matched his lifted brow with one of her own. "I thought you'd be headed back to California by now."

"Did I say that?"

Maybe she had just hoped it. Rachel felt a blush coming on, annoying but beyond her control. No doubt caused by that stupid romantic movie. It made her feel silly. It made her feel ridiculously vulnerable, and above all, it made her feel irritable.

"Can I do something for you, Mr. Stone?" she inquired, glancing at her watch pointedly.

He grinned. "Could be you can. Seems I find myself with a change in vacation plans."

Which was what he deserved, Rachel reflected, for fooling around when he should have been paying attention. He should limit his athletic feats to the movie set. "You seem to be walking, at least."

"That I am. Miss Molly wrapped me up so tightly, I'll probably get gangrene, but at least I can walk, sort of. She tells me I have a sprain. No climbing mountains or running marathons for a while, though."

"You normally run marathons?"

He snorted. "Not hardly! But I had been planning a trek along some good trout streams."

He glanced around, taking in the knotty-pine walls covered with antique photos of antique Marshes, and some recent ones as well. Rachel smiled, proud of her home and more than willing to show it off. The big star might live in a California Taj Mahal, but the Lazy M had more warmth, character, and just plain livability than any palace could boast.

The family dining room opened onto a deck through classic French doors, and huge windows overlooked the cienega. The big living room added charm, with a native stone fireplace, pine log rafters, two overstuffed sofas, a love seat, and a scattering of chairs placed for easy conversation. Directly in front of Jackson, a dark pine hallway dodged around the stairs and disappeared into the back recesses of the old house.

"Really nice place," he said.

"Thank you. We like it."

"Is there someplace private we could talk?"

Rachel sighed. She couldn't very well shoo him away without being outright rude. So she led the way through the hall to her office, then thought better of it. Her office was a chaotic mess. Call her vain, but she didn't particularly want to show off the slob side of her nature to America's heartthrob. Besides, the whole household could hear what went on in her office.

"This isn't going to do it," she told him before they reached the office door. "If you don't want everyone listening in, we'll have to go up." She gestured to the stairs.

The bedroom really wasn't where she wanted to take him, but with staff and guests making free with the house, it was the only truly private place she could offer. And after what he'd said that afternoon about anonymity, Rachel guessed her visitor didn't want to be interrupted by curious guests or staff.

"It's my bedroom." She closed the door behind them, trying to look casual about it. "But you said private, and this is about the only private space around here."

Don't explain, she told herself. Just because the country's

entire female population dreamed about getting Jackson Stone into their bedrooms . . . She squelched the thought. She didn't owe him an apology. After all, he was the one who'd shown up on her doorstep after-hours requesting a private audience.

"Now, Mr. Stone," she said firmly. "What is it that you need to talk about in private?"

His smile should have been registered as a lethal weapon. "Do you mind if I sit?"

"Of course not. Sit."

He limped toward the sofa, and as he did, Rachel spotted the cover of the DVD movie she'd been watching. It was faceup on the sofa, where Jackson Stone was bound to spot himself and his tousle-haired co-star staring at him in full-color glory.

Rachel felt her face go red. She bolted for the couch and dropped her backside down upon the offending cover. Nonchalantly, she smiled, as if something hadn't just gone crunch beneath her butt and she wasn't acting as if she'd taken a nip of locoweed.

He noticed the crunch. "Uh . . . I think you just sat on something. Nothing important, I hope."

"Oh, no. No. Nothing important."

Was that a knowing twinkle in those famous green eyes? No matter. She sat back and casually crossed her legs, ignoring the corner of *Second Sight* that was poking her in a very uncomfortable place.

Jackson sat down. "This is quite a spread you have here."

"The Lazy M is one of the original cattle ranches in this part of Arizona," she told him proudly. "Marshes have run cattle in these mountains for four generations."

"You still run cattle?"

"That's our primary business."

"So you have a full crew?"

"In the summer. We need enough staff to manage the livestock and help with the guest activities. When the cattle go to winter range and the guests go home, we cut back. The guys know this is seasonal work."

The star chuckled and shook his head. "A real ranch. What do you know?"

Rachel regarded him suspiciously. "It's all in the brochure, Mr. Stone. Could you get to the point? If you do have a point."

"Jackson," he reminded her, refusing to take offense. "Why won't you call me Jackson?"

"You seem like a Mr. Stone to me."

"You don't seem like a Mrs. Marsh to me."

Stubbornly, Rachel folded her arms across her chest.

"Okay." He grinned. "Where were we?"

"We weren't anywhere. Are we going somewhere?"

"Eventually. Aunt Molly had a lot of nice things to say about you, by the way. Is she really your aunt?"

"No, Mr. Stone. My aunt is an architect in Albuquerque. Everybody calls Molly an aunt because . . . I guess because she acts like everybody's aunt. Did she recognize you?"

"If she did, she didn't say anything. I get the impression she hasn't been to the movies since Charlie Chaplin was a leading man."

"I'd guess you're right."

"She talked a lot about you and the Marshes. How hard it is to keep the place going. How your husband was going to sell it to developers and then died. Molly figures it was divine retribution, you know. You've apparently elevated yourself to sainthood in her eyes by deciding to keep the old homeplace."

Rachel began to get annoyed. Molly should mind her own business, though she knew that was a futile hope. The old lady never refrained from expressing an opinion. "Mr. Stone, the point? Sometime before midnight, please? You jet-setters may keep fashionably late hours, but around here we turn in early."

He grinned. "Sorry. The point. Okay. Please don't take offense at this, but . . . Molly was of the opinion that you might jump at the chance of a little extra cash."

Now Rachel was truly annoyed. "You and Molly were discussing my finances?"

"Does Molly know anything about your finances?"

"No!"

"Then, no, we weren't exactly discussing your finances. She was just speculating that, in view of the ranch being in debt when your husband's parents died, and the high price of everything from chicken feed to vet services, you might welcome some extra income."

"And what prompted you to ask Molly about this?"

His brows lifted innocently. "I didn't. Molly gave me a complete rundown without me asking."

"Do tell!"

"You seem to be one of her favorite people."

Rachel began to regret sending Jackson into Molly's care. "And this is your business—how?"

"Well, now, it so happens that listening to Molly gave me an idea." He smiled in a way that hinted of trouble. "You might say I have a proposition for you."

Rachel's eyes narrowed in a way that told Jackson he was in for a challenge. The brilliant—okay, semi-brilliant—plan he'd conceived while suffering Molly's ministrations had one major stumbling block, and her name was Rachel Marsh.

Rachel Marsh, he gathered, was a woman who demanded everything make sense. And while his plan made all sorts of sense to him, to a person outside the acting community, it might not. A person who regarded the film industry as useless frivolity might even question his seriousness.

The scheme was totally serious, though. Jackson believed in making all situations work to his advantage, even when things took an unexpected turn. Unexpected turns could lead to good things.

"It's a business proposition," he hastened to assure her.

She regarded him impatiently. "I can't imagine what part of your business might involve me."

"Now, don't get all negative on me before you've heard the pitch. Actually, I want to do you a favor. It so happens I need to do some firsthand research. I'm up for a great role, a break-through role for me that could really expand my career. But it's a gritty, get your hands dirty out on the family farm sort of role in a serious film. Some idiots in the Industry are making noises that I don't have the personal background to be convincing in such a role."

"Meaning you've never done any real work in your life."

He grinned—charmingly, he hoped. "You catch on fast. Not that a good actor has to have lived a role to put himself into the character, but sometimes executive, non-actor types forget that."

"Uh-huh."

She didn't sound encouraging, but he went on. "So it occurred to me, since my vacation is pretty much ruined, why not turn this into a learning experience? I go to work for you as a regular, get-your-hands-dirty ranch hand—just for a few weeks. I'll do whatever nasty, backbreaking, sweaty jobs you tell me to do."

"And are cameras rolling to record every drop of sweat on your brow?" she asked, a definite bite in her tone.

"Of course not. Listen, Rachel, this is not some kind of pub-licity stunt. Just the opposite, in fact. The quieter we keep it, the better, because right now I want to keep Cherie out of the spotlight and away from the press. One of the reasons we were vacationing in the back of beyond was to make both her and me disappear for a while in a place the press isn't likely to be."

"We're the back of beyond, are we? How flattering."

This pitch wasn't going all that well, Jackson sensed.

Rachel gave him a narrow-eyed look. "Let me get this straight, Mr. Stone. You want to inflict yourself on my ranch so you can put dirt, sweat, and grit in your résumé and at the same time bury your daughter away from whatever trouble she's gotten herself into."

"Well, that's putting the situation in rather negative terms."

"Realistic terms, Mr. Stone. On the Lazy M, fantasy and fun are for the guests. The rest of us deal in reality."

Nope, Jackson admitted to himself, this wasn't going well at all.

———————

Sam eyed Cherie as she wandered out the front door onto the big covered porch. In deference to the cool August night, the girl had thrown a leather jacket over her shoulders. Like everything else about her attire, the jacket was black. So was the look she shot him over one shoulder.

"Your mom was blushing. Did you see that?"

Sam immediately took offense. "What do you mean, she was blushing?"

"Her cheeks got all red. Who is she trying to fool with that indifferent act of hers? She's hot for my dad just like every other woman alive."

"My mom's not hot for anybody. What's that mean, anyway?"

Cherie dropped onto the porch swing and heaved a world-weary sigh. "That means he turns her on, moron. She wants to go to bed with him."

"Why would she want to do that?"

"God! How ignorant are you, anyway? Don't you know anything?"

Sam folded thin arms across a scrawny chest and scowled. "I know a lot. A lot more'n you, I'll bet."

"Oh, *puleeeze!*" She gave him a superior smirk. "I guess since you don't have a dad, you don't know about men and women sleeping together. You're just a baby, after all."

"Am not!"

Cherie just sniggered.

"Besides, *moron girl,* I have a dad. Just because he's dead doesn't mean I don't have a dad. My mom says he watches us from heaven."

"Oh, sure," she said with a roll of her eyes.

"She says whole bunches of my dad's family are watching us. You know, this place has been in my dad's family almost forever."

"What's so great about that? Who'd want it, anyway? It's nowheresville. I'm surprised your mom stuck around after your dad died. She'll never find another man way out here."

Sam corrected her, glad to point out that the snotty little jerk didn't know everything. "We didn't *stay* here, we *came* here. My mom was vice president in charge of something at a bank. Down in Chandler." He smirked. "That's close to Phoenix, just in case you're ignorant."

Cherie snickered. "Dull. Dull, dull, dull."

Sam was tempted to turn his back and leave her alone on the porch, except that his mom said being polite to guests was very important, no matter how dumb they were. Except his mom hadn't used the word *dumb*. But that's what she'd meant. He supposed that Cherie qualified as a guest, since she didn't live here. Sometimes being polite was harder than other times.

So he stiffened his spine like a man would do, leaned on the porch railing, and reached down to scratch Chesty's head. As always, the dog was right at his side. "If you guys think this place is so lame, what're you doing here, anyway? I thought you were camping out somewhere in a fancy motor home."

Cherie shrugged. "My dad wants a place to hide out for a while, and I guess in the middle of nowhere is a good place to hide."

Sam perked up. "Hide out?" This was beginning to sound like a Jackson Stone movie. "What? Is he on the run?"

"Not exactly. I guess you'd say he's hiding me." Her jaw thrust forward in challenge.

"Why would he want to hide you? You're just a kid, like me."

"I'm not just a kid. *I* ran off with Jimmy Toledo. You know who *he* is, don't you?"

"No. Why should I?"

"He's only the lead singer in the most popular band going. Toy Boys. They got two Grammies last year."

"So why'd you go off with him? Did you join the band?" Sam thought that might be exciting, sort of like joining the rodeo circuit.

"Man oh man! You really don't know anything. We ran off to be together. We're in love. Hot for each other, you know."

Sam's eyes widened. "You're just a kid!"

Cherie smirked. "Obviously, I'm not."

"I'll bet you got in a heap of trouble."

She shrugged nonchalantly. "My dad's mad now, but he'll forget about it once he starts shooting a new film in a couple of months. In the meantime—" She sighed. "—I get dragged off to dullsville so the tabloid reporters don't hound me for the story."

Sam could understand that. "Yeah. I guess that would be real embarrassing."

"I'm not embarrassed. Let people talk. This whole stupid thing is my dad's idea."

"Your dad's smarter than you are."

Cherie snorted indignantly. "What do you know? Nothing. Moron."

That did it for Sam. His mom might want him to be polite, but this snotty girl was too much. "I know a lot, you stupid. I know you're a creep."

"*I'm* a creep? Look who's talking! With your cowboy hat and cowboy boots and"—she threw poor Chesty a disdainful look—"your stupid cowboy dog! Do you know how stupid you look? Man oh man! Stupid!"

Sam kicked the porch railing. "Oh, yeah? At least I don't look like some kind of a putrid vampire. Do you melt into a puddle when the sun hits you?"

"Very funny! Not!"

"My mom won't let your dad hide out here. That's a dumb idea. Why don't you go back to your stupid motor home and hide there?"

"Fine with me! I don't want to stay on your stupid ranch. But my clueless dad gets really lame ideas."

"Well, my mom won't let him."

Cherie laughed. "Right! She's probably melting all over herself. Women always give my dad whatever he wants. All he has to do is smile."

He gave Cherie the narrow-eyed look that Clint Eastwood had always used when he was mad at someone. "You don't know anything, creep girl. I'll bet my mom is in there right now saying no to your stuck-up dad."

Rachel stood up and crossed her arms definitively, sending a very clear message. "Sorry, Mr. Stone. The answer is no. Nada. No way. Bad idea."

She was wrong, Jackson told himself. It was a great idea, killing two birds with one Stone maneuver, so to speak. Earning calluses for the sake of a role would impress the powers at Touchstone, effectively countering Helen Gordon's snide assessment, and burying himself at Rachel's ranch would also bury Cherie. No one would think to look for them here. But he'd known Rachel Marsh would require some persuasion. That challenge didn't worry him much. A long time had passed since a woman said no to Jackson about anything.

"No. I repeat, Mr. Stone, I'm running a business here. More than one business, in fact. I really don't have time for this kind of charade."

"We won't be any trouble," Jackson assured her. "I can do a day's work alongside your hands, and Cherie can help out your housekeeping staff."

"How old is Cherie?"

"Thirteen. Almost fourteen."

"Too young. Ever heard of child-labor laws?"

"She'll just be helping out, not employed."

Rachel's face reflected how much help she thought Cherie might be. Jackson conceded that she had a point.

"I'll make sure she behaves."

"Sure you will."

The woman really made a habit of sarcasm.

"Listen, Mr. Superstar, this ranch is going to have an average of six or seven guests every day over the next few weeks. More on weekends. Do you really think these people are so dumb they won't recognize you?"

He did like the way her eyes glinted when she became intense. They were sky blue and thickly fringed with lashes that owed nothing to mascara.

"I don't think your guests or anyone else here is dumb, Rachel. Is it okay to call you Rachel?"

"You don't need to call me anything. You're not going to be here."

"Rachel." He smiled. "That's a beautiful name."

Her brow lowered dangerously.

"Rachel, people see what they expect to see where they expect to see it. No one is going to expect to see Jackson Stone the actor on the Lazy M Ranch. Are they?"

"That's because Jackson Stone the actor doesn't belong on the Lazy M Ranch."

"You didn't recognize me at first because I was out of context, right? You thought I maybe just looked a lot like a certain film actor."

She set her stubborn jaw.

"The same thing will happen with your guests. Maybe they'll think I look a bit like a guy they saw in a movie, but it won't occur to them that someone who makes millions per film would be busting his butt at a place like this."

Her eyes narrowed.

"Not that this isn't a very nice place for someone to bust his butt at."

Blue eyes chilled to glacial. "Why don't you just take your millions and escape to someplace like Rio de Janeiro?"

"Rio's not my style. Besides, I need a low-profile bolt-hole for Cherie, and I truly do need the dirt and grit on my résumé, as you say."

"I don't care about your damned résumé," she snapped. "And if you need a bolt-hole for your daughter, your motor home would work just fine, it seems to me."

"Condemning a man to days shut up in a motor home with a sullen teenager is cruel and unusual punishment."

"Your problem! Not mine!"

After a moment of tense silence, Rachel sighed. "Listen, Mr. Stone, if you're so set on spending time here, stay as a guest. I'm sure you can afford the room rates."

"Being a guest here would be a great vacation," he conceded. "But observing doesn't teach like doing."

She eyed him sourly. "I don't consider the Lazy M to be a hardship tour of duty. The bunkhouse has a television set, CD player, and a fridge with an automatic ice maker. And even here in the back of beyond, mechanization has taken the place of muscle."

"But for a spoiled and pampered actor," he said, a twinkle in his eye, "the Lazy M would be a challenge. A dip into the chilling pool of reality."

"Oh, please!"

He grinned. "Besides, it'll do Cherie good to wash dishes and make beds, be with people who . . . who . . ."

She lifted one brow. "Who don't make millions of dollars for producing a totally frivolous product?"

He tried to defuse her with his famous smile.

The stubborn woman shook her head, her expression etched in a permanent scowl. "You've got it all figured out, it seems. But it won't work."

He had to admire true stubbornness, but he wasn't about to give up. "Come on, Rachel. Consider it a good deed. Summer camp for the overprivileged."

The look he got was not encouraging.

"It's not like I expect you to hire me for real. Of course, I'll pay you for your trouble."

"I think you and Cherie would be a good deal more trouble than most of my guests. My staff doesn't have time to baby-sit you, and your incompetence would for sure affect the guests."

"Incompetence? Nah! I'm a quick-study. Your guests won't guess that I'm not a seasoned hand."

She looked dubious.

"I'm an actor. I act a real good part."

"And just how are you going to act the part of a ranch hand with a bum ankle?"

"A little gimp won't make a difference. I don't plan on hiking ten miles or climbing any mountains."

She still looked stubborn.

The time had come to break out the heavy artillery. "Three thousand a day for every day we're here. And at the first bit of trouble, we're gone. Promise."

Her jaw dropped with gratifying drama. "Three thousand a day? That's ridiculous."

"Four thousand, then." The more she denied him, the more he wanted her surrender.

"Mr. Stone, I only charge my guests one-fifty per day."

"Then this will make up for the extra trouble."

Her jaw snapped shut, a woman struggling with temptation. Jackson was very experienced in offering temptation.

"I couldn't take advantage of you like that."

"Take advantage."

She started to pace, and he couldn't help but notice the attractive sway of her slim hips, totally natural and uncultivated. No image consultants had coached her in that fine-looking walk. He'd forgotten that real women like Rachel Marsh existed.

"You'd have to work as hard as the other hands."

"Of course."

"This isn't a movie set, you know. No stunt doubles. No special effects."

"No problem."

She lifted her chin, getting set, Jackson could tell, to deliver the clinching blow. "And sooner or later you're going to have to get on a horse."

He smiled bravely. "I'll gird my loins."

"And no smart-ass remarks to your boss."

He'd won. Of course. "I'll be a model employee." He ought to get an Oscar just for convincing her to go for it. Standing, he reached out to shake on their deal. When she gave him her hand, Jackson wondered at the electricity of her touch. Rachel Marsh, in jeans and a seersucker shirt, innocent of makeup or any style whatsoever, with no allure other than what God gave her, affected him in a way that no woman had in a long time.

And she looked as if she were shaking hands with the devil.

"We'll bring our stuff over tomorrow morning, early."

She didn't look pleased. "Maybe by that time I will have figured out what to do with you."

He had a few suggestions, but guessed that she wouldn't want to hear them. So he settled for having the last word. Going out the door, he looked back and gave her his famous smile. "If the DVD is crumpled along with that cover you sat on, I'd be glad to get you another. I have an in with the distributor."

A very satisfying color rose to her cheeks.

Rachel stared at the bedroom door long after it had closed behind that infuriating man. She'd fallen prey to the almighty dollar. How humiliating. All Jackson Stone had needed to do was throw money her way, and she was in the palm of his hand. Seductive images had paraded through her mind—new plumbing, repairs to the barns and house, a truck that didn't break down every two months, and maybe a new stove for the Chuckwagon. Four thousand a day! Just think what she could do with that! The lure of temporary freedom from the monthly agony of juggling bills had done her in.

Having to surrender to that reality made her like Jackson Stone even less. Yet even as she chewed on her distaste, a niggle of doubt wormed its way into her thoughts. Had plumbing and repairs been the entire seduction? Could any woman be totally unaffected by the hint of humor in the man's eyes and the melting heat of his smile? Responding to such blatant masculine appeal didn't say much for her principles, did it?

With painful honesty, Rachel wondered who she found more infuriating—Jackson Stone or herself?

Next morning in the Chuckwagon kitchen, Rachel burned the bacon. And the cherry almond muffins came out of the oven too crusty because she wasn't paying attention when the timer dinged.

"Lord! Look at this mess!" She had no patience with people

woolgathering when they should be working, and that went double for herself. She'd been doing nothing but woolgathering since Jackson Stone had made his exit the evening before.

Her new "employee" was due to report for work this morning, if work was what he intended to do. She had a gut feeling the man was going to be much more trouble than he was worth.

But her guests weren't going to care about her distractions when they had burned bacon and crusty muffins for their Sunday breakfast.

John and Debbie Richardson were already in the dining hall. They showed up early every morning for the juice and coffee that came out of the Chuckwagon kitchen at 6 A.M. sharp. Debbie, a woman who couldn't sit still, Rachel had noted, helped Moira set the table. Husband John leaned against the pass-through into the kitchen and razzed the cook as she battled bacon smoke.

"Rachel, you should never let Joanne out of the kitchen."

Rachel sighed and brushed back a lock of dark hair that had escaped her ponytail. "You're right, John. I should chain her to the stove, but for some reason Joanne objects to that. She even insists on a day off every once in a while."

"Need help? Deb's a whiz in the kitchen."

Debbie came up behind her husband and elbowed him in the ribs. "Deb's on vacation," his wife reminded him sharply.

Rachel laughed.

"Men think vacations are just for them," Debbie told her. "Wives come along only to help."

"You tell him, Debbie! And no, John, I don't need help. Before the breakfast bell rings, you'll have crispy bacon done to a turn, fluffy pancakes, perfect scrambled eggs, and—"

"And charred muffins. I'll take one of those babies off your hands. Just to help."

Rachel grinned and tossed him one.

"John Richardson," his wife scolded, "you're going to get fat."

"I'm on vacation. Besides, I'm going to hike miles along Arizona's best trout stream today. I need the calories."

Debbie made a rude sound, then regarded Rachel with sympathy. "If you need help, Rachel, I'd be glad to—"

"Nope!" Rachel cut the offer short. "You're a doll, Deb, but everything's fine." Or it would be if she could pull her mind back into focus. Jackson Stone was already distracting her, making her life difficult, and he hadn't even arrived.

Rachel asked herself for the hundredth time why she had let herself be seduced into the man's scheme. She had done without his money until now, and she could have continued to stretch her shoestring budget. Running the ranch and raising a son at the same time allowed no time for distractions. She worked her butt off with scarcely a day off, and she didn't need to baby-sit a spoiled actor who fell off logs, turned pale at the sight of a horse, and thought the world owed him anything he wanted just because he was a film star. As if that weren't enough, he brought along a daughter who looked as if she should be swooping through the night sky with the bats.

She pulled another two pounds of bacon from the freezer and stuck it in the microwave to thaw, then searched through the cupboards for enough flour and sugar to mix up another batch of muffins. Moira was going to be making another emergency trip to the store today, it seemed. Rachel remembered when she'd lived five minutes away from a giant Albertson's grocery in Chandler. At the time she hadn't appreciated the convenience.

Debbie's voice called into the kitchen. "Rachel. Looks like you have a couple of new guests."

Rachel glanced out the Chuckwagon window. Jackson Stone's army-green Jeep had pulled up in front of the ranch house. Chesty greeted the newcomers with a chorus of barking, then broke into a joyous dance of border collie welcome. For a moment Rachel thought the man who jumped out to knock on the front door of the house wasn't Jackson, though the girl draped lethargically in the passenger seat was definitely Cherie—Batgirl revisited. The guy wasn't quite as tall, his shoulders not as broad, and he wore a battered cowboy hat that no self-respecting movie star would have touched off the set.

Terri answered the front door, broom in hand, and gestured toward the dining hall. The fellow turned, and Rachel saw that he was indeed Jackson Stone, but a slight slouch changed his whole appearance, reducing his impressive frame to one somewhat narrower and less arresting. Details of his features hid in the shadow of the ridiculous hat.

Rachel sighed. "That's not a new guest," she told Debbie. "That's a new hand I hired."

"Can he cook?" John teased, then laughed. "No offense, Rachel, but how long are you going to leave the bacon in the microwave?"

"Oh, damn!"

Jackson walked into the Chuckwagon with Cherie in tow, cheerfully greeting guests who were gathering for breakfast. His "howdy, there" rang with a slight Texas drawl. When he grinned at her, Rachel gave him a stern look. She refused to fall for that professional charm.

"Good morning, Mr. . . . Mr. . . . ." Suddenly she didn't know what to call him.

"Stoney Jackson, ma'am. At your service."

"Can you cook?" John asked.

"I surely can, sir. Just point me toward the kitchen."

"Follow the smell of burning bacon," John said with a chuckle.

Rachel glared. "Ignore John. Things are under control in the kitchen. You'll want to get your stuff settled. You and Cherie are staying in the Sitting Bull cabin." *Should change the name to Lottsa Bull.* "It's behind the ranch house, up in the trees a bit. Sam can show you the way. You'll find him out in the main barn, across from the house."

But Jackson had already waltzed past her into the kitchen. "Cherie can take our stuff to the cabin. We didn't bring much."

Cherie rolled her eyes. "Dad!"

"Hop to, kid. Go find Sam and haul our stuff up to Sitting Bull."

"Bull is right!" She gave him a mutinous scowl, then brightened. "Can I drive the Jeep up there?"

Jackson hesitated, then relented. "If you go over five miles per hour, I promise you won't get a license until you're twenty-five."

"Dad!"

"Go. Then come back here and help with breakfast."

Looking fairly pleased with himself, he rubbed his hands together and surveyed the kitchen with kingly confidence. "Okay. How many do we have eating?"

Once Jackson Stone decided to do something, Rachel discovered, he was like a tidal wave. Over her weak objections he set out to handle the entire breakfast, relegating her to kitchen helper. All the while he chatted up the guests in a Texas twang that could have come straight from Dallas. And not once did he step out of the character he'd created.

The guests, men and women alike, ate it up—both the breakfast and Jackson's act. Especially young Donna Richardson. As much attention as the man garnered, it was a miracle no one discerned his true identity. But no one did. Rachel watched his performance with nothing short of amazement.

"You've got pancake-flipping down to an art," Mary Hansen remarked as she took her plate to the pass-through for a second helping.

"It *is* an art." His grin dripped with charm. "Learned at my daddy's knee. It's even more impressive when I do it over a griddle on an open fire."

"These are some of the best pancakes I've ever tasted," John Richardson admitted.

"You've eaten enough of them," his wife complained.

"Anything eaten on vacation has zero calories," Jackson told them cheerfully. "It's the law. But maybe we should save some for the hands?"

"They ate earlier," Rachel told him. "At 5:30. When you'll be eating from now on." She couldn't keep just a bit of gloat from her voice.

"Yeah, and when Joanne isn't here they have Ted or Nathan cook for them," John said unnecessarily.

Rachel decided she'd be glad when John headed back home to Missouri.

"Well, now . . ." Jackson flipped a pancake high, caught it on his spatula, and slid it onto a serving plate. "You can't expect a woman who can ride, shoot, and run a ranch to be able to cook as well. Some chores just have to be saved for us peons."

"Well said!" Laura Boone applauded. "It's good to see a man laboring over a hot stove."

"When have you ever labored over a hot stove?" husband Tim scoffed.

"I open the frozen dinners and stick them in the microwave."

Jackson beamed at her. "Obviously another woman too busy for such a common chore."

Bemused, Rachel watched her guests respond to Jackson's charm. No one realized they were part of an exercise in character acting. No one looked past "Stoney Jackson" to see Jackson Stone pulling the strings. His hair was now black, not medium brown, and most of the length had disappeared into a rather poor crew cut. The rounded shoulders made him narrower and shorter, and a certain uneducated idiom in his speech fit exactly the role he portrayed. But Rachel still saw Jackson Stone. Whenever he looked her way his eyes twinkled with pure mischief.

She wanted to hit him for being so damned good at what he did.

As the last of the guests filed out, Moira worked at clearing the tables, and Rachel piled the dirty dishes into the sink. She decided the time had come for giving the man his due. "You are good. I have to admit it. You are very good at pretending to be someone you're not."

Leaning indolently against the worktable, he lifted a cocky brow. "I'm good at a lot of things."

"Oh, I'm sure you are."

Just then Cherie came in. "Wow! What a bunch of pigs! Look at this mess."

Jackson handed his daughter a pair of rubber gloves he'd found beneath the sink. "All yours."

"You're kidding, right?"

"Don't break anything."

"Man oh man!" she whined.

"Come on, Rachel. Show me where I'm bunking." As if he owned the place, Jackson took her arm and led her toward the door.

Rachel let him have his way. His cocksure attitude wouldn't last long. Mr. Slick Hollywood may have won this battle, but he might sing a different tune when he discovered what ranch life was really like.

She was counting on having fun at his comeuppance. As long as the man insisted on complicating her life, he might as well entertain her while he was at it.

CHAPTER 5

♡

MELANIE CARR GAVE the phone's off button an angry punch, then cursed when she drew back the stub of a once perfectly manicured nail. She scowled at the Pacific Ocean beyond her family room windows. "This is your fault, Jackson Stone! Damn you! Not only are you an oblivious, thoughtless, arrogant blockhead, but your staff is, too!"

The nerve of that little man Harvey Mathias, talking to her as if she were just anyone, as if she were one of Jackson's horde of female admirers, an ordinary pest to be brushed off as if she didn't count. She was Jackson Stone's wife, dammit! Well, his ex-wife. And glad of it. But that didn't give Jackson's personal assistant the right to brush her off.

"*Jackson and Cherie are out of town, Miss Carr,*" she mimicked in a good approximation of Harvey's high-pitched voice. "*I'm under strict instructions not to disclose their whereabouts to anyone.*"

She shouted at the dead phone. "I'm not just anyone, you dimwit. I'm Cherie's mother! Can't Jackson hire someone with the brains to exercise a little judgment?"

That's what she should have said instead of coldly and politely telling him to have Jackson call her. This truly was all Jackson's fault. He treated her as if she didn't exist, as if he could do anything he wanted with Cherie without consulting her.

And, of course, he could, legally. She'd given him sole custody when they divorced, not because she didn't love her daughter, but because she was still searching for herself, for her true inner soul and her connection with the Universe. How could she raise a child when she didn't even know her own place on the great Wheel of Life? Not wanting responsibility for Cherie, however, didn't mean that she didn't care.

Now Jackson had spirited Cherie away to who knew where, just when Melanie needed desperately to be with her daughter. And Harvey Mathias, that little twerp, wouldn't tell her how to get in touch with them. Ordinarily, Melanie would let the annoyance flow over her and be done with it, thus regaining her center and achieving harmony. But that very morning Makirah, her spiritual guide and mentor, had told her that she needed to connect on a deeper level with her only child. Cherie, Makirah had said, was an important part of Melanie's karma, and she courted disaster by not exploring the mother-daughter relationship more completely.

Melanie was nothing if not conscientious about pursuing her karmic goals, but how was she supposed to make a deeper connection with Cherie when Jackson had her hidden somewhere? The man totally overreacted to the little incident with Jimmy Toledo—acting as if Melanie had been irresponsible in letting Cherie run off with the boy, treating Jimmy as if he were some kind of criminal, and then dragging Cherie off just because the press hounded them a bit. The press always hounded Jackson. He should be used to it.

"Damn!" She inspected the ragged nail. "Damn you, Jackson! You make me mad enough to spit!"

That in itself wasn't healthy. Internalizing anger and frustration damaged the spirit and cut the soul's lines of communication to the Universe. What she needed right then was a peaceful few minutes of meditation. But first . . . "Nancy!"

When her secretary stuck her head in the room, Melanie held up the torn nail indignantly. "Emergency, Nancy. Call my manicurist and get me an appointment this afternoon."

"Yes, Miss Carr."

"And see that I'm not disturbed for fifteen minutes or so, would you?"

"Certainly, Miss Carr."

That important item dispensed with, Melanie arranged herself cross-legged on the plush carpeted floor, straightened her spine, closed her eyes, and concentrated on drifting. Breathe in, breathe out. Breathe in, breathe out. Breathe in the pure air of peace, breathe out the stale air of frustration. In, out. In, out. She imagined herself walking along her beach, listening to the sound of the waves, opening herself to the healing light of the sun. Her toes relaxed. Her ankles, calves, thighs—all let go of the tension that held her. Closer and closer toward peace she drifted . . . when a knock on the door abruptly yanked her back to the harsh world.

"Miss Carr," said Nancy's voice. "Phone call about—"

"I asked not to be disturbed."

"It's about your daughter."

"Oh!" She jumped up from the floor. "I'll take it in here as soon as I plug the phone back in. Thank you, Nancy."

Much to Melanie's disappointment, however, the voice on the phone belonged not to her errant ex-husband, but to Josh Digby. Josh worked for the *National Star,* a gossip tabloid alternately used and abused by the celebrities it featured.

"Very clever, Josh, saying you knew something about Cherie in order to get me on the line."

"I didn't say I knew something about Cherie, Mel. I just mentioned her name."

Josh was smart, and he was a shark. He'd been following Jackson practically since the beginning of Jackson's film career.

"Looking for Jackson, are you? Thinking I might know where he and Cherie are?"

"Hey, Mel, the Toledo story's still hot. All I want are a few good photos of Cherie, maybe a candid interview with her and Jackson. Is that so much to ask after all the publicity I've given the man?"

"And I suppose if you can't find them, you'll just make some stuff up to make sure the story stays hot."

"Would I do that?"

"In a New York minute. Sorry, Josh, as it happens, I don't know where they are, either."

"Come on, Mel. I'll write a good story. Make Jackson out to be some kind of hero defending his daughter. What exactly did happen, anyway?"

"You won't get it from me, Josh. Talk to Mathias."

"He already gave me the cold shoulder."

Just as he'd given her, the little snot.

"So," Digby continued, undaunted, "give me a call if you hear from your ex?"

"I'll consider it, but don't count on it."

"The *Star* can be nice to you, Mel. A lot of your fans read our publication."

"I'm hanging up now, Josh. Good-bye."

What a sleaze, she thought as she punched off. She almost felt sorry for Jackson. With that bloodhound on his trail, he wouldn't enjoy his vacation for very long, wherever he was.

Jackson decided right away that he liked the Lazy M. He liked the weathered old ranch buildings, picturesque but sturdy enough to stand for another century or so. He liked how the guests obviously felt like family with the staff and Rachel. And he especially liked Rachel. Vexing Rachel was fun. Getting her to smile—far harder than inspiring her scowl—was just as fun. With Rachel he didn't have to worry about his image. She knew who he was, and her disdain was very straightforward. After a steady diet of adulation, Hollywood style, to be barely tolerated was refreshing. Unlike most women of his acquaintance, Rachel didn't flirt, didn't assume airs, didn't size him up for what he could do for her career or could do in her bed. Instead, she sized him up for what she could do to him.

Most of the women in Jackson's life were either carved from steel ambition or concocted from froth with no substance. Rachel Marsh was neither. She projected a tough image, but

Jackson sensed a heart beneath the steel armor. He saw that heart in her eyes when she looked at her son or talked about the mountains and the picturesque ranch she called her home.

Not that he should be thinking about Rachel Marsh's heart, Jackson reminded himself. Only a few weeks before, he'd been advising Rick Carroll to avoid women who wanted commitment. He should heed his own advice. Celebrities didn't do well in committed relationships. Jackson had learned that the hard way. And if ever Rachel Marsh let a man in her life, he suspected, she would want him in her life with heart and soul. She was the dangerous kind of woman—a woman that a man shouldn't take lightly. She was a woman who could slip under a man's skin without him realizing what had happened. With those killer blue eyes and artlessly curling hair, she made a man itch to touch her, ache to kiss her.

Point of fact, Jackson found the idea of kissing Rachel Marsh dangerously compelling, even though he should know better. The woman didn't like him. She didn't like him at all. Still, how pleasant it would be to kiss Rachel until her knees turned to water and that water turned to steam, until her hair curled from the heat generated between them, until she had to admit that he was a man, a person, and not just a celluloid cutout who lacked any substance off the big screen. Just the thought made his blood run like it hadn't run in years.

If he really wanted to, Jackson told himself, he could get past Rachel's skepticism, her smug certainty that he was a fool, her determination to give him a dose of orneriness that would send him running. He could kiss her, Jackson told himself, if he wanted to.

But he shouldn't. Rachel Marsh wasn't his kind of woman, and he should leave her the hell alone.

Rachel had no intention of leaving him alone, however. That became clear his first day on the ranch. Even on a Sunday the Lazy M was a beehive of industriousness, and the boss wasted no time in putting Jackson to work. He found himself deep in more grit than he could handle when Rachel invited him in a smug tone to spend the day fixing the plumbing in the cabin where he and Cherie were going to stay. As an opening salvo, the move was a good one. It kept him away from her guests, her employees, and herself, while busying him with a grubby task that no one could enjoy. The cabin had been out of commission for two weeks, she explained. No regular paying guest would appreciate a leaky faucet and a toilet that intermittently rebelled in a fairly unpleasant manner. None of the hands had the time to look at the problem, and the plumbers in Show Low and Springerville, the nearest towns big enough to support a plumber, were backed up—along with the local toilets, it seemed—with a waiting list of at least two weeks. Sitting Bull cabin was the only place for Jackson and Cherie to stay, Rachel told him, smiling with patently false innocence. Could he dive into the problem and try to fix it?

He was sure she'd be glad to see him dive into the mess quite literally, but Jackson gave her a cheerful smile. If she thought film stars weren't accustomed to wading about in shit, then she didn't know the Industry.

Nevertheless, several times during the day he had to remind himself that he was playing the hand he'd dealt himself. He'd wanted to get his hands dirty like a real ranch worker; he just hadn't realized real ranch workers put up with this kind of dirt. Still, the nastiness of the task made triumph all the sweeter. It took him three times longer than it should have, maybe. Not to mention a few visits to the Internet via the computer in Rachel's office (surprising the things one could find on the Internet!). But success was worth the effort. Jackson savored the moment he could tell Rachel that her recalcitrant pipes were fixed. Just before dinnertime, he searched her out in the office.

"Sitting Bull is sitting pretty again," he announced proudly. His shirt bore grease smudges, and grime lodged beneath his fingernails. The dirt was a badge of honor.

"No kidding?" The surprise on Rachel's face was entirely satisfying.

"No kidding. Try the pot for yourself."

She blinked, then smiled. "Thanks so much, but you're the

one who gets to use it, so I guess if it's fixed good enough for you, that's good enough for me."

"Didn't think I could do it, did you?"

"Not really," she admitted "For some reason, I've been thinking that you Hollywood types were all pampered idiots."

He grinned tolerantly. "Nowadays I'm a pampered idiot. Once upon a time I was a poor teaching assistant who couldn't afford cab fare to class."

"Cab fare?"

"From my apartment in the city—New York. I went to the university. Had to ride the subway."

Her smile skewed to one side. "An apartment in New York. Poor fellow. Really roughing it, were you?"

He laughed "If you've never lived in a cold-water walk-up with three roommates, you don't know the half of it."

She leaned back in her chair and regarded him over the pile of paperwork on the desk. "You're just full of surprises, *Stoney.*" She gave italics to the name.

Jackson shrugged, and smiled. "I thought it sounded like a cowhand's name."

"And you didn't think anyone would connect Stoney Jackson with Jackson Stone?"

"That's the beauty of it. Jackson Stone undercover, so to speak, would never choose a name so close to his own. Not if he had any brains. So people conclude that something so obvious has to be a coincidence."

"If he has any brains . . ."

He had handed her that one, but he did appreciate the glint in her eye.

Rachel just shook her head. "Quit distracting me, Jackson. You can collect your daughter in the Chuckwagon. She and Moira are getting together the fixings for tomorrow's breakfast."

"I haven't seen Cherie all day. Has she behaved?"

"She hasn't done much other than follow Sam around and annoy him. And she and a guest—a fifteen-year-old named Donna Richardson—have been holed up in Donna's cabin, trading makeup tips, I think. Donna's parents were just as glad to have their daughter out of their hair for the day."

He couldn't help but rub it in. "See, Rachel. Everything's working out great."

She snorted. "Don't dust off a place for Oscar before you get him, my actor friend. Tomorrow is another day."

Tomorrow was also Monday, and what an early Monday it was. Even before the birds were awake, Rachel introduced Jackson to Vince, a crusty, bowlegged old fellow who had a handshake like a vise. Sitting in the Chuckwagon drinking strong coffee and inhaling the smell of bacon frying, Vince could have walked right out of an old Clint Eastwood western, maybe *The Good, the Bad, and the Ugly*. He could have done very nicely as the Ugly. Weathered, sun-seared skin, a bulbous nose, and watery blue eyes were his best features. A smile revealed tobacco-stained teeth, but the smile was friendly enough.

"Well, now . . ." Vince fixed watery eyes on Jackson where he sat across the table cradling a coffee cup in his hand. "Stoney, did you say the name was?"

Rachel, looking perkier than anyone should at five in the morning, grinned wickedly. "That's right, Vince. Stoney Jackson."

"Well, Stoney, sorry I wasn't around yesterday to break you in. We had a couple New Yorkers who wanted to ride up Mount Baldy and I had to take 'em. But I figger Miz Marsh got you broke in a bit."

"She did, at that," Jackson agreed with a crooked smile.

"I'm not generally head man around here," Vince explained. "That's my cousin Mac, but he's sittin' on a beach in Mexico with his wife, gettin' sunburned like a fool. So we're a man short for a while. Hope you don't mind hard work." He spat a stream of tobacco that splatted a neat landing five feet away.

Joanne bellowed from the kitchen. "I heard that, Vince Dugan, you old goat! You spit on my clean floor and I'm going to come in there and wring your scrawny neck."

Vince winced at the volume of the woman's threat. "Fergot," he half apologized. "Usually have my can with me."

Jackson tried to keep from smiling. He didn't know guys like Vince still existed—the genuine article walking straight from the pages of a Louis L'Amour novel. "I don't mind hard work," he assured the man. "I can do whatever it takes, in spite of this bum ankle. Just try me."

Rachel agreed with an evil grin. "Stoney's a regular John Wayne. The tougher the work, the more he likes it. Don't you, Stoney?"

"Uh . . . yeah. Sure thing."

"Izzat so?" Vince squinted at him assessingly, a slight curl of his lip expressing his opinion of the new hand better than any words. "Well, I s'pose that's good, 'cause we don't tolerate no slackers here on the Lazy M. I s'pose Miz Marsh told you that."

"Yes, sir. In no uncertain terms," Jackson admitted.

The old man turned back to Rachel. "He talks pretty highfalutin. We'll find out if he can work."

The old man, Jackson mused, was sharp as a tack in spite of his rough manners. He would have to be careful around this one.

"Okay, Mr. John Wayne, do you suppose you could manage to drive the wagon fer today's fishing picnic?"

Jackson leaped in before Rachel could say anything. "No problem."

"Good. Because George was gonna drive, but I need him to help Paul with the shoeing. And Clint ain't coming in from Greer today. He's puking his guts from a bad tamale. Ted's gonna drive the truck, and Nathan's gonna shepherd the dudes who wanna ride horseback—unless you'd rather ride horseback as baby-sitter instead of drive the team."

Jackson figured that sitting on a wagon seat was far better than sitting in a saddle. "I'll drive," he said.

"Okay, then, Stoney boy." Vince gave him a tobacco-stained grin. "Be at the barn at ten."

Rachel no longer looked perky for the early hour. She looked, in fact, a bit green.

Vince exited the dining hall just as Joanne marched in from the kitchen with mop in hand, ready to both clean up tobacco juice and give Vince a good thumping with the mop handle.

"How his wife puts up with that man I don't know," the housekeeper grumbled.

Rachel chuckled. "Why do you think he lives in the bunkhouse instead of in town with her?"

"The woman has the right idea. Kick him out."

Taking the mop from her, Rachel shooed her away. "I'll do this. The men will be in for breakfast in a few minutes. You go back to the kitchen."

As Joanne bustled back toward her sizzling bacon, Rachel mopped up the mess on the plank floor without so much as a grimace. Jackson wasn't surprised. Any pistol-packing mama who pulled calves from their mothers' wombs, shooed away marauding bears without so much as a blink, and managed to look perky at five in the morning wouldn't flinch at anything. He thought of offering to help, but she warned him away with a hostile glare.

"I suppose it's too much to expect you to really know how to drive a team and wagon?" she demanded.

He gave her the cocky grin just to see her fume. "Didn't you see the big chase in *Trueheart*?"

She scoffed. "That wasn't a stunt double?"

"Well, yeah. But I got to sit in the wagon for close-ups."

Rachel rolled her eyes. "Fine, cowboy. It's your funeral. If you kill yourself, just don't bust up my wagon and my guests while you're doing it."

Rachel wasn't about to turn Jackson Stone loose on an innocent group of Lazy M guests who looked forward to a picturesque wagon ride up to a premiere fishing spot. Rachel or any one of the hands could have driven them up to Sheeps Crossing in the ranch van, but a wagon behind a four-horse team was so much more fun. Good thing these poor city slickers didn't know their lives were in the balance.

Not that the team was hard to handle. The horses were gentle as lambs—Sam could have driven them. The greenest greenhorn on the ranch could probably have handled them. But Rachel didn't know that Jackson Stone could handle them. After all, he had fallen off a log.

So when he showed up at the barn at ten, Rachel was waiting for him.

"Do you know how to harness a team?" she asked, even though she knew the answer.

Unabashed, he smiled. "You mean they don't come already harnessed?"

She was not going to crack a smile, Rachel told herself. She wouldn't give him the satisfaction. He might have been able to charm Meg Ryan out of disliking him in *Romancing Katie*, but she wouldn't fall for it.

"You have a half hour to learn. So pay attention."

She laid out the harnesses, then greeted the big draft horses in their box stalls. These were Lazy M stock, not Paul's. Three of them had been doing chores on the Lazy M since before she had married Darin. They could find their way to Sheeps Crossing blindfolded. Loyal creatures that they were, Rachel wasn't about to trust them to Jackson's care any more than she was willing to put her guests in his hands. She could have driven the wagon herself, but that would have destroyed what little credibility the man had with Vince. Not that he deserved any credibility at all, but she did have to play fair.

"Those aren't horses, they're elephants," the star commented.

"They're just ordinary horses." She opened the first stall and expertly slipped a halter over the horse's head. Then she handed Jackson the lead rope. "This is Ben. Lead him out to the wagon."

Ben gave Jackson a white-eyed look, and Jackson flinched. The man was right about one thing. Horses didn't like him. Good thing the four-legged set didn't go to the movies. Jackson might be out of a job.

"Don't you have a wrangler to do this?" Jackson asked.

"Today, that's you. On a ranch like this, everybody has to know how to do just about everything."

"Including the owner?"

"Especially the owner."

Jackson didn't move. Neither did Ben. The scene was rather like a standoff in a western. Any minute Rachel expected man and horse to draw down on each other.

She invited sweetly, "You can always end this farce and go back to your motor home."

Jackson steeled his jaw. "Come on, horse. Giddyup."

Ben ended up leading Jackson to the wagon instead of the other way around. Rachel called after them, a laugh in her voice. "Usually we reserve *giddyup* for when we're on top of a horse."

Jackson's answer sounded a lot like a curse.

Rachel showed Stoney the basics of harnessing, then stood back and watched the team suffer his ministrations. The horses were gentle as lambs, but they knew a greenhorn when they saw one, and no horse worth his hay will turn down an opportunity to take advantage of a greenhorn. Jackson's foot got stomped on—his good foot.

"That should even up your gait," Rachel said from the sidelines. "Now you get to limp on both sides."

All she got in answer was a growl, which turned into a groan as Ben's coarse tail whipped across his face with stinging precision.

The poor horses suffered in turn. Harness straps twisted, got cranked up too tight, then eased to too loose. Rachel could have helped, but hey! The man said he was a quick study. Here was his opportunity to prove it. Fifteen minutes past the time they should have left, though, she had to give in and redo the harnessing herself. Four thousand dollars a day, she reminded herself. Four thousand dollars a day didn't come without a mess of aggravation, that was for sure.

By the time Jackson clambered onto the driver's box with Rachel beside him, both were tired, snappish, and flustered, and Rachel was beginning to wonder if the money was worth the price.

Jackson did better once he was sitting in the driver's seat

with Rachel beside him. The key was the audience, Rachel decided. Six passengers and their fishing gear loaded down the wagon. Mary Hansen and Debbie Richardson had fallen under Jackson's spell immediately, and the four men seemed to like him as well. He played the amiable cowboy very well, joking, telling bad New York City jokes for the benefit of the guest from Upper Manhattan, relating stories of his cowboying experiences—utter fables, of course, but they played very well to his audience. All the while he put on a good act of being in control of the team, who plodded along as they always plodded, three times a week, going to the same place. They were as close to being on automatic pilot as horses can get.

"I do better when the horses can't see me," he confided to Rachel in an aside. "And can't get to me."

"Is that why your knuckles are white?"

"They're not white."

"Liar. Hold the lines more loosely. Believe it or not, the team can feel your tension through the reins." To demonstrate, she lightly grasped the lines just in front of where he held them. In response, he put his hands over hers. An unexpected flutter of her heart caught Rachel off guard.

"Like this?"

"Uh . . . yes." He had big, warm hands, more calloused than she would have expected from a man who probably used a stunt double to brush his teeth. Those hands were surprisingly comfortable enveloping hers. They made her blood quicken, her pulse pound, and her breath shiver. "Do you . . . get the feel of it?"

"I definitely get the feel of it." His smile curved wickedly upward, but then, the wickedness might have been her imagination.

John Richardson called up to them. "Hanky-panky in front! What's going on, you two?"

The rest of the passengers chortled. Rachel's face heated.

Jackson called back a good-natured gibe. "Can't a man misbehave a little without you city slickers putting a crimp in his moves?"

A pudgy thirtyish fellow who had checked in only that morning offered advice. "Man, if that's your best move, you need to come up to Minnesota and learn a thing or two. We've got long, cold nights up there, and we've got the moves down to an art."

Rachel bit her lip to keep from laughing at the image of the rotund Gary Gordon, a single man still living with his parents, giving lessons in romance to Jackson Stone. But Jackson took the comment in stride.

"Us Arizona cowboys will challenge you Minnesota artful movers to a contest any day."

Everyone laughed as Rachel shook off Jackson's light grip and glared at him. His eyes gleamed in a way that was much too knowing.

"Watch the horses," she snapped.

"Yes, ma'am."

Rachel tried not to look at his smile. His smile was too distracting, too likeable. His smile tempted her to forget that Jackson Stone was an intrusion of Hollywood insanity into her peaceful, sane world.

"Watch out!" Debbie Richardson squealed from the back.

Too late. While Jackson's attention had been on Rachel, and vice versa, the team had made a wide turn around a curve where one side of the road dropped off a little embankment. Before Rachel could grab the reins and steer the team toward the safe side of the road, one wheel slipped over the edge. The wagon lurched as it high-centered on the lip of the embankment. The sudden lurch as they jarred to a precarious halt inspired Jackson to drop the reins. The team balked in confusion, whipping the reins between the traces to snake around their feet. Jackson cursed. Passengers shrieked.

"Don't panic," Rachel cautioned them all. "Just get down from the wagon." She had to bite down hard to keep her own curses from flying.

"Oops!" Jackson had the nerve to say.

Rachel couldn't answer, not without using a truckload of profanity.

Once out of the wagon, the guests calmed down. Rachel retrieved the reins from between the horses' dancing feet, and the team calmed to the sound of her voice.

"All part of the show, folks," Rachel joked. "Just wanted to keep your day interesting."

"Bull*shit*!" That from Gary Gordon.

"You trying to get us killed?" John Richardson demanded.

Rachel felt her face grow red. Carelessness like this didn't happen at the Lazy M. If Jackson Stone had been flammable, he would have gone up in smoke from the look she shot him.

The Richardsons and Mary Hansen walked ahead, saying rather curtly that they wanted to stretch their legs. Two others went off with their cameras, while Gary Gordon stalked away to use a handy bush.

"I hope those muscles of yours aren't strictly for show," Rachel snapped at Jackson. "Because you're going to lift the wagon back onto the road while I drive the team forward."

After a moment's chagrined pause, Jackson sighed. "Does this qualify as grit?"

"Don't push it, Stoney boy. You are seriously on my shit list. Quick study my foot."

"You're right," he said unexpectedly. "I screwed up."

Rachel couldn't help but admire a man who could admit to being wrong, but all the same, she fumed all the way to the picnic.

They made it to the picnic only a little late, with Jackson as grimy as any Hollywood producer could possibly want him, and Rachel in an improved mood from watching the man learn the true meaning of *sweat*. She had to give him credit. He didn't wimp out, and he kept his sense of humor. After they calmed down, the guests had poked great fun at him after the little incident. Even Gary Gordon had relaxed enough to laugh at him. But Jackson had laughed along with them, even at his own expense.

But other than those very minor good points, the man was a walking disaster.

The Lazy M's fishing picnics were just what the name implied.

Guests enjoyed a beautiful wagon ride or an equally scenic horseback ride to a well-stocked fishing stream. Lazy M hands drove the wagon, pointed out the best fishing holes to less experienced fisherfolk, and even baited hooks for the squeamish. The hands also cleaned the take, then wrapped the trout in seasoned cornmeal and fried it over a fire in a cast-iron skillet—the way a fish should be cooked.

All a guest had to do was catch the fish, and just in case everyone in the party had an off day, hamburgers and all the fixings waited in a cooler in the back of the truck driven up earlier by Ted Tyler. Rarely did the dudes dine on hamburger instead of fresh trout. The Lazy M staff knew the good fishing holes along the stream and they knew which bait worked in which place.

Rachel expected Jackson to be all thumbs with a fishing hook, so she was pleasantly surprised when he expertly threaded a squirming worm onto Mary Hansen's hook and showed a Nebraska lawyer how to cast without getting his line caught in the brush. She'd forgotten he came up here to fish in the first place.

Ted Tyler started a fire while Nathan Crosby, who had accompanied the two guests who had ridden horseback, helped Rachel haul the skillets from the truck, along with the utensils, cornmeal, and biscuit makings. "Looks like the new guy at least has some know-how about fishing," Nathan commented. "He's not much of a hand with horses. When he was staking out the team, he got ol' Ben so tangled in the harness that he like to choked."

"Who? Stoney or Ben?"

"Both."

They watched Jackson point Gary Gordon downstream toward an undercut stream bank, where trout probably lurked in the dark swirling depths.

"The guy reminds me of someone," Ted said. "What did you say his name is?"

"Uh . . . Stoney. Stoney Jackson."

"Huh! What kinda name is Stoney?" Nathan queried.

"Ain't you never heard of Stoney Burke?" Ted asked him.

"Who?"

"Stoney Burke. Old TV show about a rodeo cowboy."

"Hell, Ted, you're showin' your age. You sure that wasn't the silent movies?"

"I'd shut my yap if I was you," Ted advised. "If I ain't mistaken, you're just barely on the sunny side of forty. It's all downhill after the big four-oh, my friend."

Just then Stoney himself walked up. "Anything to drink around here?"

Ted pointed toward the cooler. "Help yourself. Coffee won't be ready for a while yet."

Jackson opened a Dr Pepper and slugged it down.

"Yikes!" Nathan said. "Don't you know that stuff rots your guts?"

"Everything I like rots your guts," Jackson replied with a grin.

"You know"—Nathan squinted at the newcomer—"you remind me of someone."

Jackson didn't even blink. "Yeah. I get that all the time. I look like that movie star Stone."

Recognition dawned on Nathan's face. "Yeah! That's it! You're right. You do look a bit like him."

"Yup."

Ted chuckled. "I'll bet you wished you had his money and his women instead of just his looks."

"Hell, yes." Jackson grinned. "You wouldn't catch me working for a living."

"Those Hollywood glamour boys don't work," Nathan grumbled. "Leastwise not real work. They're all a bunch of fairies, if you ask me."

Rachel nearly choked on the Diet Coke she'd just swallowed.

Nathan thumped her back and took her arm to steady her. "You all right, Rachel?"

"I'm"—*gasp*—"fine! Ow!" She choked. "Take it easy, Nathan. I'm not drowning."

Jackson looked on with an innocent smile.

"Anyway," Nathan continued to Jackson, "I knew you looked like someone. You could probably earn big bucks working as the man's double, ya know, if you were a few years younger."

"And maybe taller," Ted suggested.

"And maybe worked out some."

A loud "Yeehaw!" from downstream signaled that someone had pulled in a fish.

Ted rubbed his hands together. "Trout for lunch, people."

"Who gets the gut detail?" Nathan asked.

Rachel turned a slow smile on her new "employee." "Junior man gets to clean the fish."

Jackson blinked. "Clean . . . the fish?"

"You do know how to gut trout. Right?"

"Yes. . . ." His answer was cautious.

"Good. Let's hope we have a really big catch today."

An hour later, Rachel enjoyed the satisfaction of seeing Jackson Stone up to his elbows in blood and guts, with no double to take his place. Was the Hollywood cockiness starting to fray around the edges as he stabbed the knife into yet another fish belly? The man had asked for grit, and she was giving it to him. Probably his things would be out of Sitting Bull and into his Jeep less than an hour after they got back to the ranch.

That wouldn't be so bad, Rachel told herself. She could get back to her normal, predictable life. And as a bonus, she'd gotten some plumbing fixed.

She would miss that smile, though.

A small round holding pen stood about twenty feet from the barn. Right now the pen corralled four horses, three from Paul's string and one from the Lazy M's. At the beginning of the day, seven horses had crowded into the pen waiting to be reshod. Those that remained looked bored, standing hip-shot with heads down and eyes half closed. Heads came up, however, when Paul led a pretty little sorrel mare around the corner of the barn. She snorted at her friends in the pen and pranced daintily in her new iron shoes.

Paul called back into the barn. "Bring ol' Dusty next!" Then he continued toward the big pasture to turn the mare out.

The horses' heads swung in unison toward Sam when he emerged from the barn with a halter and lead rope. As he worked open the latch to the gate and let himself into the pen, they snorted and backed away.

"They don't like you," came a taunt from the other end of the pen.

Sam scowled and labored to see through the crowd of horses. There was Cherie, watching him with laconic boredom, arms and legs woven through the steel pipes of the corral.

"They like me all right. But horses never make things easy, no matter what you want to do. That's horse rules."

Cherie snorted.

"They're kinda like girls that way."

"Oh, very funny, twerp."

"Aren't you supposed to be helping Moira and Terri clean the cabins?"

"I'm not a maid, and I don't see why I should suffer just because my stupid dad wants to play cowboy."

"Your dad's gonna get after you when he gets back."

She rolled her eyes. "No one's going to get after me. I was going to hang with Donna Richardson, but she wanted to hike, and I've had enough hiking to last a lifetime." She jumped down from the railing, startling the horses into a flurry of motion, and sauntered to where she could taunt Sam from closer quarters. "What're you guys doing?"

"Shoeing horses."

"Oh, that sounds fun," she sneered.

Sam gave her his back and started toward the dust-colored palomino who was next on Paul's list. Ordinarily, Sam would have simply snagged the horse before the animal could think which way to bolt. But his spectator made all the difference. Jackson Stone's daughter was a twit, with her stupid clothes and stupid makeup and superior attitude, and her razzing made Sam want to show her how cool he really was.

So he turned and nodded to Chesty, who sat outside the pen like a silent sentinel, watching Sam for the least indication he needed a bit of border collie magic to get the job done. At Sam's nod, the border collie ducked beneath the lowest rail and reported for work.

"Get ol' Dusty," Sam told him, pointing toward the palomino. Then the boy leaned back against the fence and threw a smirk toward Cherie. "Chesty's the smartest dog in the world."

"I'm sure," Cherie drawled.

Chesty was all business. Snaking among the horses like black-and-white lightning, the dog deftly separated his target, herding the others to one side of the pen and holding Dusty for Sam's pleasure. With the horses well under his control, the dog dropped to the ground, intimidating his charges with the glare of his eyes while Sam looked down his upturned nose at Cherie.

"Told ya."

Cherie yawned. "It doesn't take much to outsmart a horse."

"Horses are smarter than you think. If you knew how to ride, you'd know that."

"I know how to ride. I can probably ride circles around you on any horse you choose."

"Oh, yeah. Sure."

"Wanna bet?"

"I have work to do." He slipped the halter over Dusty's head and gave Cherie a superior look. "Paul needs me to help with the shoeing."

"Sounds like an excuse to me. I doubt Paul needs a dork like you to help him do anything."

Sam resisted the urge to stick out his tongue. His mom insisted he be nice to girls, but this girl was really a snot. He compromised by screwing up his face at her. "Get away from the gate. I'm bringing the horse through." Once he and Dusty were out the gate, he called Chesty. The border collie gave the remaining horses a triumphant look and trotted toward his master, who rewarded him with a pat on the head. "That'll do, Chesty. Good boy."

"Good boy," Cherie sniggered. "Is that what you get for being such a suck-up? 'Good boy'?"

"You're a real creep. You know that?"

"Look who's talking." She fell in beside him as he led Dusty through the barn and tied him to a hitching ring just outside the door. George Kildare, adjusting the kiln where they heated the shoes, gave Sam and Cherie a nod.

"Are any of these horses yours?" Cherie asked Sam.

With a note of pride, Sam pointed out Thunder's stall in the barn. "That one. He's a quarter horse, and he goes like the wind."

Cherie stuffed her hands in her pockets and regarded Thunder skeptically. "Jimmy Toledo has a Ferrari. Now, *that* goes like the wind."

"A car. Big deal."

"You are so prehistoric."

George poured a fresh cup of coffee from a Thermos bottle, and Paul ambled up and gave Dusty a pat on the rump.

"I got work to do," Sam told Cherie. "So stop bothering me, okay? Go jump in the watering tank or something."

Cherie sniffed indignantly, but she retreated, wandering into the barn as the two men and Sam started fitting iron shoes to Dusty's hooves. Sam wished her good riddance as he concentrated on preventing the horse from moving while the men were working.

So he was caught by surprise when Thunder trotted from the barn, bridled and saddled, Cherie on his back. The girl waved jauntily, then turned and galloped toward the road. The look she tossed over her shoulder was pure challenge.

CHAPTER 6

♡

THUNDER'S HOOVES POUNDED in time to the drum of Cherie's heart. Wind streamed through her hair, tore away her breath, dried the sweat beading her face. She flew, free as a bird, laughing as the horse's powerful strides propelled them over the ground, hooves scarcely touching the hard-packed dirt of the road.

Sam would come after her, and he would catch her—when Cherie let him. He would be pissed off, but she didn't care. Everybody would be pissed off. That was part of the exhilaration of misbehaving. Hardly a day passed when she didn't goad someone into a sputtering, purple-faced, fist-clenching fit. That was what Cherie did best—make people mad. She sucked in anger like a Hoover sucked up dirt. Without it she would fade to nothing against the backdrop of her parents' brilliance and fame. Fade to black. That was her. She wore it proudly. One of these days all her black was going to fold into itself, sucking her down like a black hole swallowing a star. The black would still be there, but she would be gone. No one would even know she wasn't there.

But for now, anger kept her here, a real person, real to her father, who tried vainly to deal with her, real to her mother, who usually avoided her, nightmarishly real to her teachers, who shook their heads and gossiped together about what a trial she was, and real to the stupid kid who was chasing up the road behind her, yelling for her to stop.

Sometimes she wondered what life would be like if she didn't have to struggle so to be worthy of attention, if her dad weren't every woman's fantasy, if her mom didn't have conversations with Nefertiti. Her parents were so famous they could suck the light out of a room just by walking through the door. All light was reserved for them; there was none left for Cherie. So she chose the dark.

Chose the dark—and flaunted it, needling, provoking, baiting, grabbing the dark for herself, because she didn't care that all the light shined on Jackson Stone and Melanie Carr. People made it easy. They were easy to provoke, letting all their buttons hang out, just waiting to be pushed. Then they got all indignant when she had the guts to push them. Most people, Cherie mused, had their heads so far up their butt ends that they could see daylight out the other end.

She slowed Thunder's headlong gallop and reined him to a halt, deliberately letting the fool boy catch up to her. Sam cantered up on a stocky pinto, sweating and red-faced, his eyes shooting knives. Cherie gave him a smirk guaranteed to infuriate. The kid tried futilely to reach for Thunder's reins.

"Get off my horse, you stupid dork!"

"Why should I?" she taunted.

"Because he's *my* horse! Look what you've done! Got him all winded and sweaty. Get off, you . . . you . . . girl!"

"Ooooooh! What a potty mouth!"

He sputtered furiously.

"Can't you think of anything nastier than that?"

If the kid could have spit nails, he would have. Cherie was surprised he didn't take the end of his reins and hit her with them. She contemplated galloping ahead at full speed, daring him to stay with her. He'd be so mad he would probably choke. But she didn't. Both of their animals were winded. Lines of foamy sweat streaked their coats. As a rule, Cherie didn't like to afflict animals with her dark side. Though she might make an exception for the kid's snooty dog, who was sitting in the middle of the road panting, regarding her with a condescending disappointment that would do a school counselor proud.

"Get off!" Sam demanded again. "Get off or I'm gonna—"

"You're gonna what, shit-brain?" She kneed Thunder aside when the kid reached for her, then just to taunt him, she kicked the horse into a trot. *Not for long,* she told Thunder silently, *just long enough to teach that dorky kid that I don't take orders from no one, no how.*

A shrill whistle cut through the air, and Thunder stopped as if he'd hit a wall. Cherie flew over his head in a spectacular somersault, landing hard and painfully on the dirt road. For a moment she gasped for breath. When her lungs finally filled, she let loose a string of curses that should have shriveled every pine needle for miles around.

Sam came into her line of vision. He led both horses and wore a superior smirk. "Thunder's *my* horse. He listens to me, no matter who's in the saddle."

Cherie spit out furiously as she pushed herself into a sitting position. "You could have killed me, you stupid jerk! If I die, my dad's going to sue your mom for everything she has, and you're going to jail where some warden's going to kick your ass every day."

"In the old days, they strung up horse thieves. You got what you deserved, so quit whining."

"I don't whine!"

"You're the biggest crybaby I ever met!"

"You don't know anything!"

"I know a stupid girl who deserves to eat dirt when I see one. And that's you."

Chesty walked up, sniffed Cherie's knee, then barked a reprimand. She pushed the dog away and struggled to her feet, slapping furiously at the hand Sam offered. "Stupid dog, stupid horse, stupid goddamned world!" Scorching the kid with an imperious glare, she limped down the road. As Cherie knew he would, the kid followed.

"You're going the wrong way," he told her. "Home is back that way."

"Your home, not mine. I'm going into Greer to get an ice-cream cone or something. I deserve it."

He scrambled to keep up. "You are such a creep!"

"Thanks. I like being a creep."

"You can't just ride off on a horse anytime you want."

"Sure I can. I did it, didn't I? My dad's paying your mom big bucks for us to stay at your boring ranch, so I can do anything I want. You bragged about your stupid horse, and I decided I wanted to ride him. If you hadn't pulled such a dirty trick, we would have left you in the dust."

He stared at her incredulously. "Stupid! You can't just take off on someone else's horse and decide to ride somewhere for an ice-cream cone."

"Why not?" she asked airily.

"A man's horse is sacred property!"

"Where'd you hear that? A John Wayne movie?"

"What if I did?"

She laughed contemptuously.

"You don't like John Wayne? Everybody likes John Wayne."

Cherie regarded him smugly. "How would I know if I like John Wayne? I never met him. I like Clint Eastwood, though. He's kind of nice, for a dinosaur."

Sam sighed hopelessly. "You're weird."

Cherie merely shrugged. She didn't see anything wrong with being weird as long as it was intentional. "The horses have had enough rest. Let's ride." She reached for Thunder's reins.

Sam pulled them out of her reach. "No way."

Cherie shrugged. "Then I'll ride the other horse."

The kid wasn't quite as dumb as he looked. Letting her ride his precious Thunder was his only hope of controlling her, and he knew it. Reluctantly he handed her Thunder's reins.

"We're riding back to the ranch," Sam insisted.

Cherie climbed into Thunder's saddle. "I'm riding to Greer for an ice-cream cone. You can go wherever you want, little boy. And don't try any tricks. This time I'm prepared."

As Cherie had known he would, the kid rode along with her. One thing she'd learned in life: If she just kept insisting on what she wanted, eventually she got her way. That was a fact few people seemed to realize. If you keep doing what you're doing, people eventually give up trying to stop you. Usually. Sometimes that didn't apply to her dad.

Cherie would have ridden on alone, even if the stupid kid had turned back to fetch the posse. On the other hand, she didn't mind having Sam with her. He was fun to poke at, and in a way, his insults were a novelty. Everyone in her life tiptoed around her. Her dad and mom both felt guilty about making her a pathetic product of divorce—at least that was what they seemed to think she was. Both of them wanted to understand her and nurture her "self-esteem," especially her clueless mom, who was seriously into things like that. Her teachers were afraid to offend the daughter of a big star. Even her friends sometimes weren't straight with her. Her father was hot stuff, and so Cherie had to be treated with kid gloves.

But not this pint-size dweeb. He was pretty hopeless. Straight out of one of those prehistoric television series like *Leave It to Beaver* or *Father Knows Best*. Totally lame. But at least he called the shots like he saw them. He obviously didn't care that her dad was Jackson Stone.

Not that she cared about the kid with his stupid snotty dog. But it was a new and different experience having someone like Sam in her face. Different was good.

An hour's ride had them trotting down the road into a cozy green valley. Through the center of the valley, flowing over a floodplain lush with grass, ran a stream Sam told her was the Little Colorado River—as if she cared. A string of mostly log buildings stretched from one end of the little valley to the other. One narrow asphalt road was the only street.

Cherie sighed as they reined in the horses just above the town. "I was hoping Greer was bigger than I remembered. It isn't. Jeez. How retro can you get?"

"What's that mean?" Sam asked pugnaciously.

"The place looks like Davy Crockett ought to live here." She grimaced.

The kid scowled down at the town, then at her. "If *you* don't like our town, that's a good thing."

Cherie laughed. The brat had claws.

"Since you think Greer is so pathetic, we can go back to the ranch."

"No way. I want my ice cream. Besides, look at the sky. It's going to rain."

Rain it did, just as they trotted into town. Cherie pulled up at the first building with a covered porch, which conveniently happened to be a restaurant of sorts. It wasn't posh, but it was dry. She hopped off Thunder, tied the reins to the rail of the porch, covered her saddle with the rain slicker that she found tied onto the back, and hurried under cover. Sam did the same.

"I wonder if this place has ice cream?" she wondered aloud. Tables crowded the porch and a sign boasted of the best food in Arizona. Sticking her head inside, Cherie called out, "Anyone work here?"

Sam punched her shoulder. "Quit it! Just sit down. My mom's friend owns this place. She'll be out."

Politely waiting just wasn't Cherie's style. "Yoo-hoo! Sam's mom's friend! Anyone home?"

A woman styled in short red pixie hair, faded jeans, and a T-shirt proclaiming "Cowgirls Don't Take No Bull" came out of the kitchen. "Hold your horses. I'm coming." She brightened when she saw Sam. "Hi, Sam." She patted a wet border collie head. "Hi, Chesty. Who's your loud friend?" The woman quickly surveyed Cherie's dramatic fashion statement, and a twinkle of amusement lit her eyes.

Cherie's chin lifted and her eyes narrowed.

"This is Cherie," Sam said reluctantly. "She . . . uh . . . her dad sorta works at the ranch."

The woman laughed. "Sorta works? I don't know anyone who works for your mom who *sorta* works."

"This is Karen Spangler. She owns this place, and she's my mom's friend," Sam explained.

"That's a fact," Karen declared with a grin. "You two trying to get out of the rain, are you? You want something to eat while you wait it out?"

"Ice cream?" Cherie said hopefully.

"Vanilla, strawberry, rocky road, chocolate, or raspberry sherbet."

"Chocolate."

"For you, Sam?"

"Vanilla."

To suit his lame personality, Cherie thought.

They sat at a table close to the horses. Chesty, apparently sure of his welcome at the restaurant, sat between their chairs. The dog soaked up a couple of ear scratches from Sam, then butted Cherie's hand as if he wanted attention from her. Without thinking, she gave him a scratch, then pushed him away when she realized what she was doing.

"You'll hurt his feelings," Sam complained.

"Like I care?"

"Hurting a dog's feelings is mean, because a dog trusts you."

"That's the dog's problem. Dogs have no class. They take anything people dish out to them then come back for more."

"Maybe Chesty should bite you, then."

"At least that would be interesting," she sneered.

Sam leaned his elbows on the table and looked at her as if she were a fungus. Cherie was used to that kind of look. Finally he heaved a long-suffering sigh. "I think you're from another planet."

"If I were, I'd go back. Any other planet has to be better than this one." She leaned back in her chair and glanced around. A small wooden sign on the side of the log building declared this to be the Round Valley Roundup. Inside she could see wooden tables arranged around a big stone fireplace, currently cold and dark. On the porch, smaller wooden tables with battered chairs overlooked Greer's only street and the stream beyond. Hummingbird feeders hung at regular intervals from the porch overhang.

If the Round Valley Roundup was Greer's idea of a hot hangout, Cherie decided, then Greer had a major problem.

"I hope you have money," Sam grumbled, kicking the sides of his chair.

"Why should I have money?"

"To pay for the ice cream, stupid."

"We'll put it on your mom's tab."

Sam snorted in disgust, then reached into his jeans pocket and pulled out a small handful of change. Cherie deliberately ignored the production he made of a few quarters and dimes, as if the kid were treating her to lunch at the Ritz or something. Then her gaze came to rest on a newspaper someone had left at the neighboring table. The banner declared it to be the *National Star*. Civilization at last!

"That's trash," Sam said when she picked it up.

"Who says?"

"My mom says those tablets don't print anything but lies."

"Tabloids, dweeb, and your mom doesn't know anything. Man oh man! Look at this!"

Halfway down the front page, bold print announced that Jimmy Toledo of Toy Boys was threatening to sue Jackson Stone for "emotional trauma" as a result of an altercation in a Las Vegas hotel that left the poor singer both physically and emotionally battered. The article, bearing Josh Digby's byline, reviewed in imaginative detail the events of the morning Cherie's father had found her with Jimmy. Jackson Stone, Digby reported, had turned a cold shoulder to both newsmen and his fans, refusing to answer inquiries or give interviews. In fact, the star had taken his daughter and fled just days after the incident in question, which fueled speculation that Cherie Stone had somehow been involved in Stone's unexpectedly uncivilized behavior.

Looking over her shoulder, Sam blew out an amazed breath. "Did your dad really beat him up?"

"No. But he would have," she told him proudly.

A picture of Cherie accompanied the story. It was a poor picture shot the year before by a photographer who'd tailed her and her dad one day as her dad had driven her to school. She looked like a kid. Really lame. That was before she'd discovered the dramatic qualities of black.

Still, having her picture in the *National Star* was sweet. "You should have seen the picture they ran of me a couple of days after this happened. It was better. Someday my picture's going to be in the papers nearly every day. When I get out from under my dad's thumb, I'm going to be a star, and no one is ever going to write about me just because I'm Jackson Stone's daughter."

"Yeah, right. A real star."

"Well, I am!"

"Doing what?"

"I might be a singer, like Britney Spears. I'd look really good in her clothes, and, like, I could take voice lessons."

The twerp had the effrontery to snicker.

"Or I could be in films. I know absolutely everyone who's important, so I could get a break in the business really easy."

"Who'd want to watch you in a movie? Barfo."

"A lot you know, you little backwater bozo."

"I pay to get into the movies just like everybody else, and I sure wouldn't waste my money on you."

"That's because all your taste is in your mouth."

The restaurant woman came out the door, bearing two bowls of ice cream. "It's on the house today, kids."

Sam looked relieved. "Gee, thanks."

"Ice cream is the best way to celebrate a rainy day."

"Thanks," Cherie mumbled.

"What's this?" Karen lifted the *National Star* from the table. "Someone left this here, I guess. I don't know of anyone around here who sells this trash. Doggone, look at that."

Sam caught his breath. Cherie smiled. The woman would be impressed once she recognized Cherie for the celeb that she was.

"Jodie Foster is having an alien baby. And Dorothy Holmes—whoever she is—left two million dollars to her Welsh corgi. Jeez. You'd think if the woman was going to leave her money to a dog, she'd have the taste to get a real dog, like a Lab or a golden retriever."

Sam slowly released his breath. Cherie, disgruntled that she hadn't been noticed, tried to take the paper back.

"No you don't," Karen said. "You kids shouldn't be reading this drivel. It'll warp your minds. It's going in the trash, where trash belongs." She took a final look at the front page, then a long look at Cherie, but she said nothing more, just "Enjoy, you two. Say hi to your mom for me, Sam."

With a final glance at Cherie, she disappeared inside.

Jackson hunched his shoulders against the rain and tied down the tarp he had spread over the wagon. "Your brochure brags of sunny skies and clear, starry nights," he said pointedly to Rachel.

"Interrupted occasionally by rain." She secured the other end of the tarp as the wind tried to rip it away. The knots held. Grabbing Jackson's arm, she tugged him toward the trees, where everyone else had already taken shelter. "Come on. You're getting soaked."

"How come I'm the only one without a poncho?"

"Because you didn't grab one from the tack room before we left."

"Because your lying brochure said sunny skies and clear, starry nights."

"You of all people should know better than to believe publicity."

They ducked beneath the thick canopy of ponderosa pine where the others waited out the rain. The hands were unruffled by the weather. Cowboys were tougher, or at least they thought they were, than anything the weather could throw at them. The guests were happy to relax in the cool air, enjoying the fresh piney scent of rain-clean air and the satisfaction of trout-filled stomachs. Trout that they, by the way, had not been required to clean.

Perhaps that, along with the lack of a rain poncho, inspired Jackson's cranky mood. Rachel suspected she wouldn't have to worry about Mr. Megastar much longer. He was getting a craw-ful of her and her ranch, poor fellow. She allowed herself a private snicker. So much for the Hollywood tough guy image.

Jackson leaned back against a tree trunk and scowled up at the sky. "Our shelter drips." As if Mother Nature was out to get him, a fat raindrop landed square on his nose.

Rachel couldn't smother a laugh.

"Laugh it up, you over there in the raincoat."

She wished she could have a snapshot of the expression on his face. But she did have some sympathy. Taking off her poncho, she joined him at his tree trunk. "I'll share. These are one size fits all, so probably it will cover both of us. If you catch pneumonia you'll be more trouble than you are already."

He wasn't too proud to accept. Sitting on a bed of pine needles, their backs against a big ponderosa, they huddled together beneath the voluminous yellow plastic designed to protect both rider and saddle.

"This is cozy," he commented.

Unexpectedly, Rachel felt shy. She wished that she smelled of something other than wood smoke, wore something more feminine than jeans and a sweatshirt, and sported a real hairstyle rather than a tangled, windblown ponytail set off demurely by a well-worn ball cap.

For what seemed like a long while, they listened to the rain drip on the plastic above their heads. The smoky odor of her clothes battled the fish-gut perfume on his hands and shirt, but the fish had the upper hand.

"Pungent, isn't it?" Jackson acknowledged. "I did wash."

"It's the clothes."

He grinned. "I could take them off."

Rachel smiled. The whole scene approached ridiculous. With the smile came an untwisting of her gut. How many other women could say they had snuggled under a raincoat with Jackson Stone? After all, even if he was a pain in the ass, he was still America's macho hero. "I think your sitting naked in the rain might offend old Mrs. Dobson."

"Is that the blue-haired lady who rode up in the truck?"

"That's the one."

He chuckled. "She looks as if she belongs at a beach hotel in Florida. What is that one doing pretending to be some kind of Dale Evans on a ranch?"

"I could ask the same of you," Rachel reminded him. "What is Jackson Stone doing pretending to be a cowboy on my ranch?" The rain and the raincoat afforded them privacy, shutting them into their own world.

"I told you. Garnering grit," he said with a smile. "Hiding out from the press."

His eyes were startlingly green even in the dim light. She had always speculated that he wore contact lenses to enhance the color, but those eyes up close owed nothing to contacts.

"Uh . . ." She untangled herself from his gaze. "You did say that. You said Cherie had caused some kind of a stink. What exactly did she do?"

He grimaced.

"If you don't want to say . . ."

"No, nothing like that. I don't figure you'll be running to the tabloids."

"That bad, eh?"

"You know the rocker Jimmy Toledo?"

"Heard of him. Vaguely."

"Cherie ran off with him to Las Vegas. Thirteen years old, and she's sashaying around with a drugged-out piece of shit who has more damned rings in his body than he has facial hair."

Rachel grimaced. "I can tell you really like this guy. You went after them, I take it. Did Jimmy Whatshisname survive the encounter?"

"Just barely."

The look on Jackson's face made Rachel almost feel sorry for Jimmy Toledo. "So you're keeping Cherie away from the press."

"Until they find someone else to chew on. And until I decide whether I should hog-tie her in her room for the next ten years or maybe send her to military school. You think she'd look good in uniform?"

"Only if it's black."

He chuckled and shook his head. "I love Cherie. I really do. From the first moment I saw her, all red with her face screwed up and her little arms waving madly, I adored her. Still do. And I feel guilty for the divorce. Divorce is hard on a kid. Harder when your parents are on the front page of every tabloid in the grocery store. Cherie has some good excuses for being a little shit. But I swear, sometimes I think that I'm not going to survive until she's twenty."

"Does she live part-time with her mom?"

"Brief visits only," he said with certain sharpness to his tone. "Melanie loves Cherie, too, but she's not really the motherly sort."

Rachel chuckled. "The world thinks all women should be the motherly sort. Sometimes it doesn't work out that way."

He glanced her way with something like envy in his eyes. "You have a great kid, Rachel."

She nodded. "Sam is special. I worship the ground he walks on. The teenage years, though—I'm dreading those."

"He's such a little gentleman. I don't see him changing into a monster overnight."

She grinned. "Like a teenage werewolf growing fur, fangs, and claws."

"Right up Cherie's alley, though."

They laughed together. Strange, Rachel thought, how totally, ordinarily human he seemed right then, trapped with her in the rain, talking about their kids. Well, maybe not quite ordinary. Ordinary men didn't have those eyes or that heart-melting smile. She was beginning to understand why women flocked to his movies—even the "guy" movies. To be honest, she had been part of the flock. Only when he came charging into her own precious territory, bringing with him the pollution of his brassy, frenetic world, did she get on her high horse.

Could Jackson Stone really be a nice guy, or was this just a role he assumed, the caring-father image? Did actors who lived in the rarified levels of the entertainment business ever turn off the acting? Was she being treated to the down-home version of Jackson Stone, or another role he assumed as the occasion required? She hoped not, because she rather liked this version of him.

She decided to cut the man some slack. "It must be hard to bring up a kid, living in the world that you do. I mean, let's face it, the entertainment industry doesn't exactly engender kid-friendly values. It affects children living in Timbuktu, for heaven's sake. Cherie is living at ground zero."

"That's the sad truth," Jackson admitted. "But how about Sam? Living up here in all this peace and quiet, how is he going to cope with real life when he has to deal with it?"

"I do worry about that sometimes. He's lived here for three years, which a long time for a kid." She smiled fondly. "Long enough for him to think he's a John Wayne clone. And I plan to be here for a good many years to come. It's a great place to live and raise a child."

"You've only been here three years?"

"Sam and I moved here when my husband died. Three years ago. Heart attack."

"I guess I just assumed you'd lived here while you were married."

"Darin didn't like the ranch, even though he grew up here. I don't think he ever liked it, even as a kid. He wasn't like my Sam."

"Your Sam is lucky to have you as a mother."

She gave him a grateful smile, then chuckled. "Mr. Stone, you certainly do know how to get around a woman."

"That's what all the tabloids say," he admitted with a grin.

"And we know how reliable they are."

He chuckled, but the conversation dropped into a silence punctuated by the steady patter of rain. Rachel searched for something more to say. Words kept the atmosphere friendly, but not too friendly. Not that Rachel had strained herself to be friendly to the man during the short time of their acquaintance.

But instinct told her that beneath that poncho they could get entirely too cozy. Rachel couldn't help but notice the width of Jackson's shoulders, the crooked line of his nose, the down-right sensuous set of his lips. A fine mist of sweat dampened her skin, and it had nothing to do with the temperature.

"You know, Rachel, we've sniped at each other a bit—"

"Actually, I think I've done most of the sniping—not without reason," she reminded him. After all, she couldn't let him think he'd won her over.

"Well, yeah. But I want you to know that I admire what you are, what you've done with the ranch—running a business like you do and raising a kid at the same time. And I am grateful for your going along with my little masquerade."

"Angling for a raise, Mr. Stone?"

She felt more than saw his smile. "After what happened this morning, I wouldn't dare ask you to pay me what I'm worth."

She laughed, and he laughed with her. Their little shelter was growing very warm, Rachel noted. Dangerously warm. She really wanted to unbutton her shirt and let the air next to her skin. And maybe something else next to her skin as well, such as Jackson Stone's large, blunt-fingered hands, even if they did smell of fish. She was losing her edge, Rachel realized with a touch of panic, softening to the realization that the man was not only a major hunk, he was a genuine person. Most guys didn't realize that the likeability factor was a bigger turn-on for most women than all the bulging biceps and twinkly green eyes in the world. At least, it was for her.

Jackson looked a bit warm himself. His eyes had darkened and crystallized to molten emerald. He leaned toward her ever so slightly, his expression intent, charged in a way that made her heart go into overdrive.

The moment was interrupted by a tapping on the poncho. "Hey, you two," said Nathan Crosby's voice.

Rachel peeked out from the poncho and tried very hard not to blush. She felt like a teenager caught necking at Lovers' Overlook. "Hey, Nathan. What's up?"

He fixed her with a disapproving eye, or maybe that was her imagination. "Don't think this rain's going to let up any time soon, Rachel. It's getting worse by the minute. We were think-ing to pack up and get out of here before the road is nothing but mud."

Rachel sighed. "You're right. Let's head back." Just what she needed: a slick road, a wagonful of sodden guests, and green-horn Jackson Stone on the driver's box.

Fifteen minutes later, Jackson folded his arms across his chest and warily met Rachel's eyes. They had a particularly wicked gleam in them.

"You actually expect me to climb up behind you on that horse?"

"Yup."

"Why can't I just ride back in the truck with Ted?"

"Two reasons, *Stoney.* Gary Gordon is riding back in the truck with Ted and Mrs. Dobson, because Gary's feet are cold and guests always take precedence. And the second reason: Ted and the truck are driving into Springerville to pick up grain and vet supplies from the feed store. As I recall, you didn't want your face to be seen in Springerville."

He glanced hopefully toward the wagon, where guests were arranging themselves so that their ponchos overlapped. On the driver's box was Nathan, and on top of Nathan's horse was Rachel, who was looking at Jackson with that wicked gleam in her eye.

Jackson didn't really blame Rachel for not wanting him to drive the wagon back to the ranch over slick and muddy roads, but he surely didn't want to get up on that horse, especially with the horse looking at him with a jaundiced eye and its ears pinned flat in displeasure.

Horses didn't like him. Jackson had discovered that in film-ing eight different westerns in which he'd been stepped on, bitten, thrown, scraped off, smashed against walls, pinned against fences, and in one instance, kicked. And none of those stunts had been in the scripts. The horses had come up with them all on their own.

Now, it might be that horses pulled that sort of unpleasantness with anyone who didn't keep a wary eye out, but Jackson felt they saved a special animosity just for him.

The two brave souls who had ridden horseback to the picnic sat on their horses waiting for him to mount behind Rachel. Until he got on, they couldn't start for home.

"Jackson," Rachel said quietly, for his ears only, "the guests are watching. You are supposed to be a ranch hand."

She was enjoying this entirely too much. The fish guts, the rain, and now riding double with her back to the ranch. This certainly wasn't working out the way he'd pictured it.

"You're doing this deliberately, aren't you? You could have driven the wagon with me riding shotgun."

She feigned innocence. "I feel like a ride."

"Or I could ride shotgun with Nathan."

Her grin was downright smug. "I think you should stick by me. Nathan seems a bit suspicious of you."

Rachel took her left foot out of the stirrup and extended a hand to help him up. Bowing to the inevitable, he grabbed the hand, put his foot into the stirrup, and pulled himself aboard. The poncho he had borrowed from Gary Gordon flapped in the wind, inspiring the horse to prance nervously. Jackson nearly slipped off then and there.

"Hold on," Rachel instructed cheerfully. "Traveler here doesn't much like carrying double."

"Now you tell me."

She chuckled. "Come on, man. Show some backbone." To the mounted guests, she smiled. "Let's go. Move 'em out."

The two guests trotted off into the meadow, and Rachel kneed Traveler to catch up. The horse expressed his displeasure by crow-hopping for a couple of strides before settling into a long-legged, jarring trot. Jackson grabbed the woman in front of him, who at least had the advantage of a saddle.

"Loosen up. I can't breathe."

"They ought to put handles back here if they expect someone to ride in back."

"Just grab the cantle."

"The what?"

"The back of the saddle!" She reached back and tapped the raised back of the saddle seat with her hand. That cantle, however, wasn't meant as a handle. It was meant to cradle the rider's backside, and right then it cradled Rachel's backside, a backside which, Jackson had noticed more than once, filled out her jeans in a way that invited male eyes and positively beckoned to male hands. If he grabbed where Rachel told him to grab, his fingers were going to slide right under that delicious little butt. A charming idea. Not to mention tempting. But dangerous. With a woman like Rachel, a man could get into deep trouble slipping his hand beneath her butt, even if she unintentionally invited it.

Or maybe, he reflected happily, the invitation was deliberate. Together beneath that poncho, they had gotten pleasantly cozy. Had Rachel really softened, or had the sluice of hormones through his veins deluded him? Rachel was a tough lady to read. She didn't send the same signals that other women used. She was honest in her responses, and that confused him.

"Are you holding on?" she asked.

He looked at the enticing picture of her derriere caressing the seat of the saddle. Tempting, but no. Women were more dangerous even than horses.

"I'm okay."

"Okay."

The wagon and truck both had trundled down the road, leaving the riders on their own. Rachel pointed her charges toward a trail that wound from the meadow into the trees. "We're going to take a shortcut down the mountain," she told them. "It's a good trail. All the horses here could negotiate it in their sleep."

"Like the team negotiated that curve this morning?" Jackson inquired cynically.

She sighed. "All right, people. Just loosen up on the bits and let them have their heads."

Oh, great, Jackson thought. Rachel and her shortcuts. And horses sleepwalking.

But the horses were awake, and a good thing that was. The trail down through the pines and aspen was both rocky and slippery. When an altercation between two squirrels set a nearby branch to rocking, Traveler shied violently. Rachel rode out the sudden movement as if the seat of her jeans were glued to the saddle, but Jackson didn't fare as well. He hit the ground with a pained "Oof!"

The woman had the temerity to laugh. The two guests in front of them didn't even notice. They kept trudging on down the trail.

"Are you all right?" Rachel asked when she was laughed out.

"Oh, I'm just dandy," he snapped. "That damned horse did that deliberately."

"The squirrels scared him. I warned you to hold on."

"Oh, yeah." He painfully picked himself up from the wet, cold ground. "A half ton of horse scared by a five-pound squirrel. Idiot animal!"

She bit down on her lip, trying unsuccessfully to suppress a smile. "Oh, my, you are a sight."

"Thank you." He brushed at the mat of wet pine needles that plastered his backside.

"You'd better take my poncho, Jackson. Yours is now wetter on the inside than the outside. And it's ripped." She raised her arms and lifted the thick plastic folds of rain gear over her head, showing an intriguing bit of navel and midriff as she did so. Jackson was not so cold and butt-sore that he couldn't appreciate the sight. He let her get the thing off before refusing her offer.

"I'm not taking your damned poncho."

"Why not? You look about as cold and miserable as a drowned puppy."

Now, that fit his public image—a drowned puppy!

"Jackson, I don't mind riding in the rain. Actually, I like it. I'm very warm-blooded. Hardly ever get cold."

He wouldn't mind testing out just how warm-blooded she could be. Squelching the thought, he scowled. "I am not taking your poncho. And I am not getting back up on that horse."

The horse, Jackson noticed, was regarding him with rank satisfaction.

"You *are* taking my poncho, and you *are* getting back on the horse."

"I'll just walk back. You go ahead."

"Not a chance. We need to keep up with my guests, and I'm not going to hang back making sure you don't fall off another log. Besides, you shouldn't be walking such rough country with that ankle of yours."

"I'll take my time."

"Forget it." She threw the bright red poncho at him. "Take yours off and put this on. Then climb up. I'm not answering to your fans for not taking care of their darling."

The situation was humiliating. Both Rachel and the cursed horse fixed him with expressions that promised grim retribution unless he behaved himself.

"Are we playing a game of one-upmanship here?" he inquired.

Her mouth slewed into a half smile. "Could be."

"Am I losing?"

The smile became full-blown. "You definitely are."

He groused, "At least your honesty is refreshing. Not much else about this day is." He took off his muddy, torn poncho, donned Rachel's drier one, and tied his to the back of the saddle.

She gave him a half-sympathetic look. "I can see I'm going to have to teach you to ride."

"Why would you do a useless thing like that?"

"Because you're never going to pull off this act of yours looking like a half-baked jackass around horses." She flashed her teeth in a wide grin. "And I like to see you sweat."

Jackson sighed. "There's that honesty again. I'm beginning to think it's overrated."

"Just as movie actors are overpaid." She offered her stirrup meaningfully. "Get on, cowboy."

He got on, giving Traveler the same menacing eye the horse gave him.

"And hold on this time."

As Rachel put her heels to the horse's side, Jackson took her advice by plastering himself to her back and wrapping his arms around her ribs. She was warm and supple, in spite of the cold, and her damp T-shirt only emphasized the curves that made her a woman. She hadn't lied about the warm blood. Her heat infused him, made his pulse pound and his groin ache.

He forgot all about not liking the horse. Maybe this riding double wasn't such a bad idea after all.

CHAPTER 7

♡

WHEN SAM RODE into the Lazy M Ranch yard and climbed off the horse Paul had loaned him, he breathed easier to see that his mother and the guests had not yet returned from their picnic. Sooner or later his mom would find out that he had allowed Jackson Stone's creepy daughter to steal Thunder and they had ended up in Greer, where a copy of the *National Star* and a photo of Cherie lay on a table at Karen Spangler's place. The trashy paper was like some kind of a wanted poster. *Wanted, Dead or Alive, Creep Girl from Hollywood.* Of course, no one wanted Cherie dead (though Sam had toyed with the thought a time or two during the afternoon). His mom would put on her how-could-you-let-such-a-thing-happen expression when she found out, and after an afternoon of putting up with Cherie, Sam didn't feel up to explaining.

Cherie climbed down from her saddle and looked around the sodden yard. Her sullen expression was blacker than her mascara, which ran in streaks down her face. Her hair no longer stood up in perky little spikes, but clung to her scalp in a dripping skullcap. A black-painted lower lip quivered on the edge of a tantrum.

"Where is everybody?" Cherie demanded.

"In the house, or the bunkhouse. It is raining, you know."

"Like I don't know that? Duh!" Impatiently she wiped dripping water from her eyes.

"If you had the sense to wear a hat, your hair wouldn't have gotten soaked and cold water wouldn't be dripping down your back."

"Hats mess up your hair."

Sam snorted through his nose and shook his head. Girls were dumb, though he guessed they got smarter with age. He'd never seen his mom worrying about her hair. She wore a hat whenever she was outdoors.

"The saddles go in the tack room," he told Cherie as they led the horses into the barn. "And there's a bucket of brushes and sweat scrapers in there, too."

She sighed dramatically. "Get someone else to take care of it. I need a hot bath and a Coke."

Sam grabbed her arm as she started toward the door. "Come back here! When you go out riding, you always take care of your horse before taking care of yourself. That's the rules."

"Your stupid rules stink. I'm not hanging around to scrape sweat off a stupid horse. I mean, do you know who I am, moron? I live in a six-bedroom house with its own private beach. And in a town house in San Francisco. And we have a cottage on Cape Cod, and a ranch in Wyoming that's a lot fancier than this one. I have a cook and a maid and I get to shop on Rodeo Drive. Get it? I don't scrape sweat off of horses."

As if commenting on her tirade, Chesty chose that moment to trot into the barn and shake, launching a fusillade of cold, muddy droplets that plastered them both. Cherie inhaled sharply at the sudden onslaught of cold mud, then released all the air in her lungs in a primal scream. She kicked out at the dog. "Get out, you ugly, dirty dog!"

Chesty jumped back with a wounded look in his eyes.

That was too much for Sam. The stupid girl could run away with his horse, lead him a chase through the rain, and get him in trouble with his mom, but kicking his dog called for capital punishment. He yanked her away from Chesty and shoved her hard against a heavy stall door.

"Don't ever kick my dog!"

"Your stupid dog sucks!"

"Not as much as you suck, you creepy girl. You think you're

so smart! You're dumb. You're ugly. And you ride like a city slicker."

"Do not!"

"Do too!"

Cherie shoved back, then piled on when Sam stumbled and fell on his backside. The battle was on, no holds barred, no quarter given. A cheering section of one border collie barked encouragement as the combatants grappled in the dirt and pine shavings.

Rachel's shortcut got the horseback riders to the Lazy M before Nathan and the wagonful of guests got there. Arriving at the ranch's entrance archway took Rachel by surprise. She'd been riding on automatic ever since Jackson had mounted behind her, too absorbed by the experience of having his arms wrapped around her and his chest plastered against her back to pay attention to where they were. Fortunately, Traveler knew the way back to his barn. But when they passed beneath the arch, the caterwauling rising from the main barn brought her back to the moment.

"What on earth?" She kicked her horse into a canter. Jackson grabbed at her for support. One of his hands came down in a place that would have afforded them both pause had either one of them been paying attention.

"Hold on!" she warned him unnecessarily.

"No kidding!"

She reined the horse to a sliding stop at the barn door and did a flying front dismount that would have done any trick rider proud. Jackson did a spectacular dismount as well, only his wasn't intentional. Fortunately for him, this time he landed on his feet. Even with a limp, his long legs propelled him into the barn ahead of her, and by the time Rachel arrived at the battlefield, he had a kid dangling from each hand.

"What the heck is going on here?" Jackson divided his scowl between the two of them. Sam's eyes were big with alarm. Cherie just looked sullen.

"He shoved me!" the girl accused.

Rachel's brows snapped together ominously. "Samuel Tobias Marsh! You shoved her?"

Uncharacteristically, Sam showed no remorse. "She kicked my dog!"

Jackson fumed. "You kicked his dog?"

Both kids talked at once in a jumble of accusations. When Rachel managed to separate fact from exaggeration, she couldn't much blame her son for his tantrum. According to the Marsh code of right and wrong, mistreatment of animals was inexcusable. And of course Chesty was more than an animal. He was part of their family.

On the other hand, Rachel required her son to treat women and girls with respect, no matter what the circumstances.

"Sam, you know better than to hit, shove, or be rude to a girl, no matter how much you think she deserves it."

Sam screwed up his face and looked at the floor. "Yes, ma'am." His voice was contrite, but he shot a fulminating look at Cherie as Jackson released him. Jackson did not, however, release his daughter.

"You kicked a dog," he said, his tone unbelieving. "What did that dog do to you?" He glanced toward Chesty, who sat watching the confrontation with interest.

Cherie's jaw thrust forward. "He sprayed mud and water all over me. And it was deliberate."

"You are in sore need of a lesson, young lady. One of the lowest things you can do in this world is abuse a trusting animal." The rebuke on his face set the girl's lower lip to quivering, though she tried to hide it with defiance.

"What's so important about a stupid dog?"

"The same thing that's important about you. He's a living, breathing creature who deserves decency and respect. And what's more, he's never wished you or done you any harm. Apologize."

She glanced up at her father with a mixture of emotions in her eyes. "I'm sorry."

"Not to me! To the dog!"

"You're kidding!"

"I'm not kidding. Apologize to the dog."

Cherie wrenched her shoulder from her father's grip and took a step toward Chesty, who regarded her with canine condescension. "I'm sorry, dog. I'm sorry I kicked you."

As if understanding the words, the border collie's jaw opened in a doggy grin. He raised one paw in a wave of absolution.

A battle raged on Cherie's face as she fought a smile. "Next time, shake somewhere else, okay?"

Rachel clapped a hand on Sam's shoulder. "Your turn, son. Apologize to Cherie for shoving her." She could feel his reluctance in the tensing of his wiry little body. "She deserved it," he muttered under his breath.

"Samuel!"

"Well, she did!"

"What have I taught you about that?"

He beetled his brows. "Treat all females like ladies, even if they're not. Don't hit, don't shove, don't spit, don't cuss." He glared at his adversary.

"And so?" she squeezed his shoulder, feeling a bit sorry for him. If Cherie had kicked Chesty in front of her, Rachel might have reacted the same way.

"So, I'm sorry."

"For what?"

"For shoving her."

"Tell her so." She pushed him gently forward.

"I'm sorry for acting like a jerk," he said to Cherie's face. "But don't ever kick my dog again."

Jackson nudged Cherie. "Okay," she said.

"Now you two shake hands," Jackson commanded.

They did, their eyes speaking words they didn't dare say.

Jackson continued. "Cherie, as your atonement to Chesty, you'll play with him for fifteen minutes every day, throwing a ball or playing whatever game he likes."

"Daaaad!"

"I don't want her near my dog!" Sam objected.

"Then you can join them," Rachel told him. "And while you

and Chesty are at it, you can let Cherie help you train Chesty for the trials coming up."

"Ma!"

"It might help her to learn some respect for animals, and it won't hurt you to learn some tolerance. I mean it!"

The two kids exchanged speaking glances, and the silent messages were anything but polite. Rachel noticed Jackson trying hard to squelch a smile. You would think an actor would be better at hiding his amusement. "Right now," he said with as much soberness as he could muster, "it looks like you two have a couple of horses to clean up. And for good measure, you can take care of the one Rachel and I rode."

"Coats brushed, feet cleaned, fly spray applied," Rachel added.

"Yes, ma'am," Sam acceded.

"And help the guests take care of their mounts as well."

As Rachel and Jackson walked out of the barn, Rachel heard Sam's miffed whisper to Cherie. "You're never going to ride my horse again!"

"Like I care about your dumb old horse!"

Thirty minutes later, Rachel sat with Jackson in the ranch house kitchen, cradling a large cup of Earl Grey tea in her hands. She had showered, changed into clean jeans and a flannel shirt, cast aside the flannel shirt and donned a coral pink polo shirt, discarded the polo shirt for a checked camp shirt, and finally settled on a rib-knit sweater. Instead of pulling back her hair in its usual convenient ponytail, she blow-dried it into a natural tousle of curls then bunched it back with a large clip made to hold extra-heavy hair.

Curled on the bed, Fang the cat watched speculatively.

"Don't look at me like that," Rachel had chided the cat. "I am not trying to impress Jackson Stone. I don't give a fig if he likes what he sees."

Was it a crime to want to freshen up a bit after a long and tiring day?

"Looking halfway decent once in a while gives a woman a boost," she told Fang. She regarded herself in the mirror. "Do you think this sweater is too clingy? Maybe I should change to a T-shirt."

Rib-knit still in place, Rachel peered through the steam of her hot tea at Jackson, who sat across the kitchen table. The star's beverage of choice was a Dr Pepper, and he hadn't had a chance to repair himself from the fishing expedition, because he'd been busy helping the guests with their mounts and then Nathan with the team. He looked good, though, in spite of the mud and a certain fishy odor that still clung. The stubble he nurtured gave his already raffish looks a touch of spice. Long legs were encased in muddy jeans that had begun the day with the store-bought crease still sharp as a knife edge. The crease had disappeared along with any hint of new-denim stiffness. Still damp, they molded his legs like a second skin, and fine legs they were, too. Very fine. A green L.L.Bean polo shirt, crumpled, damp, and bearing unidentifiable traces of fish, dirt, and horse sweat, lent his eyes an absolutely emerald cast.

On one of the kitchen chairs he propped his sore ankle. The rest of him lounged comfortably, tipping his chair back on two legs and regarding her over his Dr Pepper with a speculative gaze. An hour ago that long, masculine body of his had been plastered against her back while one of his hands, albeit unintentionally, grabbed at her wet breast. Rachel didn't want to examine too closely how that touch had made her feel.

Somewhere in the passing hours of the day, she had stopped thinking of Jackson as a film star and started regarding him as a fairly funny, sometimes annoying, but overall very nice guy whose magnetism had nothing to do with his macho image on the screen. She no longer looked at him and saw the characters he had played—the tough Secret Service agent who had intimidated Tommy Lee Jones and saved the First Family from terrorists, the peace-loving cavalry colonel who single-handedly forged peace during a bloody Indian war, the tragic blind man who found life and love with a woman who believed in him. He was none of that, not even a star whose face had graced publications from *People* to *Time*, *The National Enquirer* to *The New York Times*. The man sitting across from her seemed like plain Jackson Stone, with dazzling eyes, a winning smile, a sore ankle, and a pain-in-the-ass daughter.

Maybe this Jackson Stone, the one who seemed almost like a real person, was more dangerous to her peace of mind than the film star was. At the beginning of the day, she had looked forward to somehow getting rid of him. Right now, in her cozy kitchen with the rain beating a tattoo on the windows, she almost hoped he would stay a while.

He raised his Dr Pepper in salute. "Thanks for the pop—and the chance to cool off a bit before I go to my cabin and string my daughter up by her black-painted fingernails."

"Sam shouldn't have shoved her."

"Hell, if I'd seen her take after the dog, I would have shoved her, too." He sighed. "I need to cut back my schedule and spend more time with her. Get her away from the group she runs with."

Rachel chuckled sympathetically. "Maybe you ought to take fifteen minutes each day to play games with Chesty and Cherie. It might do you all some good."

He barked out a laugh. "It might at that. If my boss would give me time off from driving wagons, cleaning fish, and getting stomped on by that vindictive team of horses."

"You asked to be treated just like any of the other hands," she reminded him with a smile.

"You got me there."

She stretched back in her chair, her eyes taking in his appearance. "I must say that you're beginning to look the part. Not even the direst straits in your films have made you look quite so . . . well, bad—not to mention the smell."

He grinned broadly. "So you *have* seen my movies."

"You know I have. Anyone with an eleven-year-old kid is required to see your movies. Right along with *Rocky and Bullwinkle* and *Dumb and Dumber.*"

"Ouch!"

She traced a one in the air with her finger, marking the point for her side.

"Not all my movies are made for eleven-year-olds."

One of his R-rated films—something she'd gone to see without Sam—came to mind, and immediately her face heated. At least one love scene in that thriller had made her break a sweat right there in the theater. The critics had applauded the movie for its finely honed tension and surprise ending, but women had given it five stars for something else entirely.

From the smile that spread across his face, he knew. Rachel's face got even hotter. "Score one for you."

"Thank you."

"Don't mention it."

"I don't suppose you have another Dr Pepper?"

"I guess you've earned more than one. And in deference to your poor sore ankle, I'll even get it for you. Just don't get used to this treatment."

"Yes, ma'am."

She poured herself more tea and got him a cold can from the fridge.

"I have to admit one thing," he said with a sigh. "Eight hours of cowboy work rivals a sixteen-hour day of shooting on the set. It takes the wind out of a man's sails."

"Do tell?" She popped the top and handed him the can. "Want to give up?"

"Hell, no. But I do want to go to bed, preferably with a nice electric blanket to keep me warm and a hot toddy on the bedside table. But from your sly little smile, I can see that isn't going to happen."

"Well, let's see, cowboy Stoney. Since everything got soaked today, the harnesses need to be oiled, and probably the saddles as well. Nathan will probably do his saddle, because he's picky about those things, but it wouldn't hurt to offer, because it wouldn't have gotten wet if we hadn't left his horse standing out in the rain while we broke up the fisticuffs in the barn."

Jackson grimaced.

"And Joanne reported a ripped window screen in Big Eagle cabin. The guests will be at dinner in about a half hour, so that would be a good time to fix it."

He sighed.

"Of course, I could ask Vince or George to do it, but they'll be unloading feed once Ted gets back from Springerville. Paul deals only with the horses. I suppose I could ask Dennis, but he's been working on the septic all day, and I doubt he's in a mood to do much more than collapse. This rain couldn't have made his job easier. But maybe he could manage to put in a few more hours of work." She slid Jackson a look that managed to be innocent and sardonic at the same time. "After all, far be it from me to keep a paying guest from his rest. . . ."

He held up his hands in mock surrender, but his eyes glittered, meeting her challenge. "Point me the way to the Neetsfoot Oil. I'll do the harness and the—what is it? A screen at one of the cabins?"

"You're a good man, cowboy Stoney. Play your cards right and I might actually give you a job here."

He rose to the bait. "Yeah, yeah. Laugh it up, lady."

His eyes narrowed, making Rachel's heart skip a beat. Being the subject of Jackson Stone's intense focus was more than any woman, even a sensible, realistic woman, should be expected to withstand.

Rachel was grateful when Vince interrupted, ambling through the door trailing mud and a bad mood.

"Joanne's going to have your hide, Vince. She waxed the kitchen floor just today. You'd better chuck the muddy boots."

The old man ignored Rachel's complaint and scowled at Jackson. "There you are, Stoney. Been lookin' all over for you. What're you doin' hangin' out drinkin' soda pop with the missus while there's stalls to be mucked out and tack to be cleaned? We don't pay you to sit on your butt bones like you was some guest, boy. Miz Marsh told me about your bum ankle, but that don't keep you from hobblin' over to the barn and usin' your hands for somethin' more useful than poppin' a pop top."

Rachel thought fast. Vince no doubt found this cozy tête-à-tête suspicious. She didn't normally single out employees for solitary chats in the kitchen. In spite of his grizzled old cowpoke act, the old man's mind was like a bear trap. Once it clamped on to something, it didn't let go. "I . . . uh . . . I asked Stoney to let me rewrap his ankle, Vince. So don't get after him."

Vince glanced pointedly at Jackson's ankle, which was still in his boot. Damn, but she was a lousy liar, Rachel thought.

Jackson intervened. "Vince is right. I should get back to work. Been taking advantage of your soft heart," he said with a grin at Rachel.

Vince poured himself a cup of coffee—he wasn't above taking advantage of Rachel's "soft heart"—and glowered at Jackson. "Heard about the hoo-haa with the wagon this morning. Guests are laughing about it. Who taught you to drive a team, Stoney boy? I coulda' let little Sam drive the wagon and he'd've done a better job. Surprised Miz Marsh here didn't fire you on the spot." He looked meaningfully at Rachel. "She don't usually put up with carelessness like that."

"Vince," Rachel said. "The incident was my fault as much as Stoney's. More, in fact. I at least should know what I'm doing on a wagon box."

The old cowboy raised a canny brow. "Yeah, you should."

"I think that's my cue to exit," Jackson said a bit sheepishly.

"What about wrapping his ankle?" Vince asked.

"To hell with his ankle," Rachel snapped. "Go, Stoney."

Once Jackson was gone, Vince settled himself at the kitchen table with his cup of coffee. It was a spot he'd warmed often enough. Over the years, something very like a father-daughter relationship had grown between him and Rachel. The old man took more liberties than any other employee would have dared.

"Where'd you find that ham-handed greenhorn, anyway?"

Rachel didn't think the country's biggest box-office draw would take kindly to the description.

"Sumpthin' about that guy rings a bell, but I can't pin down just what it is."

"I . . . uh . . ." She groped for a likely fib. "To tell the truth, Vince, he's my . . . my . . . cousin."

A grizzled brow went up. "Yer cousin?"

"Right. My cousin. He didn't want me to tell anyone. Probably won't even admit it, because he wants to make it on his own here. He wanted the experience of working on a ranch, and he wanted his daughter to have some time away from the city. So I decided to give him a chance."

"You never mentioned having a cousin."

"Well, I only recently met him." That at least was the truth.

"You two sure don't look anything alike."

"He's . . . like . . . a half cousin."

"Half cousin, eh?" His watery blue eyes twinkled. "Rachel, girl, I guess he can be anything you say he is. You're the boss, after all. Guess I'll cut him some slack."

A boss fast losing control, Rachel admitted privately. Life was getting very complicated.

Rachel punched her pillow for the hundredth time, then groaned and rolled over to look at the bedside clock. Four-thirty A.M., only a half hour before she usually climbed out of the sack, and she hadn't slept a wink. She yanked the covers up to her ears, dove into her pillow, and flailed morosely, trying to sleep for these last thirty minutes at least.

Fang protested the disturbance by jumping from the bed and stalking off to settle on the sofa. "Sleep," Rachel commanded herself. "Sleep, you idiot."

But sleep refused to come—all that man's fault. That man. Jackson Stone. Arrogant, cheeky, stubborn, sneaky, irritating, fascinating Jackson Stone. What insanity for her to flirt with him. Admit it! she demanded of herself. She had been flirting at the picnic, cozied up with him beneath that poncho. Then she'd ridden home with him wrapped around her like kudzu vine. Jackson Stone was like a drug—seductive and thrilling in the short term, disastrous in the long term. She should remember that next time she felt giddy looking into those captivating green eyes. Not that there was the smallest sliver of a chance that she would actually fall under the man's spell. There wasn't. Not the slightest chance. Absolutely no way. He might have devastating eyes, a hundred-megawatt smile, and a stock-pile of boyish charm, but Rachel Marsh was not a woman who could be bowled over by good looks and charm. He also had nice hands. She always noticed hands—their shape, their strength, their dexterity, callus-hard or pretty-boy soft. Jackson had nice hands, with long, blunt fingers and calluses where a man should have calluses. He had a firm, dry handshake and a solid grip, too.

But that didn't matter. None of it mattered. To get involved with Jackson Stone would be downright insane. A fast-living Hollywood actor was so not what she needed in her life. He didn't have the least bit of interest in her, anyway. He charmed women as a matter of course. It went with his profession.

She flipped over again, jerking the bedcovers with her. This masquerade of Jackson's was not going to work. She had al-ways despised deception of any kind. One of the things she ap-preciated most about living in this enclave of the Old West was the straightforward people. They said what they thought and weren't ashamed of who they were. And they were quick to sniff out a fake. Already Vince was suspicious. Putting any-thing over on that crusty old coot was nearly impossible. And some of the other hands soon would suspect something was fishy. They weren't stupid.

Jackson just wasn't a cowboy. Every time he fumbled he was going to raise brows. Every time she showed him any special notice, the hands were going to wonder what was up. Most likely she should just send Mr. Hollywood on his way and throw his money back in his face. He was all charm and no substance, a shallow, pampered weenie-boy.

Except that Jackson Stone seemed less shallow the better she got to know him. She had to keep reminding herself that she didn't like him; she couldn't possibly like him. But, damn! It was hard not to like him. Only Saturday she had picked his sorry carcass up from the side of the trail. And now it was Tuesday morning. Not even three whole days had passed, and the man already had her common sense in meltdown.

"Damn!" She threw back the covers and crawled out of bed. She deserved a sleepless night for her silliness. People supposedly grew smarter as they grew older. Didn't they ever grow wiser?

The morning was still pitch black when Rachel flipped the lights on in the barn and set about inspecting the equipment that had gotten soaked in the previous day's rain. It was spotless and well oiled. Rachel hated to give Jackson credit, but he'd done a good job. As she looked in on the drowsy horses, Chesty joined her. Trust the border collie to keep an eye out for any activity, night or day, that might need his supervision.

"You didn't wake up your boy, did you?"

The dog gave her an indignant look and went to Thunder's stall, where Sam's treasured horse dropped his big head over the stall door. Dog and horse sniffed affectionately. Only the third leg of the triangle was missing, and doubtless he would be up soon.

Rachel was suddenly very glad she lived where she did. No flash-in-the-pan movie star was going to throw her off kilter or make her pine after something she didn't need. Since Darin had died, she hadn't so much as thought of a man in that way. Her life didn't have room for romance. She didn't need a relationship, and certainly not a casual fling with a national sex symbol. The whole idea was ludicrous.

In the stall next to Thunder's, the bay mare Rachel had ridden the day she'd found Jackson pushed her nose out of the stall and whuffed in Rachel's direction.

"Hey, Sally girl."

Sally responded with an imperious stomp of a foot.

Rachel laughed. "You are full of yourself, aren't you? But you're a winner, just the same."

Sally tossed her head in agreement. Now that she had Jackson's outrageous fee coming into the Lazy M account, Rachel could buy the mare from Paul without fretting about straining her finances. She could also give the hands a raise and install new plumbing in the guest cabins.

She should thank Jackson for that and stop worrying. Jackson's stay at the ranch might be fun if only she would lighten up and stop taking everything so seriously.

Vince's gravelly voice brought Rachel back to the real world. "Well, good mornin', Rachel girl. You're out early this mornin'."

She scratched Sally's nose. "I'm going to buy Sally from Paul, Vince. What do you think of her?"

Vince scratched his grizzled chin. "She's a looker. Smart as the devil. I've rid her a time or two. Nice gaits. Strong. Got a mind of her own." He shot Rachel a fond look. "Like most'a you females."

Rachel laughed.

"You gonna turn her into a cow horse?"

"I thought I'd just keep her as a personal horse. It's a luxury, but . . ."

"You two females might get along together. You need a luxury here and there. You work too hard."

"Since when?"

Vince shrugged. "You need to find yourself a good man, Rachel girl."

"You think?"

"That so-called half cousin of yours ain't all that bad, I'm thinking. He did a pretty good job cleaning those harnesses last night. And he mucked out the stalls I set him to. 'Course, he don't know a lick of nothin', but he'd break in all right given a little time."

"Vince," Rachel said with a sigh. "Stop matchmaking. He's my cousin."

Vince snorted his disbelief.

"You and Joanne are cut from the same cloth. Can't you two just leave well enough alone?"

"Whoa there. I ain't a thing like that busybody old woman. I just have your best interests at heart."

Rachel rolled her eyes. "Just don't get nosy, okay? I don't think you'll have to put up with Stoney very long. A few days of hard work should discourage him."

She hoped. Then a wicked idea popped into Rachel's head. "And speaking of hard work, don't assign Stoney any work today. I want him to ride up to the line cabin with me. We'll fix that porch before the crew goes up there for branding."

"You could take Dennis," Vince suggested slyly. "He's handy with a hammer."

"No, I'll take Stoney."

The old cowboy's mouth twitched knowingly. "You know, Nathan don't like yer cousin Stoney."

"Really?" Rachel was surprised. Men and women both seemed to fall for Jackson Stone's charm.

Vince pulled his chin thoughtfully. "Figger you know why."

Puzzled, Rachel asked, "No, why?"

Vince's watery blue eyes regarded her with a hint of amusement. "You'll figger it out. Just think about it."

Rachel didn't have time to think about it. She gave Sally a final pat and headed out the barn door, calling behind her to Vince, "Speaking of my cousin, would you make sure he gets rousted out of bed real early—like, about now?"

Back in the ranch house kitchen, she wrote a note for Terri, who this week had pulled morning livestock chores. Terri could use a break, and after all, "cousin Stoney" had wanted firsthand experience in the grit of rural life. Rachel was just giving him what he wanted.

CHAPTER 8

♡

THE SUN WASN'T even a dim promise in the east when Jackson dragged himself up the ranch house front-porch steps and tried to snap a smart salute to the woman sitting in the porch swing drinking tea. The salute was somewhat less than snappy. The Styrofoam cup of caffeine he had grabbed in the Chuckwagon hadn't yet hit his blood.

"Vince said you wanted me." Vince had said exactly that, and with a sly twinkle that left no doubt about the double entendre. That canny old man was going to be a problem, Jackson told himself. But right then he was too sleepy to think about it. Fifteen minutes earlier he'd been enjoying a near-comatose sleep when Vince had pounded on his cabin door with a surfeit of enthusiasm. No one should be so energetic at such an early hour.

Neither should anyone look quite as fetching as Rachel Marsh did as she sat regarding him through the steam of her tea. She showed none of the pasty-faced morning trauma of most frail humans, but seemed as fresh and alive as a blossom awaiting the sun. If she could bottle some of that fresh vibrancy, Jackson thought, stifling a yawn, she could sell it on Rodeo Drive for big bucks.

One of her brows lifted expressively. "I wouldn't go so far as to say I want you."

Sass before dawn. It should be outlawed. "That is a disappointment. Does it mean I can go back to bed?"

"Nope. Is it a little early for you, cowboy Stoney?"

"Not at all." He tried to grin, but the attempt ended up a grimace.

"Well, that's good, because I told Terri she could sleep in a bit for the rest of the week, since you would take care of the chickens and eggs and goats for the next few days."

Jackson swallowed hard. "Goats?"

A few minutes later he found himself in the barn, sitting on a three-legged stool, contemplating the unmentionable parts of a goat. The goat was no happier about Jackson than Jackson was about the goat. "This is supposed to be a cattle ranch," he grumbled when for the third time the goat tried to kick him. "What are goddamned goats doing on a cattle ranch?"

"Tizzy wouldn't kick at you like that if you weren't treating her udder like it was a water balloon. Don't pull on the teats. Coax the milk down with your fingers. Gently."

For what seemed like the hundredth time, she showed him how. This was the only good part about milking a goat—having Rachel crowd behind him and place her slender hands over his, finger to finger.

"Ripple downward with your fingers," she instructed. Her mouth was close to his ear, sending pleasant shivers down his spine. "Like a wave in an audience of football fans. Understand?"

He understood she was having entirely too much fun giving him a hard time. To his regret, she moved away, leaving him on his own with the goat. Chesty sat nearby, giving him an encouraging look. Tizzy didn't look encouraging at all.

But Jackson was not going to cry uncle over a goddamned goat. His fingers did the wave down Tizzy's teat, and a thin stream of milk splatted against the bottom of the pail. He looked up and grinned triumphantly.

Rachel inched one brow upward. "There are three goats, and then eggs to gather and chickens to feed. I'd quit grinning and get working if I were you."

So much for positive feedback.

"By the way, I told Vince that you're my cousin."

"Cousin? Why on earth did you tell him that?"

"He was too suspicious about me hiring such a ham-handed jackass, if you must know."

"And being your cousin makes me less of a jackass?"

"Well, no," Rachel said with a wicked grin. "You're still a jackass. But he thinks I hired you because of family obligations. And it diverts him from thinking I have some nonsensical romantic interest in you."

From the gleam in Vince's eye that morning, Jackson didn't think she had diverted him very effectively.

"What's so nonsensical about having a romantic interest in me?" he asked in a hurt tone. "It's been known to happen."

"I know. Being enamored of Jackson Stone is practically a national pastime. But those women are interested in Jackson Stone the film star, not Jackson Stone the man."

For once in his life, Jackson didn't have a comeback. Rachel might have hit the nail right on the head. Maybe that was the problem with his love life.

"Back to the goats," his slave-driver boss insisted. "They don't care who you are as long as your hands are warm."

Emptying three goat udders took Jackson past breakfast, which he missed. The eternity spent crouching against goat bellies felt as though it went past lunch as well, but when the goats were finally back in their pen, the sun was only an inch above the horizon. Eggs still waited to be gathered. How hard could that be? Jackson thought confidently.

He hadn't reckoned with Henzilla, who didn't want Jackson's hand in her nest. The rotten biddy got the other hens upset as well. Amid much flapping, clucking, and pecking, one egg smashed to the floor and Jackson learned the true meaning of the word *henpecked*. Rachel leaned against the hen-coop door and watched with a gleam in her eyes. Jackson guessed that if she'd had a beak, she would have joined in the melee. And here he'd thought he was winning her over.

He did manage to get away with all of the eggs except the one that broke on the floor.

"You're going to have to come back and clean that up, you

know," Rachel told him cheerfully. "Can't have it lying there rotting."

As if a rotten egg would make any difference in the smell. He forced a smile. "Yes, ma'am. Whatever you say, boss." She gave him a look that made him grin. "I asked for grit, and I guess I'm getting it. Does it get grittier?"

Before Rachel could reply, a bright voice assailed them. "Good morning! Good morning!" the voice caroled. A crepe-skinned face topped with frizzy blue-tinted hair peered into the smelly hen-coop. "Joanne said I would find you here, Rachel, so I just toodled on over, and when I saw what you were up to, I decided to push my nose in. I hope you don't mind."

Apparently Mrs. Dobson was in a good mood this morning.

"When I was a girl on a farm in Iowa, we had all sorts of livestock—cows, chickens, pigs, goats, horses. Oh, look at those lovely hens and all the eggs they gave you! Collecting eggs used to be one of my chores. But goodness, young man! I see you and the hens had a set-to this morning." She clucked sympathetically at Jackson's hen pecks. "You should just tell those old girls you have a chicken dinner planned," she said with a twinkle in her eye. "That's what I used to do."

"Yes, ma'am! I think you're right." Jackson handed the basket of eggs to Rachel and took the old lady by the arm. "I could surely use a lesson in hen psychology from a farm girl like you. Maybe you'd like to come out tomorrow and show me how it's done?"

Rachel's horrified gasp was drowned out by Mrs. Dobson's enthusiasm. "Oh, my! I would love to do that, Mr . . ."

Jackson tipped his hat in a courtly manner. "Stoney Jackson, ma'am, at your service."

"You were the young man driving the wagon yesterday, weren't you?"

"That's right, but try not to hold it against me. Let me assure you, dear lady, that we at the Lazy M try to make your visit as much fun as possible, so if waking up early and sticking your hand beneath these feisty old biddies is what you want to do, then you're welcome to it. And I'll bet these hens like a sweet gal like you better than they like me."

Mrs. Dobson positively simpered. "I never sleep much past five anymore, and I'd much rather come out here than stay in the cabin and listen to my husband snore."

"Then, you come on. Have you met our goats?" Jackson felt the sting of Rachel's piercing glare, but he ignored it. "We have three of the finest goats you've ever met. Have you ever milked a goat, Mrs. Dobson?"

"As a matter of fact, I won a goat-milking contest at the county fair in Des Moines when I was ten."

"I'll bet that was a sight to behold." Arm in arm, they strolled toward the goat pen, Rachel falling in behind. The back of Jackson's neck started to sizzle. As he introduced the animals by name, the elderly lady exclaimed in admiration.

"Are they good milkers?" she asked.

"The best," Jackson lied. "The milk is sweet as butter. You can see the cream floating on top."

She looked at him hopefully. "Could I . . . do you suppose . . . ?"

"I'm sure the goats would count it an honor."

She beamed, clasping her hands in joy.

"So, we'll see you tomorrow morning about five-thirty?"

"Oh, thank you, Stoney." She squeezed his arm before releasing him. "You do know the way to an old woman's heart. And Rachel"—she grasped Rachel's hand—"you are so fortunate to have such a charming man in your employ."

Rachel's smile strained her lips. "I am fortunate."

"Bye now, you two. I'll see you tomorrow, Stoney. I can hardly wait!"

When the old lady was well out of earshot, Rachel lit into him. "If you let that lady get so much as one scratch out here, I'm going to hang you up by your . . . your . . ."

He grinned unrepentantly. "Yes?"

"Thumbs, that's what. You're going to look strange in your next film with thumbs the length of your legs. The nerve, getting a nice little old lady to do your work for you. I don't care if she did win a milking contest at some county fair, she should know better than to fall for . . . fall for . . ."

Jackson shrugged expansively.

"Fall for all that false charm." She turned on her heel, nearly spilling the eggs, and stalked off.

"The charm's not false," Jackson called after her. "And she's a nice lady just looking to revive a few memories."

"Bring in the milk buckets," she shot back at him. "And meet me at the barn at noon."

Jackson whistled at her tone. High noon at the barn. What did Rachel have planned now?

Josh Digby looked with distaste at the bologna sandwich his wife had packed him for lunch. He worked his butt off, commuted an hour each way into downtown Chicago so she and the kids could have a house in the suburbs, and all he got for lunch was a goddamned bologna sandwich. He should've gone out for lunch with Steve and Dick. But he'd stayed at his desk, working his butt off, and all he got was a lousy bologna sandwich.

He peered farther into the paper sack. One oatmeal cookie, an apple, and a bag of Ruffles. What a treat, he thought sarcastically.

"Hey, Josh!" Herman Schosser, a can of Coke in his hand, appeared in the doorway of Josh's cubicle. "Working through lunch, I see."

"Yeah."

"Gotten anywhere on that Stone story?"

Josh merely grunted. Herman was an assistant editor, and he liked to use his ever so slightly elevated position to poke at reporters' sore spots. He had just hit one with Josh.

"It'd be something if we could get a lead on Stone's whereabouts before the *Enquirer*, wouldn't it? There's always a lot of follow-up potential on anything to do with Stone. He's a sales-booster."

"I'm working on it," Josh declared glumly. "If anyone can track down Stone and that goofy daughter of his, it's me. I've been following that man around since he did his first grade-D movie, *Space Station Charlie*. Remember that one?"

"Yeah. It sucked."

"The movie did, but Jackson Stone didn't. I knew he'd be big news when his next movie came out. I knew it before anyone else."

"You're the champ," Herman agreed with an insincere grin. "You've made a lot of points with our esteemed employer digging up stories on that man."

"That's right. Me and Jackson Stone have put the *National Star* on the journalistic map. And when I get the real dope on what happened between Stone, his daughter, and Jimmy Toledo, I'm going to have another headline story. It's certainly not that pap that Harvey Mathias is feeding everyone about Stone and Toledo being good friends and a friendly discussion getting too loud. What crap! Do they think we were born yesterday?"

"And Toledo isn't talking?"

"Toledo!" Josh spat the name in disgust. "That drug-head doesn't have two unfried brain cells to rub together and produce a spark. But don't worry, I'll come up with something. Stone's daughter is a good fresh angle. People are always anxious to read dirt on the stars' kids. It makes them grateful that their own kids aren't quite as obnoxious."

Herman narrowed his eyes, like a predator scenting blood. "You have a lead?"

"I'm working on it—watching Stone's agent, hangers-on like Mathias, even his ex-wife. He's gotta be talking to Melanie about the girl."

"Yeah. Maybe."

"I'm also talking to our website people to see if we can do a better job monitoring the e-mail it generates."

"You mean people reporting sightings? Hell, we get just as many from people who've seen Elvis."

"Yeah, well, Elvis is dead."

Herman cringed dramatically. "Don't say that!"

Josh snorted "Whatever. I'll get the job done. You can bet I will. If anyone sees Stone or makes a move toward him, I'm going to know about it. And when I catch up with him, I'm going to pin his ass to the ground until he tells me the truth, the whole truth, and nothing but the truth."

"Then you'll add some spice and exaggeration to make it fit to print," Herman guessed.

Josh bit into his lunch. "They don't call me the King of Sleaze for nothing."

Damn! Here he was, working his butt off upholding the principle of the public's right to know, and all he gets is a lousy bologna sandwich.

"Well?" Rachel inquired with exaggerated patience. "Are you waiting for something?" Sitting atop Sally, she tapped a finger against the saddle horn and stifled a smile of triumph.

Jackson eyed Foxie with intense dislike, and the mare returned the regard in like measure. "Why is it," Jackson asked, "that you people with the cowboy hats always ride everywhere? There's a road to this place, right? And there's four perfectly good vehicles—a pickup, a van, an SUV, and my Jeep—within a few steps of where we're standing."

Rachel raised a brow. "First of all, I don't wear a cowboy hat. I wear a ball cap. And second, we ride because horses are more fun than pickups, vans, SUVs, and Jeeps. And third, I promised to teach you how to ride."

"You threatened."

"Whatever. I keep my promises."

The look he sent her promised retribution.

"Mount up, cowboy Stoney."

By the time Jackson put his foot in the stirrup, Foxie had started to move forward. Jackson clung to the saddle with one foot in the stirrup and the other leg swinging wildly. The free leg finally made it to the other side of the horse. Jackson landed painfully in the hard leather seat, bounced forward, and nearly impaled himself on the saddle horn. Rachel hoped none of her guests heard the cuss words coming out of his mouth as they rode down the lane toward the big Lazy M arch.

They rode twenty minutes down the trail before Jackson fell off the first time. Gentle Foxie looked back at him lying on the ground and whickered in surprise. She certainly hadn't done anything to make him go flying out of the saddle.

"Jackson!" Rachel exclaimed as she rode back to grab Foxie's loose reins. "What happened?"

"My butt just has a natural disinclination to stay in a saddle."

"That's ridiculous. No one falls off a horse at a walk. It's all in your head."

"No, it's in my butt."

She dismounted and extended a hand to help him up. He eyed her distrustfully. "Come on, Jackson, Foxie is the gentlest horse we have."

"I tell you, horses just plain don't like me."

"Well, it's no wonder if you keep jumping off and blaming them for throwing you." She pulled him up and smiled cheerily. "Just remember, the first rule of falling off a horse is to keep hold of the reins so that the horse doesn't run free. I once knew a cowboy who broke his back falling off a horse, but he kept hold of those reins."

Jackson glowered.

"But, of course, if this is just too much, you could give up and admit to those Hollywood skeptics that you're a weenie."

"Hollywood already knows I can't ride a horse. That's what stunt doubles are for. Nevertheless . . ." He eyed Rachel grimly, brushed off his backside, and marched toward the horse.

"Don't look at her like she has leprosy. You'll hurt her feelings."

"Right. Horses have feelings."

"They do. They're very sensitive creatures. Just charm her—like you would charm a woman." She shot him a challenge. "She is a female, after all. I've heard that females can't resist you."

He took Foxie's reins and met Rachel's gaze. "Just one so far."

Rachel laughed.

They plodded on at a walk because Jackson bounced off every time they broke into a trot. And he didn't once keep hold of the reins when he hit the ground. Finally, Rachel stopped in disgust. "You are the absolute worst rider I have ever seen."

"I warned you."

"You are stiff as a board when you should be loose, and loose as a noodle when you should exert some control. Really, Jackson, this is ridiculous. You're a very athletic man. And don't bring out the stunt double excuse, because it doesn't fly. I've watched you."

That admission made him smile, but Rachel ignored it.

"You are not a clumsy, uncoordinated man. You're . . . you're . . ." She wanted to say "supple," powerful, with an animal grace that would have turned women's heads even if he didn't have fame and money on his side. But he was cocky enough without her adding fuel to that particular fire. "You're nimble," she conceded, lamely.

"Nimble?"

"Yes. You know, 'Jack be nimble, Jack be quick,' and all that. Only here we'll say Jackson be nimble." She grinned impishly. "There's no reason for you to be such a klutz on a horse unless you choose to be." Rachel pulled Sally to a halt and dismounted. "Stay there," she commanded as Jackson started to follow suit. She looped Sally's reins around a tree branch. "I'm going to give you some pointers from down here. We'll just pretend this little open space is a schooling arena."

"Let's not and say we did," he suggested glumly.

"What kind of grit is that?"

"Has anyone ever told you that you're a sadist?"

"You are so negative. All right now, make a big circle at a walk. And sit up. You look like a sack of chicken feed. Head up, shoulders straight, and get that butt underneath you."

"This butt is sore."

"It's going to be sorer if it hits the ground again. Now nudge old Foxie into a slow jog trot."

He bounced like a rubber ball.

"Whoa! Stop!" She propped her hands on her hips and regarded him with a sigh. "Okay, let's do it this way. Give me a hand up." Vaulting easily up behind his saddle, she poked him in the ribs. "Let's go. Trot."

Foxie patiently endured, trotting a large circle while Rachel prodded and pushed Jackson to straighten his back, hold up his head, and square his shoulders. She placed her hands on his hips, urging him to the rhythm of the horse. "Just go with it, Jackson. Use your instinct. Move with the horse's stride." Moments later, she slapped his hard thigh. "Heels down, toes slightly out. That's right. Nope, get those shoulders square. Move, move, move. Gather up your reins. Make the horse take notice of you. That's right."

For fifteen minutes she harassed him, and had entirely too much fun at it. Sitting there glued to his strong back made her head swim just a bit, distracted her from the task at hand.

"Keep your butt under you, Stoney boy." And such a nice tight butt it was. "Chest out." Oh yes. "Head." She lost the train of thought, still thinking of tight butts and a broad chest.

"What?" he demanded.

"Never mind!" Needing some distance, she slipped off Foxie's rear and watched her pupil go around on his own. He no longer looked quite like a sack of chicken feed.

"See how much better?" she coaxed, taking a breath and bringing herself back to business.

His only response was a grunt.

"Tomorrow we'll work on the canter."

"This is another game of one-upmanship, isn't it?"

He was right, of course. Childish game that it was, one-upmanship let her maintain a distance and keep their relationship on a strictly surface level, where she wanted it. She grinned. "I'm on my way to game point, I think."

He turned Foxie toward her and pulled the mare to a halt. "Don't count your chickens before you lay an egg, sweetheart."

The endearment jolted Rachel into a laugh. Sweetheart indeed! She felt guilty at her sudden flush. Riding behind him had felt dangerously good; putting her hands on that hard, strong body had made her knees go weak. Had she been trying to reprise their horseback duet of the day before? That little scene had also smelled of danger. She felt herself wading into quicksand, slowly sinking.

Rachel batted away such thoughts. She and Jackson had work to do. He wanted grit in his résumé, and she was going to let him have it.

Another half hour of riding, during which Jackson only fell off once—a marked improvement—brought them to the small log cabin that housed some of her crew during the autumn branding, which was just a month away. George Kildare had reported several days ago that the place needed some repairs before it was used again. No surprise there. The old cabin dated from the 1930s. The log walls were sturdily built, but the floor inside and on the porch was rotting in places.

"Don't tell me the plumbing here needs repair, too." Jackson eyed the place with a certain resignation.

"Heck, no," Rachel assured him. "There is no plumbing here. You've been promoted to carpentry."

He threw her a sidelong glance, but she simply smiled.

"You did ask for it."

He shook his head in wry disagreement. "I don't think this is exactly what I asked for."

Sam sat on the top rail of the corral, watching Cherie toss a frayed tennis ball for Chesty. Her throws were halfhearted, her expression sullen. The only one enthusiastic about the game was Chesty. Sam had hoped that Chesty would turn up his nose at the stupid, snooty girl, but no. The border collie would sell his soul to play ball, even though Cherie was beneath his notice. She was beneath Sam's notice as well, but his mother had insisted that he join the "games." He would be really glad when the stuck-up loser girl went back to her mansion in California and things got back to normal around the Lazy M.

"You need to throw it farther," he advised. "He likes you to throw it really, really far."

"Like I care?" She lobbed the ball in a lackadaisical arch.

Chesty crouched, grinning, then shot into the air and caught the ball six feet up. Sam clapped and hooted.

"Big deal," Cherie scoffed. "So he can catch a ball." When Chesty trotted up and offered her the ball, she took it in two fingers, grimacing. "Do you have to slobber all over it?"

Chesty barked impatiently. Cherie threw it, watching with a sour expression as the dog shot off after it.

"Dogs are really stupid, you know? What other animal will go back and forth forever fetching a useless ball? Talk about pointless! You wouldn't catch a cat doing something like that. Even a stupid horse would know better."

Sam knew she was trying to irritate him. He considered jumping down from his perch and showing her a thing or two. His mom was gone, and there was no one to see. But Cherie would go whining to her dad. Besides which, his mom always seemed to know when he did something bad, even if she didn't see him do it. Moms were like that.

Once again taking the ball from an eager Chesty, Cherie shot Sam a look. "You think your dog is smart, do you?"

"He's the smartest dog in the world."

She smiled, a sure sign she was up to something. "Okay, if you're so sure, then let's do a bet."

"What kind of bet?"

"We'll play a game of hide-and-seek with the ball. Make the game a little more interesting than just throw and fetch. I bet I can hide it where your stupid wonder dog can't find it."

Sam narrowed his eyes. "It's got to be where he can reach it."

"Sure."

"And what are we betting?"

"If I win, you let me ride Thunder again. And you buy me another ice cream in Greer."

"How about if I win?"

She sniffed. "You're not going to win, but what do you want?"

He thought a moment. Probably telling her to go back to

California wouldn't work. But there was something she had that might be really fun. "When I win, you let me camp out for a night at your motor home, and you have to build a campfire so we can roast marshmallows, and we get to watch DVD movies on your TV and you have to fix us snacks."

She shrugged. "Okay. Dad said he wants to bring the motor home down here anyway. But I don't know how to build a fire."

"Learn," Sam said unsympathetically.

"It's not like you're going to win."

He smiled. "I hope you have Milk Duds in the motor home. I really like Milk Duds." He jumped down and called Chesty over to him. Scratching his ears, he gave the dog a pep talk. "You don't let Cherie outsmart you, Chesty. She's just a girl, and you're a border collie. You're totally smarter than she is."

Cherie smirked at them and held up the ball. "Here I go, Chesty. I'm taking your slimy old ball."

Chesty and Sam both watched as Cherie disappeared into the barn. When she came back, Cherie looked confident. "Find it if you can, dog."

Chesty barked and shot off. Unhesitatingly he went into the barn. Cherie and Sam followed. Behind his back Sam had his fingers crossed, though he felt guilty for thinking his dog might need special help. Chesty really was the smartest dog in the world.

"We should have set a time limit on this," a bored-looking Cherie said.

"Those toasted marshmallows over your fire are going to taste mighty good," Sam taunted.

With a delighted yip, Chesty darted behind a bale of hay and came out with the ball in his mouth. He pranced up to Cherie and dropped it at her feet.

"Yeah," she said glumly. "That was just the warm-up."

In the next half hour she hid the ball in the barn tack room, under the ranch house porch, inside the smokehouse, and even in the smaller barn where the wagon and heavy equipment were stored. Chesty unerringly tracked it down.

Finally admitting defeat, Cherie gave the dog a lopsided smile. "Maybe you are the world's smartest dog."

Sam refrained from crowing, though such gallantry was difficult. But a softer light had snuck into Cherie's eye as she had sought out places to hide Chesty's treasure. She'd even turned a bit playful, talking to the dog as if he were a person she was trying to outwit. During the last two hunts, Sam could have sworn that she was actually rooting for Chesty rather than against him.

When Cherie sat on the bottom rail of the corral and let Chesty push his nose into her face, Sam reluctantly admitted that the girl might be human. Not for sure, but she might.

Wiping off Chesty's kiss, Cherie nevertheless reached up and scratched the dog's ears. "Whew! Don't you ever brush your teeth, dog?" She glanced at Sam and once again assumed her snooty face. "I guess you won. When my dad brings the motor home to the ranch, I'll build you your stupid marshmallow-roasting fire and let you paw through our DVDs. And I guess you can have your stupid horse all to yourself."

Struck by the disappointment in Cherie's eyes, Sam spoke almost without thinking. "I might let you ride Thunder if you'll act nice."

She opened her mouth to retort, then snapped it shut. Sam admitted that being nice was a lot to ask of someone like Cherie.

"I'll think about it," she conceded.

Chesty barked and wagged his tail as Toby Whitman strolled up to the corral, leaning his loose-limbed frame on the rails. He focused an assessing gaze on Cherie.

"Hi, Sam. Who's your little friend?"

Cherie bristled. She stood up and returned Toby's gaze belligerently. "I'm Cherie St—"

Sam nudged her with his foot before she could spill the beans about her identity.

She recovered expertly. "I'm Cherie, not that it's any of your business. Who the hell are you?"

"I'm Toby, cowhand," he said, as if cowhand were something special. "I've been off for a few days, but if I'd known someone like you was at the Lazy M, I'd've come back earlier."

Sam saw the change come over Cherie as Toby continued to look at her. She was no longer the girl who had almost seemed like a normal kid playing with Chesty. Nor was she the sour brat who tormented him. Now she was someone else, someone slinky and hungry, looking at Toby like he was a chocolate sundae.

Sam knew Toby Whitman, and he was beginning to know Cherie Stone. And he smelled trouble in that look.

CHAPTER 9

♡

JACKSON DROVE THE last nail into the last board that would transform the dilapidated, rotting porch into something a person could walk upon without fear of losing a leg. Sweat covered his face, arms, and chest—real sweat, not the kind sprayed on by makeup artists. His shirt hung open. His hat lay on one of the cots in the cabin, and his scalp dribbled salty perspiration into his eyes. He hoped his hair dye didn't dribble as well.

The August sun was hot, and no clouds promised relief. Jackson felt grimy and sore. He'd whacked his thumb with the hammer at least once, and other parts of his anatomy complained of the hours spent crouched on the porch, prying up boards and hammering new ones down.

But damned if he was going to complain—not with Rachel working as hard as he was. She was mighty handy with a hammer and nails, handier than he was, if the truth be known. While he had labored over the porch floor, she had replaced most of the railing and reinforced the posts that supported the roof. Besides, Jackson didn't much want to complain. Not really. He'd always enjoyed working with his hands. One of the garages at the beach house held his latest project—a graceful little sailboat he hoped to launch next spring. The craft wasn't a work of art nor a boat designer's dream, but building it gave him the satisfaction of creating beauty and function from formless raw material.

Of course, breaking a sweat over sanding his boat was a

great deal more fun than breaking a sweat over this dilapidated cabin.

Rachel set down her hammer, straightened, pressed her hands to the small of her back, and stretched. Jackson wasn't too tired to notice the pull of her T-shirt across her breasts. His pulse quickened. Rachel could be covered in sweat and dressed in a flour sack and still broadcast pure, unadulterated, grade-A woman. Jackson liked women, all kinds of women— tall, short, pudgy, slender, young, old. They all had a certain charm. But a woman who looked sexy in her natural state, without artifice, exerted a special attraction. A no-nonsense woman who had eyes that could scald one moment and laugh the next, who had a mouth that said exactly what her brain was thinking, who could wear sweat or silk with equal allure—now, that was a woman a man could seriously fall for. If a man were in the market to fall for anyone, which Jackson wasn't. He couldn't for a woman like Rachel, who was likely to take love seriously when she took it at all. He wasn't a man for a lifetime kind of woman.

That didn't mean, however, that he couldn't heartily admire what he couldn't have.

She caught his glance and actually blushed. That was another thing he liked about Rachel. She hadn't learned to hide her feelings.

"Done here," he told her with a grin. "Sure you don't want me to fix the plumbing, too?"

"If the cabin had plumbing, I'd have you fix it."

"I'm sure you would."

She gave his handiwork a sharp look. "Good work, Stone."

"Hurts to admit, doesn't it?"

Her grin made her look ten years old. "It does."

"You should see the boat I'm building."

"Now you're showing off."

He shrugged. "It's just a little boat. My brother's a boat designer in San Francisco. He helped me some."

She shook her head. "Somehow it's hard to think of Jackson Stone as a person with a brother and a hobby."

He grinned. "I have a mother, too."

That got a laugh. "Stars have moms. Who woulda' thunk! I'll bet yours doesn't give you the hard time mine gives me."

"Wanna bet?"

"No bets. Are you ready for a snack?"

"You packed food?" His stomach rumbled audibly.

She laughed. "I did make you miss breakfast, if I recall. And lunch."

"Yes, you did, Simon Legree. What do we have?"

"Pastrami on rye, oatmeal cookies, a Dr Pepper for you, and a Diet Coke for me. Watch out when you open that pop. It rode all the way up here in my saddlebag, and it's—yikes!"

The Dr Pepper was better than a squirt gun. Jackson couldn't resist. Rachel might as well have pinned a kick-me sign to her backside. She shrieked as the sugary brown foam soaked her from stem to stern.

"Oh, gee! Sorry!" His laughter sputtered when Rachel returned fire with a stream of Diet Coke.

"You're a dead man," Rachel warned as he fled. Laughing, she gave chase, shaking her pop can as she went. Around the corner of the cabin Jackson met her with another barrage, the last of his ammunition.

"Aaaagh!" Gingerly she pulled her T-shirt away from skin. "This stuff is sticky!"

"You should drink something with sugar in it. All I am is wet!"

He got even wetter when she charged forward and emptied her pop over his head. No stranger to the art of infighting, he grabbed her arm and saw to it that as much of the Diet Coke went her way as his. At the end, they were both laughing so hard they could scarcely stand.

"Cripes!" Rachel complained. "I'm a mess!"

She was, but to Jackson's eyes, she looked good enough to eat, not only because she was covered with sticky sugar. Her T-shirt clung in a way guaranteed to make any man drool, and no amount of her modest plucking it away remedied the situation. Her ponytail dripped, her face wore the high color of laughter.

Jackson wanted to reach out and haul her to him. That would have been the next move in any movie script. But this scene hadn't walked out of a screenplay, and this woman was more likely to put a fist in his solar plexus than wrap her arms around him for a few moments of romance. And it was a good thing, too. Hadn't he just been thinking in terms of "hands off"?

He gave her a lopsided smile. "So much for the drinks."

"You started it."

"You invited it."

She grinned. "I guess I did." In vain she tried to shake the drips of Dr Pepper from her arms. "There's a stock tank over here. Maybe it has water in it."

The tank was a mere pond with green scum floating on top. The cold water felt good, though. Rachel didn't try to be dainty. She simply took off her boots and waded in, pushing aside the floating algae and crouching down to splash her face, shoulders, and chest. Jackson was so fascinated by the sight that he nearly forgot to wash.

"What are you looking at?" she asked tartly.

"You," he said truthfully.

"I don't see you getting very wet."

He was in only up to his knees. "That's because watching you is such a treat."

"Right," she said with a laugh.

"You think I'm joking?"

"I think you're full of enough blarney to sink Ireland."

"Don't you think a man might find you a treat to watch?"

She splashed herself again. "Don't confuse the issue, Jackson. I'm as immune to flattery as I am to charm."

Damn, but what kind of man could resist that kind of challenge? He waded forward. "Let me help you, there." Before she could move away, he cupped water in his hands and poured it over her limp, sticky hair, which defiantly curled even through the onslaught of Dr Pepper.

"What are you—"

"Tilt your head back."

"Aaaaack!"

"I warned you. Can you unfasten that cute little ponytail?"

"You are very pushy. Has anyone ever told you that?"

Nevertheless, she tilted her head back and let him rinse her hair. But Jackson wasn't fooled. He saw retribution brewing in those blue eyes, even more clearly when she straightened, squeezed the water from her hair, and eyed him like a lioness sizing up her prey.

"Thank you," she said, perfectly polite.

Then she laughed and tackled him at the knees, toppling him into the scummy green water. He flailed, then grabbed at her and brought her down with him. When the little witch dunked him, all desire for chivalry departed. He set hands on her shoulders and dunked her in turn. She came up sputtering, water streaming from dark, gleaming hair that fell in a shawl around her shoulders.

Grinning, he stood, offering Rachel a hand up. She batted it away. He grinned even wider. "You look like a drowned kitten."

"You're not exactly Neptune rising from the depths yourself. If your fans could see you now, they'd defect to Mel Gibson."

"Now, that hurts!"

"Tit for tat."

She presented him with a spectacle when she stood, though she didn't seem self-conscious about it. Perhaps only a man could appreciate how good a woman looked in wet clothes. His heart hammered in his chest, and only sheer force of will kept him from becoming a spectacle himself. Michelangelo could have cast him in bronze and titled him "Male in Lust." All his good intentions and resolve were boiling away.

"I suppose we'll dry soon enough," Rachel said with a smile. She had no idea what a sight she was. Or was she too busy looking at him?

"Uh . . ." they both stuttered at the same time. A wave of heat flooded Jackson's body. As if beckoned by his rush of desire, Rachel leaned toward him ever so slightly. He reached for her, and the space between them disappeared. Their mouths fused by common consent. Jackson welcomed her as a starving man might welcome sustenance. She reciprocated in kind, coiling about him with supple arms and legs, nestling into his arms as though she belonged there. As though she couldn't get enough of him.

They came up for air, both gasping. "This isn't a good idea," she panted. "This isn't a good idea at all."

"The hell it's not," he said, and shut her mouth once again with his own.

On the ride back to the Lazy M Jackson didn't fall off Foxie once, Rachel noted, no doubt because he was cocky about that accidental little kiss. The man was so busy congratulating himself that he forgot to be afraid of the horse. When he loosened up in the saddle, Jackson had a natural, athletic seat and a sure hand on the reins. He also had quite a kiss, Rachel admitted to herself. A lollapaloozer of a kiss.

But still, a kiss was just a kiss, as the old song went. It was no big deal—nothing more than a spontaneous reaction in a peculiar situation. Certainly that little kiss wasn't a symptom of weakening resolve or eroding common sense. Jackson might be attractive—magnetic, even. He might be sexy and funny and know just how to endear himself to a woman. But Rachel Marsh had entirely too much common sense to fall for such things. He could tease and flirt and snatch a kiss when she let her guard down, but her defenses, in spite of an obvious chink or two, were essentially intact. Or so she assured herself. That kiss didn't mean a thing.

Keep telling yourself that, a cynical voice in her head advised. *Sooner or later you'll believe it.*

When she walked into the ranch house, Sam looked up from the living room game table, where he worked on a puzzle. "What'd ya do, Ma? Take a swim in the watering trough?"

She was mostly dry, but her hair hung in undisciplined algae-crusted curls. Her jeans were damp, and they had the shrink-wrap look that came from, well, being shrink-wrapped to her form. Her T-shirt sported green lines of dried pond scum, and her face felt hot and burned—from the sun or a touch of embarrassment?

You ought to be damned embarrassed, that persistent voice chided, *wrapping yourself around Jackson Stone like a butterfly-brained woman with stars in your eyes and good old-fashioned lust in your heart.*

Rachel really didn't want to think about it.

Sam still regarded her with inquisitive eyes. "It was a hot day," she explained to her son.

"I thought you told me not to play in the watering trough."

"I wasn't playing in the watering trough. I took a swim in the stock tank up by the Tucker cabin. And just because I tell you not to do something doesn't mean I can't do it. You're eleven, and I'm thirty-one. It makes a difference."

"Yes, ma'am."

His chastened tone made her feel guilty. She let out a sigh. "Sorry, pardner. I didn't mean to take your head off. It's been a long day, and I'm tired."

And you're a sucker for a pair of green eyes, a crooked smile, and a smart mouth. A talented mouth.

No, she would not think about that.

"That's okay, Ma. You look tired. Can I go play poker with Paul?"

"As long as you don't bet anything other than matchsticks."

"What else would we bet?"

Just what stakes are you betting by playing little games with Jackson Stone?

"Oh, shut up!" she grumbled under her breath at her conscience.

Joanne emerged from the kitchen brandishing a large wooden spoon. "About time you showed up. I kept a couple of pieces of chicken hot. Checked in a couple by the name of Simon and put them in the Cherokee cabin. They signed up for a trail ride tomorrow morning and say they're going to spend every afternoon fishing, so you don't have to worry about them much."

Rachel peeled her ball cap from damp, tangled hair and tugged at her shrink-wrapped jeans. "Thanks, Joanne."

"What the hell happened to you?"

"You don't want to know," Rachel insisted.

Joanne dissected her with narrowed eyes. "It doesn't have anything to do with that good-looking new hand you went gallivanting off with this afternoon, does it?"

"We were not gallivanting. We were working on the Tucker cabin. Branding is just a month off."

"So it does have something to do with him."

How Joanne jumped to her conclusions was beyond Rachel's understanding, but the old woman always homed in on exactly whatever Rachel wanted to conceal. She sure as heck didn't want Joanne to learn about the lip lock she'd given Jackson. With the housekeeper's determination to find her a man, Rachel would never hear the end of it. "We took a little dip in the stock pond," she admitted. "It was hot out there."

Joanne's lips twitched. "I'll just bet it was."

Rachel tried to look innocent. "I'm going to take a bath and change. Then I'll eat that chicken." She felt the press of Joanne's eyes as she climbed the stairs.

The next morning her foreman, Jim MacDonald, returned from vacation, sunburned, griping about Mexican sand in everything he'd packed, and after seven whole days with his wife, ready to whip a few hands into shape. Extended time with his wife always did that to Mac, Rachel had noticed. She toyed with the idea of turning him loose on Jackson. Let Mac show the man what grit was all about

"We have a new hand," she told Mac when he came to her office a little after five in the morning. "Well, we sort of have a new hand."

A burly six-footer, Mac propped himself on one corner of her desk. "So I understand from the boys. They were talking when I dropped by the bunkhouse last night. Nathan seems to think this new guy is next to useless."

"Well, Nathan has taken a dislike to him for some reason."

Mac chuckled. "I wonder why." Mac looked as if he might know why, which was more than Rachel knew. He seemed mightily amused.

Rachel trotted out the same excuse she'd given Vince. "He's . . . a cousin."

"Is that so?" Like Joanne, Mac had been at the Lazy M forever, and he figured that gave him the right to meddle in the lives of the Marsh family.

"A half cousin," she qualified. "He wanted the experience of working on a ranch. He has a bad ankle right now, but it doesn't slow him down much. You can give him all the hard work you want. Dirty work, even. He specializes in dirty work."

"Vince told me this new guy fixed the plumbing in Sitting Bull."

"I asked him to fix it so he and his daughter could bunk there."

"Well, I guess he's got some talent."

Jackson Stone had a lot of talent—in areas Rachel didn't want to think about. A night's sleep hadn't cooled the burn of that kiss. "Uh . . . he's willing." Just thinking about how exquisitely willing he was made her want to squirm. "His name is Stoney. Stoney Jackson."

Mac's brows went up. "Stoney?"

"Yeah."

"As in Stoney Burke?"

"I'm guessing his mother was a Jack Lord fan."

Mac chuckled, then pushed on to other subjects, for which Rachel was grateful. Plenty of business awaited their attention. August was almost halfway over. In late September they would brand. Then the cattle now grazing the high range would be trucked to pastures below Springerville. In the old days, the cattle were driven—a genuine Old West cattle drive. When Rachel had first moved to the ranch, she had briefly toyed with the idea of reviving the cattle drive and opening it to interested guests who were willing to pay for the privilege of eating dust and smelling cattle for miles on end—*City Slickers,* Arizona style. But she discarded the idea when she realized how much her liability insurance would increase, so the guest ranch was shut down before the branding and the cattle were trucked every year.

This time of year meant extra work for Mac and Rachel. Extra hands needed to be hired for the branding, and arrangements finalized with the trucking company. The cowboys had to be interviewed to find out how many of them planned to return in the spring, and the cabins needed to be brought into shipshape condition to survive the winter. In addition, this week they needed to clean the equipment barn in preparation for the Lazy M's once-a-month barn dance, scheduled this coming Saturday. A band imported from Show Low would blast out everything from rock to Perry Como. People from Greer, Springerville, and even as far away as Show Low, Pinetop, and McNary came to dance and eat baked beans, coleslaw, and sloppy joes.

Thursday afternoon, Rachel enlisted Cherie to help her clean the storage barn where the dance would be held. Moira and Terri were both busy cleaning cabins, and Joanne had gone into Springerville for the weekly grocery binge. Surprisingly, Cherie wasn't as sullen about the job as Rachel had expected. While they swept the hard-packed dirt floor and spread cedar shavings, the girl turned talkative.

"I taught Chesty a new game the other day," she boasted.

"Then you probably won his heart. Chesty loves games. He has to be occupied with something every minute of the day or he goes crazy."

"Yeah, sometimes I feel like that, too," Cherie admitted. "Get all restless inside, you know? Like you're supposed to be doing something with your life that you're not doing, that you're just treading water when you should be shooting the rapids. Everybody's got you roped into place just because you're young. You know?"

Rachel could sympathize. She had felt exactly that way at Cherie's age. Probably most kids did. But it didn't do any good to tell the girl that.

"It's hard to wait. But there's lots of things you could be doing now to get ready for that day when you can launch out on your own."

Cherie snorted. "Yeah. Like gather eggs!"

"What?"

"My dad had me up this morning way, way before the sun was up. Big, special treat, he said. Turns out I got to meet a pack of goats and steal the eggs from a bunch of smelly chickens. Those chickens are mean, by the way. There was an old lady there, too. Mrs Dobson. She said my dad was a ham-handed dork and wouldn't let him milk the goats. Did it herself and acted like it was a big treat. Man oh man, you get some weird people staying here."

"We do indeed," Rachel agreed wholeheartedly, with a telling look at Cherie.

Cherie laughed. It was the first time Rachel had heard her laugh, and she was amazed at how that laugh transformed the overly made-up face to that of a happy, normal young teen.

Cherie took a bag of cedar chips and started scattering them on the swept floor, wrinkling her nose at the sharp, clean aroma. "So we're really going to have a dance here? Like, with a real group and everything?"

Rachel laughed at the tentative hope in the girl's face. "Yes, we're going to have a dance. We have one every month. But I don't know if you could call the Dirty Half Dozen a 'group.' They play oldies and country western."

"Oh." Her disappointment was obvious. Then she asked suspiciously, "You guys aren't going to do something really lame, like square dance, are you?"

"No," Rachel assured her cheerfully. "But the band does a great Hank Williams medley playing pitchforks and kazoos."

For a moment Cherie bought it, her eyes widening in horror. Then she snorted. "You had me going for a minute. This place is almost retro enough for that to happen."

"Sometimes retro is good," Rachel told the girl in all seriousness.

"You and my dad!" Cherie linked them as two objects of

pity. "You guys read from the same script, you know? He's always raving about old-fashioned this and old-fashioned that. You know he listens to oldies radio?"

Rachel was suitably horrified. "Obviously he's headed straight for the old folks' home."

Cherie made a face at her, then shot her an impish glance. "You like my dad, don't you?"

"I . . ." What could she say? She kept telling herself she didn't like Jackson Stone at all, but by now even she had to admit it was a lie. "Of course I like your father. He's a nice guy."

Cherie made a rude sound. "Right. Like that's the whole truth! You don't have to fib about it. Everyone drools over my dad. He's even been hit on by gay guys. At first I thought maybe you were gay because you didn't seem to like him, but now I see that look in your eye. You're under his spell."

"Oh, for cripes sake! I am *not* under his spell!"

Cherie grinned wickedly. "You don't need to be embarrassed about it. He's, like, irresistible."

"No man is irresistible, Cherie."

"My dad is."

"No, he's not. And I am not under any man's spell, especially his."

She didn't believe she was arguing about her love life with a thirteen-year-old. She didn't have a love life. She didn't want a love life. And in spite of the annoying smirk on Cherie's face, she was not under Jackson Stone's spell.

Two hours later, Rachel had reason to wonder about that when she left the barn to fetch a truckload of hay bales to arrange as seats for the dance. If she'd known what waited outside, she would have sent Cherie. Instead, she came face to face with two of the hands digging weeds around the barn. One of those hands was Toby Whitman, who was no doubt doing penance for smarting off to Mac. Smarting off to Mac was Toby's hobby. The other man working in the hot sun was Jackson. Mac was "breaking in" the new hand with the dirtiest possible work. On most ranches, the practice was tradition.

Ordinarily, keeping the weeds in check was a relatively simple job accomplished by mower and weed whacker, but Rachel had conceived the idea of planting bulbs along the side of the barn, with the dual purpose of providing color and keeping down the weeds. So this crop of weeds had to be dug up rather than mowed, and the hands set to accomplish the task were suffering for it under the August sun.

Jackson worked shirtless, chest gleaming with sweat, arms bulging with muscle as he wielded his shovel. If Rachel had known Jackson was outside the barn presenting such a picture of macho pulchritude, she would have stayed inside. There was no way she could walk past without being noticed.

"Hi, Miz Marsh," Toby said with a grin as he straightened from his labor. "How ya doin'?"

"I'm good, Toby. How about you?"

"Real good, ma'am."

Rachel tried not to look at Jackson, but his eyes reeled her in. There probably wasn't a woman in the world who could resist the weight of Jackson Stone's focused gaze. He smiled and leaned casually on his shovel.

She tried for nonchalant. "Working hard, I see."

He just smiled. But it was a smile that gave her a liquidy feeling in parts she'd rather not think about.

Toby took measure of the electricity between them and grinned. "Think I'll go get some cold water."

"You do that," Jackson said.

Toby trooped off, whistling.

Jackson kept looking at her, and Rachel felt her heart step up its rhythm.

"Been avoiding me these last couple days?"

"I've been busy. I see Mac put you to work."

"That he did. Good man, Mac. I like him."

"He gets a day's work out of the crew."

Jackson mopped at the sweat on his brow. "Yeah. He does that."

"Hard work," Rachel acknowledged. "How's your ankle?"

"Almost new. Believe me, this job is nothing like what the boss has put me through."

She had to smile. "Your boss must be a tyrant."

"You got that right."

"So you're overworked and abused, and you certainly look the part. Your film associates should approve."

He grinned audaciously and struck a pose that made the most of his half-dressed condition. "How about you?"

"You are insufferably vain," she told him.

"Goes with the territory. All actors are vain. Hadn't you heard?"

"And stubborn."

"Persistent."

"Stubborn."

He chuckled. "Rachel, we're well matched."

"Not at all."

He winked at her, and her traitorous body responded instantly with a blush. He reached out to touch her heated cheek, but she drew back self-consciously as Toby appeared at the dining hall doorway with two bottles of water.

"Have fun digging weeds." She managed to smile at the boy and gave Jackson a dismissive wave. "There's more work where that came from, cowboy Stoney."

The next day was Friday. Jackson Stone had been at the Lazy M just under a week, yet the guests seemed to consider him an institution. Mrs. Dobson and her husband encountered Rachel after lunch and the old lady effused about Jackson.

"Such a nice young man!" she gushed. "Where on earth did you find him? Not many fellows with a job to do will put up with a doddering old woman prattling about the good old days."

"That's for sure," Mr. Dobson agreed, rolling his eyes.

Mrs. Dobson ignored her better half, a habit Rachel suspected was one of long standing. "And he's getting to be a right good milker as well, with my help of course." The old woman's smile was beatific. Her eyes twinkled at Rachel. "And so good-looking! He reminds me of some movie star. I just can't quite think who."

"Stoney strikes a lot of people that way," Rachel said with a sigh. She hoped Mrs. Dobson didn't think too carefully on that resemblance. "I'm glad he's making your visit a pleasant one."

She had assiduously avoided Jackson all day, and still she couldn't get away from the man. Fate had it in for her.

The only answer was to flee. Vince normally drove to Greer for the mail, but today Rachel took his place. Sam and Chesty went with her.

"Has Cherie been doing her duty by Chesty every day?" Rachel asked her son."

"Yes, ma'am."

"And have you tried to be nice to Cherie?"

"Yes, ma'am."

Sam wasn't exactly talkative today, Rachel noted.

"And is Cherie being nice to you and Chesty?"

"Yes, ma'am." He looked thoughtful for a moment. "When Cherie's dad brings their motor home to the ranch, Cherie and I want to camp out in it for the night and roast marshmallows over a fire. Is that okay?"

"I didn't know he was bringing the thing to the ranch."

"He is."

"It's okay with me as long as you're careful with the fire. But you'll have to ask Cherie's dad."

"If it's okay with him, it's okay with you?"

"Yes."

"Cherie says her dad will let her do anything she wants."

"I doubt that's true, Sam. No dad lets his kid do absolutely anything. That wouldn't be responsible."

"Well, maybe he's not responsible."

"I think probably he is."

He thought for a moment more. "Do you think Mr. Stone would mind if Cherie was getting funny with one of the hands?"

That sounded ominous. "What do you mean, getting funny?"

"You know." He made a face. "Making google eyes and talking all syrupy like."

"Who with?"

"Toby."

"Ah. Our resident ladies' man. I don't think Cherie's going to get very far with Toby. Toby and I had a little talk a few days back."

"Oh. Okay. You know . . . Cherie can be pretty nice sometimes, for a girl. And then she'll get real stupid, like when she starts talking about what a big shot she is or when Toby comes around."

Rachel shook her head sympathetically. "Girls can be like that, Sam. Get used to it."

When they pulled up to the post office, Sam and Chesty shot out of the truck to run up to the riding stable. The stable's owner, Roy Kimble, was organizing the local rodeo and Greer Days festival for the end of August, and Sam was dying to help him. Rachel went to check their post-office box and say hello to Molly.

Molly looked up from sorting packages when Rachel walked in. "Well, if it isn't Miss Rachel herself. Where's that old codger Vince today?"

Rachel smiled. Vince might be twenty years younger than Molly, but his irascible nature made him an old codger in Molly's mind, and at eighty-plus, Molly called 'em as she saw 'em.

"I made Vince stay home, much as he'll miss seeing you. To tell the truth, I needed an excuse to get away from the ranch for a while."

"Don't blame you," Molly sympathized. "That place keeps you so busy you don't have time to sneeze."

"Something like that." She pulled a stack of envelopes from the Lazy M box—bills, bills, two offers for credit cards, a note from a former guest, and more bills. Thanks to Jackson Stone and the big bucks he was paying her, the bills would get paid without Rachel finagling money from savings and contemplating selling the household furniture.

"Did that young fella with the ankle find you last week?" Molly asked, a gleam in her eye.

Rachel considered the possibility of diverting Molly from

this particular subject. She decided the chances were slim. "He did," she admitted.

"Right good-looking man. You know who he is, don't you, Rachel?"

Rachel's heart thumped. "What do you mean?"

"Why, he's the big movie star Jackson Stone. Don't tell me you didn't recognize him!"

Jackson had met Molly before he assumed his little disguise, but he had been confident the old lady hadn't recognized him. It wasn't the first time someone had underestimated Aunt Molly. So much for Jackson's precious anonymity. Maybe now he would leave and get out of her hair.

The possibility didn't please her as much as it should have.

"I know who he is," Rachel admitted reluctantly. "Have you told anyone?"

"Of course not," Molly said indignantly. "I figure a big star like him, when he's off doing private things, doesn't want the TV and newspaper people following him around. I know when to keep my mouth shut, young lady."

"Don't get upset, Molly. I didn't mean to imply that you didn't. It's just that right now, he particularly doesn't want the press hounding him. He . . . uh . . . he's taken it into his head to be a real cowboy for a little while."

"Now, don't that just beat all!" She shot Rachel a canny look. "What are the chances he's set his sights on something out at that ranch of yours? He was mighty interested in hearing about you, Rachel girl."

Great. Now even Molly was matchmaking.

"Not a chance," Rachel said emphatically. "He's definitely not my type."

Molly chuckled. "Back when I was still young and spry, I wouldn't have let a fine-looking man like that one come courting without nabbing him. No, ma'am!"

"Molly, the man is not courting."

The old postmistress didn't listen. "Take it from someone who's been on this planet a long time, Rachel. Some things only come around in this life once. You have to snap up those opportunities."

"You're impossible, Molly Satler."

"I'm just the only one around here with common sense."

Rachel smiled. "I'll send him for the mail tomorrow, and you can have him."

"Might take you up on that. He's got mighty fine legs, he does. I've always appreciated a man with fine-looking legs."

Cupid had it in for her, Rachel decided. She couldn't get away from Jackson even in town. Her next call was at Karen's restaurant, the rendezvous spot with Sam. Sam wasn't there when she stuck her head through the door, but a dozen or so tourists were. She decided to order a sandwich.

"Can a person get food around here?" she called into the back.

"Keep your shirt on." Karen came from the kitchen wiping her hands on a dish towel. Today her T-shirt declared that "Cowgirls Do It With Horses." She spotted Rachel and smiled. "Hi, stranger. Long time, no see."

"Sam been in yet?"

"Nope. Want a sandwich?"

"Chicken salad on wheat?"

"Coming up. Come on back to the kitchen."

"You're busy today," Rachel noted as she pulled up a stool beside a worktable.

"Making money hand over fist. But it'll end come Labor Day. Season's about over. I'm glad the rodeo and festival are coming up. It'll bring in some extra cash."

"You coming to the dance tomorrow?"

"You know it. Can't miss the last dance of the summer. Understand you have a new man out at the ranch. Got to look him over. New men out this way are rare specimens."

Rachel sighed. Not again. "How'd you know?"

"Met his lovely daughter," Karen told her with a wry smile. "She and Sam were here for ice cream the day it rained so hard. I got the impression they weren't exactly buddies."

"The scamp. I'm going to nail Sam on this one."

"Don't be such a hard-ass. The boy was trying to cope with an 'older woman.' What's the dad like?" The silence gave Rachel away. Karen's brows rose a notch. "That good, is he?"

"Aaaaagh!" Rachel collapsed face first onto the worktable and covered her head with her arms.

"Wow! *That* good?"

If she couldn't confide in her best friend, then who could she confide in? "He's walking temptation, Karen. And totally what I don't need."

Karen hooted in delight. "Excellent!"

"Karen!"

"It's about time you got back in the game, Rachel!"

"Sheesh! Why does everybody think romance is a game of chance?"

"Well, isn't it? Have you kissed the guy?" Karen asked, setting a chicken salad sandwich in front of Rachel.

Rachel temporized by taking a bite and chewing slowly. Karen was having none of the delay.

"Well?"

"Well, yes. I have."

"And is he a good kisser?"

Rachel rolled her eyes.

"I take that as an emphatic yes. Have you slept with him?"

"Karen!"

Karen gave her a look.

"No, I haven't slept with him," Rachel admitted in a low voice. "And I'm not going to. I have more sense than that. Besides, sleeping with a guy is not a casual sport."

"Did I say it was?" Karen poured half a Diet Coke in a glass, set it in front of Rachel, then took a drink from the can. "You might fall in love. You might marry the guy, in spite of his weird daughter. You're not a doddering widow of ninety-nine, you know. You still have some juices running through you."

Rachel laughed. "I'm certainly not going to marry this one! I don't even like him. That is, I like him all right. He's a nice guy, but totally not my type. I don't like him in *that* way."

"What way?" Karen asked innocently, grinning.

"*That* way. You know."

"No spark, huh?"

Rachel frowned.

"No chemistry? Fluttery stomach, pounding heart, hot blood pumping through your veins?"

"Stop it."

Karen raised a brow. "You're blushing, kiddo."

Rachel grimaced. "It's hot in here. That's all."

"Bullshit."

Just then Sam came in. "Hey, Miz Spangler. There's a guy out there who wants more iced tea."

"I'm on it, pardner."

"Hey, Ma."

"Hey, Sam. Want half of my sandwich?"

"Yeah. You oughta see the two new quarter horses Roy bought! One's almost sixteen hands! He's huge! And the rodeo's gonna be really cool. Races, and bulldogging, and bucking horses. Roy said I could ride in the parade, and maybe Chesty and me—"

"Chesty and I," Rachel corrected automatically.

"Maybe Chesty and I could demonstrate sheepherding. Wouldn't that be cool?"

"Way cool."

By the time Karen returned from the dining room, Rachel had to leave. She was almost grateful. Karen would give her no peace until Rachel told her more about Jackson. She paid for lunch and promised to tell all by the time Karen came to the Lazy M to help with branding, as she did every year. By that time Jackson would be gone, and Rachel could laugh about how silly she'd been.

As Rachel and Sam climbed into their truck and drove away, Karen stood on the Roundup's porch and looked after them with her hands on her hips. She did love secrets. They intrigued her. A secret to Karen Spangler was like a mystery to Sherlock Holmes. She was absolutely unable to resist investigating.

Back in the kitchen, she opened a drawer and took out the

issue of the *National Star* that had been left on a table the day of Sam's visit during the rainstorm. There on the front was the fuzzy photo of a girl who looked remarkably like the girl who had sat on her porch eating ice cream. The photo was too blurred for Karen to be certain, but the girl who had been with Sam looked a good deal like Cherie Stone, which would mean that her father, and Rachel's guy, was . . .

Karen smothered a laugh. It couldn't be, just couldn't be. This was a secret worth digging into.

CHAPTER 10

♡

THE BARN DANCE Saturday drew a crowd. Summer was ending and everyone wanted to stave off the coming of winter with a bit of celebration. The smaller of the Lazy M's two barns, normally used to store tools, extra harnesses, a horse trailer, the wagon, and other miscellaneous items that needed to be kept from the weather, was swept clean, the dirt floor strewn with cedar chips, and the rafters festooned with colorful paper lanterns and crepe streamers. A huge sheet of plywood atop four sawhorses served as a table. On it was the result of Joanne's labor—cold cuts, crackers, cheese, fresh cut vegetables, corn chips, salsa, onion dip, baked beans, sloppy joes, and coleslaw. Coolers held iced pop, beer, wine coolers, and sun tea. Along the walls, hay bales provided seating. The Dirty Half Dozen, the band from Show Low, played everything from imitation big band to nineties rock, but their specialty was country western. A musician couldn't live in the Arizona mountains without specializing in country western.

All but one of the Lazy M's rooms were full, and all the guests had dressed in their western finery for the dance—shiny new boots, jeans that still had store-bought creases, and cowboy shirts with mother-of-pearl snaps. The ranch hands showed up with their hair slicked back and fingernails scrubbed clean. Nathan Crosby had gone so far as to don a new shirt and a turquoise bolo tie. Vince had shaved—for him, an extraordinary concession to good grooming. Clint, the Lazy

M hand who commuted from Greer, had brought his wife, a sociable young woman who had assigned herself the task of teaching the guests to line dance. Vince's and Mac's wives had also trailed along with their husbands.

Folks from Greer and Springerville came as well. The banker who had loaned Rachel the original capital to make improvements on the Lazy M had brought his wife and son. The manager of Joanne's favorite grocery store was there with his girlfriend. Aunt Molly sat enthroned on a bale of hay, captivating guests with her tales of the real cowboying days of Arizona's White Mountains. Karen showed up in tight red jeans and a silver sequined top that would make Elvis himself blush. She toured the barn several times, her eyes trolling for Rachel's new ranch hand.

"He's not here," Rachel told her with a playful poke in the ribs.

"What? Did you lock him up?"

"No. Maybe he doesn't feel like mingling." She hoped. Jackson's fast-growing beard did give him a different enough look that, along with his dyed hair and semi-slouch, might keep him safe. None of the guests who had almost daily contact with him seemed to suspect he was anything other than a good-looking, somewhat bumbling cowboy. In the week he'd been at the Lazy M, Jackson had become a favorite with the guests. He thrived in front of an audience. Wisely, he didn't try to pretend cowboy macho. Instead, he made a joke out of his small incompetences. The guests thought it was all an act, and they loved it.

The guests loved Jackson in other ways as well. He had made a regular show out of the predawn goat and chicken chores. Rachel was astounded at how many guests actually rose from bed at such an unholy hour to experience a bit of down-home farm chores. Most of the "city slickers" turned out to be better milkers than Jackson, and Jackson seldom had to squat beside a goat or reach his hand under a chicken. The guests competed to do it for him.

Rachel acknowledged that the Lazy M might actually miss Jackson when he left.

"This is a disappointment," Karen complained. "I was hoping to meet your new heartthrob."

"Quiet! He is not my heartthrob. Now I wish I'd kept my mouth shut."

"No, you don't. You love being mysterious."

"I don't!"

"Okay." Karen grinned. "Maybe it's me who loves being mysterious."

Nathan Crosby interrupted the interrogation when he pulled Rachel away to dance. "Gotta take a dance when I can get it," Nathan told her. "I know how busy you get at these parties."

"You're right. I usually have so much to do that I don't have time for fun. You look really nice tonight, Nathan. I like that bolo tie."

"Thanks. And you're beautiful, as usual."

Rachel laughed. "Beautiful, is it? When an employee calls the boss beautiful, expect a request for a raise to follow."

"No, ma'am. You're beautiful without a raise. Don't you ever look in the mirror?"

Rachel began to feel awkward. "You guys are getting a raise next season, actually. We've had a few financial windfalls, and I figure you all deserve it."

"Everybody will be glad to hear that. I think most of the boys are counting on coming back next spring."

"That's good to hear."

They two-stepped around the big open dance space to the strains of an old Charlie Daniels hit. Nathan was a good dancer. He didn't hold her too loosely, as did almost every other crew member who worked up the nerve to dance with her, and he didn't crush her as Darin used to do when they danced.

"There was something that I wanted to talk to you about," Nathan admitted as he guided her around the floor.

"Yes?"

"Uh . . . I haven't made any definite plans for the winter yet, so if you need someone to stay here and help out around the place . . ."

"That's really nice of you to offer, Nathan. But you know, there's not a whole lot to be done during the winter other than shovel snow. Toby and Vince are going to keep an eye on the herd down below Springerville, since they both live close by. I'm sending all but two of the Lazy M horses off with the herd, and of course, Paul will have his string down in Scottsdale."

He looked disappointed. "Just thought I'd ask."

"Well, as I said, it was nice of you to offer." She was a bit surprised. Most of the men in the bunkhouse fancied themselves footloose and fancy free. They were generally happy to move on in the fall and come back in the spring. At least most of them came back. One or two might find greener pastures.

"Guess I'll spend the winter driving trucks over in Albuquerque, then. Come back in the spring." His eyes probed her expression. Rachel didn't know what he hoped to find. She was grateful when someone tapped Nathan's shoulder to cut in—until she saw who the someone was. Jackson had the nerve to show up after all.

Jackson pulled her out of Nathan's arms and into his own. Nathan scowled and said something under his breath, but Jackson quickly danced her beyond the cowboy's range of retrieval.

"What did he say?" she asked Jackson.

Jackson smiled grimly. "You don't want to know."

"Nathan's in a strange mood tonight." She looked over her shoulder at Nathan as he sullenly retreated to the refreshment table.

"Don't worry about Nathan," Jackson warned. "No man likes to be cut out when he's dancing with a beautiful woman."

"Beautiful, am I?" She laughed softly. "You fellas certainly are generous with the compliments tonight. Someone must have put something in the punch."

Something in the punch—that would explain the giddiness that warmed her blood and made her heart pound as they moved around the dance floor. "Cowboy Stoney" was looking very handsome tonight. He'd trimmed his incipient beard, and his hair, buzzed into a cut unworthy of a national sex symbol, had grown out a bit in the week he'd been at the Lazy M. Rachel had an insane urge to run her hand through that hair.

Worse, trapped in Jackson's arms, she was an easy target for his smile. His wasn't a big grinning smile, or even a bold blatant smile. It was a private smile, just between him and her, a smile that warmed his eyes and made Rachel's insides turn to liquid.

An ache of guilty longing almost made her stumble. "You're looking quite handsome yourself tonight. I'm surprised someone doesn't recognize you."

He didn't look worried. "Everyone here knows exactly who I am—Stoney Jackson. Like I said before, if you don't expect to see something, then you generally don't. Besides, this new beard of mine has grown in pretty well. I figure I'm damned close to being unrecognizable."

"I have to admire your overconfidence."

"I'm glad to hear you admire something."

What was it about the man that made her want to kick him in exasperation and smile at the same time? "What is it about you that lets you get away with just about anything?"

"Something I learned years ago in the Industry. Godzilla-size egos are rewarded with success. Without a certain amount of boldness and arrogance you get nowhere."

"Then it's no wonder you're such a huge success."

He gave her a wry smile. "Ah, Rachel, I do enjoy your claws. One of the many things I enjoy about you. I couldn't hole up in that cabin while all these guys in here got a crack at you."

"Get a crack at me? You have to be kidding!"

"Nope. More than one guy here has an eye on you. Including me," he added with a wicked grin, then swung her out and twirled her under his arm, ending with her pinned securely against his chest. For a moment her heart fluttered against his, then he loosened his embrace. Nevertheless, she needed to catch her breath. Coming up hard against that wall of muscle had somehow knocked the air right out of her lungs.

She suddenly had a desperate need to reassert herself as the one in charge. "If you have this much energy left after the way Mac has made you work, maybe I'll tell him to put you on weed detail again next week. Or maybe all the hay bales and grain sacks in the barn loft need to be rearranged."

"Bring it on," he invited.

Nathan was back, and now he served Jackson the same treatment Jackson had given him, slapping him hard on the shoulder. "My turn again, guy."

With an easy smile, Jackson gave her up. A twinge of annoyance took Rachel by surprise as he melted into the crowd. She wasn't irritated that he was gone, she assured herself uneasily, just that she hadn't had time to quiz him about that "including me" comment. He was teasing her, of course. Merely teasing.

"That guy's way too full of himself," Nathan said as he danced her around the floor.

Rachel agreed, of course. But somehow she didn't like Nathan commenting on it.

"He going to be around next summer?" Nathan asked.

"No. Definitely not."

"Something real familiar about him. Vince says he's your cousin. Is he really?"

Just what she needed was one of the cowboys suspecting Jackson's masquerade and starting a bunkhouse rumor. "Why do you care?"

"Call it my protective instincts."

"Just who are you protecting?"

"You, of course."

Rachel sighed. Men! Sometimes they weren't much better than a pack of contentious dogs. Their snarling wasn't much more subtle. "Nathan . . ." she began.

Before she could lower the boom, Vince cut in. "My turn, you young pup."

Nathan handed her over with more grace than he had with Jackson.

"Thank you," Rachel sighed as Vince grinned at her.

"Having a problem with the menfolk, are you?"

She shook her head. "I don't even want to talk about it."

He chuckled. "That's what comes of bein' young. You oughta get married, Rachel girl. That'd settle the bucks down all right."

"Is that a proposal?"

"Hell. If I could get rid of the old lady, it might be." He went on chuckling. Vince always appreciated his humor more than anyone else did.

When the band ended one piece and swung into another, Vince swung her right along with them. His style of dancing resembled an aimless shuffle around the floor. Rachel never knew which way he would lurch.

"You're steppin' on my toes, Rachel girl. Thought you were a better dancer than that."

"You old coot," she said fondly. "If you would move to the music, your partner would know where your toes are, so as not to step on them."

"Excuses," he said. "You tired of dancing? How 'bout some eats."

Rachel breathed out relief. "That sounds good."

At the refreshment table, Vince's wife, Sharon, greeted them.

"The old man talked you into dancing with him?" Sharon chortled. "You ought to know better, Rachel."

"You wimmen jest don't know how to dance," Vince complained. But he smiled wickedly. "That cousin of yers looks like he dances right good, Rachel."

From the gleam in Vince's eyes, Rachel guessed that he suspected something.

Just then Mac and his wife, Helen, joined them. "Who is that new fellow that you're all gossiping about?" Helen asked.

"We aren't gossiping," Rachel hastened to deny.

"He looks familiar," Helen noted. "Has he been here before?"

Sharon shook her head. "Couldn't have been. Him, I would have remembered."

"He's a hunk," was Helen's opinion. "I swear I've seen that face before."

"He's Rachel's cousin," Vince said, saving the day. But his eyes twinkled.

Both wives looked at her questioningly.

"A half cousin," Rachel said lamely. "Distant."

Helen frowned. "What's a half cousin?"

"Kissin' cousin, maybe?" Vince asked.

Rachel gave him an exasperated look. "You and Joanne! Why are you two so anxious to pair me up with some man?"

"We figger it might sweeten your nature some," Vince teased.

Sharon barked out a laugh. "If anyone around here needs a sweeter nature, old man, it's you."

Vince snorted at his wife and took Rachel's arm. "Come on, Rachel. Let's dance."

"Oh, no! I came over here to eat." She grinned at Sharon. "You dance with him, Sharon. You married him."

Vince tugged his reluctant wife onto the dance floor, and Rachel slipped away for some cold cuts and privacy.

The barn was crowded, the music loud, and everyone seemed to be having a good time. Jackson lurked on the edges of the crowd, not nearly as brave as he put on. Cherie also graced their little dance with her presence. Rachel wasn't surprised. She couldn't picture the teenager passing up the chance for a good time. Currently she danced a slow dance with Toby Whitman, plastered up against him like wallpaper on a wall. Rachel recalled Sam's comment about the girl and Toby. After Rachel's lecture, Toby should know better. But perhaps not, Rachel noted. Toby looked to be off in a world that only an eighteen-year-old on a testosterone high can visit.

Rachel made a mental note to drop a word of warning in Jackson's ear. She would have to say something to Toby as well. She expected he would come down off that testosterone high quickly enough when he learned that Cherie was only thirteen. He'd better! Jackson had troubles enough with his daughter without Toby making more.

Actually, Rachel had to give Cherie credit. The girl had settled in better than Rachel had expected. Every day the teenager and Sam tried to invent a new game for Chesty, who invariably trumped them both. And Cherie generally hung on the fence whenever Sam worked with the little herd of sheep he kept specifically for Chesty's training. Sam's immediate goal was to not make a fool of himself in the rodeo demo, but real sheep trials were not too far down the road. While Cherie pooh-poohed the importance of a herding demo, or even real sheep trials, she did concede that Chesty pushing about a bunch of spring-loaded sheep was pretty cool—cool enough that she coaxed Sam into letting her try her hand at playing the role of shepherd. After getting mowed down by the sheep for the third time, she gave up and watched from the sideline. But she was a surprisingly good sport about it.

"Looks like another successful bash." Karen slipped up beside Rachel and stole an olive from her plate.

"Get your own, you mooch."

"Good idea." She left briefly and came back with a bowl of chili. "I see Morticia the Younger is here." She cocked an eyebrow upward. "That must mean Daddy's here, too." She gave Rachel an expectant look.

"Karen . . ."

"Don't be coy. This is your best friend talking. Friendship carries certain serious obligations."

Rachel did not want to point Jackson out for Karen's sharp-eyed perusal, but she didn't really have a choice. "Over there," she said, pointing surreptitiously with her chin. "The guy with the beard."

Karen homed in instantly. "Hubba hubba."

"Don't be juvenile."

"Nothing juvenile about it. I have a very mature appreciation for a guy who looks that good. Is it the light, or is his beard a slightly different shade than his hair?"

"Lots of guys' beards are a shade different than their hair."

"Hm." She turned that sharp-eyed look on Rachel. "You wouldn't be keeping secrets from your best friend, would you?"

"I don't know what you're talking about." Rachel tried to sound innocent, but her acting wouldn't earn her any Oscars.

"Hm," Karen said again, then smiled. "You know, Rachel, a hot little affair wouldn't do you any harm. Might loosen you up a bit."

Rachel practically slammed her plate on the table. Good thing it was a paper plate. "What is it with everyone around here wanting me to take up with some man? Any man."

Karen jerked her head toward Jackson, who was being literally dragged onto the dance floor by Mrs. Dobson, the Polk County champion milkmaid. "That man would be good."

"And I do not need to loosen up."

"Yes, you do. Why don't you go save the poor man from that old lady he's dancing with? I bet he'd rather dance with you."

"Mrs. Dobson is a very nice woman. He's gone out of his way to make friends with her, and so he ought to give her a dance."

"Then he's got to be a treasure, Rachel. How many men like him take the trouble to make friends with old ladies?"

"Oh, for heaven's sake. Go dance with him yourself if he's such a treasure."

Karen's face lit up. "There's an idea. I think I will."

Rachel watched Karen weave through the crowd toward her prey. She began to think she should have locked Jackson in his cabin.

Cherie slumped against a prickly backrest of hay bales and sipped from a can of Mountain Dew. Toby sat beside her, admiring her with his eyes. At least Cherie assumed that puppy-dog gaze of his was admiration. In this backwater, Cherie was probably hotter than any other girl he could hope to meet.

Right then, however, Cherie wasn't all that interested in Toby. She was more interested in the expression on Rachel Marsh's face as she watched Karen Spangler go on the prowl for Cherie's dad.

"You know?" she began to Toby, "I really think those two are hot for each other."

Toby followed the direction of her gaze. "Who? Miz Spangler and your dad?"

"No, idiot! Rachel and my dad."

His face puckered with doubt.

"Duh! How could you miss it?"

"Miss what? Just because they danced together? Everyone dances with everyone at these things. It don't mean nuthin'."

"You are, like, so blind! Look at Rachel looking at Karen."

"So what?"

"Karen is about to pounce on my dad and drag him away from old lady Dobson. Rachel's standing there with her face full of food, trying to look nonchalant. But she's worried, see? Just enough green is coming out of those eyes to reveal her true feelings."

"Rachel's eyes are blue."

Cherie rolled her eyes. "The green-eyed monster, you know? She's jealous. I swear she's jealous."

Toby snorted. "You're imagining things. Harsh Marsh jealous? Not likely."

Cherie glanced at him in surprise. "What did you call her?"

"Harsh Marsh. It's what the guys call Rachel when she isn't in earshot. It's not like they don't like her or anything. But, you know, she's all nose to the grindstone and superserious and all. She don't date. She don't even notice if one of the guys gives her the eye. Like poor Nathan. He's a good-lookin' guy, you know, for a middle-aged dude. And he'd walk through fire for Rachel. But she doesn't even know he's alive. And she certainly don't got no sympathy for a man's needs, you know? No understanding at all."

Toby stuck a piece of hay in his mouth and slid a sideways glance at Cherie to gauge her reaction to mention of a man's needs.

Men were so obvious, Cherie reflected. "Go on," she prompted.

"What I think is that Rachel's—" He lowered his voice dramatically. "—Rachel's all dried up, you know? Got no soft womanliness about her anymore. Hell, she's old enough."

Cherie snorted her contempt. "Toby, you confirm my opinion of men."

He stuck out his chest a bit.

"And it's not good," she added, puncturing his posture. She had a curious desire to defend Rachel. "Classy women fall for classy men, and I don't see many classy men around this place."

"Huh?"

"Rachel's classy, even if she is sort of old. I like her. She knows how to handle herself. Doesn't lose her cool. She's not crazy like my mom or totally into herself like some of my dad's girlfriends."

Toby looked impressed. He was easily impressed. That was why Cherie tolerated him. He was unsophisticated, too thin, and too pimply to be of much interest, but he believed nearly everything she told him.

"Your mom's crazy?" he asked, making it sound like having a crazy mom was something special.

"Certifiable," she assured him. "At least as far as I'm concerned."

"Bummer! Is that why your dad divorced her?"

Cherie shrugged "Dunno. That was, like, years ago. Most everybody I know has divorced parents."

"Mine aren't divorced. I don't even know any divorced people."

"You're kidding!"

"No."

"This place is, like, prehistoric."

Toby puffed out his chest again. "My ma says there's nothing wrong with having standards. When I'm ready to settle down, it's gonna be forever."

"Yeah. Right."

" 'Course, I've got some wild oats to sow first."

He was pathetically transparent, Cherie thought. As if Cherie Stone, who had made off with the hottest rock star going, would even consider a skinny, pimply cowboy who would probably never have two dollars to rub together. Still, it was sort of nice to have someone to talk to. Someone who thought she was hot. Someone who was anxious to lend a sympathetic ear.

"So you want Rachel to hook up with your dad?" Toby asked. "That would give you a mom who wasn't crazy."

"Like I need a mother. Get real!"

"And you'd get to live out here." He sounded eager. "My pa says this is God's country, you know? We're lucky to live here."

"Your 'pa' needs to get a life."

That was the question, though, Cherie acknowledged reluctantly. How would she feel if Rachel and her dad got it on? Got it on seriously. Her dad had never shown signs of wanting to settle down with any woman, but then, Rachel wasn't like the other women he dated, and there was that gleam in his eye. What would it be like if they actually—God forbid—got married?

Rachel was okay. Actually, she had kind of a steady, quiet, solid air about her that Cherie almost envied. She wouldn't mind being a bit like Rachel when she was that old. Self-assured. Someone to reckon with. Of course, Cherie would take a lot more care with makeup and hair, and she'd never let herself get so casual about fashion.

Then again, Cherie figured she was borrowing trouble. Probably nothing would happen between her dad and Rachel. After all, her dad was star class. A premier catch. What would he want with Rachel, even if she was sort of steady and solid and listened to a person like she was really listening? That would be the mismatch of the century.

Jackson rather enjoyed dancing with Alice Dobson. She was a spry old gal with a lively sense of humor, and treating him like a son seemed to amuse her. But they didn't get to dance very long before a woman in tight red jeans and a spangled top playfully tapped Alice on the shoulder.

The old lady was a good sport about it. "You can have him for a while, dear," she said. "He's plumb worn out my feet."

"Hello," his new partner said as she slipped into his arms. She was thirtyish, with red pixie-cut hair, teasing brown eyes, and a wide smile. "I'm Karen Spangler, Rachel's best friend, and owner of the best restaurant for miles around."

"Hello, Karen Spangler." He laid a megawatt smile on her. "I'm Stoney Jackson."

She chuckled. "Of course you are." Her eyes said that she didn't believe him, and Jackson began to think that Rachel was right about him being overconfident. He probably should have stayed in his cabin tonight instead of slicking himself up and trying to impress Rachel.

How long had it been since he'd had to make an effort to impress a woman?

"I must say," the spangle-topped pixie commented, "you really are the hottest thing we've seen around here for decades. Imagine something like you landing on Rachel's doorstep."

Karen Spangler wasn't a bit shy, Jackson noted. "Rachel's doorstep isn't a bad place to be," he answered warily.

"Rachel Marsh's doorstep is a very good place to be, but I'm impressed that you realize that, Mr. . . . . Jackson, is it?"

He smiled ruefully. Obviously, he'd been very overconfident.

"You can tell Rachel you have my seal of approval, if you like. And if she doesn't want you"—she smiled impishly—"you can drop by the restaurant and give me a chance." On that note, the pixie whirled away from him, leaving confusion in her wake. These down-home Arizona women, Jackson decided, could teach Californians a thing or two about keeping a man off balance.

"Hey there, Stoney boy. Having a good time?"

It was Vince. Just what Jackson needed—another keen-eyed character with a suspicious mind.

"Hey, Vince. Sure thing. Who could not have a good time at this bash?"

Vince clapped him on the back with more force than a puny-looking old man should have been able to muster. "Let's hit the vittles. Whaddya say?"

"Uh . . . sure." The glint in Vince's eye made Jackson uneasy, but he could think of no polite way to ditch him.

"You clean up pretty well, son. Saw you dancing with Rachel a few minutes back. The two of you were cutting a fair step out there."

"She's a good dancer."

"She's a good woman." Vince grabbed a bowl and ladled it full with chili. "Want some?"

"No, thanks. Chili doesn't set well on my stomach."

"Gives ya gas, eh? Can tell you're not from around here, Stoney boy. We grow iron stomachs by the time we're out of short pants. Let's sit a while. I been wantin' a word with you."

"Actually, Vince, I have to . . . uh . . . get back to the cabin. I need to check the plumbing again."

Vince waved his greasy spoon, dismissing the excuse. "You fixed those pipes just fine, son. It's one of the few things you've done right around here."

This, Jackson thought, could be ugly. He definitely should have stayed in his cabin.

Vince went on. "I just want you to know that I don't buy that crap about you being Rachel's relation. No, sir. I know damned well and good why she hired you."

Jackson cursed to himself. He wondered what it would take for the old man to keep his mouth shut and not go to the media.

"Yessir. She's taken with you, and any fool can see you're taken with her."

"What?"

"No shame in admitting it, son. You seem to be a good man, in a sort of citified way. In fact, I pulled you over here to give you some good advice."

Jackson didn't give in to relief. The gleam in Vince's eye said the old man knew more than he was letting on.

"Our Rachel's a good, solid woman. You ain't the first fella who's set his sights on her, you know."

Did he have his sights set on Rachel, after all his warnings to himself? Those warnings seemed so easily forgotten whenever Rachel was within flirting distance—or kissing distance. "Vince, I don't think—"

"That's your problem, son. You do think. Both of you think too damned much. Sometimes you need to be bold, ya know? Bold! Quit namby-pambyin' around and let nature take her course. You young people think everythin' to death. It's no wonder nuthin' in this world gets done anymore."

Jackson crooked a smile. "Be bold."

"Sure thing! Get her to notice you for more than falling off a damned horse and talking a line. Ain't no shame in settin' yer eye on a woman, but you gotta do more'n talk. Rachel's like most women. She's stubborn and set in her ways. And she's stubborning herself into a lonely life, I'm thinking. It's occurred to me that maybe some fella like you might come along and make her see that lonely ain't that good. But you gotta do a lot more'n talk about it."

Jackson chuckled. "You're quite a guy, Vince Dugan."

"Yup, I am. And just you remember . . ."

"What?"

"You be careful with that girl, Stoney boy. She's like my own daughter, you understand. Make her cry and I'll hang you up by your unmentionable parts. You can count on it."

Jackson blinked. The man sounded serious. "Be bold," he said with a nod. "But be careful."

The night was full of strange encounters, Jackson reflected as Vince wandered off for a second bowl of five-alarm chili. But maybe the grizzled old cowboy had a point. Jackson had been warning himself away from Rachel because she wasn't his usual kind of woman, and at the same time he'd been teasing, flirting, and sparring with her like a man on the road to seduction. Rachel was under his skin, making him itch, and he wasn't doing much good forbidding himself from scratching.

No doubt Vince was right. Jackson was overthinking this. Maybe life was too short to pass up the chance to be with someone special, even if you could be with them only for a short time. He needed to make up his own mind and let Rachel make up hers.

Deep in this attractive line of thought, Jackson was drifting back toward the food table when Nathan Crosby caught his attention with a comradely punch to the shoulder. "Hey, Stoney boy. Boss lady wants to see you." His breath reeked of beer.

Jackson guessed the guys had a six-pack or two in the bunk-house, even though Rachel didn't permit alcohol at the dance

"Where is she?" Jackson glanced around. Rachel wasn't anywhere in sight.

"Outside," Nathan said. "Better come. She don't like to be kept waiting."

Jackson followed him out the door, into the dark, where the punch that met his jaw was anything but comradely.

CHAPTER 11

NATHAN REVELED IN the intense satisfaction of his fist connecting with Stoney Jackson's face. The other man's grunt of pain was music to his ears. He hit him again, in the gut. And again, aiming once more for the face. This time the son of a bitch blocked and took a swing of his own.

Like everything else he did, Stoney boy was a wussy fighter, no match for a real man who had been jumping into brawls since he was fifteen. He landed one pounding blow into Nathan's midsection, but in the process, he left himself open to Nathan's left hook, which staggered him. Nathan followed as his victim stumbled backward, delivering a fist to the side of the head, a blow to the ribs.

Lord, but it felt good to deal out this load of punishment, to let loose the anger and frustration. Nathan couldn't stand to see this incompetent loser insinuate himself into Rachel's life and Rachel's heart. Nathan had worked his butt off for the Lazy M for two seasons and hadn't gotten anything more from Rachel than a friendly smile and offhand praise for a job well done. Praise wasn't what Nathan wanted from Rachel. What Nathan wanted from Rachel Marsh was the same exact thing that Stoney wanted, but if the way Rachel looked at the wuss was any indication, Stoney was rounding third base while Nathan couldn't even get to first. The injustice of it made Nathan's blood boil, and the only cure was to feel a few of Stoney's bones break under his fists.

So he pounded away and ignored the blows the other man managed to land. Wuss-boy had strength behind his fists, but he hadn't learned to fight in the no-holds-barred arena of cowboy bars and trucker dives. Blood ran from his nose and a cut on his head, and the sight of it drove Nathan to greater fury.

Then someone grabbed him from behind. Vince's voice growled in his ear. "Settle down, boy."

Rachel came from the barn. He saw her jaw drop, her eyes widen. "Jackson!" She rushed to wuss-boy. The loser staggered against her, and she caught him with a little cry. "Jackson! Omigod! What the hell is going on?"

Nathan struggled to free his arms. Frustration almost made him want to hit Rachel as well as Stoney. "Lemme go, dammit!"

Vince growled. "Not till you cool off, ya damned fool."

Rachel rounded on Nathan like a bitch defending her puppies. "What the hell did you do? What brought this on?"

Nathan gave her sullen silence.

"I know Jackson didn't start this fight!"

"He had it coming!" Nathan grumbled.

Wuss-boy, hand cradling his jaw, mumbled something unintelligible.

Rachel was merciless. "You're fired, Crosby. You know my policy on fighting. Get your things together and be out of here by morning."

She glanced at Vince, and Vince nodded approval. When Nathan shrugged off his hold, the old man let him go.

"You women are all the same," Nathan shot at her. "You don't know a good thing when you see it. Bitch."

That riled the wuss. He lunged forward, but Vince caught him. The man's glare burned between Nathan's shoulder blades as he stalked away, savoring the small victory of having the last word.

Nathan's insult hit Rachel like a physical blow. She was used to her employees liking her, in spite of the occasional grumbling about "Harsh Marsh." She felt stunned and stupid.

"Rachel . . ." Jackson's voice, hoarse and harsh.

Rachel winced at the look of him. She'd seen him more battered in his films, but what he wore now was real blood, not makeup. "Hospital," she ordered "Now."

He shook his head, then grunted in pain at the movement. "I'm . . . okay."

She wasn't having any of his nonsense. "We'll see. Let's take a look at you in the light.•Get your butt into the kitchen."

Jackson went, slowly, his steps punctuated with inarticulate grunts that sounded faintly like cussing. When Rachel started to follow, Vince caught her arm.

"Cut the man some slack, Rachel girl. It's not him you're mad at."

Rachel took a couple of deep breaths, trying to settle herself. "You have any idea what happened here?"

"I saw Crosby point Stoney outside, and I figgered he was up to no good on account of how he'd been lookin' when you and Stoney was dancing."

"How he was looking?"

Vince shook his head ruefully. "Nathan's a good man, mostly. But he can get purely mean when he's jealous. It's sort of his weak spot."

"Jealous? Of Stoney and . . . and . . ."

"You got it, Rachel girl. Hell, ain't anyone missed which way the wind is blowin'. When you smile at that man, it ain't no cousinly smile."

Heat rushed to Rachel's cheeks. "It's no kind of smile, Vince Dugan. Jackson and I . . ." She gritted her teeth and closed her eyes. That was not the first time tonight she'd called Jackson by his real name in front of Vince. In front of Nathan, also, which was even worse. Her composure was shot, and she could almost hear the shards of her mind rattling around her empty head like shattered glass.

"Stoney and I," she corrected carefully, "are distant cousins. That's it."

But Vince's eyes were twinkling. "Whatever you say, Rachel girl. Whatever you say."

This was not a good Saturday night, Rachel reflected with a sigh. Not a good Saturday night at all.

Miles away, someone else also suffered from a bad Saturday night. It was a hell of a thing, Josh Digby thought, when a man had to spend the entire weekend at his office instead of going to a ball game with his kid or relaxing in front of the television. But success required work, even in the tabloid game. Contrary to public opinion, sleaze wasn't that easy to come by.

Interest in the latest Stone doings was dying, and Digby couldn't allow that to happen. He'd strung along his audience with interviews of the Vegas hotel staff, speculations from Jimmy Toledo's band members, and quotes (misquotes, actually) from Harvey Mathias, who wasn't saying anything of interest, which was why Josh had to add a bit here and subtract a bit there from what he did say. He'd even cornered one of Cherie's schoolmates, Cyndie Roth, the one who had called with the original tip that Cherie Stone was up to something in Vegas with Jimmy boy. That tidbit of information had sent Josh flying off to Vegas, only to end up trying to pry a story from hotel bellboys and desk clerks. But since then Cyndie hadn't provided anything hotter than Cherie being in the doghouse with her dad. Though the teen—she couldn't have been older than fourteen from the sound of her voice—seemed enamored of the image of herself as the tabloid version of Deep Throat, she was better at giggling than telling a coherent story.

Soon Josh had to come up with something juicy or move on to something else. He would hate to move on to something else. Jackson Stone was his specialty, his hallmark.

Dark had closed in hours ago, and beyond the window, the lights of downtown Chicago were bright smears in a rainy night. Fluorescent lighting fought its way through the cigarette smoke in Josh's office to reflect annoyingly off the screen of his computer monitor. The reflection was more than enough to make him grumble. His current project would keep him at his desk until well after midnight. Dinner had been a candy bar from the vending machine, and the evening's entertainment included virtual reams of e-mail concerning Jackson Stone, most of it useless.

Much of the mail he collected off the *National Star* website fell into the same category as Elvis sightings. Most of these people had as much chance of sighting Stone as they did the King. At least Stone wasn't dead—at least not as far as Digby knew. And wouldn't that make a fine story! ACE REPORTER TRACKS DOWN JACKSON STONE, FINDS STAR DEAD IN HOTEL ROOM AFTER DRUG AND SEX BINGE. Or better still: REPORTER FINDS STONE BATTERED TO DEATH BY DAUGHTER AND ROCK-STAR LOVER, HELPS POLICE COLLAR FLEEING COUPLE.

Take that, *National Enquirer*! He would get the raise of the century, his own office with a view of Lake Michigan, and a company car. He'd make it a Lexus.

Josh grimaced. He had to get out of the tabloids before he went insane and started taking himself seriously.

"Hey, Josh!" Steve Malinsky, fellow reporter, stuck his head into the cubicle. Steve spent many of his nights at the office, mostly because he goofed off during the day. "Working hard, or hardly working?"

"If I weren't working, would I be sitting in this chair while everyone else is home relaxing?"

"Got anything new?"

"No," Josh growled.

"Stone story's dying down. People are more interested in Tom Cruise's hot new romance."

"Cruise, schmooze. When I find Stone, I'll make sure there's eye-catching interest. Depend on it."

"Did you see the story about aliens landing in Montana?"

"Montana? They can have it."

"Walker got sent out to interview the people who saw 'em. Lucky stiff. He took his fishing pole."

"Good for him." Digby's eyes didn't leave his computer screen.

"Well, I'll let you work. I'm headed home to dinner and re-runs."

Josh merely grunted, scarcely noticing as Steve departed. Here was something at last, a name that triggered a spark in his brain. Greer, Arizona. Some woman had written from Greer asking if the photo of Cherie Stone on their website was recent. (It wasn't. Stone was assiduous about keeping his daughter out of camera range.) The query sounded innocent enough. Probably from a Stone groupie. But Greer was a hole-in-the-wall little mountain town where Stone sometimes vacationed. You would think a guy with his bucks would go to Rio or the Caribbean or Tahiti, but Stone was one of those macho types who liked dirt beneath his nails and wood smoke in his eyes.

Maybe Jackie boy had dragged his kid off to the mountains, thinking no one would find him hiding among the rednecks. Could be this e-mail inquiry was from someone who had spotted Cherie and was trying for a surefire ID. The more he thought about it, the more Digby convinced himself that the query was a legitimate lead.

This is why he was a great reporter, Josh told himself. His mind was like a trash bin, overflowing with bits and pieces of information that no one else thought was important. One never knew when one of those bits was going to complete a puzzle that was worth big bucks. Big bucks in circulation. Big bucks in status. Big bucks in salary. Too bad there was no Pulitzer for trash.

Greer, Arizona. Nowheresville, but if Stone was there, the little burg was where Josh wanted to be. Still, the lead was a slim one. The boss wasn't going to cough up bucks for a plane ticket because of one query.

He wasn't going to give up, though. *You're in trouble, Stone,* Josh silently warned the star. *Josh Digby's on your trail, and you sure as hell aren't going to get away.*

Rachel found Jackson sitting at the kitchen table, holding an ice pack to his jaw. When Rachel walked in seething, Joanne made a tactful withdrawal.

"Damn!" she said. "You wanted some grit on your résumé, did you?"

He grunted miserably.

"How bad are you?"

Jackson leaned back in the chair and gingerly lifted the ice pack from his face. Rachel winced. The left side of his jaw was turning purple along with his left eye. A cut above his temple still dribbled blood.

He groaned. "Where are the damned stunt doubles when you need them?"

"In Hollywood. Where you should be. Why the hell didn't you yell for help?"

"Too busy getting hit," he slurred.

"Dammit! Look at you!" Gently she probed his jaw.

Jackson tried to dodge her hand.

"Hold still, would you? What a mess. Doesn't look broken. Still have all your teeth?"

"Yeth."

"Very funny." She leaned over him and brushed his hair away from the cut on his head. It was shallow but ugly. "You could probably use a couple of stitches there."

His answer came as a gust of warm breath against her breast. Suddenly aware of her position, she jerked back. He managed a smile. She had to admire a man who could still flirt after the drubbing he'd taken.

"Stitches, Jackson."

"No hospital."

"Jackson . . ."

He reprimanded her with a wagging finger.

"Then, Molly."

"No Molly. Sleep."

"Damned stubborn fool. At least let me look at the rest of you. Take your shirt off."

His slow smile told her exactly what he was thinking.

"Oh, give it up! Men!" She helped him unbutton his shirt and carefully worked it down his arms. "You'd still be posturing at death's door. Ouch! Look at that bruise!"

Jackson Stone definitely did not need a body double for skin shots. He had classic washboard abs and a chest taut with muscle. If Rachel hadn't been so worried about broken ribs she would have been more appreciative of the scenery.

"No way to tell if something's broken in there. You need a doctor."

"No. S'okay."

He was the most stubborn man she'd met. "It's time we ended this masquerade anyway."

He raised his arm and pressed two fingers to her lips to quiet her. Impulsively, she took his hand. The sound of throat-clearing alerted her to Joanne's presence in the doorway. Rachel promptly released Jackson's hand, letting it fall into his lap.

"Ow!" he complained.

"What?" she asked.

"Every damned thing on me hurts. Sleep. That's all I want. Sleep."

"None of that," Joanne said, briskly taking charge. "You might have a concussion. You shouldn't be going to sleep alone."

Jackson managed a grin as he peeked at Rachel from half-closed eyes. "Sounds good to me."

Before Rachel hit him with a well-deserved retort, Joanne clarified. "He needs someone around to check him every hour or so, wake him up and see if he still knows up from down."

"Cherie?" Rachel suggested hopefully.

"If you ask me, that girl doesn't know up from down herself."

Joanne and Jackson both pinned her with their eyes. It didn't matter that Jackson's were half closed. Rachel could have felt the pressure of his stare through closed lids. She felt herself being sucked into a tunnel whose only exit was temptation.

Jackson spent the night in the ranch house living room, sleeping on the couch with Fang the cat curled on his stomach. Rachel blew up an air mattress, fetched a sleeping bag from the closet, and made herself a bed on the floor beside the couch, like a faithful guard dog.

"Come up here," Jackson mumbled sleepily. "It's a big couch. There's room for you, me, and the cat, too."

Rachel merely snorted. "You did get a knock on the brain, didn't you?"

His answer might have been either a chuckle or a groan. Rachel couldn't tell which. She lay there in the dark, listening as Jackson's breathing evened into a quiet rhythm. She could still feel the frantic fear inside her—echoes now instead of the real thing. When she had seen Nathan beating on Jackson, alarm had escalated to frantic terror in seconds. When had the man wormed his way so deeply into her concern?

The entry light snapped on as Joanne came through the front door. She peered into the dark living room. Rachel rolled wearily off her mattress and reported in.

"He's sleeping."

"Good. Sam and Cherie are settled in just fine."

Cherie hadn't wanted to spend the night alone in the Sitting Bull cabin, so Sam was doing a sleepover to keep her company. He'd volunteered, and Cherie had welcomed the idea, so Rachel had okayed it. She knew fully well that putting those two kids together might be like putting a match to a fuse, but she was too tired to worry about it. Chesty was with them, and he would make a good referee.

"Thanks," Rachel said. "See you in the morning."

Joanne still looked worried.

"I'll check him every hour on the hour. Promise. Or maybe you'd like the job?" This last rang with annoyance.

"I'm too old to be waking up every hour," Joanne said. "He's all yours."

The housekeeper had a glint in her eye, Rachel noted. "Oh, go to bed," she told the older woman.

Joanne patted her arm and smiled toward the dark lump that was Jackson. "Such a nice man. I hope he stays."

Rachel waved her away and stumbled back to her little pallet. "You're hopeless," she muttered. In her state of weariness, she didn't know whether the statement referred to Joanne's matchmaking, Jackson's stubbornness, or her own faltering determination to steer clear of entanglement. "Hopeless," she repeated as she collapsed upon her air mattress.

She had a little alarm clock beside her, but she didn't really need it, because sleep wouldn't come. Every hour she shook Jackson awake and asked him how many fingers she held up, what day it was, and where he was. She learned something important from those sessions. Jackson Stone was cranky as a bear when awakened from a peaceful sleep, and crankier still when he didn't feel well.

The first time she conducted her little test, he impatiently pushed her hand with its two raised fingers away.

"How many fingers?" she insisted.

"Eighteen. Let me sleep, dammit."

She clucked like a mother hen. "There's always the hospital."

"Two," he muttered.

"What was that?"

"Two goddamned fingers. You're enjoying this, aren't you?"

"I'd rather be up in my bed."

One corner of his mouth pulled upward. "So would I."

"Go back to sleep, Don Juan. See you in an hour."

Rachel still didn't sleep. She lay listening to Jackson's quiet breathing, her feelings softened somehow by weariness and the comforting darkness of deep night. Sometime in the small hours she brewed a cup of tea and returned to her post beside the couch to drink it. Sitting cross-legged on her air mattress beside the sleeping man, Rachel learned that Jackson Stone snored. It was not a little, quiet snore, but a full-throated, bear-size snore. So much for the romantic image of America's heartthrob. She speculated, however, that his other qualities compensated for the snore.

There in the darkness, close enough to feel the heat from Jackson's body, Rachel had no trouble listing those qualities. There were the obvious good looks, fame, and fortune, of course, but those things were superficial. The sense of adventure and good humor. Jackson could even laugh at himself, his own shortcomings. And heaven knew Jackson had enough short-comings as a macho cowboy to set the whole ranch to laughing.

What else? she pondered. He easily won the hearts of chil-dren—always appealing in a man. And he was fierce in his protection of his daughter. After all, his hide-and-seek game with the media was for Cherie's sake, even though Cherie didn't seem to appreciate the effort.

Sometime during her ruminations in the dark, Jackson tossed in his sleep and muttered a nearly unintelligible word that sounded like her name. His hand, deliberate or uncon-scious, landed on her shoulder where she leaned against his bed. His fingers brushed against the bare flesh of her neck, sending a shivery thrill down her spine. Such a simple thing, a man's touch. She missed it.

Don't go there, Rachel, her inner voice warned. *Don't even start down that road.*

But that road was so damned tempting!

Sitting Bull cabin normally housed guests, not staff, so it in-cluded the standard guest amenities, including a midget-size fridge and a tiny microwave oven. The fridge supplied Sam and Cherie with a six-pack of Coke—Diet Coke for Cherie—and the microwave was just big enough to pop a bag of pop-corn. The cabin had no television, though, so the kids could either go to bed or talk.

Sam didn't mind the lack of entertainment. Staying in one of the guest cabins was entertainment in itself, especially since no grown-ups were around. Cherie certainly didn't count as a grown-up. He wasn't sure what she was—a creature different than anyone he'd met before. But she was at least entertaining.

He tossed Chesty a kernel of popcorn. The border collie had made himself at home on the sofa while the kids sat cross-legged on the floor. His eyes tracked the journey of every piece of popcorn from bag to mouth. Cherie also tossed the dog some tribute. Sam figured that if anyone understood Cherie, it was probably Chesty.

"I'm bored," Cherie complained.

"I could go to the house and bring back some of my comic books," Sam offered with a shrug.

"Comic books! God, you are such a baby. We need a television."

"My mom says television rots young minds. She won't let me watch half the stuff that's on."

Cherie made a rude sound. "Your mom can be really prehistoric, you know? At least nineteenth century. Sometimes my dad's like that, too."

Sam figured all parents were like that. Maybe things were different when a kid had the full set—two parents. Maybe a mom and dad together would be so occupied with themselves that a kid could get away with more. His mom certainly seemed to be distracted whenever Jackson was around. And speaking of Jackson . . .

"It's really weird that Nathan beat up your dad. Nathan's usually a pretty nice guy."

Cherie sniffed contemptuously. "You are such a lamebrain. It's so obvious."

"What?"

"Nathan has the hots for your mom. Anyone with brains could see that. Your mom has the hots for my dad, so Nathan tried to get my dad out of the picture. He was underhanded about it, too. If he hadn't jumped him all sneaky like, my dad could've taken him."

Sam didn't like anyone talking about his mom like that. "My mom doesn't have the hots for anyone."

"A lot you know. Women sense these things."

"You're just a kid, not a woman."

"Thirteen is not a kid. Back years ago, women used to get married at thirteen. Even younger. In the Middle Ages. Besides, I'm almost fourteen."

Sam giggled, picturing Cherie in a black wedding dress complete with black veil and makeup. "The bride of Dracula. That's what you'd look like. He wouldn't care if you were thirteen or thirty."

Cherie threw a handful of popcorn at him, and the melee began. Chesty joined in, eagerly disposing of popcorn that landed on the floor, the sofa, the desk, and under the table.

When the ammunition ran out, they were still high on silliness. "I know what we can do," Cherie said with an evil smile.

"It's probably time for bed," Sam suggested virtuously.

"Don't be a dweeb. I want to get back at that Nathan for hurting my dad."

"My mom fired him."

"So what? Like working here is so great? He'll just get another job."

Sam could see the thoughts ticking through Cherie's mind. He began to feel sorry for Nathan.

"He has a truck here, doesn't he?"

"Yeah. An old Ford. Cherie, you'd better not get in trouble."

"You are such a goody-two-shoes. Trouble, my boy, is my middle name. Only dorks go through life treading the straight and narrow."

In spite of himself, Sam felt a spark of interest. "What're you gonna do?"

Narrow-eyed, she looked into the bathroom "See my dad's shaving foam?" Grinning wickedly, she outlined her strategy.

Even to Sam, the idea sounded delicious. He who had behaved all his life felt the first joyful stirrings of mischief in his soul.

Cherie held up one finger. "Let's say we make it more interesting, okay? If we get caught, I take all the blame."

That might not be chivalrous, but it sounded right to Sam.

"And if we don't get caught, I get to ride Thunder."

With such action before them, even that sounded acceptable. Sam stuck out his hand to seal the deal, and Cherie took it.

Jackson woke slowly from heavy slumber. He felt drugged, chased by dreams he only half remembered. Rachel had played a prominent part in them; of that he was sure. His lips still curved in a vague smile.

Then he moved, and aches and pains overwhelmed the wispy bliss left over from sleep. He hurt everywhere. Absolutely everywhere. His teeth hurt, his jaw, his head, his chest, his back, his hands. And speaking of hands, one of his was tangled in silk, it seemed. He moved his fingers experimentally. Hair slipped across his roughened skin. Silky hair. Rachel's hair.

Bliss returned, even through the pain of lifting himself to see her there, fast asleep, propped against the couch with her head pillowed on a cushion. She looked as though she'd had a hard night. Pale, with tousled hair, and shadowy circles under her eyes, she certainly wasn't a picture of slumbering beauty. But he loved the lush thickness of lashes against her fine skin, the silky feel of her hair twisted around his fingers. The curve of her lips, turned slightly upward in sleep, was absolutely delicious, and the faint spattering of freckles across her cheeks and nose made him smile. She reminded him of sunshine, blue skies, and laughter. She was a breath of fresh air in a world gone stale with ambition, get-ahead-itis, meaningless fame, and empty values.

To top it off, she was goddamned sexy in spite of her tousled weariness. Rachel Marsh would still be sexy when she was seventy-five—she was a lifetime kind of woman with a lifetime kind of beauty. Not for the first time Jackson wished he were the kind of man who could share his life with such a woman— all of his life, day in and day out, year in and year out, with the steadiness and attention that made those forever relationships thrive.

But celebrity had a price, and that was one. Romances abounded in his world, but the stress of fame very seldom allowed romance to grow into true, steady love. Jackson wondered if fame was worth it.

The light in the entry hall came on. "Isn't this a touching scene?" Joanne said from the living room archway.

Jackson could see the twinkle in the woman's eyes.

"I see you're still among the living." She walked to the couch and looked down at the two of them. Jackson hadn't bothered to move his hand. It felt too good twined in Rachel's hair. "She looks kind of tuckered, though."

"She deserves to be ragged out. Every hour on the hour she woke me up and harassed me."

"She was supposed to."

"Well, she enjoyed it."

Joanne's satisfied smirk was a silent comment on just who had enjoyed what.

Their conversation finally roused Rachel, who sat up and looked around blearily. She started in surprise when Jackson loosed his grip on her hair. Running her hand through tangled tresses, she scowled. "Cripes. What time is it?"

Joanne said briskly, "I was beginning to think you two were going to sleep until noon. I have biscuits and gravy in the kitchen if you'd care to eat." She looked sympathetically at Jackson. "I sent Terri to do the goats and chickens. Your helpers will be disappointed."

He grimaced and was instantly sorry. "Ow!"

"I think Stoney's off duty for a few days." Rachel gave him a look that squelched his instinct to argue. "Do you think you can eat?"

"I can always eat."

In spite of trying to maintain her gruff attitude, Rachel fussed over him at breakfast, plying him with aspirin along with orange juice, hot biscuits, and savory bacon gravy while Joanne wrote down the ingredients for a poultice to put on his jaw, which was a colorful display of bruises and swelling. His teeth were all still in his head, Jackson was glad to note. His agent would have given him hell if he'd shown up with one or two missing. His ribs felt better as well. He didn't think any were broken. He had busted two ribs several years ago taking a fall during a sequence where he should have used a stuntman. That hurt a lot more than this did, so he guessed that the most Nathan had managed to do was bruise, not break.

"Are you sure you won't see a doctor?" Rachel asked when Joanne had left. "You look like hell."

"Look on the bright side," he told her. "Now people really won't recognize me."

"It's not funny."

"Don't make a big deal out of it, Rachel. Don't your men ever mix it up?"

"I don't tolerate my employees fighting," she said stiffly. "I fired Nathan. I don't understand why he took leave of his senses like that."

"The man was jealous. I'd be jealous, too, if I thought some other guy had the inside track with my girl."

"I am *not* your girl."

"Didn't say you were. But Nathan thought you might be."

"I was not Nathan's girl, either. I'm nobody's girl."

He wagged his eyebrows in spite of the pain. "A sad statement if ever I've heard one. You should be somebody's girl."

She actually blushed. He loved it when she blushed.

"Even if I were your girl, as you put it, I doubt you would have jumped another man and beaten him to a bloody pulp if you suspected he had designs on me."

"Nathan didn't beat me to a bloody pulp, colorful as that sounds."

"He would have if Vince and I hadn't come along. Didn't you ever learn to box or anything?"

"Nathan wasn't exactly fighting by the Marquis of Queensbury rules. Besides, he took me by surprise."

She smiled. "It wasn't in the script."

"Touché."

She was saved from answering by Sam and Cherie tumbling through the door with the remarkable energy of youth.

"Awright!" Sam exclaimed. "Joanne's biscuits and gravy!" He told Cherie, "Joanne makes the best biscuits and gravy in the universe!"

Cherie wrinkled her nose. "Is that real bacon? Do you know how many grams of fat are in that? Gross!"

"It's real bacon," Jackson said with considerable satisfaction.

"Gee, Mr. Stone," Sam said, "you look awful."

"Yeah, Dad. Awful. I guess Jimmy really shouldn't have been worried about your whupping his butt, huh?" She chuckled.

"Oh, yeah," Jackson said with certainty. "He should have." He noticed that despite her protestations, Cherie tucked into a plate of biscuits, gravy, and bacon with enthusiasm. She'd forgotten her makeup this morning, and her looks were much improved. If he mentioned it, for certain the black mascara and lipstick would appear within the hour, so he kept quiet.

"Uh . . ." Sam began, looking a bit embarrassed. "I told Cherie I'd take her riding up to Hay Lake today, Ma. Is that okay?"

"If it's okay with Cherie's dad."

Jackson nodded.

"And I said she could ride Thunder."

Rachel looked surprised. Cherie was being accorded a great honor.

"So can I ride Sally?"

"Sally's a handful," Rachel reminded the boy.

"I know. I've ridden her. And I'll be careful."

"You're a good rider, Sam. I know you can handle the mare. Just don't start fooling around between the two of you and get careless."

Cherie chimed in, "I'll watch out for him, Rachel."

Jackson sensed Rachel's struggle to keep her expression serious. "Thank you, Cherie. I'll count on it."

"Well, where did that come from?" Rachel wondered aloud when the kids had trundled off to their adventures.

Jackson sighed. "Don't ask. Running around with Sam can only be good for Cherie. They're not going to meet any bears out there, are they?"

Rachel chuckled. "I doubt any of the bears around these parts could hold his own with Cherie."

His laugh ended abruptly in a curse. "Damn, that hurts!"

"It looks like Sitting Bull is all yours for the day. Why don't you try to get some real rest? There's no way I'm letting you do any work around here for the next few days."

Suspicious, Jackson probed a bit. "You're being an awfully good sport about this."

"What do you mean? It wasn't me who got my clock cleaned."

"I did not get my clock cleaned. I would have gotten my act together eventually and taken him down."

She smiled. "Right."

"What I mean is that you haven't once, last night or this morning, suggested I throw in the towel and retreat to my RV. You just scored a touchdown in that game of one-upmanship and you don't even bother with the extra point."

She smiled. "I hate to kick a man while he's down. But now that you mention it, how about that motor home? Ready to throw in the towel?"

He snorted. "What do you think?"

"I think—" She hesitated, then shook her head. "—I think you are one of the most stubborn men I've ever met. Don't you think you've proved your point to whomever you're trying to impress?"

"What if I'm trying to impress you?"

At that, she laughed. "I'd be impressed at a show of common sense."

"Which has never been my strong suit," he admitted with a grin.

"So you're going to plow ahead."

"I'm just enjoying myself so much, I can't quit. I'll be back on the job the moment you say. Fixing sewers, mending porches, driving the team, gutting fish. You name it."

She lifted an admonishing brow. "Brave words when I've already said I don't want you working for a few days. Your looks alone would scare the guests into demanding a refund."

"Thank you."

"Just telling the truth."

He mopped up the last dollop of gravy with a piece of biscuit. A scheme was forming in his mind. It was sneaky and devious. Downright wicked. Definitely cheating. And very bold.

Vince would approve. He had decided, sometime during the long night, that the crusty Mr. Dugan was right. He was over-thinking this whole thing between him and Rachel. For better or worse, Rachel was in his blood, and if he blew the opportunity to be with her, for however short a time, he would kick himself for the rest of his life.

The problem now, of course, was to get Rachel to see things the same way.

"I know the ranch can run without me—with difficulty," he added with a grin. "But how about it doing without you for a few hours?"

Rachel looked suspicious. "Why should it?"

Casually, he shrugged. "All this talk about my motor home reminded me—my fees are only paid up through tomorrow at the campground. Since I can't have my usual good time bust-ing broncs and reaming out plumbing, maybe you could drive me up there so I could bring the rig back here." Perfect inno-cence. All those acting lessons were good for something be-sides an Oscar.

"I suppose I could manage that. But how are you going to explain an ordinary ranch hand owning a mobile mansion like that?"

"What makes you think it's a mobile mansion?"

"Would Jackson Stone, megastar, drive around in a beat-up pickup truck with a camper shell?"

"You've got me there. I'll say that it belongs to a friend in Springerville," he said with a perfectly straight face. "He's park-ing it here for a few days so I can work on the engine in my spare time."

"You expect anyone to believe you know anything about engines?"

"Stranger things have happened."

"Not in my lifetime."

He grinned. "There's those claws again."

Rachel gave him a look.

"Come on, Rachel. It's not that unbelievable. These people around here have more important things to do than try to poke holes in my story. The ones most likely to suspect already know who I am, probably. I don't think I've fooled Vince for one minute, yet he hasn't blown the whistle. Your friend Karen smells something fishy, but she's given me the Good Housekeeping Seal of Approval. She said I should tell you that, by the way."

Rachel crinkled her nose. "She did, did she?"

He smirked. "She did."

"She's got a nerve."

"Jealous?"

"In your dreams, cowboy."

"Take me to get the RV?"

She shook her head. "Your friend's RV, you mean."

"That's exactly what I mean."

"It's your funeral, I guess. Just remember, you can't fool all of the people all of the time, or something like that."

He dismissed the risk with a wave. "I'm not looking for all of the time. Just a little more time."

On his way out the front door, Jackson caught Joanne's canny look. He had no doubt the housekeeper had been listening in on the entire conversation.

"You're a sly one, Stoney." Her smile took any reprimand from the comment. "Go for it, boy."

He grinned and gave her a thumbs-up. No wonder he liked this place so much.

CHAPTER 12

♡

JACKSON'S MOTOR HOME was a revelation to Rachel. A tent camper herself, she'd never been inside one of the big bus-size behemoths.

"You could live in this thing," she said, marveling at the queen-size bed, fully appointed bath, modern kitchen, and semi-spacious dining area. "I mean, you could live in it full-time, like a house."

"Some people do. Modern gypsies."

"I'll bet those gypsies don't have kids. It would be impossible to raise a kid that way."

"I'm beginning to think it's impossible to raise a kid just about any way."

She laughed. "You have a point. Wow! Is this a convection oven?"

"Yup."

"Satellite television. Full entertainment center. Plush carpeting. Cripes, Jackson. You go all out, don't you?"

He grinned. "Occasionally."

"A wine cellar! Omigod, you have a wine cellar!"

"More of a wine cupboard."

"But all the bottles are in these cute little holders."

"So the corks stay wet."

"These aren't exactly from Ernest and Julio, are they? Nineteen-fifty? Cripes, this wine is more than fifty years old."

"For special occasions."

"How many special occasions can there be in a motor home?"

"You'd be surprised. Catch a big fish, roast the perfect marshmallow—so many things call for celebration."

She smiled warmly. "You're right. I should remember that."

Jackson as he looked right then didn't appear to be someone who would own a rig like the one they were sitting in. He more closely fit the role he had been playing for the last week—an itinerant cowboy who didn't have two bucks to his name between paydays, who lived day to day on charm and brass, and, incidentally, had recently gotten walloped in a brawl.

"You look dead on your feet," she said. "The pale shows right through your tan, and through the purple and blue as well."

He cautiously touched his jaw, just exactly where Rachel wanted to touch him, to soothe, to . . . She wouldn't think about it. Absolutely would not. She would keep her hands to herself, where they belonged.

"It doesn't feel as bad as it looks," he told her. "But I guess I still feel a bit rocky."

"In the movies, you can take a much worse drubbing and still chase after the bad guys. Which film was it where you were all shot up, blood everywhere, and still ran along the roofs of moving cars to chase down the villain?"

"*Nights of New York*. That was a while ago." He chuckled. "And here I am, weaving on my feet like an old man after a little mix-up at a barn dance. Not exactly the real thing, am I?"

A sudden warmth flushed Rachel's face. "I don't know that I would say that. Maybe you are the real thing in the ways that are important."

His eyes were entirely too penetrating. She abruptly got up from the sofa. "Maybe you should lie down for a bit. If you have any food in this rolling Taj Mahal, I could fix us some lunch."

He took her up on the suggestion. While he retreated to the bedroom, Rachel rummaged in the refrigerator and cupboards.

She came up with a can of tuna, an unopened bottle of mayonnaise, pita bread, limp celery, and a couple of packaged fruit cups. Not a feast, but it would do for lunch.

The simple domestic task of preparing tuna salad sandwiches didn't keep her mind from the oddness of her situation. Reality, she reflected, was a peculiar thing, because it constantly changed. Or perhaps only her perception had changed. A month ago, if someone had told her that she would not only feel comfortable with someone like Jackson Stone, but genuinely like him, Rachel would have laughed out loud. She would have denied adamantly that she, a woman who disdained appearances, who considered flash and glamour mere silliness, who valued substance over facade, could be seduced by Hollywood good looks and practiced charm.

Was that what had happened? Rachel wondered. Had she been sucked in by good looks and practiced charm?

The thought made Rachel pause in the middle of stuffing tuna salad into a pita pocket. Admit it, she chided herself. She had fallen for Jackson Stone, his cocky smile, his cockeyed attitude, the way he could go from joking to smoldering seriousness in the blink of an eye. His brass, his teasing, his concern for Cherie—all that made her heart melt. Hell, she even liked his frustration with Cherie, because it made him more human, less like an icon of the silver screen performing feats of derring-do.

This whole week she had desperately tried to dislike him, to dismiss him as an icon of a frivolous, self-indulgent culture, a troublesome invader in her plain and peaceful world. And all along she'd been sinking deeper and deeper under his spell.

Cripes, but she was a fool!

Not that it really mattered. Soon he would be gone. Any day now he would grow bored with his role at the Lazy M, bored with provoking her, bored with taking lip from Mac and Vince and the other men. His ankle didn't really keep him from doing what he wanted. He could stay in this fancy motor home, fishing and hiking as he'd originally planned for his vacation. Soon he would leave. And once he was gone, Rachel wouldn't be confronted with his tempting presence. She could resume her normal mundane life, get back to the business of running a guest ranch and dealing with an eleven-year-old. Her ordinary little world had plenty to occupy her. Jackson Stone would fade from her mind and become just another larger-than-life movie hero who made tabloid headlines and box-office block-busters. She would get over him. Or so Rachel told herself.

She poured herself a glass of lemonade—she'd found frozen concentrate in the freezer. A half hour had passed since Jackson had disappeared into the bedroom. Rachel wondered if he was feeling better. Lunch might put color back into his face—at least that part of his face that wasn't showing too much color to begin with.

Quietly she tiptoed through the narrow corridor into the bedroom. Jackson sprawled across the bed, looking dead to the world, one arm thrown across his eyes, the other flung out in an attitude of complete relaxation.

"Jackson?" she whispered.

He didn't stir.

"Jackson, lunch is ready."

Perhaps she should leave him be, Rachel thought. She took a knit throw from the foot of the bed and carefully spread it over him. Suddenly the arm that had covered his eyes moved to grab her upper arm. A slow, heated smile spread across his face. "You don't really want lunch right now, do you?"

Taken by surprise, Rachel opened her mouth, but nothing came out.

"I didn't think so," he said in a satisfied voice.

He pulled her onto the mattress, where she landed beside him with a soft thud. All thoughts of tuna salad fled. "I . . . I thought you were asleep."

"I'm not. Obviously."

"Obviously," she agreed somewhat breathlessly. "There's . . . in the kitchen . . . uh . . ."

"What I want is right here."

The fire in his eyes made Rachel incapable of moving. He had propped himself on one elbow, looking down at her, his solid width blocking the world beyond. Reason, bit by bit, sifted from her mind, leaving only raw emotion behind.

"Here we are." His voice was soft, but it possessed a quiet intensity that made her nerves stand on end.

"What are you . . . we . . . you doing?"

"We." He smiled. "Definitely we."

Jackson's fingers still circled her arm, but Rachel didn't feel restrained by anything but her own hammering heart. Slowly he lowered his mouth to hers, kissing her at first lightly, deliciously, then more thoroughly. One of his hands slipped beneath her backside to pull her closer to him. The heat of their contact penetrated to the very core of her, melting anything that resisted their mutual hunger.

Rachel felt her body soften and warm. Every instinct within her strained toward him. The feel and taste of him, the scent of desire, both his and hers—all seemed so right. More than right. Necessary. Imperative.

When they came up for air, she looked at the face hovering so close above hers. She'd seen it there in her dreams, looking just like it did now, the green eyes blazing with need, mouth curving in affection. But the purple and blue jarred her out of the spell. She stroked his poor jaw with one hand. "Oh, Jackson. All your aches and injuries. We can't do this."

His eyes crinkled in silent laughter. "Rachel, sweetheart, my jaw is not the part of me that aches." He stroked a warm line with one finger, tracing her jaw, trailing slowly down her throat, playing over her collarbone, then exploring the open neckline of her cotton shirt. His voice thick with building desire, he said, "You are the most beautiful woman I've ever met."

A twitch of her lips expressed disbelief, but he stilled the skepticism with a light kiss.

"Where else would I find anyone like you, who makes me feel . . . Lord, I don't know what I feel." His hand slipped beneath her shirt and cupped a breast through the filmy material of her bra. "But this feels so good."

With delicious deliberation, he got rid of their clothing piece by piece. Each expanse of her skin that he exposed seemed a marvel to Jackson, a gift to be explored and savored. For her part, Rachel lost herself in the wonder of him. Shyness and hesitation burned to cinders in the heat of sudden passion. Her breath left her lungs, and her whole body turned to warm, sweet butter, wanting more of him still. Naked together with him, Rachel gloried in desire. Her legs wrapped around him, urging him even closer.

"Sweet girl," he murmured, soothing and exciting at the same time. His hand traveled, caressing, teasing, soothing, igniting. From throat to toes he explored, and all places in between, following hand with lips, until Rachel thought she would explode with need.

When finally he took her, the world blurred. This man was the world, the whole world. Jackson, just Jackson. No thought intruded, no doubt, no iota of sanity. Just desire, soaring joy, and an almost painful pleasure. Rachel clung to Jackson as her only anchor. He steadied her, folded her inside his strength, kept her aloft until her every fiber succumbed to pure rapture. Slowly the world became solid again. Ecstasy faded to bliss, bliss softened to warm satisfaction. The feverish energy of passion cooled, leaving Rachel limp, helpless against emotions that assaulted her on all sides.

When Jackson finally spoke, his voice was a husky, breathless whisper, as if he'd run ten miles. "You are . . . you are quite a woman, Rachel."

Still lying beneath him, her legs tangled with his, she could only smile.

He caressed her face, a touch of affection rather than passion. "You are just about anything a man could want, sweetheart. You take the act of love and turn it into love itself. You know that?"

She didn't know that, didn't quite understand it, and certainly couldn't muster the energy to think about it. Lovingly she touched his cheek with her fingers, but Jackson said no more. His face peaceful, his breathing even, he was sound asleep.

Warm lassitude suffused Rachel's body and mind, a comforting cushion that allowed her to regard the need for panic in fairly calm detachment. She had just indulged in some serious stupidity. Truly serious stupidity. Jackson had taken precautions against physical consequences. But what of the consequences to her heart?

Rachel was not a woman who casually made love with a man. She had married at nineteen—something she did not regret, because her marriage had been a good one. Nevertheless, it was a union that had grown out of friendship more than passion. While her friends were experimenting with love and learning the rules of romance, Rachel had been caring for a child, making a home, and struggling to finish college.

When her husband had died so unexpectedly, Rachel had stumbled into the world of singlehood unprepared and ignorant of the rules. Dating required more attention than she could spare. The rules were complex, the rewards elusive. Early on, Rachel had decided that she didn't have time for the game.

But now she was in the game, outclassed and outgunned. A goose flying wing to wing with an F-16 would have an easier time keeping pace than Rachel Marsh running along Romance Road with Jackson Stone.

She should have stuck with common sense. But here on this bed Jackson had stolen her common sense.

Lying next to Jackson made serious fretting impossible, however. Right then, with his breath ruffling her hair and his arm heavy across her stomach, Rachel knew that whatever the price to her heart, making love with him had been worth it. Jackson Stone was a special man with a caring and tender spirit. He knew the way to a woman's heart was through a smile, a light touch, a word whispered in her ear at the right moment, not through spectacular sexual gymnastics. Not that his lovemaking left anything to be desired Oh, no. Not at all. Rachel's smile widened as she remembered.

What would she do about her folly? Nothing. Nothing could be done. She would enjoy heaven while she could and endure the aftermath when Jackson left.

The man beside her moved. His arm shifted, tightening its hold on her, but his eyes remained closed and his breathing evened out once more. Rachel smiled at him, putting all her love into a smile that he couldn't see.

Love doesn't conquer all, the voice in her head reminded her. *Don't let your heart fool you into thinking it can.*

With a resigned sigh, she covered his hand with hers. His eyes opened and found her own.

"Is it morning yet?" he rumbled quietly.

Rachel laughed. "Morning? Do you know where you are?"

"I remember where I was." Sliding his hand from her stomach to between her legs, he caressed her ear with a husky whisper. "I was right here, loving you. Have I told you lately that you're beautiful?"

Desire jolted through her like a fork of lightning. She went with it, letting it carry her.

"Or that you are the sexiest woman alive?"

She opened to him His fingers worked magic.

"Or that you are the most incredible woman that I've ever met?"

Almost breathless, she choked out, "I think you have." She swallowed hard. "Don't . . . don't stop."

He smiled. "Not a chance of stopping before I do this." He moved so that he was on top of her, parting her legs with his hips. Deep inside, bliss spread in a warm flood. "And this." He kissed her mouth, her throat, and other parts that very much needed kissing. "I love you, Rachel. Goddamn, but I love you."

She let the wave take her, not caring where she washed ashore.

Rachel stopped the truck in front of the garage as Jackson parked his mobile mansion beside the main barn. A reception committee awaited them. Checking herself in the rearview mirror, she felt like a teenager who had parked in Lovers' Lane and needed to hide the evidence. Her cheeks were flushed. Her hair was in semi-disarray. Her eyes had a suspicious sparkle, and her smile was definitely suspect.

When he climbed down from the RV, Jackson looked as he always looked, no hint that thirty minutes before he had been heating up a bed to the point of combustion. But then, he was an actor, Rachel told herself. She began to understand why he'd been awarded that Oscar.

Paying no attention to the RV, Dennis stumped up to her the minute she stepped from the truck. He looked as though he'd been grinding nails with his teeth. "There you are! Thought you were only going to be gone an hour."

Rachel struggled to come up with an adequate lie. Jackson saved her, sort of. "Had trouble getting her started." He patted the side of the RV, but his eyes twinkled at Rachel. "She'd been left alone too long."

Rachel just barely kept herself from kicking him, but Dennis didn't notice the undercurrents. He held out his hand for the truck keys.

"I need to take some lumber up to the number two windmill."

"Sorry." Rachel stepped out of the way as Dennis hauled himself into the truck and started the engine.

"Didn't run the tank dry? Nope? Good. See ya."

As Dennis drove off, Jackson laid a hand on her shoulder. The hand rested lightly, but the touch scorched. "Didn't run the tank dry, did you, Rachel?"

"You are cruising for more bruises than you already have," she warned. But stern was hard to capture when she actually wanted to laugh.

"Oh, there you are!" This time it was Mrs. Dobson, who dithered up in a flurry of concern. "I missed you in the barn this morning, Stoney. That girl—Terri is her name? Yes, Terri. She's nice, but I don't think she was expecting all of us at milking time. Poor thing. Threw off her timing with the goats, if I do say. Good thing I was there to help."

Rachel gave her a smile. "Alice, I don't know what we'll do when you're not here." She really did have a warm spot in her heart for the old lady.

"Stoney, you look like a mule ran over you, then kicked you a few times to make sure he did the job right."

"That's not far off."

"Well, dear, next time keep your guard up better and watch out for the left hook. Looks like he caught you a zinger." The old lady winked and patted his arm.

From around the corner of the barn galloped Sam, Cherie, and Chesty. "Hey, Ma! You're home!"

"Hi, Rachel! Wait'll you hear what Chesty just did!"

"Wow! Is that the RV?" Sam said at the same time.

"Hold on, you two!" Rachel corralled Sam before he could bounce off to admire the RV. "You know better than to interrupt like that, Sam!"

Jackson had reined in Cherie and stood with hands planted firmly on the girl's shoulders.

"Sorry," a chastened Sam said. "Hi, Mrs. Dobson."

Responding to a squeeze from her father's hands, Cherie echoed Sam. "Hi, Mrs. Dobson. Sorry we stepped on your conversation."

"That's quite all right," Alice said. "It's time for me to be off, anyway. The husband just got back from fishing, and he'll want to tell a few fish stories." She patted Jackson's arm again. "Remember, dear, what I said about the left hook."

As soon as Alice walked away, Sam got his bounce back. Eyes wide, he rushed to the front of the RV and peered in the huge front window. "Wow! Really cool!"

"Take a look inside," Jackson invited.

"Thanks!" He disappeared around the corner of the bus-size vehicle, followed by Cherie and Chesty. "Ma!" came his voice from inside. "They have a bigger television than we do! Did you see the cool hideaway table?"

"I think he's impressed," she told Jackson.

"His mother should be so easily impressed." His wicked grin sent her thermostat inching upward.

"I wouldn't worry about it." She sent him a teasing smile. "You did your best."

Sam popped into sight again, tumbling out the driver's door. "Ma! This is great. Cherie and me want to spend the night camping out in this. Okay? Cherie's going to build a fire and we're going to toast marshmallows."

"I trust that fire isn't going to be on the living room carpet." Jackson raised a brow at Cherie as she climbed down from the cab with a bit more dignity than Sam had managed.

"Dad! How stupid do you think I am?"

"Just checking. You're going to build a campfire, Cherie? You?"

"So? I can do stuff like that."

Jackson shook his head wonderingly.

"Well," Rachel said, "if it's all right with Cherie's dad, I guess it's all right with me."

Joanne joined them in time to hear the end of the conversation. "What are those two getting into now?" she asked Rachel.

"They're going to camp out in the RV tonight."

Joanne eyed the big motor home. "That's quite a rig, Stoney."

"Belongs to a friend in Springerville," he said without missing a beat. "I'm going to do some work on the engine."

The housekeeper snorted. "You don't say."

Cherie frowned in puzzlement, then understanding inspired a conspiratorial smile. The girl was a true offspring of her dissembling father. Sam, however, wasn't so fast on the uptake. But when he opened his mouth to say something, a sharp jab from Cherie's elbow brought him into line.

Rachel quickly changed the subject. "Do we have any marshmallows?"

"Marshmallows?" Joanne scowled. "You're giving a marshmallow roast for those two scamps, after what they did last night?"

Rachel couldn't remember anyone ever describing Sam as a scamp, not until he'd met Cherie. She wondered if he didn't need a little scamp in him. "What did they do?" Rachel and Jackson asked at the same time.

Sam attempted to slink back to the RV while Joanne recounted the kids' late-night adventure, but Jackson foiled his escape with a firm hand on his shoulder. Cherie, who had drifted unobtrusively into the motor home, didn't escape, either. When she peeked out the window, her father beckoned imperiously.

"So," Joanne concluded, "when Nathan got ready to take off mid-morning, he found that old truck of his full of shaving foam." She lowered an accusing look at Jackson. "Yours, I assume. It must have been a full can, because the stuff was everywhere—on the seat, the dashboard, the steering wheel, the front window. They didn't miss much of anything."

Cherie oozed quietly from the RV and eyed her father with misgiving. Sam studied the ground.

"Shaving cream in Nathan's truck." Rachel bit her lip.

Jackson had less success in stifling a laugh. He ended up choking.

"He had it coming," Cherie muttered.

"Yeah," Sam agreed quietly. "He shouldn't have jumped Cherie's dad."

Rachel tried to get serious. "You can't appoint yourself judge and jury just because you don't like what someone has done."

Sam gave her a plaintive look. "Does this mean we can't camp in the RV?"

She glanced at Jackson, who had managed to wipe the humor from his expression. His eyes twinkled, though. How Rachel did love those eyes!

"Please," Sam pleaded "Cherie and me had this bet, and Cherie lost, so I get to stay in the RV and she's gonna build a marshmallow-roasting fire all herself."

"You had a bet, did you?" Jackson queried.

"Yeah," the kids both answered.

Rachel smiled. "Well, I guess you can't renege on a bet, can you?" She caught Jackson's grin, and her smile widened. "If you want to stay in the RV tonight," she told the culprits, "then you think of a different punishment for your little prank. In two hours, you tell Cherie's father and me what that punishment is, and if we think it's fair, then you can stay in the RV."

Sam immediately brightened. "Okay!"

The two kids were off like arrows shot from a bow, Chesty galloping behind. Rachel and Jackson both laughed. Joanne regarded them with disapproval.

"If I'd ever done anything like that, my pa would've beat my butt black and blue."

"Would that have stopped you from doing it?" Jackson asked her.

" 'Course not." She sniffed. "Rachel, you got two new guests. They're off with Paul on a trail ride, and they signed up for the fishing picnic tomorrow."

"Good. I'll say hello to them at dinner. Anything else?"

"Nope. The kids caught a load of fish up at Hay Lake, and I'm cooking them up for dinner along with some other fish the guests brought in. So tonight's trout night. Sam helped me gut them, and Cherie shucked a tub of corn." She gave Jackson one of her rare smiles. "She ain't a bad kid, you know."

"Thanks," Jackson said. "I know."

Joanne shook her head "Can't stand here talking all day. Got things to do. You need me, I'll be in the house."

Life was back to normal, Rachel mused, full of minor crises and demands. Nothing had changed, and yet everything had changed. She longed for a moment alone with Jackson. She wanted to touch him and talk to him without others looking on. She wanted to lean against him, feel his breath in her hair, and together explore the relationship that had changed so drastically. But she couldn't do that. She didn't dare let the intimate smile she felt inside find expression on her face.

"Jackson," she said quietly now that they were alone for a brief moment, "I—"

He shook his head in warning, just in time for Rachel to bite her lip before Mac was upon them.

"There you are!" he bellowed.

Those words seemed to be the greeting of the day, Rachel

thought wryly. She couldn't disappear so much as an hour without everyone considering her AWOL.

"Here I am," she replied with a sigh.

"Not you, Rachel. Stoney here. Stoney, would you run a message up to Vince for me? He and Toby are up at stock tank number two trying to fix the windmill. You can take my horse. He's already saddled."

Rachel looked a question at Mac, and he shrugged. "I need to run into town for a while, so I can't go. Vince needs to call his wife. She sounded pretty anxious to talk to him."

"Uh . . . why don't you drive?" she suggested to Jackson.

"I'm taking the van," Mac told her. "Everything else is gone."

"Stoney has a Jeep."

"I wouldn't take even a Jeep over that road to the windmill. Not unless you want to lose an axle."

"It's okay," Jackson said. "I'll take the horse."

"Better get going if you're going to be back in time for dinner." He gave the RV a curious glance. "What's with the motor home?"

"Belongs to a friend of Stoney's."

Rachel thought she didn't sound very convincing, but Mac seemed satisfied. "Nice rig," was all he said.

As Jackson strolled to where Mac's gray gelding was tethered to the hitching post in front of the barn, Rachel wanted to tell him that he didn't need to prove himself, he wasn't a cowhand, he wasn't a horseman, and perhaps the time had come to end these foolish games.

Which foolish games? the voice from inside asked *The silly cowboy pretense, or the fool games you both played in Jackson's mobile bedroom?*

Rachel told her alter ego to shut up. She had problems enough without trying to deal with an interfering conscience.

"Would you look at that?" Mac tilted his hat back on his head to get a better view. "Where's that man's mind? Do you believe he actually tried to get on the wrong side? He's lucky old Tumbleweed's a forgiving sort of horse."

Rachel wanted to hide her eyes.

"He's got it now." He shook his head. "I hope you're not paying that guy much."

"Actually," Rachel admitted with a sigh, "he's paying me."

"Sounds about right," Mac said with a grin, then with a casual wave headed for the van.

Standing alone by the motor home, with no one there to see, Rachel could finally let loose the goofy smile that simmered inside her.

That smile was still on her face eight hours later when midnight found her waking from a light sleep full of entertaining dreams. Languidly, she rolled over and looked at the bedside clock. Sleep beckoned temptingly. The mother in her, however, knew why she had wakened. When she had checked on Sam and Cherie before climbing the stairs to her bedroom, the kids had still been toasting marshmallows over the little fire they'd built beside the motor home. Sam had showed Cherie how to dig a fire pit and line it with rocks. Rachel had overheard a few of Cherie's cracks about caveman technology, but Sam had held his own in the crack department. Her little boy had both wit and grit, and wouldn't you just know it took a female to bring them out, even at his tender age.

Rachel rolled out of bed. No mother could sleep through the night without making sure that fire had been properly extinguished and the kids safely tucked away in bed, or at least safely watching movies in the motor home. She slipped on moccasins and a jacket and tiptoed out into the night.

The ranch was quiet and dark. A couple of the guest cabins showed lighted windows, but the little campfire was doused and the motor home showed no signs of life. Apparently even the lure of the DVD couldn't keep Sam and Cherie awake after the way they'd plowed through the day. Rachel shook her head and smiled, thinking of Nathan's truck. For that stunt the kids had endured KP duty in the Chuckwagon, but Rachel felt like thanking them instead.

When she headed back to the house, she glimpsed through the pines a soft glow illuminating a window in Sitting Bull cabin. Jackson was awake, then. Could thoughts of Rachel Marsh be keeping him from sleep?

More likely his sore butt was keeping him awake, Rachel mused. He had returned from his ride to the windmill in one piece, Mac's horse still with him. That had been a bit of a surprise.

Sam wasn't the only one around here with grit.

Before she knew it, Rachel found herself on the path to Sitting Bull instead of the path to the house. As a conscientious and caring employer, she really ought to make sure Jackson was okay.

He answered the door bare-chested and barefooted. A flush heated Rachel's cheeks at the slow smile that greeted her.

"Hi," she said.

"Hi yourself."

"I . . . I just wanted to make sure you're all right, uh, after riding to the . . . you know."

"Didn't fall off once."

"Congratulations."

He gestured her into the cabin. Rachel hesitated. She should turn around and go back to her own bed. More foolishness would just make the situation worse.

Jackson took her arm and pulled her inside, closing the door behind her. "Now that you ask, Rachel, I don't think I am quite all right."

Instantly concerned, she turned toward him, only to find herself trapped in his arms. "You're . . . something's wrong?"

"Yeah. I'm addicted. Most powerful drug in the world. You."

She pushed at him. "That is so lame."

"Really?"

"It's a good thing you don't write your own lines in the movies."

"Stop trying to get away. It's not going to work."

She gave up trying. His embrace was too tempting. "I really should go." Token resistance.

"No, you shouldn't." He kissed her hair, then her temple. Breathing became difficult.

"I should."

"We have all night." His voice was pure enticement. "All night. Just you and me together."

Breathing became impossible. His hands massaged her backside, bringing her close against the unmistakable evidence that here was one fire not yet extinguished. She wanted to crawl inside him. She wanted him to crawl inside her.

He picked her up and carried her into the little bedroom, and very shortly, the light in the window of Sitting Bull cabin went out.

CHAPTER 13

♡

ANOTHER DAY, ANOTHER picnic. Jackson clucked to the team and gave the reins a shake to get the horses moving. He felt good. Damned good. Ten days had passed since Nathan had tried to rearrange Jackson's features with his fists, and most of his bruises and aches had disappeared. The morning was beautiful, with just a hint of cool in the air. The blue of the sky was so deep and pure it made his eyes ache. The breeze whispered a song in the pines, and wildflowers splashed the landscape with color.

On a day like this, rational thought blew away on the fresh breeze. Birds sang, butterflies flitted to and fro, and the day's first puffy cloud floated across the sky like a great ship under full sail. Add to that the warm bubbling of Jackson's spirits and you had a recipe for flights of fancy, woolgathering, and impossible daydreaming. The mix included not a single dollop of rational, adult, common sense.

The sight of Rachel riding just ahead of the team only helped the daydreaming along. Rachel Marsh looked great on a horse, great from all sides—front, profile, and rear. The rear view was especially enticing, and that was the view Jackson enjoyed as his wagon rolled along. Rachel fit very well into her saddle, he noted. Rachel fit very well just about anywhere, and one place she especially fit was in his bed. Every time she touched him a current flowed between them, and sometimes she didn't have to touch him, just look at him. The current was warmth, desire, laughter, loving—yes, loving was a real part of it. He might as well admit it to himself, Jackson thought. He might have intended to just stick his toe in the water, but right now he was flailing in the current and heading for a waterfall, about to cascade right off the edge of a cliff into unknown territory.

"Hey, Stoney!" one of his passengers, a dentist from Payson, interrupted his reflections. "They let you take off the training wheels today?"

Stoney swiveled on the driver's box and gave the man a good-natured grin. "Yeah, Doc. What's the matter? Don't you feel safe?" Dr. Payne had been on the last fishing picnic, when Ted had sat on the driver's box with Jackson, and the story of his first ill-fated attempt at driving had quickly become legend.

"Wasn't it you who couldn't get the team to go forward last week where the road crosses the stream?"

"Now, Doc, these horses were just having a little fun with me. They love me like a brother."

A twenty-something woman who had been more than a little friendly with him, or at least would have if he had so much as turned an eye her way, said with a laugh, "Last week, Cass Robbins saw him try to get on a horse backwards."

"Trick riding," Jackson announced. "My specialty. I do one of the most spectacular flying dismounts you've ever seen."

"What part of your anatomy do you land on?" Twenty-something asked

"Whichever hits the ground first."

Everyone laughed.

Today for the first time Jackson was alone on the driver's box. He didn't jump to the conclusion that Rachel trusted him with the team. More likely she and all the hands thought the team was far smarter than he was, and those faithful, reliable beasts wouldn't let him get into trouble. When they were displeased with his handling, the horses simply stopped in their tracks.

Still, being in charge of the team, pretending like he knew what the hell he was doing—it felt good. What felt better, though, was watching Rachel as she rode ahead, Rachel of the supple form, looking like part of the horse, curly ponytail flying out behind her in a glossy dark banner.

Lord, but she looked good. He would love to show her off in L.A.

Rachel in Los Angeles? The thought took Jackson by surprise. But the notion hadn't dropped on him out of the sky. The kernel of it had been sprouting for days, ever since he and Rachel had first made love. Since then the game he'd been playing with romance had taken a serious turn. His mind was running with new storylines involving Rachel in L.A. Rachel at the beach house. Rachel and Sam helping him sand his boat. Rachel on his arm at the Golden Globes.

The images were tempting—so damned tempting! The intensity of longing surprised him. Jackson had known from the first that Rachel was dangerous territory—a woman very unlike the fast-living, fun-loving ladies he most often favored. Rachel was a breath of fresh air to a man steeped in shallow encounters and casual love games.

Maybe Jackson had thought he could take a deep breath of that freshness and not get hooked, and now he'd learned the truth. Rachel Marsh was a drug more powerful than any substance circulating at an L.A. party. Rachel Marsh was downright addictive.

Sadly, like all addictive drugs, this one was going to exact a painful price, because the more Jackson visualized making Rachel a part of his life, the more he realized the relationship would never work. Along with romantic images of Rachel running with him on the beach in front of his L.A. home were less fanciful scenes: Rachel facing the flashbulbs and pushy demands of the paparazzi; Rachel reading whatever unpleasant observations about her that slime Josh Digby might write in the *National Star;* Rachel breathing L.A. smog and fighting L.A. traffic.

And there the director yelled "Cut!", the film of his imagination snapped, the screen went black. Nothing about the plot rang true; Rachel and Jackson as a couple simply wouldn't

work. Rachel would hate his life, hate the frenzy and the false-
ness, the glare of constant public spotlight. She loved her
ranch, her mountains and clean air and fresh breezes. She
loved her dog and her goddamned horses, her snowy winters
with hardly anyone about, her sane and sensible world where
what mattered was what you did, not who you were and who
you knew. His world would seem superficial to her. It was superficial, and sometimes he hated it, too.

His mind looked that stray thought in the eye and shied
away like a gun-shy horse at the crack of a rifle. What was he
thinking? He'd known Rachel Marsh not even a month, and already he was conjuring ways to make room for her in his life.
Such foolishness would get him in trouble. He liked fun
women, women who didn't take life seriously, women who
laughed and loved and took what he could give without expecting his heart and soul.

Rachel wasn't a good-time girl. Sooner or later, she would
expect a man's heart and soul. She would expect marriage and
permanence. Years ago Jackson had learned that marriage
didn't do well in the celebrity spotlight. The film industry was
littered with broken marriages, one of them his. He wouldn't
put Rachel through that hell. He wasn't going through that hell
again himself.

Right now he and Rachel were having a great time. Neither
of them had expectations beyond today. If he tried to stretch
things out, the relationship would get complicated. Better to
leave it here, where it was fresh, pure, and simple, than try to
drag it with him when he left.

They arrived at their destination without a single incident
marring the trip. Jackson gave the team a silent but heartfelt
thank you when they stopped of their own accord at the now
familiar picnic site. Vince took the lead horse's head. He and
Dennis had driven the truck with food and fishing gear, and
they already had a cook-fire going. "You didn't lose anyone, the
horses didn't run away, and you didn't all wind up at the bottom of a cliff. Not bad."

"He's joshing, folks," Jackson assured his passengers.

"Yeah," Vince said with a grin. "Just kidding. There's coffee over by the fire, and your fishing gear's in the back of the truck. Go to it, fishermen."

While Vince secured the team, Jackson assisted the guests from the wagon. Twenty-something climbed down last, and what a climb it was. Clasping her hands behind Jackson's neck, she clung to him while undulating her way to solid ground.

"Thank you," she purred.

Jackson was an expert in escaping overenthusiastic women. He slipped deftly out of her grasp, making it seem as if she were the one who had done the slipping.

"Oh, my," she breathed. "All that jouncing about in the wagon has made my legs really wobbly." She took his arm and pulled him toward the fire. "Do you know, Stoney, I haven't ever fished before. If I catch a fish, will you take it off the hook for me?"

"Believe me, Maria, whatever you catch on your hook, I'll make sure it gets off."

"Oh, good!" She sent him a simmering look, then frowned. "I just know that I've met you somewhere before, somewhere else. You look really familiar."

"I don't think so, darlin'," he said in an easy cowboy drawl. "I for sure woulda' remembered."

At least that was the truth, Jackson thought as he headed back to the wagon. Maria was just his style, a good-looking girl on the prowl for a good time. She'd been flirting with him since she checked in two days ago, yet he could scarcely remember her name.

Rachel Marsh had taken his criteria for a good time and shaken them up like dice in a cup. At her toss the dice had landed on edge, still spinning. A good time would never be the same again.

Jackson unhitched the team and pulled a tarp from beneath the driver's box to spread across the seats. The day was beautiful, but that first puffy white cloud sailing across the sky had gathered others in its wake. Now a whole flotilla floated across the blue.

He remembered huddling beneath the poncho with Rachel during the rainstorm of his first picnic. He'd almost gotten to kiss her beneath that poncho. Lord, he prayed, send more rain. More rain and a single poncho for him and Rachel Marsh.

Lost in such intriguing thoughts, he shook open the tarp and flipped it over the wagon seats—just as Rachel rode by on Sally. Sally reared back, showing the whites of her eyes, then launched into a jolting rodeo act that sent Rachel flying. She landed with a thud that made Jackson wince. He knew exactly how she felt.

Throwing the tarp aside, he hurried forward, frightened that she might actually be hurt. The guests babbled in alarm, but Vince and Dennis hooted with laughter. Rachel pushed up on her elbows and squinted at them sourly. "You could show some sympathy, gentlemen."

Vince grinned so wide his face nearly split in two. "I knew that mare was gonna unload you one of these days!"

Rachel still clutched the end of Sally's reins. She had once sternly lectured Jackson that a good horseman never let go of the reins, even if he landed headfirst in nettles. Vince walked over and relieved her of them. He gave the mare a friendly slap on the neck. "Good job, Sally girl. Ever' once in a while the boss needs to eat a bit of humble pie, eh?"

Cautiously, Jackson offered Rachel a hand up. At her ferocious glare, he grimaced apologetically. "Uh . . . oops?"

She growled. "Oops scarcely covers it." Her eyes narrowed suspiciously. "Was that deliberate?"

"I would never!" he declared sincerely. "It was . . . it was sheer stupidity."

She looked startled, then laughed. "It was, you booby!" She kept laughing. "Oh, damn! What a sight that must have been. I'll bet I sailed ten feet into the air."

"Just feels that way," Dennis commented with a chuckle.

She took Jackson's outstretched hand. "You, I'm going to dock a week's pay."

Since Jackson's pay was zero, that didn't hurt much. "You're a hard woman, Rachel Marsh."

"Ouch!" She came up less than gracefully. Twisting to regard her backside with disfavor, she noted, "Something back there is creaking."

"You're lucky something back there isn't broken." Jackson brushed sticks and dirt from the back of her shirt. He wisely left the seat of her jeans for her to clean. "You all right? Really?"

She grinned. "I'm fine."

Vince handed Sally's reins back and, with an instructive brow raised in Jackson's direction, left them alone—man, woman, and horse. Rachel's attention seemed to be all for the mare, whose nose she stroked fondly. "Did that scary fella flip a tarp in your face, poor sweetie? Is he an idiot?" she cooed. "Yes, he is!" But the sideways look she sent Jackson's way was as good as a smile. "You are so in trouble."

He tried to look humble. "I'll let you pelt me with pine cones."

"Hmmph!"

"Beat me with a willow stick?"

"Not good enough."

He raised a brow. "I could give you a nice massage where it hurts the most."

She laughed softly and kissed Sally's velvety nose. "It's a good thing I love you, you idiot."

Jackson's heart jumped. She had kissed the damned horse but looked straight at him with one of her sneaky, impish, corner-of-the-eye whammies. "I'm never going to catch up to that horse in your affections, am I?"

She smiled smugly. "Face it, my friend. A man is just a man, but a horse . . . well, a horse is a horse!"

He laughed.

"Git along, now, Stoney boy. Don't you have work to do?" Limping only slightly, she led Sally toward where the other horseback riders were dismounting. Sally's broad rump swung around and nearly knocked Jackson off his feet. The mare gave a snort of satisfaction as Rachel led her away. Jackson had to laugh. Looked like it was going to be that kind of day.

The day didn't turn out to be that kind of day, however. The tarp incident didn't affect Rachel's good cheer. Vince and Dennis joshed Jackson for about five minutes, then forgot it. They were accustomed to his blunders. If he had walked barefoot through the cook-fire they would have simply shrugged and commented that Stoney was at it again. Achieving such bumbler status didn't exactly make Jackson feel good, but it didn't make him feel as bad as it might have. Nothing much could make him feel bad as long as Rachel was still smiling and in one piece. The panic he'd suffered when she hit the ground still had his heart racing.

That in itself was downright scary, now that he thought about it.

What seemed to be chaos became order as Vince handed out fishing gear and bait to the guests. Dennis tended the fire, and Jackson gave advice to the fishing virgins about hook-baiting, casting, and the best places to drop their lines. Twenty-something pleaded prettily for him to find her a good fishing spot and help her bait her hook. Jackson figured that once he disappeared into the brush with that lady, he would be lucky to make it out with his virtue—what was left of it—intact. He recommended Dennis as a much better man with barbed hooks, worms, and salmon eggs. Twenty-something went away looking miffed.

When the last guest had left to catch lunch, they all four unloaded the coolers from the truck.

"Water's still muddy from last night's rain," Vince commented. "Won't be great fishing today. We'd better get out the hamburgers and start them thawing."

Jackson's mind turned back to the night before, when he and Rachel had managed some private time in her bedroom. The memories made him smile. Rachel smiled also, though she tried hard to avoid meeting his eyes. "Did it rain last night?" he asked. "Didn't hear a thing."

"You deaf?" Dennis asked. "That one lightning strike must have been no more than a mile from the ranch."

"Thunder and lightning. Do tell."

Rachel bit her lip, trying to hide a smile.

Vince looked from Jackson to Rachel and back again. His tongue clucked like a hen. "So . . . I guess Stoney boy gets gutting detail again, eh?"

Rachel nodded, and smiled. "Sounds right."

"He's a pretty good gutter," Vince said, eyes twinkling above his scruffy beard. "Maybe we should put him on permanent detail."

"Good idea," Rachel approved. "Keep him busy and out of trouble."

Dennis and Vince laughed, and Rachel joined in.

"Yuk it up, you three. I'll have you know that it'll take more than gutting fish to keep me out of trouble."

Rachel laughed harder. "I was afraid that might be true."

Cherie lounged on the couch in Rachel's office, the phone in her hand. With Rachel and her father both on the picnic, Joanne in town shopping, and Terri and Moira both making beds and cleaning cabins, Cherie couldn't pass up the chance to get at the phone. Her cell phone didn't work in this back-water. She was surprised the Lazy M had telephones at all. Smoke signals and mirrors would be more in keeping.

Smiling in anticipation, she punched the long-distance number. Rachel would wonder about a Beverly Hills call on her bill, but by that time, Cherie would be safely away. She would mail her an explanation along with payment for the call. Rachel would understand about cabin fever. After all, the cow-girl probably hadn't been out of the sticks for years.

"Deanna!" she squealed when her friend answered the phone. "It's me! Cherie!"

"Cherie!" Deanna squealed back. "Dudette! I thought you dropped off the planet, you know?"

"I did almost. Girl, you should see this place my dad dragged me to! You will not believe when I tell you!"

"What are you in, like, Alcatraz?"

"Just as bad!" Okay, Cherie admitted silently, that was an ex-aggeration. Some things about the Lazy M were marginally okay, but Deanna would never understand. She would think Cherie was a dork for liking anything about a place like this.

"You're coming back in time to go with us to Europe, right? I told my folks you were coming with us, and they were cool with it, you know? You have your passport, right?"

"It's still good. And yeah, sure, of course I'm coming with you. I wouldn't miss a chance like that!"

"All right! Girlfriend, spending all that time with just my parents would be sooooooo boring. I'd die before two weeks were up, you know? Just literally die."

"All I have to do is soften up Dad just a little more."

A slight hesitation, then, "You mean, he hasn't said yes yet?"

"Don't worry! I'll work it out. He's in a pretty good mood lately. Met a woman. You know how that goes. And if he gets stubborn, I can use the guilt angle. That always works."

"Awesome! I wish my parents were divorced."

"No, you don't," Cherie said, suddenly serious. She liked Deanna's mom and dad, even if they were a bit old-fashioned and uptight. In a way her friend's mom reminded her of Rachel, except Marjorie Cohen was dumpy and talked too much. But she was sweet and smart and would walk through fire for Deanna if she had to.

"So, when will you be back, girl? We need to do serious shopping, you know, before we go."

"I'll be back in time. I'll call you again when I know for sure, if I get the chance. My cell phone doesn't work here, and I have to sneak in to use the phone."

"Serious bummer! Where are you? The moon?"

"Just as bad. Arizona. Would you believe a dude ranch, with cowboys, and horses, and little log cabins, like right out of the Stone Age?"

"Totally gross!"

"Yeah. Kinda. You should look up the website so you can see where I am. LazyM.com. Dad and I are staying in a cabin called Sitting Bull. And this weekend we're going to a dumb stupid rodeo. It'll be so lame that it's fun, kind of. But I'll be glad to come home."

"I'll bet! Wait'll I tell you about this guy I met! He was on *Gladiators*—you know, that new reality show with the huge ratings. Did you see that? Anyway, my mom won't let me go out with him, but . . ."

Cherie let Deanna ramble on. It was so good to hear her voice, even though the things she wowed over were sort of boring. Not long ago Cherie hadn't thought they were boring. She had better get back to the real world pretty soon, Cherie decided. Fantasy Cowboy Land was warping her values.

At the picnic, fishermen began to trickle in to drop rainbow trout into the pan of fresh water. Maria of the simmering eyes sidled by with no fish at all, just to let Jackson know she was back. When he started to clean the first trout, however, she fled. Fish guts, Jackson guessed, sort of ate away at his sex appeal. Too bad.

"Hey, Rachel." He caught her attention as she walked by with Mrs. Calloway, who had come along on the picnic to add to her pine cone collection while her hubby fished. Mrs. Calloway hastened in the other direction when she saw Jackson's task, but Rachel ambled over and gave him the superior look of a woman who knows she has the upper hand. A direct challenge, Jackson figured.

She glanced at the two trout he had already cleaned. "Neatly done, Stoney. Nice work. Must be nice to know you have such a talent to fall back on."

He returned her wicked smile with one just as wicked. "My talents are many and varied."

"So I've noticed."

"It seems a shame to squander my talents by keeping me up to my elbows in fish guts."

Her eyes twinkled. "I don't know, the job seems to suit you. After all, the fish are dead already. You can't hurt them by screwing up. Besides, think of all the firsthand grit you're collecting."

He shook his head ruefully. "I gave you a fine weapon with that grit thing, didn't I?"

She laughed. "A woman needs a weapon against a man like you."

"You think? Interesting." He gave her his famous lopsided grin. "You know, Rachel, if you helped me with this pail of fish, we could take a short walk by the stream and discuss other weapons you might have, in illustrated detail." He proffered a slimy twelve-inch trout. "Grab a knife."

She backed up a step. "I haven't ever cleaned a fish," she admitted, her expression screwing up in distaste. "And I'm not going to start now."

"You mean Rachel Marsh, archetype country girl, gives her catch to some poor cowboy to gut?"

Her jaw thrust out pugnaciously. "For your information, I've never caught a stupid fish."

Jackson lifted a brow dramatically.

"I don't like putting the poor worms on the hook, and I don't like the look the fish give you when they come out of the water."

If he laughed as hard as he wanted to, Jackson probably would have stabbed himself with the gutting knife. So he settled for a broad smile. "Rachel Marsh is a weenie-girl."

She turned a very satisfactory shade of pink.

He had to laugh at her. "No fish, and no fish-gutting. Rachel has a squeamish spot in her armor. I love it."

She gave him a haughty look and turned on her heel. "I don't have to put up with this."

Before she could stalk away, the words just slipped out of his mouth—almost as big a surprise to him as they were to her. "I love you, Rachel."

She froze. Seconds ticked by before she finally turned back to him. "Say that again."

"You heard me." Jackson shrugged, trying to ignore the sinking feeling in his gut. When had he last said those words to a woman—right out in plain daylight instead of in a moment of passion, when they really didn't mean the same thing? Years ago, he had told Melanie he loved her. He'd meant it. But love didn't last. Did it ever? He managed an insouciant pose. "They're not original, of course. You said them first, if you remember."

Her face told him that she did indeed remember. "I was talking to the horse."

He smiled. "Right." They both knew the truth.

"My brain had just been jarred."

"More than my brain has been jarred in the last week or two."

She abandoned pretense. "You mean it?"

"I said it," he confessed. There was no going back now.

For a moment they eyed each other uneasily. Then Rachel smiled a smile that rivaled the sun. "I do believe you're leering."

He picked up a limp fish and slit it open. "Lovers of my quality do not leer."

"That's what you think."

"If there were any privacy around here I'd show you a real and actual leer."

She laughed. "You keep those fishy hands away from me. And don't even think of doing anything wild with those fish guts."

He grinned.

"I don't want you close to me, mister, until you've taken a shower."

"And then you want me close to you?"

"What do you think?"

He liked the sassy smile she shot at him as she turned to walk away. She wanted him. Oh, yes, she wanted him. And he wanted her so bad he was practically foaming at the mouth, wanted more than just a night in bed. He wanted it all. He wanted it so bad, he could taste it.

Out the corner of his eye, Jackson caught Vince's smile. Jackson wasn't the only one watching Rachel's departure. Vince's knowing look shifted to Jackson, who could almost hear the old man's gritty chuckle.

That obvious, were they? Hell, yes, they were. Rachel positively glowed, and Jackson's frustration no doubt showed through every smile. For a moment he wished his deception at the Lazy M were real, that he was an ordinary ranch hand working to make something of himself, so he could set his sights on Rachel Marsh as a permanent fixture in his life. Would that life be a more satisfying one?

What the hell had he done to himself?

Despite the muddy stream, the guests brought in enough fish that hamburgers were not needed. Rachel whipped up Dutch-oven biscuits while Dennis and Vince rolled the trout in cornmeal and put them in a cast-iron skillet to fry. Jackson buried the fish entrails, then went to the stream with a bar of biodegradable soap and lathered his hands and arms. Someday he would learn to bring a change of clothing to these picnics.

Then he remembered—very shortly, the picnics would be doing without him. This next weekend was the last one in August. In September, he and Cherie would ride off into the sunset, so to speak, and resume their real lives.

Cherie would pretend to celebrate, though Jackson suspected she would miss Sam and Chesty. And Rachel, too. For a kid who thought that everyone over the age of twenty was "prehistoric," Cherie got on surprisingly well with Rachel. And Cherie and Sam, though they constantly sniped at each other, were never far apart. Could be letting those kids together was dangerous. He smiled, thinking about Nathan's truck. Cherie's mischief wasn't usually so innocent. And he suspected that Sam pretty much didn't get into mischief at all. Between them, the kids had forged a middle ground. Maybe that was good for both of them.

By the time he had finished washing up, the ranch guests were eating, seated on logs, tree stumps, or the folding chairs Vince had brought in the truck. The Calloways took advantage of the chairs. Maria and Dr. Payne sat on the truck tailgate. John Wakes, the attorney from Scottsdale, had plopped down with his wife on a cushion of pine needles. Rachel sat cross-legged on the bare ground and looked perfectly content to do so. Jackson started to walk in her direction, but he was intercepted by Dennis, who thrust a plate of food at him. "Better eat, Stoney. They'll be wanting to head back soon." He offered to share the log where he was sitting.

"Thanks." Jackson sat down, and tucked into tender trout, baked beans, potato salad, and a huge Dutch-oven biscuit. Gourmet meals were part of his lifestyle in Los Angeles, but they couldn't compare with this fare. The pure blue sky, the pine-scented air, the peaceful rippling of the Little Colorado River twenty feet from where he sat—all that couldn't be imported, no matter how much one was willing to pay. Nor could one buy such company. The hands working the Lazy M were genuine. Vince, Mac, Dennis, Ted, Toby, and the others, they didn't pretend to be what they weren't. Well, Toby pretended to be a ladies' man, but he hadn't yet figured out that he wasn't. Even Nathan, absent and unlamented, had been honest about what he was and what he wanted.

In fact, the only one pretending was Jackson Stone, and that little act didn't sit too well with him at the moment. He liked this place, liked this life, and somehow his fakery cheapened it. He wanted these people as his real friends. And he just plain wanted Rachel.

Sometimes the price of being Jackson Stone was too high.

CHAPTER 14

♡

AMONG THE VARIOUS pens and pastures of the Lazy M stood what the cowboys called the "big arena," where a rail fence encompassed a considerable area of packed dirt. Connected to the arena at one end was a smaller pen securely fenced with wire field-fence between the rails. Paul used the big arena to give guests horseback riding lessons. The cowboys used it occasionally to school a new horse, and twice each summer the local 4-H group gave a horse show there. On the Thursday before Greer's rodeo, Sam and Chesty were in the big arena practicing their herding demonstration. Cherie watched, standing with feet on the bottom rail and arms wound around the top.

She hated to admit that the dorky kid was good. But the kid was good, and so was his dog. Sheep were dunderheads, and persuading them to do anything wasn't easy, as Cherie had learned when she had tried her hand at the job. She'd gotten in Chesty's way and in the sheep's way, and finally the stupid woolly beasts had mobbed her, knocking her on her butt in the dirt. The sheep and Chesty had regarded her with the snide sympathy reserved for losers.

So she really did have to give Sam credit. He made the job look easy as he and Chesty moved the woollies in a predetermined path around orange plastic cones and through a series of gates and chutes that were set out in the arena for that purpose.

After successfully completing the course for the third time, Sam trotted over to the fence with Chesty at his heels. "How'd it look?" he asked Cherie.

"Sweet. But you'd better be careful."

"Why?"

"People are going to think Chesty's smarter than you are."

Sam grinned. "Chesty thinks so, too."

"It looked good." Cherie didn't mind giving him a little encouragement. He was a dweeb, but he wasn't a total loser. "Everybody's going to be impressed."

"You really think?"

"Well, sure. I mean, look who's going to be in the audience. These are *not* people from, like, L.A. or New York City, you know. These are hicks. They should think a bunch of smelly sheep running around plastic traffic cones is totally awesome."

Sam squinted at her as he always did when he didn't quite catch the subtle edge of her comments.

"It's cool," she assured him in a weary voice.

But Sam's attention had shifted from Cherie. "That's Dr. Fox's truck driving in. He's come to look at Thunder's pastern." He gave the sheep an anxious glance. "Cherie, would you put them back in the pen for me? I gotta go talk to the vet."

"Me?"

"Chesty will do all the work. All you have to do is open the gate to the pen, then close it behind the sheep." He bounced on the balls of his feet with anxiety to get to his horse. "Come on! Chesty could do it all on his own if he could work the gate latch. I gotta be with Thunder when the doc looks at him. Thunder will think I've deserted him. And if I leave sheep loose in the arena, Mom will string me up. Really!"

"Oh, go on!" she told him crossly.

Chesty stood in the middle of the arena and watched Sam leave. True to the border collie code, he wasn't about to leave his charges unattended, even to follow his boy. When Sam disappeared into the barn, Chesty changed his focus to Cherie.

"If you were truly smart, you could open and close the damned gate yourself."

Chesty replied with a low woof.

"You've got answers for everything, don't you?" Reluctantly she climbed down from her perch. "If you let those ugly, smelly sheep knock me on my butt, I'm going to personally see to it that you get a poodle cut and a bow in your hair. Then let's see you look so superior." It was an empty threat, but one that made her feel better.

She waded through the sheep, who glanced at her with only mild interest. "Come on, girls. Let's get in the pen. You are all girls, right? How do you tell with sheep?"

The sheep didn't follow her. They always followed Sam like a pack of puppies, but then, Cherie had never lured them from their pasture with a bucket of Purina sheep pellets. She marched toward the gate anyway, scowling Chesty's way.

"What are you waiting for? Head 'em up, move 'em out!"

The dog did what Cherie asked. The sheep, however, liked being loose in the arena, and Chesty was working with half a team. The human half was in the barn paying attention to a horse. In spite of that, Chesty would have penned the sheep on the first try had Cherie not eeeked in alarm the first time a woolly charged her way. Her cry scattered the beasts, who bounded in all directions. Chesty gave Cherie a disgusted look.

"You're the expert," she grumbled. "You get them back."

On the second attempt, the sheep headed peacefully back to captivity, but Cherie failed to open the gate in time. The latch stuck. She was still wrestling with it when a herd of anxious woollies arrived, butting her in the backside, pressing against her legs, stomping on her feet with sharp little hooves. Fifteen feet away, Chesty crouched, holding the sheep with a stare that promised instant retribution to any that made a break for freedom.

"Wait a minute! Wait a minute! Ouch! Quit!"

A particularly nervous old ewe panicked and fled. This stringy old girl didn't care about border collie retribution, and she nearly ran the dog over. Chesty's startled snarl goaded her into great leaping bounds of panic. The rest of the herd followed suit, taking advantage of the dog's distraction to break free.

"Man oh man!" Cherie wailed. "I thought you were supposed to be good!"

With an embarrassed glance at Cherie, Chesty took off like black-and-white lightning to round up his charges. Already in a dither, the sheep charged for the pen as if it were their only safe shelter against ravenous wolves.

Unfortunately, Cherie hadn't learned the trick of standing behind the gate for protection. The sheep mowed her down as they crowded into the enclosure. As a panting Chesty crouched threateningly, keeping the sheep penned, Cherie just barely had the presence of mind to reach out from her spot in the mud to swing the gate shut. Crawling on all fours to the gatepost, she pulled herself up—trying to ignore the sucking sound as the mud reluctantly released her—and closed the latch.

"Oh, sure! You can do it on your own! World's greatest sheep dog? I don't think! A poodle could have done a better job!"

Chesty gave a bark of protest, which startled Cherie right off balance and landed her once again in the mud. The string of words that resulted were not really fit for a teenager. And to make things worse, someone was leaning on the fence, a witness to her humiliation. Wiping the mud from her eyes, Cherie saw that it was Rachel. She looked ready to laugh.

Suddenly everything was just too much—staying on this stupid ranch, eating food cooked by someone who had never heard of low fat, much less nouvelle cuisine. Doing stupid housework, putting up with a stupid eleven-year-old with a stupid smart-ass dog. No movies, no television, no restaurants, no malls, no friends. And she couldn't do anything right. Stupid old Moira was never satisfied with her sweeping and dusting. Terri laughed at her clothes—as if that loser had any fashion sense! Sam called her a creep and said she was weird. Toby said she was just a kid. Her dad still hadn't forgiven her for the Jimmy Toledo thing, and he would probably never let her go with Deanna to Europe. And now she got mowed down by a herd of stupid sheep. She was thirteen years old, and likely she was never ever going to have sex, get a driver's license, or wear anything bigger than an A-cup bra, because she was going to kill herself before she ever made it to fourteen! Then everyone would be sorry!

Cherie hadn't realized that she was babbling her complaints aloud until Rachel squatted down beside her.

"Cherie, take it easy. You're going to get through this and back to your normal life before you know it."

"My normal life sucks," Cherie growled. She was not in the mood to be comforted.

"Well, join the crowd. Everybody's life sucks to a certain extent."

That took her by surprise. What kind of comfort was that?

"And things always suck a lot more when you're thirteen. When a girl is thirteen, Mother Nature tests her to see just how much she can take. Then, when you've passed the test, she starts to let up a bit."

"Really?"

"That's the way it works. Boys don't get tested, because Mother Nature already knows they can't pass."

"She's got that right!" A laugh escaped her, but not for long. She wasn't going to be talked out of a sulk that easily.

Rachel stood up, smiling at Cherie's abrupt about-face. "Don't glare like that," she advised. "It makes you look as old as I am."

That was pretty old. The glare faltered. "I have a right to be mad. I'm covered with muck because of that stupid dog. He did it deliberately."

"Sometimes Chesty has a weird sense of humor. Besides, there seems to be an epidemic of people landing on their butts lately."

"Sam thinks his stupid old dog is perfect," Cherie griped.

"Nobody's perfect. Not me, not you, not Sam, not Chesty. Though Chesty's pretty close." She offered a hand up. "Come on, or that mud's going to set like concrete. Wait a few minutes and we'll have to crack you out with a chisel."

Cherie smiled before she caught herself. She did appreciate Rachel not fussing. If Cherie's mother could see her, the hysterics would have been earthshaking. "This muck smells like sheep pee," she complained.

"Probably because sheep pee is the liquid component."

Cherie groaned and glared anew at Chesty. "Next time you and Sam can do without my help, you mangy mutt."

She took Rachel's hand and pulled herself up. The mud released her with a sucking sound.

"We need to get you cleaned up," Rachel said.

"Before my dad sees me. He'll laugh like a jackass. My dad sometimes has a weird sense of humor, too."

"I've noticed that," Rachel said wryly.

The cowgirl sounded as though she liked a certain amount of weirdness, though, Cherie noted. Right now, she ached too much to think about her dad and Rachel. "Man, I wish the cabin had a tub. I'd kill for a bath, and bath oil, and a big, fluffy towel." Limping dramatically toward the fence, she groaned again.

"For a price," Rachel said slyly, "I might be able to arrange for that tub with steaming water and bath oil. Even the big fluffy towel."

Cherie's brows snapped together in suspicion. "What price?"

"A smile?"

Lame. But what could one expect from someone who lived out in the sticks? For a hot bath, Cherie could wrestle her mouth into a smile.

"Not a grimace. A smile. Big one. Lots of teeth."

Cherie tried again, with more success.

"Doesn't that make you feel better?" Rachel cajoled.

It did, actually, though Cherie wasn't about to admit it. There was nothing worse than having some bit of cheerfulness come along to spoil a perfectly good funk.

Rachel picked up Cherie's muddy clothing from where the girl had thrown it on the bedroom floor. From the bathroom came the sounds of happy bathing—splashing, giggling, and an occasional snatch of song. Cherie had a pretty singing voice and an infectious laugh. Sometimes liking the kid was hard, but not liking her was harder. Rachel remembered being thirteen—hormones running wild, puberty taking its toll, childish cuteness transformed to humiliating gawkiness. She had sulked the entire year, Rachel remembered, and much of year fourteen as well. Nothing had pleased her. She'd hated her hair, her skin, her figure, her parents, her school, and her life.

How much harder must it be for Cherie, who dwelt in the shadow of beautiful and famous parents, who spent her days in a segment of society where drugs, promiscuity, and self-indulgence were the norm? Even adults had trouble avoiding the maw of that maelstrom. What chance had a child, even a child with a father like Jackson, who seemed determined to defend his daughter from any and all comers?

Rachel smiled at the thought of Jackson. He was a good father, a good man.

She knew stereotypes were the lazy man's effortless characterization, and the modern world, including herself, depended upon them far too much. But Jackson wasn't anyone's image of a big movie star. He wasn't really temperamental, egotistical, self-indulgent, demanding, or anything else that supposedly came with stardom. Not that he didn't sport his share of faults. The man was stubborn, proud, and sneaky. Getting Mrs. Dobson to do most of the morning chores had been a prime bit of sneakiness if Rachel had ever seen one, despite Alice's delight in reliving her girlhood farm experience.

Her train of thought derailed when Cherie opened the bathroom door and emerged in billows of steam, a towel her only garment. "I just thought of something!" she told Rachel, big-eyed. "I don't have any clothes! Even in the cabin. I was going to do laundry tonight."

Rachel measured Cherie with her eyes. "I think my stuff will fit you pretty well. It'll be a bit big, maybe, but it will cover what needs covering."

Soon Cherie was dressed in clean blue jeans and a T-shirt declaring her to be the property of the Phoenix Suns. The jeans were too long, but they fixed that by turning up the cuffs.

"Wow! Retro!" Cherie said when she examined herself in the mirror. "Totally big, though."

"News for you, girl. Jeans aren't supposed to be a second skin. That's how they're supposed to fit."

"No way. Not unless you're totally over the hill. Like, maybe, twenty-five."

Rachel laughed. "I'm totally over that hill, that's for sure. But really, Cherie, doesn't it feel good to be able to move around without getting pinched eight ways from Thursday?"

Cherie wriggled experimentally. "Yeah. It does. But man oh man, the guys wouldn't even look at me if I wore stuff like this to school or to the mall."

"Someday you're going to want guys to admire you for something other than your shrink-wrapped jeans and padded boobs."

Cherie looked down, sheepishly regarding the nearly flat plain of her cotton T-shirt. Rachel patted her shoulder comfortingly. "Sweetie, soon you won't need to pad. Believe me, you should appreciate that young, unencumbered body while you still have it." She smiled as Cherie examined herself critically in the mirror. "You know, without all the junk on your face, you truly are cute."

Cherie sighed. "Cute is definitely not the look I'm going for."

"Dracula is?"

The girl rolled her eyes. "Black is very in."

Rachel suffered a sudden urge to show Cherie that cute wasn't all that bad for a thirteen-year-old. When she had been thirteen, cute hadn't been an option. She'd had braces and pimples. For Cherie to possess such potential and throw it away on the Morticia look seemed such a shame.

"Let me do your hair and face," she suggested. "And I challenge you to not like the results."

Cherie scowled suspiciously. "What're you, some beauty school dropout?"

"Worse. I always wanted a daughter. Sam won't let me do his hair and makeup."

Cherie giggled. "Sam in drag! I love it."

"You," Rachel told her with a grimace, "are way too old for your age."

"That's what my dad says." She gave Rachel a measuring look. "Okay, here's the deal. You do me, if I do you."

"Me?" Rachel pictured spiked hair and black eye shadow.

"You could use a few hair care and makeup tips, you know."

The girl looked so serious that Rachel couldn't resist. "Okay. It's a deal." She figured that no matter how bad the results, makeup washed off easily enough.

"And you have to go to dinner like I fix you."

That was asking a lot. "Dinner in the kitchen."

"Dinner in the Chuckwagon."

Rachel sighed. Cherie smiled triumphantly.

They went to work. Rachel gave Cherie's hair another shampooing. All the gunk the girl put in it wouldn't come out in just one wash. Bent over with her head in the bathtub, Cherie complained loudly. "Don't scrub so hard! I'm going to have a bloody scalp!"

"You're going to have a clean scalp. The basis of beauty is cleanliness."

"Ouch! What fortune cookie taught you that!"

"You're going to be cute. Just you wait."

Cherie's response sounded very like a growl.

Once the hair was squeaky clean, Rachel slathered it with conditioner and rinsed. When she finally wrapped a towel around the girl's wet head, Cherie didn't complain. She just scowled.

Next came just a touch of styling gel.

"Is that all you're going to use?" Cherie asked.

"We are not doing spikes here."

"I like spikes."

"You'll like this better."

"Wanna bet?"

Rachel turned on the blow dryer to drown out the rest of Cherie's objections. The hair was short, so styling didn't take long. Rachel worked it into a soft, full 'do fringed around the ears. It moved silkily with every movement of Cherie's head, flattering, natural, youthful, yet feminine.

"Like it?" Rachel asked hopefully.

Cherie looked in the mirror and crossed her eyes. "I look like Mary Poppins."

"You do not. You look wonderful. Not that there's anything wrong with Mary Poppins."

"Only you would say that."

"What color is your hair really?"

"Like my dad's. Boring brown."

"Nothing about your dad is boring," Rachel said carelessly, then realized just how those words sounded.

Cherie smiled craftily into the mirror. "That's okay, Rachel. I know you lust after him."

Rachel exhaled a frustrated huff. "You really are way too old for your age. And for your information, there is a big difference between lust and . . . and . . ."

"Love?" Cherie asked with a grin.

"High regard. Respect. Fondness."

"Yeah, right. All that." She grimaced. "What about makeup? You're not going to make me go barefaced, are you? Gross."

Rachel smiled tolerantly. "I wouldn't make you do that. Wrinkled and ancient as you are, you wouldn't want to show your bare face in public, would you?"

Cherie rolled her eyes. "You are so not funny."

Rachel did have makeup, though she seldom wore it. And she knew how to apply it. Up until a few years ago, she had been a bank vice president in Chandler, and bank vice presidents do not show up for work *au naturel*. For Cherie she stuck to the minimum. No foundation. That glowing youthful skin didn't need Revlon or Max Factor to hide anything. Just a touch of mauve eye shading brought out the color of her eyes. A little subtle blush contoured her cheekbones, and a dusting of loose transparent powder gave her a finished look. Add tinted lip gloss, and the job was finished.

Rachel stood back and regarded her masterpiece with satisfaction. "Ta-dah!" she proclaimed. "You're cute, and beautiful, too."

Cherie gazed at herself in the mirror, smiled experimentally, frowned, grimaced, and gave herself an arch, superior look—trying out every expression she could think of.

"Well?" Rachel prompted.

"It's different."

"When you go downstairs, you'll see everyone's face light up when they look at you."

"I really have to go downstairs like this, huh?"

"Yes."

"I feel naked."

"That's because you're letting the real, beautiful you show through."

Cherie sighed. "Rachel, you're too weird. But for an older woman, I guess you're okay. My dad could do worse."

Rachel's surprise showed, and Cherie smiled. "So now"—she got up and gestured for Rachel to sit in the hot seat—"we're going to make you into something my dad can't resist."

"Now, Cherie. Your father and I are not . . . not . . ." She was going to say "an item," but the lie stuck in her throat. She didn't know what she and Jackson Stone were. They made glorious love. They bantered, teased, and flirted. They talked about their kids, Jackson's boat, politics, falling off horses, films, the ranch, and the upcoming Greer rodeo. One thing they didn't talk about was the future, because of course there was no future for them. How could there be, with Jackson wedded to Hollywood and Rachel longing for the simple life?

But how did one explain that to a thirteen-year-old child, even a child as worldly as Cherie?

"I like that," Cherie said. "You can't tell a lie. Almost everybody lies, you know. Now sit down—no, wait, don't! I had to endure torture by shampoo, and so do you!"

Rachel let Cherie have her fun. She had agreed, after all, though she was sure to regret it. To make things worse, Karen Spangler walked into her bedroom just as Cherie had finished scrubbing her scalp raw and getting liberal amounts of soap in her eyes.

"Hi, Karen," said Cherie, not a bit diffident. "We're doing makeovers."

"You look absolutely great!" Karen told the kid.

"You think so? I haven't decided."

"I think so."

"I'm going to give Rachel some style. Want to watch?"

Karen smiled wickedly. "Wouldn't miss it. I came for dinner. Didn't know I was going to get a show, too. A comedy, no less."

Rachel sent Karen a warning glare as Cherie pushed her down into the chair in front of the mirror. "Don't get sassy, my friend, or Cherie will do you, too."

"Be quiet," Cherie warned Rachel. "You're lucky. One of my friends' moms is a makeup artist at Paramount. I'm almost a professional. Where do you keep your scissors?"

"Scissors?" Rachel suffered a twinge of panic.

"You need a serious new 'do."

"I didn't agree to let you cut my hair!"

Karen laughed. "Oh, be a sport, Rachel. I'll bet she does a great job." To Cherie she confided, "I've been trying to get her to cut that mop for years."

So out came the scissors. Rachel told herself that she was insane for allowing a thirteen-year-old anywhere near her hair. Not that it was exactly a crowning glory, but when Cherie finished, Rachel would most probably look like an overage rocker. "Don't you dare give me spikes!"

"I won't give you spikes."

In the mirror, Rachel watched Cherie comb the wet snarls. Was that a wink the little hellion gave Karen? She knew and feared that wicked grin of Karen's. Those two were about the same age, despite the nearly twenty years separating them.

"No back-combing. I hate that. And don't clot it up with gel."

Cherie sighed with long-suffering patience. "Did I bug you when you were doing mine?"

"Yes."

"Well, I had reason to bug you. Whatever I do to you, it'll be an improvement."

Karen giggled. "Well, it would have to be, wouldn't it?"

"Karen," Rachel said sweetly, "how many customers do I send to your restaurant every summer?"

Karen feigned contrition. "See how she is? Guess I'd better behave."

The scissors worked diligently at the uneven ends of Rachel's wet corkscrew curls, and out of the corner of her eyes she saw masses of dark hair fall to the floor. Rachel closed her eyes. Better not to look. After an eternity listening to the ominous *snip-snip* and her tormentors' barbed quips, Rachel heard nothing but silence. She opened her eyes to see considerably shorter hair curling just past her shoulders.

"Blow dryer," Cherie declared.

"Definitely!" Karen seconded. "And a curler. Rachel, I know you have a curling iron, even though you never use it. Where is it?"

"My hair is too curly as it is!"

"Where is it, girl? Ve haf vays uf making you talk."

"Sheesh! Beneath the sink."

When they were finished, Rachel's shining dark hair curled in graceful layers around her face, neck, and shoulders. The effect, Rachel had to admit, was quite pretty. But it certainly didn't look like her.

"Now to makeup," Cherie declared happily, examining the scant supplies that Rachel had used on her. "She must have more than this around here."

Rachel covered her face with her hands. What a punishment for plucking the girl out of the mud!

Thirty minutes later, Cherie was gone, having declared that she was going to try out her new "babyface" on the guests. Rachel, still stunned by the stranger who stared at her out of the mirror, scarcely noticed the girl leave.

When the door closed behind Cherie, Karen chuckled. "The kid's pretty good. She can do my hair anytime."

"The hair is okay," Rachel admitted. "But if I smile, my face is going to crack."

Karen dabbed at a bit of mascara that had flaked onto Rachel's cheek. "She did sort of lay it on with a trowel. But hey! If you wanted to pose for *Streetwalker Weekly,* this look would be just the thing!"

"You're not helping."

"And you did promise the kid that you'd show off her work at dinner, right?" Karen snickered.

"You're not helping at all."

"Jackson Stone is going to love it."

Rachel nearly choked.

Karen gloated. "Oh, come on! He might be able to fool your city slickers, but an Arizona cowgirl knows bullshit when she sees it. You were going to tell me, right?"

"After he was gone!"

"I love it! My best friend is sleeping with a movie star! You are sleeping with him, right? At the barn dance I gave him my seal of approval."

"So I heard."

"He used me as a reference? Wonderful. Imagine me being a reference in romance for Jackson Stone!"

"Did it ever occur to you to just leave my love life up to me?"

"Your nonexistent love life, you mean?" Karen smiled innocently. "Of course I can't leave it up to you. What are friends for? He was obviously smitten, and you were being your usual starchy self, about to miss out on a great romantic adventure."

"Cripes!" Rachel buried her face in her hands. This day was getting worse and worse.

Dinner wasn't as bad as it could have been. Karen helped Rachel soften the makeup job a bit—not really enough to be technically breaking her promise to Cherie, but enough not to totally raise guest eyebrows. Cherie, who was helping Moira and Joanne serve, scarcely noticed. She was too busy basking in the compliments of people who had only seen her in gel-spiked hair and Death by Revlon.

It was Karen's birthday, and Rachel had invited her to the Lazy M for the occasion. Joanne had baked a spectacular cake—German chocolate with dark chocolate icing—and had kindly left off the candles.

"There are too many these days to blow out, anyway," Karen complained. "And all that wax ruins the icing."

A fiftyish accountant from Seattle advised her, "Once you're past thirty, it's easier to represent the decades by a single candle."

"Past thirty?" Karen gasped. "Oh no no! We stopped counting long before then!"

The whole table laughed. Rachel laughed along with them. Though she didn't always join the guests for meals in the Chuckwagon, she generally enjoyed them. She occasionally daydreamed about having the Lazy M all to herself, but at moments like these, she knew she would miss the company.

In spite of a certain awkwardness over the new hair and the plastered face, Rachel had fun. But something was missing. Jackson was not there. He had eaten with the hands, who were served at an earlier sitting. And while Rachel was grateful for not having to bear his scrutiny of "the new Rachel," a small part of her felt less than complete without those green eyes watching her, that mouth curling into a wicked grin. She hadn't seen him all day, and after spending almost the entire day before trading barbs with him at the fishing picnic, she missed him to an alarming degree.

Soon Jackson Stone would be back where he belonged—in

the limelight. And Rachel Marsh would still be where she belonged—at the Lazy M, enjoying a quiet winter preparing for the next tourist season. She was a fool to let her heart attach itself to a man who would never be a real part of her life. Cripes! She was even becoming fond of his crazy daughter. Why else would she be sitting at dinner looking like an Avon lady gone wild?

Karen didn't stay long after dinner, only long enough for a glass of wine in the ranch house kitchen and another round of teasing about Jackson Stone. Halfway through the wine, Sam and Cherie came in to wheedle another night's stay in the motor home. Sam had motor home fever; he'd decided the mansion on wheels was much more fun for sleep-outs than a flimsy tent.

"You'll have to ask Cherie's father," Rachel temporized.

"He said it was okay," Cherie told her. "He's in the shower, complaining about a bunch of hay bales."

"Can we, huh?" Sam pleaded.

"No fire or marshmallows this time," Rachel said.

"That's okay." Sam led the way toward the door. "We can watch *X-Men* on the video."

"That is a really boring movie," Cherie complained. "Besides, we can get the *Friends* festival on the satellite dish. That's totally better."

They went out arguing, but Cherie looked back over her shoulder and winked at Rachel. "You look hot," she said with a grin.

"She's corrupting both Sam and me," Rachel observed wryly.

"You like her," Karen said.

"I'm a sucker for kids."

"Good thing, since the hunky Jackson has such a difficult one."

Rachel gave her a look. Karen merely grinned and slugged down the rest of her wine. "I'm leaving. Got to set up for breakfast tomorrow." She gave Rachel a wink similar to Cherie's. "Be careful, girl. Practice safe sex."

Rachel threw a wadded-up napkin at her as she ducked out the doorway.

With Karen gone, Rachel wasted no time retreating to her room to peel off what felt like a rubber mask covering her face. During her bank days, she had spent twenty minutes every morning applying just the sort of stuff that now felt so foreign. She hadn't gone to the extremes that Cherie favored, but still, she had used foundation, eye shadow, mascara, blush—the whole nine yards. A few years of freedom had spoiled her. Men, she reflected as she searched for a jar of makeup remover, were totally spoiled. You wouldn't catch a man plastering his face with goo just to conform to *Cosmopolitan*'s concept of elegance.

She finally unearthed an old jar of facial cleanser at the back of a bathroom drawer. The stuff was so old that the outer edges had dried, cracked, and turned brown. She set the jar on the bathroom counter and stared at herself in the mirror.

Actually, Cherie hadn't done that bad a job. Her head felt lighter with a few inches of hair trimmed off, and the layering gave the once unruly mane more discipline and form. The curling iron had tamed her riotous curls into graceful waves. Not bad. The makeup job, on the other hand . . . Well, it was different. She batted mascara-thickened lashes. They looked long enough to create a breeze. The eye shadow made her eyes look huge and dramatic, and the blush actually gave her cheekbones.

The women who hobnobbed with Jackson Stone were probably done up far fancier than this, however, if one believed magazine interviews and the "candid" shots appearing in the papers.

"Well," she told Fang the cat, who watched contemptuously from the bed, "that's their problem, isn't it?"

Fang merely yawned.

A soft knock sounded at the door. "Rachel?" Jackson announced. "It's me."

Rachel looked at her mirror image in wide-eyed panic. She contemplated throwing a towel over her head, or perhaps just pretending not to be there. But she did want to see him. How she wanted to see him!

"Rachel? Are you there?"

"I . . . yes. I'm coming."

Her sense of humor kicked in as she headed for the door. Why not give the guy a good laugh? It was the least she could do.

CHAPTER 15

♡

HE DIDN'T LAUGH—quite. But almost. His eyes widened slightly and one side of his mouth twitched. "Ah," he said.

"Your daughter," Rachel informed him. She certainly wasn't going to accept the blame for this.

"Was this some kind of female bonding thing?"

"It's a long story. Have you seen her?"

"I almost didn't recognize her. So it was you who wrought the miracle."

"A temporary miracle, I'm sure."

"And she . . ." His hand waved vaguely toward her face. "I really like the hair."

"Actually, she didn't do a half-bad job."

"And the . . . the face, well, it's a real different look for you."

She smiled. "The soul of tact. I was just about to start peeling off the layers of goo. Come in, if you want."

He did, but stiffly. "Joanne said you might have some liniment. I must have unloaded a hundred hay bales today. Then Mac had us unloading poles to replace some of the rotten stuff in the arena. I thought a shower would loosen up the kinks, but it didn't."

Rachel grimaced in sympathy. "Jackson, why don't you give this up? You've proven your point, don't you think?"

He shrugged. "I'm actually getting to like it."

"And I actually don't believe you. You are stubborn as a mule."

"Me? Stubborn?"

She just shook her head and went looking for the liniment. Unlike the makeup remover, a jar of A-1 Muscle-Rub, guaranteed not to sting, stain, or cause a rash, occupied a prominent spot in the medicine cabinet. "A bath in Epsom Salt might help."

His slow smile was warmer than called for by the mention of Epsom Salt. "Are you offering your tub?"

"Only if you scrub out the ring that Cherie left."

He did, then scrubbed it yet again after he'd climbed out and donned Rachel's terry-cloth bathrobe, whose sleeves reached just below his elbows. The hem fell short of his knees.

"That's lovely on you," she teased, but thought with a smile that any man who scrubbed the tub after a bath was worth his weight in gold. Some things were more important than looks and money.

He looked down at the robe. "I think it works. Don't you?"

She held up the jar of liniment. "If you want to turn around and drop it, I'll do the honors."

"First"—he took her by the shoulders and turned her toward a mirror—"we clean you up."

"I cleaned up."

"You missed at least half a dozen places and probably one whole layer. I'm an expert at taking off makeup." He pushed her down into a chair and tilted her face up and back. "Trust me."

After pinning a towel around her hair, he greased her face with the makeup remover. Then her throat. She sighed in deep relaxation as his hands massaged tenderly—face, throat, collarbone, down the sternum, and . . .

"I don't have makeup down there," she said in a lazy voice.

"I know." His voice had grown husky. "But what you do have down there is pretty interesting."

"You're bad," she teased.

He put his lips close to her ear and whispered, "A while back you thought I was good."

He was good, in so many ways. So many, many ways. The magic he worked was lovely and wicked. She should stop him,

Rachel thought vaguely, but she didn't. Finally, he used a warm washrag to wipe her free of grease, unwound the towel from her head, and fluffed her hair with his fingers.

"You'll never starve," she assured him. "If you ever get tired of the movie business, you could get a job in a spa giving facials."

"I also give a mean massage. Care to try one?"

A wave of delicious lassitude washed over her at the very thought. No woman in her right mind would turn down such an offer. However . . .

She got up from the chair and waved the tube of liniment in front of his face. "You're the one with sore muscles, remember?"

He stretched those wonderful broad shoulders, grimacing. "Yeah." He looked at the liniment, then at her, his eyes warming with a wicked glint. "Can you think of anything creative to do with liniment?"

She gave him a sizzling smile. "We'll just have to see, won't we?"

As a matter of fact, they both got very creative. By the time Jackson had gotten his "massage," the liniment tube was empty, the bedsheets were a greasy mess, and so were they—greasy, tired, and sated. Jackson looked down at her from his superior position and grinned.

"It's lucky we both took our clothes off."

"Yes, indeed." She laughed. "For several reasons."

"That was quite a massage."

"Do you feel better now?"

"You have no idea how much better." He rolled off her, bringing her with him so that she ended up looking down at him. His hands stroked her back and came to rest possessively on her backside. "You feel like a greased pig."

"A very romantic thing to say!"

"That's why I'm a big-ticket item in Hollywood."

Her nose twitched. "Unfortunately, I smell like a greased pig, too. You're no better."

"There is sort of a locker room atmosphere in here." He chuckled.

"It is strong, isn't it? What do they use in this stuff, anyway?"

"I don't know, but from now on, that smell is going to bring some pretty vivid images to my mind." One hand moved, teasing her with a graphic reminder of at least one of those images. She exhaled a startled breath and dropped her head to his shoulder. "Yes," she breathed. "There was that."

He kissed the top of her head. "That bathtub of yours has room enough for two, don't you think?"

"Only if the two get really cozy."

"We could manage that."

They did, sitting in a tangle of feet, legs, and other parts, hot sudsy water up to their necks, smiling at each other through clouds of steam. Rachel was perfectly content to lean back, close her eyes, and enjoy complete absorption in the moment.

"This hits the spot," Jackson rumbled lazily. "Do you suppose I could get away with spending the night here without alerting the troops?"

"Mmmmm." Rachel savored the picture of a whole night lying in Jackson's arms. "I think I've stopped caring."

He looked up in surprise.

She poked him in the chest with her toe. "Blockhead. I haven't stopped caring about you. Just about your stupid secret, our secret—anybody's secret. I've always hated secrets." She opened her eyes enough to see his lazy, satisfied smile.

"Come here, gorgeous." He reached out and pulled her toward him, creating a tidal wave that slopped over the edge of the old-fashioned claw-foot tub.

"We're making a mess!"

"Then quit struggling, and we'll stop making a mess."

She obeyed, coming to rest astride his lap with their faces close enough for him to kiss her, which he did. "You're totally spoiled," she complained with a smile.

"And you're totally beautiful."

"Oh, right. You've been in the sticks too long, Jackson Stone. Of course I look good next to a horse or a cow, but hold me up beside your other ladies and you'll be singing a different tune."

He chuckled. "My other ladies?"

"Oh, yes. You have quite a rep as a Don Juan."

He tightened his arms, bringing her closer. Rachel couldn't help but savor the slippery, sensuous feel of skin on skin, her breasts brushing over the hair of his chest. Damn the man for making her want something she couldn't have, at least not forever.

"Don Juan, hm?" He sighed dramatically. "Would you believe me if I told you that I was filling a lonely life with shallow, meaningless relationships?"

She laughed, then kissed him lightly on the mouth. "No."

"No?"

"You heard me."

"Then, how about this? I've just been waiting for a sterling woman like Rachel Marsh to lure me into domesticity."

She kissed him again. "No."

Another wave slopped over the side when he dumped her off his lap and caged her in his arms against the end of the tub. "You are one tough customer, Rachel Marsh."

"The men do call me Harsh Marsh, you know."

"I'm beginning to see why. You don't think I'd make some lucky woman a fine catch?"

"I suppose that depends upon what she wanted to catch. You are sort of . . . public property, you know. And a man like you, surrounded—admit it—by certifiably gorgeous, sophisticated, talented friends and lovers is not going to easily settle for something rather ordinary. Someone used to seven-layer double chocolate cake is not going to be content very long with vanilla pudding."

He laughed at that. "You think of yourself as vanilla pudding?"

"Maybe with sprinkles or brown sugar or something."

He pushed himself back to his own end of the tub and regarded her with warm eyes. She steeled herself. One of them had to be sensible, to be strong enough not to believe the seductive fantasy.

"You are pretty insane, you know that?" he asked cheerfully.

"Certainly not. You're the one who doesn't understand. You see, Jackson, I rather like being vanilla pudding, with or without sprinkles."

"You definitely have sprinkles," he told her with a grin.

She tried to look stern. "You're being obtuse."

"No," he insisted. "You're buying into the fame and glamour thing. It's all bull, you know. Just as superficial as that stuff we wiped off your face." One corner of his mouth lifted in a wry smile. "And if you think I spend my time surrounded by beauty, talent, and sophistication, then you've never worked in the Industry."

Rachel sighed and slipped deeper into the warm water, which had shallowed up quite a bit from being dumped overboard. She felt herself slipping into more than deep water. She didn't know exactly where Jackson was going, but he almost sounded serious—about her, about their relationship. Crazy, she told herself. Impossibly crazy. She shouldn't listen. She should just close her eyes, shut her ears, and enjoy the contentment of this almost perfect moment.

But, of course, she couldn't do that. Rachel made a habit of confronting issues head-up and face-on. It was a hard habit to break.

"Jackson?"

His foot stroked her hip, making confrontation more difficult. "Hm?"

"What exactly are we arguing about?"

"We're not arguing. We're discussing."

"Don't evade, cowboy. What is the central question here?"

He sighed, no longer joking. "There is no question. There's a . . . let's say an epiphany, on my part. Cherie and I have to leave in a week or so, and I've come to realize that I don't want to leave. It's not that I don't want to go back home, back to work, back to my life, but . . ."

She finished for him. "But the summer fling ends."

He didn't look pleased. "You don't mince words."

"I believe in facing reality."

"Reality," he said firmly, "is that I don't think what we have is a fling. It shouldn't be just a fling. Sweetheart, I know about reality just about as well as anyone does, and I'm not trying to sell you on happily ever after or our names signed on the dotted line. But couldn't we try at least for semi–happily ever after?"

She looked at him with wide eyes, not knowing what to say.

"I love you, Rachel. You've got to know that. And you love me, too. You can't hide anything, you know. You're as transparent as a piece of glass."

She felt exposed by far more than the lack of clothing. "I do love you," she admitted. "If someone can learn to love someone else in such a short time."

"Sometimes good things happen in the blink of an eye, just like bad things. We have to endure the bad things, so why not enjoy the good ones while they last? If we don't take the risk and grab them, we could miss something wonderful."

This whole conversation was insane. In her world, if people fell in love, they married and started a life together, making adjustments to make that life possible. They were serious about family and community, about commitment and growing old together. Could she settle for semi–happily ever after, as he put it? "Jackson, what are you leading up to with this? What do you want?"

For a few heartbeats he didn't answer. He looked as if he might like to beat his head against the lip of the tub—frustration, chagrin, confusion, even anger chasing across his face in rapid succession.

"What do I want?" he repeated, then sighed, seeming to deflate as he sank more deeply into the water. "Good question. I don't know what I want. No, I do know what I want. Right now I want you, for as long as I can have you. I want you to think about me as more than an inept temporary cowboy who limped into your life one day and back out again a few weeks later. I want more time, to not just discard a good thing when it's barely beginning. We are a good thing, Rachel."

Her heart gave a thump. She couldn't imagine anything more ridiculous, or more seductive.

"As for me, I'm getting wrinkled before my time, and the

water's getting cold, so . . ." Untouched by modesty, he hefted himself out of the tub. Water ran in rivulets that outlined muscle and sinew and a natural, God-given masculinity that took her breath clean away. But it was the man who drew her more than the body, the man that shone from those famous green eyes and nestled in the captivating smile. His public didn't really know the man, but Rachel Marsh did. Or so she thought.

She almost feared to think on his words. They were too different, too stubborn, too entrenched in their own lives to have a real relationship. Yet the thought of losing him sliced her heart, especially now that the possibility of somehow keeping him—for a while at least—dangled tantalizingly before her eyes.

He wrapped a towel around his middle and regarded her with a warm sizzle in his eyes. "I think it's your turn for a massage." With a wink, he turned and went into the bedroom. "See you in bed."

Josh Digby sat in his office tapping a pencil against the edge of his desk in bored contemplation. He considered persistence to be one of his virtues. That and ambition made him a true bloodhound of a reporter. If any story could be tracked down, Josh Digby could do it. If any truth needed ferreting out, Josh Digby was your man. And if the truth needed a little embellishment to make it interesting, no one was better at subtle, or in some cases blatant, creativity.

Still, even Josh had his limits, and sadly enough, he had reached those limits on this latest Jackson Stone incident. The story was all but dead. Jackson and Cherie were holed up heaven only knew where. Well, Josh Digby knew where, actually. At least he strongly suspected. But he didn't have enough evidence to convince his boss. The boss man didn't think one e-mail query plus a reporter's gut instinct justified the expense of a plane ticket.

Nope, Josh thought ruefully. Time to move on. There was that Congressman caught cross-dressing in San Francisco. He ought to pursue that. Everyone else was. And the medium who claimed two days ago that he actually talked to God. That was worth some attention. And of course Oprah's latest heartache. He might get some mileage out of that.

But he preferred to stick with Jackson Stone. Digby was a Stone specialist. He sort of admired the guy, liked most of his movies, and thought the star was probably a pretty decent guy, overall. Not that Josh cut him any slack. He was a professional, after all. As far as Josh was concerned, celebs were the meat and he was the grinder. The resulting hamburger paid the bills. But curiosity about what made Stone tick made pursuing that particular celeb less boring than harassing others.

Still, this time the story wasn't going to work. Too bad. Good try, Josh told himself. Maybe he could get a line on that flying saucer supposedly harassing ranchers in Wyoming. Chasing aliens might be easier than chasing a Hollywood icon.

Josh shook his head ruefully. He had to get a real job one of these days—before he started believing his own copy.

Just then the phone rang.

"Yeah?" He answered it laconically, but he came to attention when he heard the voice on the other end. "Jake! How are you, buddy?"

Jake Carver was Melanie Carr's publicist. He and Josh had a good deal going between them. Josh gave Melanie good coverage in the *Star*—lots of front-page stuff, photos that made her look good, a push for her films when they came out—and Jake fed Josh tidbits of information when he had them. Those tidbits had led to a good story more than once.

Josh waited patiently through the preliminaries—weather, families, the sad state of the new movie releases—before getting down to business. "What's up, Jake? You got something for me?" He listened avidly. "A helicopter, eh? Does she usually tell you where she'll be?" He nodded. "Uh-huh. Sounds like something's going on. I'll look into it. I owe you, buddy."

He smirked in triumph as he hung up the phone. Melanie Carr had chartered a helicopter in a great hurry, and she wouldn't give her publicist a specific destination. The wilds of Arizona, Mel had told Jake, but refused to give him details.

Well, Josh knew right where she was going, and with this bit of information he might be able to pry a plane ticket from his tightwad boss. Deftly he flipped his pencil into the air and caught it, then sent it point first into the poster of Jackson Stone that was pinned to his cubicle partition. The pencil struck Stone in the nose.

Josh smiled. "Gotcha!"

Saturday morning graced the little town of Greer with crystal-clear air and the crisp nip of coming autumn. The town made Jackson believe he'd walked through a time warp back to the 1950s. Perhaps that was why he liked the place so much. Here, the world moved at a slower pace. A crowd was more than three people in front of the post office. Noise pollution was the natural sort—thunder rumbling during an afternoon rainstorm or squirrels scolding passersby from the branch of a tree. The most serious crime might be someone fishing without a license.

On this late August Saturday, however, people lined the streets and sat on the front porches of the general store, post office, art emporium, and Karen Spangler's Round Valley Roundup to watch the town's big doings. Roy Kimble, the owner of the local riding stable, had organized Greer Days with the help of every businessperson in town. A pancake breakfast at the old schoolhouse led off the day, followed by a parade down the town's one and only street and a rodeo of sorts in Roy Kimble's arena. This was not your standard rodeo with bucking broncs, snorting bulls, and rodeo clowns, however. The printed program boasted of pig wrestling, egg races, and a herding demonstration by Samuel Marsh and his border collie, Chesterfield. A bit more traditional were the calf roping, barrel racing, and rescue races.

All in all, Greer Days promised almost more fun than a man

could tolerate, or so Jackson thought as he lounged in a canvas chair on the Roundup's porch. Rachel had had the nerve to suggest he spend the day at the ranch, out of sight of the crowds. He would be bored, she warned. This was strictly small-town games. She still didn't understand, Jackson reflected. This place and these people didn't bore him. Small-town games didn't bore him, especially when they included Rachel.

Jackson wasn't the only spectator sitting on Karen's porch. A half a dozen people—mostly out-of-towners—sat in the chairs Karen had set in front of the tables, which had been pushed back for the occasion. She had left out a gigantic pot of coffee and Styrofoam cups before leaving to mount her horse for the parade. He hadn't known Karen had a horse, but he wasn't surprised. Everyone in this town had a horse. A horse, a fishing pole, and hiking boots were household staples.

"Howdy, there," said Molly Satler's gruff voice.

Jackson tilted back his dilapidated felt hat so he could look up at the old woman. "Howdy yourself, Aunt Molly."

When he started to get up and offer his seat, Molly waved him down. "I'm not so old that I can't get my own chair, young man." She grabbed an empty chair and set it down next to his. "A lot better sitting here in the shade drinking Karen's good coffee than riding down the street in Roy's old wagon, decked out like some Vegas showgirl."

"Vegas showgirl?" Jackson inquired as she settled into the chair.

"Roy wanted me to be grand marshal of this hoopla. Was gonna tow me down the street with that draft team of his—as if it takes two of those Percherons to haul me down the street. There ain't been a single day in my life I weighed over a hundred pounds. He was gonna dress me up in one of those fancy banners"—she swept a wrinkled hand from left shoulder to right hip—"declarin' somethin' or other. I'm too old for such nonsense, I tells him."

"Might have been fun," Jackson opined.

"More fun sittin' in the shade. How's the ankle?"

"Near perfect as an ankle can be, thanks to you. Didn't give me much trouble, to tell the truth." He pulled his hat back down to shade his eyes from the morning sun.

Old Molly gave him a sly look. "You think that hat and those whiskers are gonna keep people from knowin' who you are?"

The hand that was lifting a cup of coffee toward his mouth froze.

Molly chuckled. "Caught ya with that one, eh? Shucks, boy, I knowed all along who you was. I may be old, but I ain't blind. Just goes to prove that most folks look at something without really seeing it, but not me. When you've been around the planet as long as I have, you come to figure out that some things ain't what they claim to be." Her face creased in a smile. "Don't look so nervous there. I ain't gonna blow the whistle. Figure famous folks need to get away from themselves sometimes, just like we all do."

Jackson resumed drinking his coffee. "You're a sly old woman, Molly Satler."

"That's me."

Jackson found that he didn't care all that much if Molly "blew the whistle," as she put it. The role he played was beginning to wear.

"Though I'll admit," Molly added, "that you do look like a pretty typical no-account bum with those whiskers scraggling all over your face."

He chuckled. "Thanks, I think."

"Don't mention it. Here they come. Roy talked Charlie Swetman down at the general store into riding in his wagon and being grand marshal. Don't see that they put no stupid banner on him!"

"He doesn't have the figure for it."

She eyed him suspiciously, then grinned. "I like a man that can give some back."

"And I like a woman who can dish some out."

"That must be why you're hanging around our little Rachel. There's a gal who can dish it out by the shovelful if she has to."

"Guess I can't hide anything from you, Aunt Molly, can I?"

"Heck, no. And speak of the devil, here she comes, right behind the Springerville High marching band. You know, there's
nothing that gets the blood to thumping like a good marching
band. Or at least a loud one." She chuckled. "But you're not
paying a bit of mind to the band, are you?"

Rachel and Sam rode together, with Sam on his faithful
Thunder and Rachel on a flashy chestnut gelding belonging to
Paul. A banner draped over the chestnut's haunches boasted
the Lazy M logo and phone number. If she'd tried to put that
banner on Sally and take the mare into a parade behind a
thumping, tooting band, she would have staged a rodeo all on
her own.

Chesty trotted beside Thunder and once in a while gave the
crowd a friendly wave of his tail, but mostly his eyes fixed on
Sam. Right behind Rachel and Sam rode none other than
Cherie Stone on a little pinto mare that also belonged to Paul.
She had begged Jackson to ride in the parade with her. Jackson
had assured her that he was not about to give some horse the
chance to dump him on his butt in front of such an audience.
That's what stuntmen were paid for.

"That's your daughter, is it?" Molly asked.

"How'd you know?"

"The way you're looking at her. Besides, she looks like you.
Pretty little girl."

Jackson had no fear that anyone else would recognize
Cherie from the photos that had shown up in the news. The
new image had edged out the Addams Family look, at least for
now. Her hair blew softly in the breeze and just a touch of cosmetics added color to her face. Maybe, Jackson hoped, she
would really take the plunge and let her hair go back to its natural soft brown. But that was hoping for a lot.

"She's a good kid," he told Molly. "At least she's a good kid at
heart."

"How old?"

"Thirteen."

Molly nodded complete understanding.

The parade was short. The local 4-H had decorated a horse-drawn wagon for its members to ride in. An equine drill team from the town of McNary pranced down the road doing serpentines, pass-throughs, and crossovers. Generally speaking, the horses kept their lines straighter than Springerville's marching band, but then, they didn't have to play tubas at the same time. Most of the local businesses, including the Art Emporium, the general store, Pete's Garage and Gas Works, and a fishing resort up-valley on the Little Colorado River were represented by riders on horseback, including Karen Spangler, of course, advertising "the best home-cooking in Arizona." It was actually a poor excuse for a parade, but Jackson wouldn't have traded his canvas chair on the Roundup porch for a front-row seat at the Rose Bowl Parade. The Rose Bowl had glitter. Greer Days had heart.

What it had, Jackson admitted, was *his* heart. Without Rachel Marsh, it would have been just another small-town parade.

After the parade, Jackson gave Aunt Molly a ride in his Jeep to the arena, where a very small set of bleachers overflowed with spectators. Fortunately, Rachel and Karen had managed to snag seats. They waved to Jackson and Molly and motioned them over.

"Is there room for this old woman to sit with you?" Molly asked the girls.

"You know there is, Molly." Rachel patted the space beside her, and Karen directed Jackson to sit between her and Rachel.

"Squeeze tight," she advised him in an undertone "I'm sure you won't mind."

"What man would?"

"Keep your leers for someone who appreciates them, fella."

"You're a hard woman, Karen." Jackson wedged himself between Rachel and Karen, feeling ridiculously lighthearted. All three women knew who he was, and who he was didn't make any difference to them. None of these ladies would ever hit him up for an intro to an agent, a part in a movie, an interview for a magazine. They would never contrive to get their photo taken with him or hang on his arm just to be seen with a star.

To them he was a real person. To Rachel, he sensed, he was not only a real person, but a real problem.

Since their conversation in the tub two days before, she'd grown subdued and a bit wary. He saw his own dilemma reflected in her eyes, the frustration of wanting him, yet also wanting to keep her safe, familiar world intact. He read the emotion in her voice, her touch, the looks she gave him when she thought he wasn't looking.

Her pain only added to his frustration.

"Where's Cherie?" he asked.

"With Sam," said Rachel.

"And Sam is . . . ?"

"Giving Chesty and the sheep a pep talk about the herding thing. And trying to talk Cherie into entering the egg race."

"You're kidding."

If Cherie so far forgot her teen angst to enter an egg race, then he would proclaim Rachel and Sam miracle workers. Not only had Rachel wormed her way into his heart, she and her son were good for Cherie.

A sudden rush of longing made Jackson almost weak. He wanted all this—Rachel, Sam, days just like this one, friends like the people who sat beside him. But those things came with a price, and he'd found out in his years with Melanie that the price was too high. Could the second time around be easier? Or would it just be more painful?

"Here comes the Grand Entrance," Molly said, clapping. "How they got old Charlie on that horse would have been a thing to see. Hope he doesn't fall off."

The Grand Entrance swept around the arena with flags waving. Charlie Swetman, in spite of Molly's remarks, looked at home in the saddle. Karen whispered into Jackson's ear, "Molly and Charlie have this thing going. Rivalry or love, we can't decide. The whole town has a bet going about whether they'll kill each other or get married."

Next on the agenda was a performance by the equine drill team, the Arizona Hoofers by name—all schoolkids concentrating fiercely as they put the horses through their impressive

paces. The parents of these children, Jackson thought, probably didn't lose sleep over their daughters eloping with rock
stars or their sons piercing various body parts. But they probably worried about their kids every bit as much as he did. Nothing was as simple as it seemed.

"Why isn't Sam on that team?" Jackson asked Rachel.

"He wants to be, but I don't have time to drive him to McNary
for twice-weekly practices."

The calf-roping competition reminded Jackson why he
didn't want to be a real cowboy. The winner was the Lazy M's
own foreman, Jim MacDonald, who roped and tied his calf just
hundredths of a second faster than Nathan Crosby, who also
competed. Nathan had found a job with a spread over by
Springerville, Jackson had heard. They had exchanged un-
friendly glances by the hot-dog stand behind the bleachers.
The man was an ass, but Jackson had to admit that he was
damned good at roping cows.

Mac didn't seem to mind that his tussle with the calf plastered him in dirt and other animal-produced stuff that Jackson
didn't even want to think about. He came up into the bleachers
to show off his trophy, then took himself off for refreshments
without so much as a glance at soap and water. That, Jackson
mused with a smile, was carrying grit a bit too far.

Sam climbed up the bleachers toward them and squeezed
himself between Jackson and Rachel. "Ma! Didn't Mac do
great?"

"He did!" Rachel agreed.

"Thanks for letting me and Chesty ride in the parade."

"No problem, pardner."

He didn't kiss his mom. Eleven-year-old boys don't do that
in public. But he grinned hugely. And Rachel glowed. The
warmth in her eyes when she looked at her boy forced Jackson
to bite back a smile. His smile muscles had worked so hard
these last weeks that they were getting stiff. How could any
man not love this woman? How could any man not want her?

"Cherie's gonna enter the egg race," Sam informed Jackson,
then turned back to his mom. "Can I do the pig wrestling, Ma?

You should see those cute pigs they have over there in the pen. They're just baby pigs, Ma. It'll be fun."

"I think you have enough to do with your herding demo, kid."

"But Jack Kimble is entering, and he's a whole year younger than me."

"Jack Kimble doesn't have Chesty and six sheep to deal with."

Sam slipped a look at Jackson, as if he might lend support. Jackson gave him a sympathetic shake of the head. The boy grimaced, scowled down at his boots for a moment, then brightened. "They're selling hot dogs over by the stable office."

Rachel forked over some money. "Ask Cherie if she wants one, too."

"I will!" he promised. "Bye, Ma. Bye, Miz Spangler. Bye, Aunt Molly and Mr. Jackson." He gave them all a wave, clambered to the ground, and disappeared.

"That kid's got more energy than a pack of monkeys," Molly commented with a smile.

"I promised him a bowl of ice cream if his herding thing goes okay," Karen said. "Cherie, too. She's brave to enter the egg race. I wouldn't be caught dead. Those eggs are raw, you know."

Rachel laughed ruefully. "Ice cream. That's what they need after today's excitement. Sugar."

Sam's part of the rodeo went very well indeed. Chesty wasn't a bit fazed by the audience, and if Sam was nervous, he didn't show it. The sheep, however, were very frazzled by the unfamiliar arena with its strange noises and smells. They huddled in their pen, not wanting to go through the gate into the arena, until Chesty waded in among them and gave them a push. The audience was suitably impressed, and the demonstration hadn't even begun.

Jackson felt Rachel's tension as the announcer explained the goal of the exercise—to take the sheep as a controlled flock around a set course of orange traffic cones, through a free-standing gate at the far end of the arena, then back through the cones to a chute where Sam would safely pen the animals. It sounded easy, but sheep are contrary creatures. Rachel had confided her fears that Sam would screw up and be mortally embarrassed as only an eleven-year-old could be embarrassed. Now she sat tensely as Sam gave Chesty the command to start.

Jackson took her hand and squeezed it. For a moment her eyes left her son and met his. She smiled. Lord, how he wanted her.

"He'll do fine," Jackson said in a low voice. "And if he doesn't, we'll get him ice cream anyway, and I'll tell him about the time I totally blew a scene when I was playing the Music Man in summer stock."

Her hand curled into his as if it intended to stay there. He wanted to raise her fingers to his mouth and kiss them, but he couldn't. Not here. Rachel's attention turned back to Sam. Karen and Molly both gave him knowing grins.

Sam and Chesty worked like a couple of pros, and the audience applauded wildly in appreciation. When Sam and his dog joined the group in the bleachers, they both walked on air. Jackson made room for them between him and Rachel. Karen left to buy drinks. Charlie Swetman came by to take Molly away. Jackson, Rachel, Sam, and Chesty remained to watch the egg race, where contestants balanced a raw egg upon a spoon and raced each other to a finish line at the far end of the arena. Anyone dropping his or her egg was disqualified. To make things harder, they had to climb over and through a series of obstacles blocking the course.

The local kids didn't have a chance. Cherie, who had studied modeling, dance, and gymnastics practically since she was born, left them all in the dust.

"She's incredible!" Rachel shrieked as Cherie crossed the finish line, held up her intact egg, and did an end-zone dance worthy of professional football.

"Sweet!" Sam shouted. "Way to go, Cherie!"

They were just like a family, Jackson noted—the kind of family that wasn't supposed to exist any longer, the family that died with *Leave It to Beaver* and *Father Knows Best*. What he would give, Jackson reflected, to have such a gem of a family. Such a family would be worth giving up a lifestyle, turning a world upside down, reinventing priorities. But if he did all that, would it change the central problems? He would still be in the spotlight, and Rachel would be right there with him

Such blessings as these could be achieved if one were a carpenter, attorney, nurse, or construction worker—someone with a private life. But Jackson lived constantly in the glare of media scrutiny. Any time taken strictly for himself required an elaborate escape such as the one about to come to an end. Private relationships did not thrive in such conditions. Friendships were hard. Love affairs could be tucked into a corner of life for a while, but even they were difficult. Something as committed and consuming as marriage was all but impossible.

He thought he had accepted that fact when he and Melanie had crashed. It had been a spectacular, painful crash, made even more spectacular by the sensationalist media. Since then, for Cherie's sake, he and Mel had sorted out a workable friendship, but the lessons learned were not forgotten. Asking Rachel to share his life even for a while was incredibly selfish. Asking her to share it forever would practically be a crime.

They met Cherie behind the bleachers. Flushed with victory, she showed them what she'd won, a blue ribbon rosette, a coupon for two free hot dogs, and a plastic, gold-painted trophy. From the shine in her eyes, Jackson speculated that cheap plastic trophy would be on the mantel right beside his Oscar.

While Cherie showed off her trophy to Rachel, Jackson thought he saw a familiar face in the crowd. His heart jumped wildly before he decided he was mistaken. Josh Digby couldn't be in Greer. There was no way that vulture could have tracked them down.

The face disappeared. Jackson refused to think about it, to spoil this perfect day. He was going to preserve this day in his memory, keep it whole and bright to pull out when being Jackson Stone, superstar, got too much for him.

They drove back in Jackson's Jeep, all four of them. Five, counting Chesty, who sat in the backseat between Sam and

Cherie, drooling on both of them. Cherie enjoyed making a fuss about the dog drool, and Sam enjoyed egging her on. The mock battle went on most of the way home, but it stopped abruptly when they drove through the big Lazy M arch and caught sight of the pasture behind the barn. Sitting in the pasture was a sleek helicopter.

Many of the Lazy M guests were still enjoying Greer Days, but those who had stayed at the ranch were gathered in a little knot on the front porch of the ranch house. A khaki-clad stranger in dark glasses leaned against a porch pillar, and holding court on the porch swing was a woman anyone in the country would have recognized—even Rachel.

Cherie groaned. "Man oh man! What's my mom doing here?"

CHAPTER 16

♡

HELL DIDN'T BREAK loose until Jackson ushered Melanie into the privacy of his cabin. His ex had her dander up; Jackson could tell from the snap of her jewel-green eyes. During their eight-year marriage, every fight—and there had been a truckload of them—had been prefaced by that distinctive glitter.

She started on him as soon as the door closed behind them. "How dare you kidnap Cherie and drag her off without telling me what you were doing! Or even where you were going! I've been frantic! Out of my mind with worry! Especially after what happened with Jimmy Toledo! Look at me! I'm a mess, and it's all your fault. My chakras are out of balance, my energy is totally drained. If you could see my aura right now, do you know what it would look like?"

Jackson took a guess. "Fire-engine red?"

"What?"

"The color of explosions, firestorms . . ."

She scowled ominously. "Jackson, you are so not funny! I have every right to be furious. Cherie is my daughter! My only child! How could you make me worry so?"

Jackson wasn't buying the devoted mother act. "Melanie, just how long have you known that Cherie and I weren't in L.A.?"

She shrugged. "Long enough to be truly frustrated when I couldn't track you down. Mothers need to know their children are safe in the nest. It's an instinct thing."

"Right. This is me you're talking to, Mel. Me, not some doting reporter. You call Cherie maybe once every couple of months, have her visit once or twice a year. How many birthdays have you forgotten? Two years ago you even forgot how old she was."

She waved a dismissive hand. "Trivial. She's my child, and we have an elemental bond of the spirit. I don't see Cherie as much as I'd like, but that's no excuse for you to act as if you own her."

"I don't own her, Mel. I'm her father. I also have sole legal custody, something you willingly ceded when we divorced."

"Giving up custody doesn't make me any less a mother! I love Cherie!"

"I didn't mean to imply that you didn't. Only that Cherie isn't a huge part of your life."

"Jackson, that's not my fault. You know me. I live at two hundred percent. My career, my studies into Spirit. I scarcely have time to eat and sleep. It doesn't mean I don't think about her or worry about her."

"So you hopped in a chopper and flew out here to do what? Rake me over the coals for not consulting with you about getting out of town?"

Her chin lifted to a familiar fighting angle. "Partly."

"And to convince yourself that you're an attentive mother?"

"That's unfair, you jackass." She sniffed indignantly. "I am an attentive mother. My attention isn't overt, that's all. Something can be subtle and understated and still be real. But I wouldn't expect an icon of macho shoot 'em ups, chase scenes, and fisticuffs to understand that."

Jackson snorted.

"Besides"—she gave him a tolerant smile—"I was led here."

"By something other than a desire to annoy me?"

For a moment her eyes twinkled mischievously as she admitted, "That, too, perhaps. But . . ." Her expression became solemn. "But I was led here by something far more important than simply annoying you."

"And that would be?"

"My spiritual adviser—Makirah Moonwalker. He works with a lot of the more advanced souls in L.A. San Francisco and New York also. Anyway, Makirah says I need to connect more with my child, that she's an important part of my karma. Then right after I talked to Makirah, Josh Digby called and started pumping me for information on where you'd disappeared to with Cherie. It was like a sign from the Universe reminding me that I didn't know nearly enough about my daughter's welfare. And when I couldn't track you down and no one seemed to know where you and Cherie were, I just got frantic. I thought of the years that—okay, you're partly right—I didn't pay nearly enough attention to Cherie. And it occurred to me that maybe the Universe was teaching me a lesson by taking away my child because I hadn't recognized her worth. Truly, Jackie, I was frantic. I thought for sure something had happened to you both."

Jackson almost understood the rambling account, which only proved he had lived with Melanie much too long. Pinching the bridge of his nose between finger and thumb, he sighed. What a time for his ex to suffer an attack of maternal fervor. "You can stop being frantic, Mel. The Universe doesn't have Cherie in its clutches. I do. To tell the truth, I didn't even think about telling you my plans. And if I had thought about it, I probably wouldn't have. You're not discreet with the media, and I wanted to get Cherie away from the cameras and microphones. Letting you know where we were would have brought the reporters in a rush."

"That's not true! You're paranoid about reporters. Cherie is a child of Hollywood. She needs to learn that a few photos and stories aren't going to hurt her."

"That's one place where you and I disagree."

"If you wanted to avoid publicity, you shouldn't have behaved like a schoolyard bully to poor Jimmy Toledo. You were the one who invited the press to a feeding frenzy. You never have known how to handle the media, Jackson."

"I handle the media just fine."

"By running away?" She shook her head in sympathy.

"Jackson, Jackson, when will you learn? You can't run away from problems. If you manage to avoid them in this life, you'll meet them again in the next."

Jackson answered with a sigh. Discussing anything with Melanie gave him a headache. When they had divorced, the aspirin industry had lost its best customer. "Mel, spare me the philosophy. How did you find out where we were?"

"Cherie called Deanna and told all, and Deanna spilled her guts to her parents, who in turn spilled their guts to me."

Jackson massaged his temples. "Sheesh!"

"And I, of course, chartered a helicopter to rush here and see for myself. I don't believe in sitting around to let problems prey upon my mind. As it is, I'm going to have to meditate for a week to get my vibrations back into a balanced energy."

"Tell me you didn't spill the beans to Digby."

"I'm not dense, Jackson. Of course I didn't. I didn't tell anyone anything." She backtracked with a grimace. "Come to think of it, I might have mentioned Arizona to Jake Carver, but Arizona's a big place. Besides, Jake won't tell anyone."

Jackson sighed wearily.

"Oh, quit with the heavy sighs! You'd think you were running from hit men, not innocent reporters."

He shot her a look. "All right, Mel, now you know where Cherie is. If you hop back into your helicopter and fly out of here, maybe the whole world won't share that knowledge."

"Fine by me. Have Cherie pack. She can fly back to L.A. with me for a while. Makirah says I need to make the effort to reconnect with my child, and that's exactly what I'm going to do. Besides, Cherie has tons of shopping to do before she can go to Europe with Deanna and her parents."

"Melanie . . ." Jackson sighed. "Be reasonable for once and just leave. Cherie isn't going back with you, and I haven't yet decided if she's going to Europe. In a week or so we'll be home, and then you can come to the house and visit for a few days if you want. Last time she stayed with you, she ended up in Vegas with a rock star who wears rings in his nipples."

Melanie's eyes narrowed. "Jackson, I do believe you're

jealous, jealous of a mother-daughter relationship. You resent the fact that I can relate to Cherie on a much more basic level that you do. Shame on you for being so small-minded."

Jackson shook his head hopelessly.

"Don't be jealous, dear. Cherie and I are both women. We share the goddess gift. It's a primeval thing. I'm not trying to take Cherie away from you, poor man. A few days with me isn't going to threaten your masculine dominance over our child."

"Melanie, you are so far into fantasyland that Tinkerbell should be riding on your shoulder. I am not jealous, not threatened, and Cherie isn't going back to L.A. with you."

His ex propped hands on slender hips and regarded him with a scowl that simply made her look that much more adorable. Everything Melanie did made her look adorable, a trait that made staying mad at her almost impossible. "Stubborn jackass," she said, almost affectionately.

Jackson flashed her a winning smile.

"Then I'll just stay until you decide to go home. I'll spend time with Cherie right here. That might even be a good thing, to commune with each other in a primitive place where the vibrations of nature facilitate spiritual empathy." She brightened. "This is a guest ranch, right? Maybe it'll be fun." She smiled her adorable smile, but those green eyes still glittered. "You don't mind me sharing your cabin, do you?"

Cherie perched on the ranch house living room sofa and stared morosely into the cold fireplace. Ankles crossed, folded legs drawn tightly against her chest, she crowded herself into the smallest possible space. The arms wrapped around her legs almost made her feel hugged. Almost. Not quite. She could have used a hug right then, but everyone was totally too occupied with their own concerns to pay much mind to her. Wasn't that the way it always was?

She watched surreptitiously as Rachel puttered about the room trying to look as if everything were okay. The cowgirl wasn't much of an actress, though. A crease between her brows revealed a scowl just waiting to break through. Cherie understood perfectly. Rachel was making serious time with her father. The lovers thought no one knew, but no one could mistake the hot way they looked at each other. Her dad had been in a goofy good mood ever since he'd first set eyes on the woman, and Rachel had been walking on air for days.

Now Cherie's mom had appeared—poof!—as if she'd beamed down from Spaceship Beautiful. That would shake up any woman, but especially someone like poor Rachel, who was very nice and all, but not exactly a walking love goddess. Whereas Cherie's mom—well, Melanie Carr combined cute, winsome, and just plain old drop-dead gorgeous into one package. She carried good looks to a new level, with skin that really didn't need makeup, hair that looked sexy even if she just ran her fingers through it and let the wind dry it after a wash, and a figure that needed no help at all from Maidenform.

Having such a mother was downright humiliating. All Cherie's friends thought she was so totally lucky to be the daughter of two icons of sexiness. They didn't understand her parents were a total drag. Her dad cared too much what she did, and her mom mostly didn't care at all—except maybe once or twice a year when the motherhood bug bit her. And when either one of her parents were around, Cherie became invisible to just about everyone.

Rachel stopped puttering and sat down beside her. Her eyes were sympathetic as she reached out to place a hand on Cherie's hunched shoulder. "Are you okay, Cherie?"

Cherie shrugged. "Sure. Everything's cool." Rachel bit her lip, as if she didn't believe that everything was cool, as if maybe she cared at least a little bit. Cherie's heart expanded a small notch. "Maybe not," she confessed. "My mom can be a downer."

"It must be tough to have such famous parents."

"Famous, beautiful parents."

Rachel smiled. "You've got their genes. Give yourself a few years and you'll be a stunner."

At least Rachel didn't prattle on about beauty coming from inside instead of outside. "Yeah, yeah. But I feel like, you know, an also-ran sometimes. And my mom, she totally thinks I should play devoted daughter whenever she pops up. I wish she'd just stay away."

Rachel didn't look too happy herself. Adults could get a case of the dumps, too, Cherie realized, and decided to give the cowgirl a break. "You don't have to worry about my mom, you know."

"Worry about your mom?"

"Yeah. You know, about her horning in on what you've got going with my dad. My mom is totally weird. Totally. And she drives my dad right up a tree. When they're together, all they ever do is fight. Mom thinks Dad is a stodge, and he thinks she's an airhead."

Rachel would never make it in acting. Her relief wrote volumes on her face.

"'Course, my dad sort of is a stodge. That's the truth. And Mom isn't really an airhead. She's *mucho* smart, just kind of . . . well, different, you know? She likes to keep an open mind about stuff. A really, really open mind. Plus, she's tight with a bunch of real crazies. They're so interested in past lives and spirits and stuff that half the time they forget what's happening right here in this life, you know?"

Rachel folded her legs up beneath her chin in a position similar to Cherie's. Cherie figured that was a sign that they both felt equally low. She patted Rachel's knee. "Believe me, Rachel, beside my mom, you look really good to any man who isn't interested in terrific looks."

Rachel choked, then laughed. "Cherie, you are quite a kid."

"Yeah," Cherie grumbled. "Unique. I can't believe my mom showed up here. She's probably afraid the reporters will catch up to us and she won't be part of the story, you know?"

Rachel shook her head. "I'm sure that's not it, Cherie. She's your mom, and I'll bet she was worried about you."

"Right. You don't know my mom at all. Half the time she forgets I'm alive. She's too busy meditating on her former lives.

Don't get her started on the royal dynasties of ancient Egypt. She was an Egyptian princess ages ago and bores everyone silly with her dumb stories of having to marry her brother. Gross."

Rachel's brows lifted a bit, but she didn't say anything. Cherie was grateful. The cowgirl knew when stupid platitudes and reassurances weren't going to do any good. Then a dreadful thought bolted into her brain.

"Man oh man! Total stupidity! I know how Mom found us." She slapped her forehead hard with the heel of her hand. "Deanna! I'm going to throttle Deanna! She has such a mouth on her. I should've known better than to call her, the moron!"

"What?"

"Nothing," Cherie growled. "Never mind." Rachel didn't need to know about the excursion into her office to call California. Her dad was going to kill her when he found out. Not only had she sneaked a phone call, she'd brought her mother down upon them like a plague of killer bees. She was going to be grounded for the next ten years, and her chances of going to Europe had just plunged to zero.

Rachel sighed. "Guess I'd better tell Joanne to add another chicken to the pot. I'm sure your mom will want to stay for dinner."

Rachel truly was clueless if she thought they'd get rid of her mom after dinner, Cherie thought dejectedly.

"Well, I'll be hog-tied and horsewhipped for a fool," Joanne said as she and Rachel diced celery for that night's chicken stew. "I knew there was something fishy about that man. Besides him not knowing one end of a horse from the other, I mean. Kept thinkin' I'd seen him before, but couldn't quite place him. Guess that's why he gets all those acting awards, eh? Jackson Stone, as I live and die, right in our backyard." She shot Rachel a sideways look. "And our little Rachel reeling in a genuine movie star. Who would've thought it?"

"I haven't reeled in anybody," Rachel snapped.

Joanne snorted. "You must think this old woman was born

yesterday, missy. I know spoonin' when I see it. Times was when I was a young woman myself, and I did my share of it. Enough so I can recognize it when I see it."

It was Rachel's turn to snort.

"Nothing to be ashamed of, girl. It's about time you loosened up your garter belt, if you catch my meaning. A woman your age ain't meant to be livin' like a nun, not unless she is one. If I was you, I'd be proud. Almost like makin' time with Cary Grant or Gregory Peck. Not quite, but almost."

Rachel shook her head. There was no reeling in Joanne's free spirit. Or zipping her mouth, either. "Joanne, what am I going to do with you?"

The older woman laughed. "Nuthin' you can do, missy. I been here too long."

"And what would I do without you?"

Joanne just smiled.

Rachel got back to business. "If you want to get the room under the stairs ready for Miss Carr, I'll finish up here and then look in on Moira and Terri in the Chuckwagon kitchen."

Joanne wasn't so easily diverted. "Ain't she sumpthin', droppin' out of the sky like that? Melanie Carr in the flesh. She must be richer than the devil. Looks better in real life than in the movies, even. It's just not fair that some women get hair and skin like that and the rest of us have to spend two hours in front of a mirror just to look half that good."

Rachel made a wry face. This wasn't what she needed to hear.

Joanne dumped a pile of diced celery in the stew pot and started on the onions. Then, knife poised in midair, she cursed. "God love me for a stupid old woman. Here I am carryin' on about that piece of fluff bein' so gorgeous and you're probably feelin' like a drab little mouse beside her."

She didn't need to hear that, either.

"Just remember, missy, that beauty comes from the inside, not the outside. And if mister hunky movie star is worth having at all, he knows a good, solid, down-to-earth woman is worth twice some flashy sex kitten."

Rachel had to laugh. "Sex kitten, Joanne?"

"Well . . ."

"I don't think Melanie Carr can be dismissed as a mere sex kitten. She really is a very talented actress, and from what I've read, she has a very active social conscience. She gives huge amounts to charities, sponsors events for women's health awareness, does public service spots for education, things like that."

"Well, la di da!" Joanne refused to give Rachel's "rival" any credit.

When the housekeeper left to prepare a room for their surprise guest, Rachel finally was able to release the morose sigh that had been building since Melanie Carr had so precipitously dropped into her life—a calamitous ending to a wonderful day.

The day had started out so well, with perfect weather, good friends, the fun of a parade with its wagonloads of 4-H kids, and Sam perched so proudly upon Thunder. Sam had looked cute enough to make Rachel's heart melt even if she hadn't been his mother. And Jackson—he'd been pretty cute himself sitting beside her watching the rodeo, joking with her friends, proud as punch when Cherie had won that stupid race. His thigh had pressed warmly against hers. Her heart had warmed as well. They had seemed almost like a family, Jackson and Rachel, Sam and Cherie. She had let herself drift off to Fantasyland just a little. Maybe more than a little.

Now enter Melanie, dropping from the sky like an omen. Her very presence had to remind Jackson that he belonged in another world, that he commanded the affections of women who were extraordinary in both beauty and talent. And she illustrated for Rachel the sort of woman that Jackson had loved in the past and would probably love in the future. No wonder Jackson had avoided any mention of marriage or any other kind of commitment when he'd talked about stretching their relationship to a "semi–happily ever after."

Not that Rachel had for one moment considered taking him up on that crazy idea. Call her old-fashioned, but she thought two people in love should at least try for the happy ending. Commitment might not be "in" in Hollywood, but commitment was what drove Rachel's life—commitment to her son, her home, her guests. She wasn't sure she wanted to commit to Jackson, but she sure as heck wasn't going to string along in some kind of fuzzy, indefinite relationship just because they were a "good thing."

An abrupt ending like this was better for everyone concerned, Rachel told herself. They could scarcely carry on with Jackson trying to deal with Melanie, Cherie sinking once again into teenage angst, and the guests all atwitter about the celebrities in their midst. Actually, having the silly fling over was a relief.

And there's a bridge in Brooklyn you can get for a bargain! her pesky inner voice mocked.

A hesitant knock on the front door interrupted her gloomy musing. She opened it to see Jackson waiting on the porch, his expression as sheepish as his knock. Beside him, not looking sheepish in the least, was Melanie Carr.

"Hi," he said, a faltering smile on his face.

"Hi," she said back.

"You've met Cherie's mom?"

Rachel unwillingly shifted her gaze to Melanie Carr. How ironic that now, when she had just admitted the fallacy of stereotypes, up popped a walking, breathing Hollywood star, complete with glitz and glitter. Jackson's ex-wife presented a perfect picture—her blooming skin, her trim, perfectly toned figure, her artfully tousled blond hair. What's worse, the smile she gave Rachel was warm and sincere. Bad enough that the witch was beautiful. If she was genuinely nice as well, then the universe knew no justice.

"We said a brief hello when she first came. It's nice to meet you, Ms. Carr. We assumed you'll be staying for dinner and threw another chicken in the pot."

"How kind." The star displayed perfect teeth in a friendly smile. "As a matter of fact—"

"As a matter of fact," Jackson interrupted, though he looked as if he'd rather be fleeing to the north forty, "I've come to ask you if Mel might stay a night or two up here at the house, since the cabins are full."

Rachel sympathized with his embarrassment. "We anticipated that as well. Joanne is making up a room."

"My goodness, Mrs. Marsh, it's no wonder you're such a success out here. You think of everything and make a person feel so welcome."

"Of course you're welcome. I just hope you find the room comfortable. It's probably much smaller than you're accustomed to."

"I'm sure it will be very cozy."

Like a shadow stalking in from the dining room, Cherie slipped around the doorway. Her mouth was sullen even as she gave her mother a brief peck on the cheek.

"Cherie, darling, you look so sweet! Absolutely precious. And so healthy. I see the outdoor life agrees with you."

Cherie simply snorted and scowled. Melanie seemed to be used to such responses, because she didn't take offense. Cherie pointedly turned away and addressed Rachel. "Is it okay if I help Terri and Moira serve in the dining hall and then eat with them over there in the kitchen?"

"Don't you want to spend some time with your parents?" Rachel asked, just as pointed.

Cherie looked ready to give a curt no, but Rachel drilled her with stern eyes. "Maybe later," the girl compromised. She gave her mother a reserved smile and left. Melanie didn't seem a bit surprised. "What thirteen-year-old wants to spend time with her parents?"

"Let me show you to the room," Rachel offered. "Do you have luggage?"

"It's still in Jackson's cabin. I had the helicopter pilot take it over there before he took off to go back to L.A."

So they were stuck with her for a while, Rachel thought, laboring to keep a smile pasted on her face. Was Melanie protecting her territory? Were the two of them still involved, despite what Cherie had said? Could any man look at Melanie Carr and still care that any other woman was on the planet?

Get over it, she told herself sternly. Why should she care? She had known from the beginning that Jackson Stone was a brief indulgence.

So why did her heart sink into her stomach?

Melanie continued chattily, "I told Jackson I could just bunk in with him. There's no need to bother you with cleaning up an extra room." She smiled impishly at her ex. "But Jackson is such an old fuddy-duddy. He says if the press got wind of us bunking together they'd have rewedding plans in the very next issue of *The National Enquirer*. He hasn't noticed that there aren't any reporters here."

"I doubt your arrival went unnoticed," Jackson said dryly.

"Oh, Jackson! Come out of your shell. A little publicity never killed anybody." She flashed Rachel a woman-to-woman smile. "He is such a twit when it comes to privacy."

"Uh . . . right. The room is this way."

Rachel guided Melanie down the short hallway from the kitchen. Jackson followed silently. It was over. Over was over. Fini. Kaput. Welcome back to the real world. Rachel resisted the temptation to look back at Jackson, to discover if she could decipher the emotions on his face. "I'll have Sam fetch your luggage," she told Melanie.

Melanie waved away the idea with a graceful, elegantly manicured hand. "Don't do that. It's so heavy. I really didn't know how long I'd be here, so I packed just everything. Jackson can fetch my bags, can't you, Jackson. Put those showy muscles of yours to some use."

A muscle twitched in Jackson's jaw, and Rachel felt the air crackle. "I may need to hitch the team to the wagon," he grumbled. "Mel doesn't travel light."

Melanie just laughed as he stalked out the door. "I'm bad. I shouldn't tease him, poor man, but he's so fun to bait. Such a spoiled little boy. But then, I'm more spoiled than he is. Why, this room is absolutely darling," she exclaimed as Rachel showed her into the smallest of the two guest rooms in the ranch house. The larger one was currently occupied by a chiropractor from Oregon and his wife. "So down-home cozy. Did you decorate this yourself, Mrs. Marsh?"

"Call me Rachel. Absolutely no one calls me Mrs. Marsh."

"Rachel, then. You have wonderful taste. The room feels so real, so genuine."

Rachel didn't know how a room could feel other than real.

"The vibrations here are so peaceful." Melanie kicked off strappy little high-heeled sandals and padded about the room barefoot. Not that there was much padding about to do, as the room was painfully small. Melanie seemed genuinely charmed, though, as she plunked her lissome self onto the bed and smiled warmly. "So, tell me what Jackson and Cherie have been up to?"

The question caught Rachel off guard. "Well . . . uh . . ."

"Cherie looks absolutely wonderful. And Jackson—" She laughed an open, musical laugh. "—Jackson looks as if he's been run over by a bus."

The friendly sparkle in her eyes was hard to resist, all the more because it was so unexpected. Rachel couldn't stop a smile from spreading across her face. "You should have seen him when the bruises were fresh."

"I'll bet. What did you do? Hit him? I know he deserves thumping about ninety percent of the time."

Rachel laughed. "I've been tempted a time or two, but no. One of the hands sort of ambushed him. The man's gone now. I fired him."

Melanie gave her a canny look. "Let me guess. Jealousy?"

Rachel blinked.

"Don't look so surprised. Guy fights are either about money or women. Given the way you and Jackson look at each other, jealousy was the logical choice."

Rachel struggled to think of something to say.

"Don't look so stricken," Melanie advised. "Jackson and I divorced years ago, and though occasionally we still vibrate on the same frequency, separation truly is the best thing for both of us. Don't believe all that trash in the tabloids about us getting back together. We can't even have an innocent lunch together without someone like Josh Digby scribbling lies made up from his hot little imagination. Frankly, I would be absolutely relieved to see Jackson fall for someone as grounded and centered as you are."

"Uh . . . centered?"

"Don't deny it. I'm very perceptive. Psychic, even. Three hundred years ago my friends and neighbors burned me as a witch at the age of twenty-six, leaving two orphaned children to be abused by unenlightened zealots." She sighed. "But that was then, and this is now. Now I'm not considered dangerous." She grinned impishly. "Just eccentric."

How did one express sympathy to someone for being burned three hundred years before?

"So don't let me interfere with what you have going on with His Nibs. If you can stand him, you're welcome to him. Just don't make the mistake I did when I married a Mandarin in eleventh century China . . ."

Melanie nattered on, and Rachel settled herself in a chair to listen, feeling rather like Alice falling down the rabbit hole. It was going to be a long night, but what the hell. The way things stood, she didn't have anything better to do.

The hour was past midnight, but Jackson knew Rachel was still awake. Her bedroom window was the only one in the ranch house still lit. He sat on the dark porch of his dark cabin watching that window, trying to decide if he should take the chance of going up there. Cherie was asleep inside the cabin. She wouldn't wake. Sam was sleeping in the motor home. He treated it like most boys treated a tent in their backyard. The bunkhouse was dark. The dormer ranch-house windows that were Joanne's, Moira's, and Terri's showed no sign of life. No one would see him if he crossed to the ranch house and climbed up to Rachel's room—just to talk. They very much needed to talk. Mel dropping into the scene had changed everything for him. His ex brought with her an epiphany of sorts, one that made him see how absolutely dense he'd been for the last few weeks, maybe for the last few years. Sometimes things right in front of your face are invisible until a small shift in perspective allows you to suddenly see them.

That's what had happened when he'd seen Mel and Rachel together. He'd been barking up the wrong tree and hadn't realized it until this afternoon.

But he stayed where he was, sitting in his chair, wondering why courage had deserted him. Because Rachel had turned white as one of Joanne's freshly laundered sheets when Mel had showed up. Because he knew she didn't really want to see him right then. She had always hated the deception of his role-playing, hated the complications, hated the lies, even though they were white lies. Rachel liked things honest and straightforward, not complicated and convoluted. Mel's coming had made things very complicated indeed.

Jackson's whole life crawled with complications, like snakes in a pit, but he'd learned to live with them. Time to make a change. He remembered talking to Rick Carroll—it seemed years ago instead of weeks—warning him away from women who thrived on commitment. Dangerous women indeed. They could bring a man down, and lift him up, before he knew what had hit him.

The front door of the ranch house opened and shut quietly. Milky moonlight revealed Rachel as she crossed the yard to the corral just off the barn, where she leaned against the fence and stared out at the moon-silvered cienega. As Melanie would have put it, the Universe had just told him what to do.

Rachel didn't turn when he came up beside her, but she gave him a diffident "Hi."

"You okay?"

"Of course."

Jackson folded his arms across the top rail and stared with her into the night. "I guess the jig is up. Stoney Jackson is dead. Long live Jackson Stone."

"Long live Jackson Stone," Rachel repeated with a sigh.

"The guests seem to be thrilled. I'm sure most of them went up the hill tonight so they could get a cell signal to call back home and let their friends know the whole story."

He heard the dread in her voice and couldn't resist putting a hand at the base of her neck to massage away some of the tension. "Rachel, love, I'm going to get Mel out of here before the press arrives. You can deny I was ever here if you like. I'm going to take Cherie back to L.A. so she can go to Europe with her friend. I guess Europe is the safest place for her right now."

"She'll be over the moon with glee."

"Then I'm coming back, so don't think you're getting rid of me."

She dropped her head onto the hands that were resting on the rail, then raised it again. "I like Melanie. She told me all about her life as an Egyptian princess."

Jackson chuckled. "I'll bet."

"She knows we've been . . . sleeping together. I didn't bring it up, certainly, but she knew."

He sighed. "Mel's like that. Not all of her New Age stuff is posturing."

"But I like her."

"I like her, too, when she's not making me crazy."

Rachel talked to the night, not to him. Not once had she met his eyes. Jackson took that as a bad sign.

"Melanie seems to think I'm perfect for you," she said, an odd little smile lifting her mouth.

Jackson let out a long breath. "You are perfect for me, Rachel."

Rachel pushed back from the rail and ran a hand through her hair, which for once was loose and ruffled softly in the night breeze. "Melanie also thinks she can talk to animals and was burned as a witch three hundred years ago."

"Well, she can't be right about everything."

Her voice cracked. Apparently she didn't see the humor. "Jackson, don't do this. I can't do this. We're too different. We want different things. It's just as well that it ends right now.

Don't you think so? I'd been hoping for a few more days, but then Melanie dropped in, and . . ."

Even in the faint moonlight he could see her jaw clench with emotion. His heart sank. Now he remembered why he dated good-time girls who didn't want emotional investment, who expected little and gave little in return. Emotional investment hurt. It hurt like hell. But now his heart was tangled with this woman. Now he had found something he really wanted, and he wasn't about to give up. "Rachel, love, you're not getting off that easily."

She looked up at the edge in his voice. "I beg your pardon?"

"I thought I could walk in here, do a bit of research, romance a pretty woman, and have a good time. But the pretty woman turned out to be more than I bargained for. You've put hooks into my soul, sweetheart, and they're not going to rip loose any time soon."

He read the protest on her face, but he didn't let her give it voice.

"I know we've got some issues to work out—different priorities, different expectations from life. But Rachel, I mean this: I'll do whatever I have to do to keep you and Sam with me, to make you happy, to convince you that deep down inside, we've got more in common than you believe."

He put one finger across her lips as she started to speak.

"Come to L.A. with me this winter. Bask in our warm sunshine and let me corrupt you with a little easy living." He grinned. "Give me a chance to convince you that you can't live without me."

"L.A.?" she choked.

"Just for the winter. This place closes to guests in a couple of weeks, and your crew handles the fall branding, right? You don't really need to be here. Sam could go to Cherie's school. It's a good school, in spite of what you might think from looking at Cherie."

She laughed weakly. "You're every bit as insane as Melanie, you know that?"

"I'm as sane as the day is long. In the Industry, I'm known as the guy that can make even an impossible plot work. I can do that with us. Trust me on that. I'm going to make you so happy that you'll be begging me to marry you—at the same time I'm begging you to marry me."

Her eyes widened. "M-m-m-marry?"

He waited for her to recover before he kissed her, but didn't allow for such complete recovery that she could put up a fight. That wouldn't do. He kissed her thoroughly, so thoroughly she had no means of escape, no room to deny that he meant every syllable, every letter of the word *love*.

"I love you, Rachel. For years I've avoided entanglement, telling myself that marriage just didn't work for people who live the kind of life I live. But when I saw you and Mel together, my stupidity hit me. How could I have thought that life with you would be anything like life with Mel? How could I have believed that? We could make it work, you and I, if we tried hard enough."

He kissed her again, brief but thorough. Her lips melted under his. So sweet, so warm.

"You do love me, don't you?" he asked when they came up for air.

"You make it hard not to." Her lips pressed against his throat as she said the words, because he wasn't letting her get more than two inches away from him.

"That's good, because I love you a lot."

"I don't know, Jackson. I do love you, but . . ." She sighed. Not the happy sigh he had hoped for. More a sigh of resignation. He would fix that, Jackson told himself. Things were confused now, but soon they would be better. They would be a family—Jackson and Rachel, Cherie and Sam. And maybe another kid or two. Or three. Somehow they would work it out.

"I'll be back," he told her, better than Schwarzenegger had ever said it. "I'll be back."

CHAPTER 17

♡

GOD SAVE THE world from small towns, Josh Digby thought sourly. He sat on the porch of the Roundup, scowling out upon Greer's one street while taking apart his omelet. He hated onions. Why did everyone think onions were a natural part of everything from sandwiches to omelets? They gave him heartburn. This town gave him heartburn, with its frontiersy log buildings and its one street crowded with tourists and craft booths and vendors left over from the rodeo.

Just his luck that he would come to this backwater when the local yokels chose to invite every tourist within a hundred miles to clog their streets—make that *street,* singular. Josh had thought that his quarry would stand out like a sore thumb in this quiet little mountain burg. Or if he had holed up somewhere, the locals would know where he was. Jackson Stone couldn't show his face in L.A. or New York City without being instantly recognized. He certainly couldn't hide in a prairie dog–size town in Arizona.

The rodeo and festival had spoiled everything. The town was actually crowded, and a good part of the crowd seemed to be tall, lanky men wearing cowboy hats. Who knew what their faces looked like beneath those Stetsons? And the locals were all so busy making money that they didn't have time for his questions.

So Josh had endured the rodeo, prowling the stands to spot a familiar photogenic face, unsuccessfully. All he'd seen was a colorful mix of tourists in shorts and T-shirts, kids eating ice-cream cones and hot dogs, and a smattering of cowboys who were the genuine article, not the big-screen version. He'd seen one or two guys who looked like Stone—sort of, but not close enough. And one of the kids in the egg race could have been Cherie's younger sister. But not Cherie. Fate had it in for him, Josh had decided.

Showing Stone's photo to people got him nowhere. Of course everyone recognized him. And of course no one had seen him except on the big screen. "Is *he* going to be here?" asked a middle-aged woman with a son whose cowboy hat was bigger than his whole head. "When? Will he be signing autographs? Did you hear that, Denton? Jackson Stone is going to be here at the rodeo!"

Josh had just sighed.

The day after the rodeo, the town was nearly as congested. Vendors of jewelry, crafts, and artwork had set up a street fair in the open lot across from the post office. There was even a booth set up by the local Avon lady. The tourists were eating it up as local color. And there was still no trace—not even a rumor—of Jackson Stone.

Stone's elusiveness frustrated Josh no end. Actors were not supposed to make life this hard for reporters. Their relationship was a symbiosis of sorts. The stars might play games of hide-and-seek, but the games weren't supposed to be this difficult. He knew Stone was around here somewhere. Somewhere close. Every line of evidence pointed to Greer, Arizona. So did gut instinct, and Digby's gut was seldom wrong. Stone was here, dammit! But he couldn't find the bastard.

"How's the omelet?" The waitress's inquiry broke into his brooding. She was a good-looking woman with pixie red hair, a western shirt with mother-of-pearl snaps, and shorts brief enough to demonstrate that her legs went all the way up to . . . well, to wherever. A man couldn't complain about onions to a woman who looked like that.

"It's great."

"More coffee?"

"Sure." He decided for one more try, pulling Stone's photo, now creased with much use, from his pocket. "You live around here?"

"Sure do. I own this place."

"No kiddin'? Congratulations." He flashed the photo. "Seen this guy around by any chance?"

The woman studied the photo. Her only reaction was a blank face. "Isn't he in the movies?"

"Jackson Stone. Big star."

"Of course I've seen him. I go to the movies in Springerville every once in a while."

Pretty, Josh thought. But definitely a hick.

"Have you seen him around here? You know, in the flesh."

She laughed. "Around here? This isn't exactly Hollywood, mister. You want to see someone like him, head west about six hundred miles."

Josh sighed. Why didn't he just go back to Chicago and admit failure, be satisfied with his stinking little cubicle for the rest of his dreary career, or move up to a publication that wouldn't require him to chase after frigging movie stars for a living?

"I've seen the guy," said a gravelly voice from over Josh's shoulder.

"Huh? What?" Josh twisted in his chair. The sexy waitress glared at the newcomer, who was a forty-something fellow with dusty brown hair and a sun-lined face.

"Nathan Crosby," the waitress said in a grim voice, "you mind your own business."

"I figure this is my business. Besides, it ain't gonna be a secret much longer. Saw Dennis in town this mornin', and he's got quite a story to tell. Seems not only is Mr. Swanky Stone gracing us with his presence, but his ex as well. Cat's out of the bag. I knew I recognized that son of a bitch from somewhere."

Josh's ears perked up like a dog's. Suddenly the world grew brighter. "Mister, if you can tell me where to find Stone, I'll make it worth your while."

Nathan pulled out a chair and sat down at the table. "This is your lucky day," he said. "I can tell you exactly where he is."

If this was the first day of the rest of her life, Rachel complained to herself, then she might as well just shoot herself right now. She trudged across the kitchen with a stainless-steel pail of fresh goat milk. The poor creatures had bleated loudly about full udders when Rachel had discovered mid-morning that no one had bothered to milk them. Terri, who had milking duties this week, had apologized profusely to both Rachel and the goats. She and Moira were so agog with the revelations of the day before that they had both done nothing but giggle the entire morning, forgetting chores as well as good sense. Rachel had warned them to get their heads screwed onto their shoulders, but she had ended up milking the goats.

Joanne followed her into the kitchen and helped her sieve the milk. "If those two flibbertigibbets don't start paying attention to work, I'm going to take a skillet to their behinds, I swear. Moira spent more time in the Chuckwagon giggling and laughing with the Olsons' daughter than she did in the kitchen. And Terri has her head somewhere in the clouds."

Rachel snorted. "The guest schedule is in chaos because no one wants to do anything but hang around and wait for a chance to pester Jackson or Melanie. Speaking of our leading lady, have you seen her yet this morning?"

"Not a peep out of her, unless she snuck out when I was over at the Chuckwagon."

"Hm." Rachel glanced at her watch. "Maybe I should take her some breakfast."

"There's good poppy-seed muffins in the fridge," Joanne told her. "And the orange juice is fresh made this morning."

When Rachel knocked on Melanie's door, she got a sleepy invitation to enter. Catching sight of the muffins, orange juice, and tea, Melanie smiled in delight. She sat at the dressing table in a patterned silk robe, looking better than any woman who had just climbed out of bed had a right to look. "You brought me food! And you even remembered that I like herbal tea. Bless you, Rachel. But you don't need to serve me in my room."

"I know, but I thought with all your new fans ready to pounce the moment you make an appearance, you might like breakfast first."

"What? Oh, your wonderful guests." She chuckled. "I love the attention, in case you didn't notice yesterday. If I weren't basically an attention sponge, I would have gone crazy in this business by now. But morning definitely is not my best time of day. I'm a night owl, not an early bird."

Rachel set the tray down. Her nose twitched at the room's strange odor. "Is something burning?"

"Incense," Melanie told her. "I was meditating, and incense helps me center myself. There's been a lot of stress in my life lately, and I need to meditate at least three times a day to keep myself in tune with the universe. Do you meditate regularly, Rachel?"

"Well, uh, no."

"No wonder you look so stressed. You must start, really."

"I'll think about it."

"I may need another session before I start the day. Dealing with Jackson can be so difficult. He's stubborn as an ox. Turn your back on him for a minute and he gets away with murder. Everyone spoils him because he's such a charmer. He smiles and every woman in L.A.—hell, every woman in the whole damned country—falls at his feet.

"But this time I'm giving him a piece of my mind. Really, dragging poor Cherie off to imprison her in a place like this— no offense intended, Rachel. This is a charming place, but young people like to be out partying where the bright lights shine, and making Cherie endure this will just make her even more rebellious."

"Partying and bright lights? Cherie is only thirteen."

"Thirteen is a lot older today than when you and I were thirteen. Kids grow up fast these days, especially in L.A. Cherie needs the guiding hand of someone more spiritually aware than Jackson. I plan to take a much more active role in her education from now on, and this peaceful retreat of yours is the perfect place for us to renew the mother-daughter connection." She finished her muffin, brushed crumbs from her hands, and emptied a small suitcase full of cosmetics onto the dressing table. "Time to put on the face. Such a bore."

Rachel's eyes widened at the sheer volume of makeup.

Laughing at Rachel's expression, Melanie spread a moisturizer over her face. "One of the disadvantages of being a celeb," she explained "Cameras are everywhere, and as soon as I go someplace looking less than fabulous, a photo of me looking my true age will show up in a newspaper or magazine. You don't know how lucky you are not to worry about wrinkles and bad-hair days."

And that comment was supposed to improve Rachel's mood?

"And by the way, Rachel, you must let me know the charges for the room before I leave."

"Believe me, Jackson has paid enough for the both of you."

"I hope he's paying you a small fortune, considering the trouble I'm sure he's put you through. We movie people are so high maintenance, aren't we?"

Melanie, at least, was high maintenance. Rachel left her alone with her incense and mountain of cosmetics and tried to find refuge in her office, where a mound of bills waited to be paid. Because of Jackson Stone's generosity, for once the bills would be paid without hair-pulling and juggling of accounts. Jackson—why couldn't he be easy to dismiss, easy to forget, easy to lose? Just hours before, standing beneath the midnight stars, loving him, even marrying him, had seemed possible. The seductive night had veiled the complications of the world. The temptation to hide herself in his arms had overwhelmed common sense. In the light of day, however, with the peaceful Lazy M tumbling into chaos, impossibilities once again paraded through her mind.

All the man has to do is smile, Melanie had said, *and women all over the country fall at his feet.* Rachel was certainly not an exception. Where was her good sense? Even more important, where was her survival instinct?

"Ma?" Sam stuck his head in the door of her office. "Can me and Chesty come in?"

"Chesty and I, and of course you may."

"Right. Chesty and I." He clumped in, cowboy boots dragging along the floor, and collapsed onto the couch. "Cherie's acting like a shit again."

Rachel's jaw dropped. "What did you say?"

"She's acting like a—" He had the grace to look sheepish. "—a dope?"

"Samuel Tobias Marsh, why did you use such a word?"

Sinking deeper into the couch, as if a piece of furniture could defend him, he shrugged. "I slipped?"

Rachel glared.

"Cherie uses it all the time," he said with a touch of belligerence.

"Don't use that tone with me, young man."

"Sorry."

"And you're not to use that word again until you're at least thirty."

His up-and-down friendship with Cherie had injected a bit of the devil into her son. It was good for him, Rachel decided.

Just as Jackson was good for her? Was Jackson good for her?

"Okay, pardner, what's Cherie done now to make you say she's behaving like a dope?"

"She's locked herself in the RV and won't let me in."

"Sam, it's her RV. Hers and her dad's. She doesn't have to let you in."

"And she looks like an alien from outer space again."

Rachel smiled. She had caught only a brief glimpse of Cherie that morning, but a mere glimpse was enough. The Morticia look was back, and so was the crown of gel-stiffened, lacquer-sprayed spikes. Spikes shot from her eyes as well. "Sam, I think Cherie isn't happy about her mother coming here, and probably she wants to be alone in the motor home to, well, just be by herself. Girls are like that." Rachel could remember being like that at thirteen. She could even remember being embarrassed by her mom. "Honey, don't let it bother you. It doesn't have anything to do with you."

"She's being a dork."

"That's enough, Sam. Just leave Cherie alone. Why don't you and Chesty go out to the barn and make yourself useful? I'm sure Paul would be grateful for your help worming a couple of the horses today. Or start on that new Harry Potter book we got in the mail last week."

Sam sighed and made a face. "Yes, ma'am."

Taking his cue from the boy, Chesty looked equally forlorn as the two of them dragged out.

Sam was going to miss Cherie—spikes, black lipstick, moods, and all. He would miss Jackson as well. Her son needed a permanent man in his life.

And you don't? the inner voice asked.

Maybe she did, Rachel conceded. Maybe they both did. But they needed a man, she told herself sternly, not an icon. Not a movie idol. She was moved beyond words that Jackson wanted to marry her, that he was willing to make changes in his life to make her happy. But should he have to change? And could she meet him halfway, which was only fair? Jackson ran with the jet set, while Rachel and Sam preferred to live life at a horse's pace. Was there a happy medium somewhere in between?

You do love me, don't you? he had asked the night before.

Yes, she loved him so much it hurt, even though she'd known the man not even a month. She loved him with a longing that tossed good common sense out the window.

That's good, because I love you a lot.

Her heart picked up its pace at the memory. He loved her, truly loved her. How extraordinary was that? How wonderful. But love wasn't everything. Love was just the beginning of a long, difficult journey. A couple needed more than love to carry them through. What else did Jackson Stone and Rachel Marsh have to sustain them in the trials of everyday life?

Rachel dropped her head down on a pile of bills, longing to

pound her forehead against the desk. Why couldn't she fall in love with someone useful, like a carpenter or an accountant?

Jackson stood on the little front porch of Sitting Bull cabin, his home for the past few weeks, and looked out upon the Lazy M. Paul's horses lazed in the corral, idly swishing flies with their tails. Toby and Dennis, also idle, lounged in the shade of the bunkhouse. A guest or two was in sight. They seemed happy to be doing nothing. What occupied everyone's time, it seemed, was watching him. Overnight Jackson had graduated from the Lazy M's worst cowboy to its main attraction.

Jackson had never been so reluctant to give up a role. Sometimes in making a film, he got so involved with his character that shedding the persona actually hurt. Getting back to living in his real skin took an effort. This was worse, though. Stoney Jackson was dead, and Jackson felt as though he'd lost a part of himself. He'd enjoyed joking around with the guests, working with the hands as one of the guys. He'd even come to appreciate the early mornings spent outwitting hens and coaxing milk from goats—when he couldn't rope one of the guests into doing the chore.

Unfortunately, Stoney Jackson hadn't been one of the more convincing roles of his career. He hadn't really been one of the guys. His incompetence had made him a mascot of sorts, the butt of good-natured teasing from both the cowboys and guests—quite a change from the celebrity deference he received everywhere else. No one would dare treat a star with the brutal straightforwardness Jackson had enjoyed at the Lazy M.

That honesty was one of the things he would miss, honesty and a lot of other things. He wished this interlude didn't have to end, wished he were just arriving and could live it once again.

In the distance he saw dust rising through the trees where the road from Greer climbed out of the valley. Some lucky bastard was headed for the Lazy M to begin his stay. Lucky, lucky bastard. He would be here, and Jackson would be gone.

Jackson would be sweltering in L.A., missing the cool stillness of the mountain mornings, the uncluttered vista of meadow, pines, and blue sky. He would miss Vince's complaints about his arthritis, Mac's resigned sigh every time Jackson did something stupid, Toby's boasts about his romantic conquests, Dennis's staid good nature.

One person he refused to miss was Rachel, because he was determined not to lose her. He was almost glad Mel had shown up when she had. Otherwise the obvious might never have hit him over the head—that his misgivings about marriage and permanence were all based on Melanie and women like her. How could he have thought that marriage to Rachel would be anything like marriage to Mel, or any other of the tottering marriages bred in Hollywood? Rachel was unique, and their marriage would be unique. Unique, and good, because Rachel Marsh was a once-in-a-lifetime woman, a forever kind of woman. She made him smile, laugh, wake up every morning thanking the universe for another day. She brought him down to earth, reined him in when he was galloping off half-cocked, and still managed to keep his head in the clouds and his heart singing.

Not to mention the sex. Jackson had always thought sex was entertaining, but not until Rachel did he realize that it could be earth-shattering. All those hyperboles in literature and film weren't exaggerations after all.

Nope, he wasn't going to give up Rachel, even though Rachel had her doubts. Rachel might have good sense on her side, but Jackson had persistence, and he'd put money on persistence any day.

Right then, though, he had to stir himself to get Mel, Cherie, and himself out of this place before a swarm of killer media descended upon the Lazy M and left behind scorched earth, metaphorically speaking. Mel drew the media like hounds after a fox. And after her spectacular entrance, the guests would be spreading the story as soon as they could find a signal on a cell phone. Jackson and his little entourage needed to escape before the swarm descended. Once they were discovered it would be too late.

His ex, as far as he knew, was still sawing logs in the ranch house, and his daughter had spent the morning sulking in the RV. He'd spent too much time waiting for them to come out of their holes. If they were going to get off the ranch that morning, he needed to go in after them.

He decided to tackle Cherie first, thinking she would be the easier task. He'd had experience dumping Melanie out of bed when she wanted to sleep and still flinched from the memories.

Jackson knocked on the door of the RV and said in a no-nonsense voice, "Cherie, if you don't come pack your stuff, we're leaving it behind."

"I can't."

"Why not?"

"I'm sick."

"Then we'll stop at Show Low and take you to the doctor."

"I don't need a doctor."

"Are you really sick?" He tried the door. It was locked, of course. She wasn't sick, she was sulking. "Cherie, unlock the door. Ever since we got here you've wanted to leave. So now we're leaving. You should be happy."

"I want to stay."

He would never understand females. Never. "We'll come back to visit."

Silence.

"Unless I'm forced to send you off to military school. Locked military school, with retired marines as teachers. You won't get vacation until you're twenty-five."

Cherie's sigh was so huge that Jackson heard it through the closed door. The lock clicked and the door opened. "You're just kidding about military school, right?"

"I don't know. You could use a little spit and polish."

"Dad!"

"Go pack. You have fifteen minutes before we're out of here." He put a hand on her shoulder, prepared to force-march

her to the cabin if he had to, when Cherie seemed to wilt beneath his touch. "Uh-oh!" she groaned.

Uh-oh indeed! Coming toward them were the two women
Jackson least wanted to see keeping each other company. No
man in love wanted an ex-wife prattling about his faults to the
woman of his dreams. And Mel did love to broadcast his faults
far and wide.

At least he wouldn't have to pry her out of bed.

"There you are," his ex greeted him with a bright smile.
"Rachel was just showing me around the place. I hoped we
would stumble on you somewhere."

"Just the people I wanted to see," Jackson lied. Rachel he
was delighted to see. Mel he just wanted to handcuff to the
motor home and get her out of there before the press arrived.
"If you'll get your stuff together, Mel, we can hit the road."

"Don't be ridiculous, Jackson. I'm not going anywhere." She
gave the motor home a contemptuous glance. "Especially in
that. I need some private time with my daughter, and I've decided that this a good place to do it."

She must be between films, Jackson thought. Too much time
on her hands always brought out the troublemaker in Mel.

"Also, I'm still waiting for an apology from you about dragging poor Cherie away without telling me where you were
headed. I don't want you thinking you can get away with this
sort of thing as a matter of course. Just because I gave you custody does not make you Lord High Poobah where our daughter is concerned." She tossed Rachel a glance, as if to say,
"Here's how to handle the man, dear. Take notes."

"Mel, if you want to visit with your daughter, then pack
your things, because Cherie and I are out of here in fifteen
minutes."

"Kidnapping her again?" Mel replied sharply.

"I didn't—damn! Melanie, just pack!"

Their conversation was drawing an audience. The yard had
been nearly empty when Jackson had crossed it a few minutes
ago, but now a number of guests and crew wandered here and

there, attempting to look casual and uninterested. But all had ears pricked in the direction of the motor home.

Rachel gave all those curious ears a worried frown. "Jackson, maybe you and Melanie should discuss this in private. And Cherie can come with me to say good-bye to Sam."

"No!" Cherie declared. "I don't need to say good-bye, because I'm not leaving. I'm not ready to go home yet. We need to stay longer." Her chin lifted defiantly—so like her mother, the similarity was downright scary.

This whole scene was just crazy enough to be a dream, Jackson decided. He tried to remember waking up that morning. Maybe he was still asleep.

"Cherie, get back in the motor home and stay there. I'll pack your things."

If she actually obeyed, he would know for certain this was a dream.

She didn't. Her lower lip crept out in a belligerent pout, and her eyes told him to stuff it. Mel's expression looked very much like her daughter's. Nope, not a dream. He held out a hand toward Rachel, his port in a storm. "Would you take Cherie into the motor home while I help Mel get her things and we hash out a few points?"

An all too familiar click brought Jackson's head whipping around, to see Josh Digby, one foot still in his Hertz rental car, grinning behind the lens of a camera. The colorful words that escaped Jackson's mouth caught even Cherie's world-weary attention. Scratch the plans for escape.

Digby's sudden appearance on the scene was just the beginning of the nightmare. Word of Jackson's whereabouts spread at the speed of light even before Digby's photo hit the presses. And what a photo that was, an innocent scene caught by the camera in a way to intrigue the most salacious imagination: Jackson reaching out to Rachel; Rachel gazing intently—some might say longingly—at Jackson; Melanie and Cherie both looking on with daggers in their eyes. Jackson Stone, lecherous rake, flaunts new lover in front of brokenhearted ex-wife and daughter. The press didn't care if Digby's photo created a totally false impression, and neither did the public, really.

The day after Digby's photo opportunity, the Lazy M was under siege. Jackson and Mel were cornered; to run once they'd been spotted, Mel confided to Rachel, would start a chase that would make a feeding frenzy of sharks look civilized.

Rachel hid behind the closed door of her office and looked at the photo splashed across the front page of the *National Star.* Other tabloids had moved like lightning to pick up the story. Rachel was cast as the villain—the other woman who stood in the way of an anticipated reunion of America's leading movie idols, the opportunistic hussy who seduced Jackson Stone even while his daughter looked on.

The lies shouldn't hurt so much, Rachel told herself. No one believed tabloid trash. And even if they did, why should she care if strangers thought she was some kind of sexual opportunist? If anything, notoriety would help her business.

But the lies did hurt. Rachel's stomach roiled and her heart ached. Her mother had called in the late morning to demand an accounting, and shortly afterward, her aunt from Albuquerque had checked in. They both had been indignant for her; being family, they had to be indignant. But even in them, her only relations, she had detected a bit of lurid curiosity. All in all, she felt rather alone in a world of staring, hostile thrill-seekers.

Well, not quite alone. Jackson was there for her, sympathetically trying to jolly her out of her black frame of mind. But she wasn't in the mood for humor. When she'd first read the *Star* story with its damning photo, Jackson had teased, "You'd better marry me now that the whole country, nay, the whole world, sees how you lust after me."

She'd turned away, refusing to respond. Even he couldn't completely understand how she felt. After all, Jackson Stone was accustomed to this sort of thing. He had turned serious then and kissed her, assuring her that the camera rarely pictured truth, and everyone knew it.

Melanie also teased Rachel about the photo. She had tsk-tsked when she'd first seen it. "Look at that lovelorn expression on your face, Rachel. You truly are a goner, aren't you, dear?"

"The camera rarely pictures truth," Rachel quoted Jackson.

"The camera almost always pictures truth," Melanie replied with a smile. "It's just that truth is open to interpretation. The truth in your universe is not necessarily the truth in mine." She had tapped Rachel's image on the newsprint. "But that needs no interpretation."

When Rachel had snorted fire, Melanie put a calming hand on her shoulder. "Don't fret, dear. Don't worry about these gadflies from the press. They're annoying, but not fatal. If you're going to link up with Jackson, you'll just have to get used to it."

Rachel wasn't sure she could get used to it, or that she even wanted to.

The press descended like a swarm of locusts before the morning was out. "You could leave," Mac had suggested to Jackson.

But Jackson refused to leave Rachel to the predators' mercy. Most of them would have followed the stars upon their departure, but some would stick around to pester the "other woman."

"Don't worry," he told Rachel. "A month from now, no one will remember your name."

So Jackson stayed, ostensibly to defend Rachel. Cherie hadn't wanted to leave anyway, or so she'd declared. And Melanie seemed perfectly content to linger and soak up publicity. Even this kind of publicity. And there was certainly lots of publicity to be had. Camped where Melanie's helicopter had landed just two days ago were reporters from *The National Enquirer, The Globe, Entertainment Weekly, People,* two television crews, and, of course, the *National Star's* Josh Digby, who seethed that his exclusive was no longer exclusive. The crowd actually pitched tents in the pasture between the cow pies, horse leavings, and rocks. They were prepared to stay until they got the interviews they wanted. A few sightseers had joined them. Groupies, Melanie told Rachel.

Rachel felt as though she should apply to the United Nations for help. After all, her home was under attack by a hostile force. And so was she. How celebrities lived in this prurient, hostile spotlight was beyond her understanding. These reporters had no respect for the truth, for privacy, for dignity, for a person's reputation. Everywhere she went, cameras were in her face and questions pounded her ears.

"Don't be surprised if some of these gossip rags use doctored photos to make things a little more spectacular," Mel had warned her at breakfast that morning.

"Why can't I just throw the jackasses off my property?" Rachel asked.

"You'd need an army of security guards to do it, and then you'd need to build a ten-foot wall around the whole ranch. Don't let it bother you," Melanie advised. "No one believes them anyway. Just keep your chin high and spit in their eye."

Rachel didn't want to spit in anyone's eye. What an awful way to live.

A knock on the office door distracted her. "Come in," she grumbled. "Oh, it's you."

"Good day to you, too." Jackson's smile was cautious. "Joanne thought you might need a bit of cheering up."

She gave him a jaundiced look and waved the newspaper under his nose. "I've had to give three refunds this morning. The guests were charmed to have the stars drop by to entertain them, but they don't feel so charitable about your army of followers."

He grimaced. "I'm sorry, Rachel. I really am. I'll make this up to you."

"My phone is ringing off the hook—curiosity-seekers. I'm in the phone book and on the Internet as well, and everybody in the world seems to be looking up the Lazy M. Not to make reservations, unfortunately."

He dropped his tall frame onto the couch. "I never meant this to happen, goddammit. I'd take Mel and Cherie and leave, but that would only make it look as if something lurid is going on with you, me, and Mel. Hell, knowing how these guys think, they'd probably include Cherie, as a foursome. They're blowing this way beyond Cherie's little adventure with Jimmy Toledo."

Rachel slapped the newspaper onto the desk. "This is such bullshit."

Jackson managed a grin. "Speaking of bullshit, I've done my best to convince them we're here on sort of a fractured family vacation. You figure in as a family friend. Some are buying it. No doubt you'll see speculation that Mel and I are getting re-married. That's been a favorite theme of these guys since Mel and I got divorced. This time they'll probably drag Cherie into the story as well."

"So you spin even more lies to get them off your trail. Jackson, is there any truth in your life at all?"

He grimaced. "You make it sound worse than it actually is, Rachel."

"Sorry." She massaged her temples, where a headache was clamoring for attention. "I have no call to climb up on my high horse. Actually, I'm amazed at how well you weather this sort of thing. Doesn't it make you grind your teeth to have people writing this crap about you?"

"I've been dealing with the media for a long time. It's not my favorite part of the job, but you do get used to it."

"You shouldn't have to. Even celebrities are entitled to a certain amount of privacy."

The understanding and sympathy in his expression nearly did her in. Her stomach flip-flopped. She wanted to sit down beside him, rest her head on his sturdy shoulder, and let his arms comfort her. She wanted a kiss from him that would dispel this black mood.

But whatever comfort he gave her would be only temporary, so she stayed where she was, elbows on the desk and lips touching her steepled fingers, almost in an attitude of prayer. The parade of thoughts racing through her brain was not a happy one.

She'd known from the beginning that Jackson Stone was trouble, and she'd been right. Not only was her ranch suffering, but her heart was in shreds. Saying yes to him would be so easy, and so wrong for her and Sam. They had a wonderful life at the Lazy M. What would they have with Jackson? Could she give up the simple life to join him in his glittery, fast-paced world, dodging cameras, living behind a privacy barrier built of small deceptions and convenient spin?

And then, of course, there was Sam. Sam wouldn't like the California smog, earthquakes, and crowds. He wouldn't like a place where he couldn't ride Thunder with Chesty trotting alongside. And he wouldn't grow up among straightforward, plain people who valued him for what he was, not how much money he had or how famous his stepfather was. Even if Jackson made his home here and commuted to California, the Hollywood craziness would follow him. The last two days had amply demonstrated that.

Love didn't conquer all. It couldn't protect a fish out of water. It couldn't make this fish want to jump out of the water. Rachel had to stay in her own quiet pond and let Jackson go back to his rapids.

"I do love you," she said softly. "I love you so much. Even though I've only known you a few weeks, it seems I've known you for eons."

She looked up cautiously, avoiding his eyes. The smile that spread across his face froze when she clenched her hands into fists.

"I do love you," she repeated dully. "But I can't live your life."

"What do you mean?"

Her fists clenched even more tightly. "Look at you, Jackson. You're rich and famous, at the top of your career. Yet the very reason that you're here is that you needed a place to hide. And now the hounds have found you, and look what happens."

He explained patiently, "It's not always like this, Rachel. The Jimmy Toledo thing sort of set a spark to tinder, and now they're looking for more, just to keep the story going. But usually the press isn't this bad. And when they do get too pushy, you learn to brush them off. Kind of like flies."

A tear fell on her hand. She tried to blink away those that welled up behind it. She was Harsh Marsh. She shouldn't cry about doing the right thing.

"I can't live that way, Jackson. My home is here. My life is here, and it's a life I chose. You live in a madhouse."

His mouth thinned to an ominous line, but she ignored it. Finally she found the courage to meet his eyes.

"Is stardom worth the price, Jackson? Is it worth being hounded, having no privacy, no life that's just your own and not your public's?"

He didn't answer, just fixed her with eyes that looked more black than green. Then he shook his head and turned to go.

"Jackson." Rachel stopped him as he opened the door. "Now I understand why you wanted to be someone else."

He nodded, unsmiling.

She bit her lip hard enough to bruise. "I wish to hell you were someone else."

Then he was gone, the door closed firmly behind him, and Rachel buried her face in her hands.

CHAPTER 18

♡

"YOU'RE WEIRD," SAM told Cherie. He sprawled beside her on the floor in front of the motor home's television set. Every once in a while she offered him some of her popcorn, but more often she shared with Chesty, who lay between them with his head on Cherie's lap. "And you're going to get in really big trouble." He was glad to be finally permitted into the RV, where Cherie had been hanging out for the past two days, but he wasn't going to toady up to her. She'd gone back to her vampire getup and snooty ways, and he didn't like it.

She gave him a royally disdainful sniff. "I'm in big trouble already, so it doesn't make any difference. Besides, once this thing is settled, everyone will be so relieved, I'll look like a hero."

"Will not."

"Will so. And you will, too, if you have enough guts to act like a man instead of a weenie."

"I'm not a man. I'm a kid."

"You're a weenie kid. A scared little weenie kid."

"I'm not scared. I'm sensible."

Cherie shook her head knowingly. "You're too young to be sensible. If you ask me, you're too young to be much of anything."

That hurt. But maybe she was right. Sam had always tried to be what he thought his mom wanted him to be. Cherie, however, was exactly what she wanted to be no matter what anyone else wanted. She had led him into trouble a couple of times during the last few weeks, but a little mischief wasn't the end of the world. Before Cherie came, Sam had thought it might be.

As if sensing his wavering will, Cherie pressed on. "It's not that big a deal, Sam. We'd just be helping your mom and my dad get what they want. Personally, I'd rather have my mom gone, but I'll settle for getting rid of the reporters to begin with. Maybe my mom will follow them. She likes to go where the publicity is."

"I don't think your mom is so bad. She says she can talk to Chesty, you know? She just looks in his eyes and kind of hums and stuff."

"Yeah. That's my mom." She made a face. "What does she think Chesty says?"

Sam shrugged. "Your mom says Chesty and me were brothers in another life, whatever that means."

"Don't ask her. She'll explain—and explain, and explain."

"Your mom is nice, though."

Cherie heaved a long-suffering sigh. "Retardo-boy! You've got a mom who at least gives a fig about you. Try putting up with mine sometime! Compared to mine, your mom's downright cool."

Sam popped a kernel of popcorn into his mouth. "You want your dad to marry my mom?"

Cherie made a face. "Marriage is a bit extreme, you know, but I could put up with it if necessary." She noted his confusion with a snicker. "Think about it, kid. My dad and your mom are mostly in good moods when they're together. I don't want to live with my dad if he doesn't settle things with your mom, and I'll bet your mom won't be easy to live with, either."

Sam felt compelled to disagree. "My mom is always nice to me."

"Even when she's just broken up with a boyfriend?"

"She hasn't had any boyfriends."

"Man oh man, are you in for a surprise. My dad—well, he doesn't get nasty or anything like that, but he gets grumpy when some bimbo gives him a hard time."

"What's a bimbo?"

She gave him a tolerant look. "Never mind. Anyway, none of those women meant anything to him, and your mom, well, your mom is different. He's gotten real goofy over her. If she gives him the boot, he'll be a grump for a year. Not only will I not get to go to Europe with Deanna, he'll probably send me to military school for real."

"No kidding?"

"Well, maybe." She scooted around so that she lay on the floor with her head resting on Chesty's back. Sam was a bit jealous of his dog being so tolerant. But Cherie did have the bag of popcorn, and even border collies could be bought. "It's not that I'm being totally self-centered," Cherie explained, throwing a piece of popcorn Chesty's way. "I want my dad to be happy, and your mom's fairly human, you know. She treats me like I'm a real person, and she doesn't act like she's totally clueless. I figure my dad is bound to marry someone, eventually, and I'd rather have your mom than a lot of other women who might apply for the job."

Sam was silent.

"And while this place is pretty lame, we could modern it up a bit. Money can do wonders with almost anything, you know, and my dad has so much money he doesn't know what to do with it. As long as I didn't have to be here all the time. God! A girl could grow mold on her soul, living here full-time."

Cherie was talking about things that hadn't crossed Sam's mind. He liked Jackson. Jackson was cool, even though he was a city slicker. That was what Mac called him, but he said it in a nice way. Everyone seemed to like Jackson.

But did Sam want Jackson to marry his mom? The two of them were pretty old to be doing stuff like that.

"So, anyway," Cherie continued, "my life's going to be a lot easier if my dad gets your mom. Of course"—she made a face at him—"if they get married, that means you'll be my dorky little brother and I can boss you around whenever I want."

"Just try it," Sam warned. "If you were my sister, I'd sneak into your room at night and cut all those silly spikes off your head."

"Then you'd be the one headed for military school."

"Wouldn't."

"Would."

"You don't know anything," Sam declared.

She was weird. An alien. An escapee from a vampire movie. Still, having her around wouldn't be all bad. When she wasn't in a mood, Cherie was okay. She had won the egg race, after all. Chesty liked her, and Chesty only liked good people.

Cherie picked up the remote and switched off the television. "Are you in, kid?"

"Are you sure about this?"

She gave him a smug smile. "What I'm sure about is this: Those reporters are messing up things for my dad and your mom, and therefore for you and me. I can take care of them, but your help would make things easier. This is what I have in mind. . . ."

Sam listened, and a smile gradually spread across his face.

Rachel contemplated hiding in her office all evening. In the two days since Melanie had shown up, life had bounced from one emotional trauma to another. Saying no to Jackson had been the absolute hardest thing she'd ever done. But saying no was the right decision, she kept telling herself. One of them had to stay rooted in reality.

She picked up the guest schedule she'd been staring at and crushed it in her fist. Crushing something felt good, and the schedule was meaningless anyway. Half of the guests had left, and those still here had joined the press in being obnoxious. What had happened to her calm, ordered life? What had happened to her peace of mind? The ranch was in chaos, the hands were picking fights with the reporters, Moira and Terri did nothing but giggle all day long, Joanne claimed that a nervous breakdown was right around the corner, and the reporters

were sending heaven knew what kind of drivel for their newspapers and tell-all television shows to broadcast. Now that
she'd been cast as the Arizona Jezebel, as one reporter had
dubbed her, she was fair game every bit as much as Melanie
and Jackson. What's more, she was fresh meat for them to
chew on. Jackson at least kept some of the worms out of her
face by interposing his physical presence between her and
them.

Jackson and Melanie put up a front that they were simply
visiting a friend at her guest ranch, routinely denying lurid
speculations, and refusing to talk about Cherie and Jimmy
Toledo. The circling hyenas left them unruffled.

But they left Rachel endlessly ruffled. She wanted them
gone—the reporters, Melanie, even Jackson and Cherie. She
wanted her life back. She wanted the Lazy M to be hers again,
quiet, organized, peaceful—boring.

Boring? Since when did she think of the Lazy M as boring?

Rachel refused to pursue the thought. And she refused to
hide for the rest of the evening. Dodging unpleasantness
wasn't really her style.

She emerged from her office to find Melanie sitting in the
living room. Keeping her company was one of the few ranch
guests who hadn't fled with refund in hand. She was a fortyish
lady pharmacist from Albuquerque who seemed one of the
more sensible people on the ranch.

"Hello, Rachel," the pharmacist greeted her. "I was just
telling Mel about the screenplay I've written."

So much for sensible. Rachel pasted a smile on her face.
"You've written a screenplay? How interesting."

"It would be a perfect vehicle to showcase Mel's talent."

"Ah."

Melanie was perfectly cordial as the pharmacist made her
pitch. When the pharmaceutical screenwriter left, Rachel
dropped wearily into an overstuffed chair by the window. "I'm
sorry," she said to Melanie. "I should be keeping my guests
away from you."

"Oh, no!" Melanie replied. "Fans are fans, even if they have screenplays in hand, or a niece trying to break into show business, or a charity cause that needs a sponsor. Don't worry, I get it all the time."

"You are amazingly patient."

Melanie laughed. "With some things I am."

"With some things you're what?" Cherie asked as she came in with Sam trailing behind. It was the first time Rachel had seen the girl all day. Given the hovering press, Jackson had been content to let her hide in the motor home.

"Patient," Melanie told her.

"Oh. Yeah, I guess."

Sam asked hopefully, "Can me and Cherie have some of that fudge Joanne cooked today? And maybe some milk?"

"What a good idea!" Melanie said brightly "That does sound good!"

Cherie sent her mother a look that said plainly that mothers were not invited, but Melanie ignored the message. "I've been trying to have some time with Cherie ever since I got here, and this is just ideal. Fudge and cold milk: the perfect bonding facilitator for mother and daughter. It's been so long since we truly connected heart to heart, spirit to spirit."

Cherie rolled her eyes. "My spirit's turned in for the night, Mom."

Mel laughed. "Oh, you! You should really come with me sometime soon to meet Makirah, dear, to learn what Spirit really is. It's so important that a young person, a still-growing person, connect with the Inner Soul. Especially a female. We are so much closer to Spirit than males."

Melanie flashed Rachel a look that clearly asked for privacy, and Rachel was glad to grant it. She felt a touch of sympathy for Cherie, but even more for Melanie. The kid would tangle the mother in her own "connections" inside five minutes.

"Come on, Sam. Let's give these two ladies some privacy."

"But . . . !"

Rachel saw the hope of fudge and milk fade from her son's face. "We'll fetch them some fudge from the kitchen, then have some ourselves."

He brightened, but gave Cherie an uncertain look.

Later, the girl mouthed, as if adults were too dense to read lips. Rachel wondered what the two of them might be up to.

Once in the kitchen, however, she was distracted from suspicion by an unexpected query from Sam. As she sliced the fudge into equal squares, he asked, "Ma, are you going to marry Cherie's dad?"

Rachel nearly sliced her own finger. Her mouth fell open, but nothing came out.

"'Cause Cherie thinks maybe you should. And it's okay with me. Mr. Stone's pretty cool, even if Cherie's kinda weird most of the time. I just wanted you to know, if you want to marry Mr. Stone, I'm willing to put up with dumb Cherie."

A lump clogged Rachel's throat. "That's very big of you, son. Mr. Stone is very nice, and I do like him a lot, but some things are just so complicated that they're downright impossible. I think Mr. Stone and me getting married is one of those things."

Sam looked both disappointed and thoughtful as he fetched milk glasses from the cupboard. "You're always saying that something worth having is something worth working for, aren't you?"

She couldn't deny it. "You're right. That's what I always tell you."

Sam gave her a look, the same look she gave him when she wanted him to comprehend an obvious point. Rachel wondered if the child wasn't wiser than the mother.

Sam went straight to bed when his mother told him to. But he didn't shed his clothes and don his Davy Crockett pajamas. Nor did he sneak a flashlight beneath the bedcovers to read another chapter of his Harry Potter book. On this night he couldn't afford to waste time on such childish things. Operation Stampede was going down tonight, and he had to be ready.

So he lay in the dark and watched the clock beside the bed

tick away toward the magic hour. The time he and Cherie had agreed upon for the caper was still five hours off. That was a long time to stay awake. Suppose he went to sleep? A guy never knew when sleep would sneak up on him in the dark, and Chesty's warm, snoring bulk curled against his legs already had him drowsy.

With a sigh, Sam set the alarm clock for the agreed-upon hour. For a moment he stared at the clock, then reached out and tucked it beneath the covers. The alarm sounding off at that odd hour of the morning might wake someone—like his mother. That wouldn't be good. Not good at all. He was doing this for her—mostly. But she might take a pretty dim view of the plan until she saw for sure how well it worked. Then he would be a hero. Cherie, too.

With the clock tick-tocking against his ribs, Sam's sleepiness fled. He stared into the dark and thought about his mom, who had looked mighty stern these past two days. Cherie was right. For a girl, she seemed to be right a lot. His mom might start smiling again if she married Mr. Stone. Having a movie star as a dad might not be too bad. Sam might get to meet Arnold Schwarzenegger or Clint Eastwood. He'd seen all of Clint Eastwood's old movies on tape. He might be dead now, like John Wayne. Dead or really, really old. But Sam still wanted to meet him. He'd introduce him to Thunder. Sam figured Clint Eastwood would appreciate a good horse when he met one.

And Hollywood might be fun to visit. Not to stay there, of course. Sam and his mom would have to come back here, because this was where they lived. But if Mr. Stone married his mom, probably he could live here and fly to Hollywood in a helicopter like the one Cherie's mom had used. And maybe Sam would get to ride in it sometimes. How cool was that?

Sam took the flashlight from the drawer of his bedside table and shone it under the covers at the alarm clock. Only a half hour had passed since he climbed into bed. He wished time would fly, so he could get to work and do his part to help his mom and Mr. Stone. Now that he'd considered the situation, he knew that he and Cherie were doing the right thing.

Besides, this caper was going to be really, really fun.

The morning sun hadn't yet peeked over the horizon, but the potential spectacle in the pasture where reporters had pitched tents had already drawn a fair-size audience. The show was about to begin. The press was still asleep. Several of the tents vibrated with snores.

Among those gathered at the fence were Sam and Cherie. Cherie wore a huge grin, no makeup, and hair that ruffled softly around her face. She'd been too busy for the past two hours to bother with cosmetics and hairspray. Already she congratulated herself on the success of her scheme. Dragging out of bed in the wee hours of the night wasn't her idea of a good time, but this show was going to be worth it. She couldn't have let Sam handle it alone. He was just a kid, after all.

Everything had gone like clockwork, thanks to her organization, Sam's cooperation, and Chesty's talent. Even better, with the first morning light, the hands had noticed what was going down and several of them had ambled over to watch the fun. Mac, Vince, and Dennis wore grins as big as Cherie's. They had no use for these guys with their cell phones and laptop computers and in-your-face nosiness. Just the day before, Mac had punched out a guy from the *World News Tattler* for calling him a rustic redneck.

Nosirree. When the hands saw a flock of nosy sheep grazing, peeing, and pooping among the reporters' tents, they had no sympathy at all for the members of the press. Instead, they gleefully hung around to watch the fun. These spring-loaded sheep were going to provide some great entertainment when the tents burped a bunch of reporters into their midst.

"Whoo-whee!" Dennis said. "Look at that! Pooping right on that guy's doorstep. Nothing like waking up to a pile of sheep berries."

"At least it ain't cattle," Vince commented. "I'd ruther be shit by sheep than some damned old soupy cow."

"You got a point," Mac said, then cast an eye on Sam. "You do this, boy?"

Sam looked a bit uncertain of his ground, so Cherie took over. "Both of us, and Chesty, of course. Couldn't have done it without Chesty," she said, generously giving credit.

Mac grinned. "Good job."

As the sun broke free of the horizon, the sheep began to bleat indignantly. They were accustomed to Sam giving them a portion of grain when the sun rose, and this morning no grain came their way. Grass was all very well and good, but a morning without grain was not a good morning to a sheep's way of thinking. A few tried nibbling on the tents. Others simply stood still and baaed plaintively. One woolly old biddy expressed her displeasure by butting a neighbor. The altercation that followed sent the two into the side of a tent, where they sat down abruptly. Miffed, the sheep gave the tent, and presumably its occupants, a couple of hearty kicks. The loud exclamation from inside the tent startled the other animals, and the sudden noises and stirrings from other tents made them even more nervous.

With a happy bark, Chesty bounded over the fence and circled around the frazzled flock so they couldn't bolt for open pasture. With the pasture fence on one side of them and Chesty zealously guarding the escape route, the sheep trotted about bleating and butting, stepping on tents and people emerging from tents, nervously peeing and pooping—often where the denizens of Tent City might least want them to pee and poop.

"That Chesty's one smart dog," Dennis observed.

"Smart as a whip," Vince agreed.

Sam beamed proudly, and Cherie glowed. This stunt was going better even than she had imagined. Even the cowboys thought it was cool. Very cool.

Vince shouted a warning to the guy from the *National Star*.

"Careful, there, guy! Don't get too close to 'em. There's Mad Sheep disease in this county."

"What the hell? Owww!" the man from the *World News Tattler* yelped as Ramon the Ram decided to use the reporter's rather large backside for target practice. The sheep were not happy.

"Big sheep escape last night," Dennis called out, laughing. "Don't let 'em slobber on you. Mad Sheep disease!"

"Oooh! Too bad about that laptop!" Mac chortled.

Sam called Chesty in, but by then the sheep had gotten into the swing of things. They were having too much fun to leave their playground of tents, sleeping bags, tin plates, and soda cans. By the time Sam and Cherie left for breakfast and the hands departed for their chores, the pasture was in a shambles and several of the reporters scrambled for their vehicles. Sam and Cherie shared a high-five while Mac grinned and gave them a thumbs-up.

Rachel had her attention on scrambling eggs for breakfast when Terri burst into the ranch house kitchen bubbling with laughter. "Rachel! Did you hear what happened in Tent City?"

Rachel gave her a pained look. "I try to ignore Tent City as much as possible."

"You'll like this! Ever hear of Mad Sheep disease?"

"You mean Mad Cow disease."

"Nope." Vince sauntered into the kitchen, a wicked grin on his face "Mad Sheep disease."

"What are you two talking about?" She reduced the heat under the eggs and took a pile of plates from the cupboard. "Vince, do you want something to eat?"

"Nope. Ate already. Take some coffee, though." He sat and tilted his chair back on two legs, looking smug. "That was some scene this mornin'. Glad I didn't miss it."

"All right," Rachel relented with a sigh. "What happened in Tent City?"

Terri grinned. "Poof! Totally flattened."

"Kicked about," Vince added.

"Peed on."

"Chewed up."

"Pooped on."

"Scared the living daylights out of those sorry-ass reporters."

Rachel held up her hands for silence. "Wait a minute. Mad Sheep disease?"

"That was Vince's idea," Terri said. "And Mac's. And those press idiots actually believed it."

"What do sheep have to do with any of this?"

Vince chuckled. "You need to ask your boy about that. Didn't think the little nipper had it in him."

Right on cue, the "little nipper" made his entrance, Cherie at his side. Chesty pranced in behind them, his tongue lolling happily. Rachel fixed both youngsters with a stern eye. Sam's ebullient bounce instantly slowed to a cautious tread, but Cherie marched in like a conquering heroine. She gave Terri a high-five and grinned at Vince.

"Sam!" Rachel pinned him with narrowed eyes.

The boy crooked a little grin. "Yes'm?"

"Explain!"

The tale made her almost choke on her eggs and bacon. She didn't know whether to scold or laugh, and looking suitably stern was nearly impossible as Sam boasted of Chesty's prowess in moving the sheep to the pasture from their pen in the moonlit hours before dawn. Cherie claimed creative credit for the scheme and also creative liberty in describing the chaos when sheep met newshounds.

"It was sweet!" she declared. "I wish I'd thought to bring my video camera."

"It was awesome!" Sam added. "And the reporters are leaving!"

"Yeah, and a couple of those guys are going to have to wipe their hard drives before using their laptops," Cherie chortled. "And I do mean wipe!"

Sam giggled.

Rachel's heart swelled. Losing Jackson would be so much

easier if what they had together was just passion, just them. But what they had together was more than passion, more even than a growing love between the two of them. They had a potential family, involving all of them. All of them with connections, as Melanie might put it, binding them, wrapping them about in a cocoon that kept the world's loneliness at bay. Mad Sheep disease indeed!

It won't work, her good sense warned her. *You're looking for an excuse to do something stupid, and it won't work.*

Joanne clumped into the kitchen and joined them, dishing herself a plateful of scrambled eggs and toast. "We have half our usual crowd in the dining hall," she complained, "but they take an extra hour at breakfast just gossiping about movie stars and such. And that nonsense in the pasture this morning. None of them were up early enough to see it firsthand, but the story's gettin' passed around like buttered popcorn at the cinema." She grunted something that might have been approval. "We're well rid of that set, I tell you."

Cherie and Sam exchanged a smug glance. Rachel told herself that she really should deliver a maternal set-down. These two were entirely too full of themselves.

She was saved the trouble by Jackson's entrance. He clumped into the kitchen with a thundercloud riding in brow. Apparently he'd seen the remnants of the press camp, and he was not amused. Silence dropped like a dark curtain at his scowl. Sam bit his lip and kept his gaze glued on a spot under the table. Cherie squared her jaw and looked a challenge at her father. "I did it," she confessed, anticipating his question. "It was my plan, and it needed to be done." Her tone was martyred—Joan of Arc at the stake. "You wanted to get rid of the reporters, so I got rid of them."

A plea for understanding bled through the defiance, but it met with Jackson's granite glare.

"Cherie, how would you have felt if one of those reporters had been hurt? And are you going to pay for the damage to their equipment?"

Cherie sulked. "Everyone else thinks it's funny."

"Everyone else is not responsible for your behavior. Apparently you aren't responsible for your behavior, either. You and I need to have a talk, in private." He pointed in the direction of the living room.

Cherie's jaw grew firmer. Like a prisoner headed for execution, she followed her father out of the room, brushing past Melanie, who was just now coming from her room.

Melanie lifted one finely drawn brow and tsked sympathetically. "Such a fierce scowl that man has." She turned a smile upon Rachel and said blithely, "If you marry him, dear, remember that he has no sense of humor in the morning."

All eyes turned Rachel's way. She sighed. Too bad the kids hadn't turned a herd of sheep loose in Melanie's room.

The sun was still high in the sky, but for Cherie the world was dark. Dark as night, dark as a dungeon, dark as her father's insensitive, ungrateful, unyielding heart. Cherie's mood had progressed from black to blacker as the day grew older. Now she sat cross-legged on a hay bale in the equipment barn, keeping the ranch machinery company. The tractor and wagon pressed her with no expectations, so she liked their company just fine. The horse trailer didn't care if she came or went, lived or died, and that was fine as well. It was great, in fact. Just great. People were always telling her to do this, think that, dress this way, talk that way, and she was tired of it. She did her best to be clever, and good, and cool, and what did she get? She got crap. All the time, crap. And she was tired of it.

Her dad was not happy with her, and that was putting it mildly. He cut her no slack, no slack at all. She hadn't intended any real harm. The sheep hadn't done that much harm, really. It wasn't like anyone got hurt. And everyone else seemed to think the whole thing was a hoot. Even Rachel. Sam's mom had tried to look mad, but Cherie had read the laughter in her eyes. Her dad was just being cranky, taking everything out on her, as if all this were her fault. If it weren't for her, he never would have met Rachel, and if not for her, those creepy reporters would still be slinking all over the ranch bugging people. Her dad gave her no credit. He called her irresponsible and thoughtless and accused her of never thinking about consequences. It wasn't fair. He wasn't fair, and life wasn't fair!

A shadow moved in the corner of the barn. Cherie hoped it was the Boston Strangler come back to life. At this point, she figured, nobody cared if she lived or died. She could get herself strangled, her mutilated body dropped on the doorstep, and her mom would probably say something like "Served the little monster right," and her dad would just be glad he didn't have to deal with his rotten daughter anymore. Or maybe they would be sorry that they hadn't treated her better. Her mom would regret making her nothing more than a hobby, and her dad would shed tears over being such an ogre. They would be sorry then.

"Come and get me!" she invited the Strangler.

The figure that emerged from the shadows wasn't the Boston Strangler or even the Lazy M Lacerator. It walked on four legs, had a lolling tongue, and ears that couldn't decide if they wanted to stand up or droop.

"Chesty." Cherie greeted the dog with a sigh, then she patted the hay bale beside her. "Come on up, mange-ball. If it were anyone else, I'd tell 'em to get lost. But you can stay."

The border collie jumped up beside her and shoved a wet nose beneath her arm.

"What's the matter? Did you get in trouble for siccing the sheep on those dumb reporters?"

She wondered how much grief Sam had gotten. She hadn't seen her partner in crime since that morning. He'd be okay, she decided. His mom wasn't nearly the toad that her dad was.

"Well, that was a great job you did with those sheep." She curled her fingers through the black-and-white fur and pressed her forehead to a shaggy shoulder. "You're smarter and better than anyone around here, Chesty. Man oh man! How pathetic is it that my only friend is a dog!"

That was what she got for trying to help, for being selfless and making the effort to do something for others. She had wanted to grease the skids for her dad and Rachel, and now both of them were ticked off. Well, she wasn't going to bother them anymore! She wasn't even going to think about them, and she certainly wouldn't care what they thought of her. If she knew how to find the freeway, she would swipe the Jeep keys and drive herself back to L.A. Or take the motor home. That would be cool. Maybe she would stay at her mom's place until she could take off for Europe with Deanna and her parents. Or maybe not. Her mom was on a motherhood jag. Melanie had cornered her for a whole half hour over fudge and milk the evening before, trying to fill her brain full of mother/daughter/goddess/Spirit crap.

What lame luck she had in the parent department—a dad who thought she was a total loser and a mom who wanted to strangle her with New Age flakehood. Right now probably neither one of them would let her go with Deanna. She might as well run away. She would take one of her dad's credit cards and make him really sorry he'd been so unjust.

Cherie sighed into Chesty's fur. "They'd be really sorry. All of them would be sorry. I don't know why I thought Dad should stick with Rachel, anyway. We'd have to spend time at this lame ranch. The only cool things here are the horses and you, you old dog, you." She thought a moment, screwing up her face. "Okay, there's some other stuff, too. The rodeo was sort of fun. And Sam is okay, even though he's a dweeb. And a couple of the hands are cooler than they look, even if they are really prehistoric."

The idea came to her like an explosion in her brain. The hands . . . That was it! She gave the border collie an enthusiastic squeeze that made him yip.

"You're a genius, Chesty! This is, like, telepathy, right?" For a moment she grew thoughtful, and then her eyes narrowed. "I know just the person who can help!"

CHAPTER 19

♡

SAM LAID LOW all day long. After lunch he retreated to his room. He told his mom that he wanted to finish the new Harry Potter book. His mom was always happy to see him reading something, and Sam figured he needed to earn a few attaboys to offset Operation Stampede. The next best thing to staying out of maternal sight was sticking his nose in a book. Both strategies kept him out of the way of trouble.

Though Sam had suffered a mild scolding, his mom hadn't really seemed all that upset by the sheep thing. Vince had told him once that his mom was a "no-nonsense kind of woman," but Sam knew that she did like nonsense every once in a while. Besides, she didn't like those nosy reporters any better than Jackson did, and Sam had heard her talking about getting the sheriff to make them go away. But Jackson had warned her that throwing the reporters off would bring a whole army of them to the ranch. Reporters were like hyenas, he'd told her. The scent of a fracas would attract a whole pack of them.

But those pesky reporters sure hadn't liked the sheep. Watching those woollies flatten Tent City had been one of the high points of Sam's life. His mom might have laughed out loud if she had seen it firsthand.

Still, adults were unpredictable, and a kid couldn't be too careful after pulling a stunt like Operation Stampede. Poor Cherie had really caught it from her dad. Jackson had really looked grim when he marched Cherie out of the kitchen, and

Sam had seen only glimpses of Cherie since. All day she had slunk around looking like a zombie. Sam didn't blame her. He wouldn't want Cherie's dad mad at him, that was for sure. He remembered how Jackson had looked in the movie *Trueheart* when he had faced down those Comanche guys who had killed his horse. He could really look scary when he wanted to.

Not that Cherie couldn't be downright scary herself. Sam figured she and her dad were about evenly matched in that regard, but Jackson was bigger, and he was a grown-up. That gave him an unfair advantage.

In any case, Jackson appeared to have won this round, because Cherie looked as if someone had taken all the stiff out of her spine. Sam had thought about seeking her out, but he was close enough to being in trouble himself that getting next to Cherie would probably earn him a chewing out.

For a while Sam managed to leave his real-life troubles behind by diving into the world of Harry Potter and his friends. He wished that he could have mail delivered by an owl and hop on a flying broom to zip around the sky. He wished that he were brave enough and smart enough to save the world from evil wizards and their nasty minions. Some kids had all the luck!

When a scratch at his bedroom door pulled him away from the realm of magic, Sam was surprised to see that it was almost time for dinner. A whine from outside the door told him he had locked out Chesty.

He apologized profusely as he opened the door. "Sorry, bud. I didn't mean it."

Chesty gave him a forgiving lick on the hand, then whined anxiously and looked toward the door.

"Not quite dinnertime yet. But I could probably find a dog biscuit in the kitchen." The coast would probably be clear. He'd heard Jackson tell his mom that he was taking the motor home into Springerville to get an oil leak fixed, and this time of day his mom would be helping Joanne in the Chuckwagon kitchen.

Now that the reporters were gone and things were back to

normal, Jackson was taking Cherie and the motor home and heading for home. And a helicopter was coming early tomorrow morning to pick up Cherie's mom, who didn't think the RV was cool and wouldn't ride in it. Things would be back to the way they were before Sam and his mom had found Jackson and Cherie on that afternoon a month ago. Soon the Lazy M would close for the season. After branding, most of the hands would leave. No more guests until spring. Paul would take his horses and head for warmer country.

Sam tried to ignore the sudden chill of loneliness, but he quickly gave in to the sudden urge to find Cherie. She was probably feeling pretty low, he reasoned, and when a person felt low, that person needed company, even if the person didn't know it.

Besides, Sam needed a bit of company himself. With Chesty beside him, he quietly left the house and looked around the ranch yard. No one was in sight, though voices and the clanking of pots and pans drifted from the Chuckwagon. In the barn, Paul said something to Vince and a horse whinnied. But neither man took note of Sam and Chesty slipping past the open door.

Boy and dog checked out their own favorite hiding spots— the smokehouse, the equipment barn, under the Chuckwagon porch. No Cherie, though. Finally, a hint of voices from behind the bunkhouse led them in that direction.

Bingo! There was Cherie talking to Toby. Sam hid himself behind the corner of the building. Ordinarily he would have walked up to them bold as brass and asked what was going on, but a feeling in his gut told him he wouldn't be welcome.

"Is that all you're taking?" Toby asked Cherie. They stood beside Toby's old beat-up truck, and Cherie had a duffle bag in her hand.

"My dad will grab the rest of my things. This will get me where I need to go."

"Okay. Whatever."

Toby had that dopey look that men sometimes got around the ladies. Not that Toby was a man, really. He was more like an overly tall kid. And Cherie certainly wasn't a grown-up lady, for all that she sometimes acted flirty and stupid. Sam could see that something was going down. Toby and Cherie were going to get in big trouble.

"Let's go," Cherie said. Her mouth curved downward in a sullen sort of bow that told Sam she was in a really bad mood. "We need to get out of here before my dad comes back."

"For sure."

"And you're not going to say a thing, right?"

"For you, darlin', I'd let them pull out my fingernails and stretch me on the rack."

Cherie rolled her eyes. "Right. Let's go."

"I gotta get my wallet."

"Sheesh!" Cherie threw her duffle into the back of the pickup and followed Toby into the bunkhouse. Sam knew what he had to do, though the prospect of such boldness was scary. Still, would Harry Potter balk at helping friends who were headed for trouble? Would Harry Potter wimp out because he might get a scolding? No, Harry wouldn't, and neither would Sam.

"You stay!" he ordered Chesty. "Stay here, and don't tell!" Trying not to think about what his mom would say, Sam climbed into the bed of the truck and hid himself beneath a canvas tarp—just as Toby and Cherie came out of the bunkhouse. Next thing he knew, the truck was bumping along the dirt road that led to the highway, and from there who knew where?

Rachel watched the motor home drive in beneath the Lazy M archway and bit her lip as Jackson parked it beside the barn. Her stomach was churning, her palms sweating. All day she had suffered a similar distress because Jackson was going back to California, walking out of her life, leaving a woman who no longer knew herself or what she wanted, a home that would be empty without him, and a heart that threatened to shrivel in his absence. Worse, it was she who sent him away, she who refused to give love a try, she who thought her life was so hunky-dory that any change had to be for the worse. She had been at war with herself all day, one camp telling her to shun temptation, another shouting at her to give it a try.

All that had been bad enough, but this was far worse. As Jackson climbed down from the motor home and walked toward her, smiling that lazy, sensual smile that made her heart pound, Rachel wished with all her heart that she didn't have to pile one more thing upon the burden he already carried.

"Come to your senses yet?" he asked.

"Jackson . . ."

He stopped in his tracks, his smile flattening. "What's wrong? I can see from your face that something's wrong."

"I can't find Cherie. Not anywhere."

"She was sulking in the equipment barn when I left. Knowing Cherie, she's still hiding in there dreaming up ways to spit-roast me over a slow fire." He grimaced. "I was a bit hard on her this morning. Maybe I need to go and mend some fences."

"I checked the equipment barn, Jackson. I checked your cabin, the main barn, the guest cabins, the house. Melanie hasn't seen her. Neither have the hands. Not since mid-afternoon. I even telephoned Karen in Greer to see if she might have hitched a ride into town."

"That little idiot! When I find her . . ." He darted a suspicious glance toward the main barn. "The horses are all accounted for?"

"Yes. And Paul hasn't seen her."

"The ranch vehicles?"

"All here."

Glancing over to where his Jeep sat next to Rachel's van in front of the garage, he ran his fingers through his hair. "She's got to be around here someplace. She wouldn't have taken off walking. Walking isn't Cherie's style. What about Sam?"

"Sam's been reading in his room all afternoon. He's been avoiding me like I'm poison—probably afraid that I'm going to take after him more than I already have."

"We could at least ask him." Jackson took her arm and

guided her toward the house. "And another word with Mel wouldn't hurt. She claims to be psychic. Let's see if she can find her missing daughter."

"I talked to Mel. She said not to worry. Cherie is just working off her negative energy and will come back when she's ready."

He snorted. "Yeah. That sounds like something she would say."

The door to Sam's room was shut. Frowning, Rachel knocked. "Sam, open up, pardner. I need to talk to you."

Jackson wasn't so polite; he simply opened the door. The room was empty. Harry Potter's latest adventure was facedown on the rumpled John Wayne bedspread. A plate dotted with cookie crumbs sat on the desk beside a half-empty tumbler of lemonade. But no Sam.

"I was sure he was up here."

"Funny thing about kids," Jackson said sourly. "They can disappear faster than snow in L.A."

"He hasn't disappeared. He'll be in the barn with Paul, or maybe down by the arena. I should have looked for him before this." Sam, she thought with a hint of nervousness, wasn't like Cherie. Sam wasn't a problem child who wore trouble like a badge of honor. Sam was quiet and obedient, considerate, trustworthy.

And gone. He wasn't in any of the places that they searched. With every place that Sam wasn't, Rachel's panic escalated. "I don't understand!" she said as much to herself as to Jackson. "He can't just be gone. I didn't scold him that harshly. He didn't have reason to be upset."

Jackson sat down heavily on the steps of his cabin. "She could've walked out to the highway and hitched a ride, I suppose, but I can't picture her taking Sam, even if he wanted to go."

Rachel thought she might choke on frustration. Her stomach churned with acid. The very thought of her Sam somewhere where she couldn't find him, couldn't protect him, made her want to throw up.

"Hey, hey, Rachel." Jackson's arm went around her. His eyes

warmed. "It's okay, sweetheart. Sam's probably with Cherie, and Cherie will look out for him. She's a tough little devil."

She tried to answer, but her throat clogged with emotion. How could he be so calm when he had to be as frantically concerned as she?

For a brief moment Jackson pulled her against him, his arms circling her in comfort. His chest was a wall of strength that invited the tears she finally allowed to spill.

"It'll be fine," he said, his lips against her ear. "Take it from a guy whose kid is world class at the sport of parent baiting. We'll call the sheriff and get them working on it."

That inspired a fresh deluge of tears. Right now, Rachel, who prided herself on self-reliance and strength, needed someone to prop her up, and Jackson's steady calm kept her from melting into a useless puddle of frantic, blubbering, maternal panic.

They were walking back to the house to call the sheriff when Rachel heard the bark. "That's Chesty."

Another bark.

Rachel's heart pounded. "Where Chesty is, Sam will be, too. Come on."

They followed the sound to the rear of the bunkhouse, where they found Chesty standing among the weeds and oil stains that decorated the ground where the hands parked their vehicles—the site of the Great Shaving Cream Escapade, Rachel remembered with a painful lurch of her heart. To her intense disappointment, Sam wasn't with his dog, a thing ominous in itself. Chesty looked woebegone, ears pinned back and tail limp, but there was no trace of either Cherie or Sam.

Jackson gave Chesty a sour look. "Nothing. He was barking at a rabbit, most likely. Come on, Rachel. Let's go call the sheriff."

Chesty barked in a tone that clearly called Jackson's judgment into question. Jackson expelled a frustrated sigh and turned to go.

"Wait!" Rachel forestalled him. "Where's Toby's truck?"

Parked here were Vince's truck, Mac's motorcycle, and Dennis's little Hyundai. Toby's truck should have been there as well.

Jackson turned slowly, his expression darkening. "Toby?"

"He wouldn't have," Rachel said, mostly to herself. "Toby wouldn't have gone off with Cherie. He fancies himself a ladies' man, but he knows that she's only thirteen. And he certainly wouldn't take Sam. He knows I'd have his hide off him in strips."

"That's child's play compared to what I'll do to him if he's gotten either one of those kids in trouble." He scratched Chesty's ear. "Did they leave you behind, big fella?"

"Oh, Lord!" Rachel said quietly. "Sam warned me weeks ago that Cherie was playing up to Toby. Why didn't I listen?"

Fifteen minutes later, no doubt was left. None of the hands had seen Toby for over two hours. Mac said the boy was supposed to be painting the sheep pens, but he hadn't seen him, either. They found a can of white paint and paint-stiffened brushes by the arena. Toby's gear was still in the bunkhouse, however. Only his truck was missing—along with two children.

"Where the hell would they have gone?" Jackson fretted as they emerged from the bunkhouse. His arm was around Rachel, and she leaned into him, uncaring of who might see. Some situations brought life right down to the basics—who you loved, who loved you back, who you wanted beside you when the world went crazy. These were the important things. Other details were merely clutter.

"This couldn't be another elopement," Jackson added. "Even Cherie isn't that demented."

"And they would scarcely have taken Sam as chaperone."

As if in answer to their question, Joanne shouted from the house. "Phone call! It's Sam!"

Jackson prayed that the state troopers patrolling between Greer and Springerville were somewhere eating donuts, because he was breaking every speed limit. Springerville was a forty-minute drive from the ranch at sane speeds; he intended to make the distance in much less time.

Rachel sat beside him as the Lazy M van flew over the asphalt. Her hands clutched each other, knuckles white—not because of his speed, Jackson knew, but for worry about their children. At least now they knew where they were.

"Sam ought to get a medal for this," he told Rachel. "Not every eleven-year-old would have the presence of mind to stow away in a runaway's car and then phone back information."

Rachel moaned and massaged her temples. "When I think of him alone at the bus station . . . I swear I'm going to ground him until he's forty for taking off like that. He should have told an adult when he saw them leaving."

"By the time he could have found someone, the culprits would have been out of sight. We wouldn't have known where they were. Besides, it's the Code of the West, isn't it?"

"What?"

"You don't rat out your friends."

She laughed shakily.

"Don't come down too hard on the little guy," Jackson advised. "If I ever have the good fortune to have a son, I couldn't ask for one better than Sam."

A tear dribbled down Rachel's cheek, and he wiped it away with a thumb. How very beautiful she was, this ostensibly ordinary woman who would never make cameras flash nor fans hover. Any producer in the country would look at her and pronounce her not young enough, not thin enough, no style, no aura, no flash. Yet in his eyes she was as close to perfect as a woman could get. True star quality. She had character, compassion, humor, and wit. Her smile made his heart beat, her body made his blood run hot. This was a woman to love for a lifetime and beyond.

"You were right, you know, Rachel. It's past time I made serious changes in my life."

"Did I say that?"

"Not in so many words. But I got the message. My daughter

is a mess—for several reasons. One is that she has too much money and gets too little attention from me. And she lives in a world that thinks beauty, fame, and wealth are the ultimate goals of existence. Her friend Deanna's family is about the only normal family she knows."

"That's rough."

"Not to mention that nowhere in the country can I so much as take a leak without ten reporters popping out from behind the urinal."

For that she granted him a small smile.

"You know what I mean."

"After the last few days, I do."

"Somewhere along the way I regressed from a fairly sane, mature, hardworking man into a spoiled prima donna who thinks he can walk into anyone's life and rearrange it simply for his own entertainment."

"I wouldn't paint you quite so black."

"You wouldn't?"

The warmth in her eyes could have been compassion, but Jackson hoped not. He didn't want her sympathy; he wanted her. If he could go back in time to the day he first met her, he would do things differently. His pursuit of Rachel had been a good-natured joke, an entertaining challenge. How stupid was that? He should have recognized right off that a woman like Rachel was rare as a perfect diamond, more precious than an Oscar, and worth ten times any other woman who had ever walked into his life. He hadn't thought to look for permanence with anyone. His stab at permanence with Melanie had convinced him that a stable married life was impossible. Somewhere along the way he had bought into the Hollywood version of romance, not the one projected in films, but the one the filmmakers lived in their everyday lives. Love was for excitement. Love was for fun. Love was for image, sexual recreation, and even challenge. But love wasn't forever.

A few short weeks at the Lazy M had brought him back down to earth. Rachel Marsh had latched on to his heart and reminded him that sometimes love was forever. But not until he'd seen Mel and Rachel together had the contrast between what had been and what could be hit him between the eyes. He had clung to old fears while the future slipped through his fingers.

If he had wised up earlier, could he have persuaded Rachael to marry him? Could he have repaired the image she had of a spoiled, thoughtless superstar wed to fame, money, and irresponsible bachelorhood? Could he still convince her that he would much rather be wed to her?

"Cherie needs a different sort of life," he continued out loud.

"Jackson, don't beat yourself up about Cherie. Basically she's a good kid. There's pure gold somewhere beneath the spikes, hairspray, and mascara."

"And attitude," he said glumly.

"And attitude," she agreed.

"I'm not blaming my daughter for her problems," he assured Rachel. "The fact is, I need a different sort of life, too."

Her only response was, "Turn here to get to the bus station. And you'd better slow down. I'm sure the local police would just love to give Jackson Stone a traffic ticket."

The bus station smelled like a bus station. It wasn't crowded. A young man carrying an Arizona State University backpack slept on one of the benches. Sprawled across another bench was a young couple, their unhappily shrieking baby, and the pile of paraphernalia that always accompanies an infant. A gentleman who looked to be at least a hundred mumbled to himself as he examined the bus schedule, and a middle-aged lady barricaded by suitcases read a paperback mystery and ignored all who passed.

Nowhere was there a lanky, arrogant kid in a cowboy hat or a teenage girl sporting spiky hair and goth makeup. And nowhere was Sam.

"She's in the snack bar, if you're looking for your daughter." The information came from behind Jackson, delivered in a Midwestern twang spiced with insolent relish.

Jackson whirled to confront Josh Digby, who gave him a little salute. Just his luck a reporter would be here, and Josh Digby, of all people. The whole ugly mess would be recorded for the papers in great detail.

"And the little kid—the one who set the damned sheep on us—he's hiding in the phone booth. He probably can't see you from there."

Rachel uttered a little cry and gave Digby a spontaneous hug. "Thank you, Mr. Digby! Thank you so much!" Biting her lip, she rushed toward the pay phones, but Digby put a hand on Jackson's arm before he could follow.

"A twerpy cowboy brought her in here. He's in the snack bar, too." At Jackson's hard-eyed look, he shrugged, almost an apology. "Don't worry about it, Stone. Cowboy brawls in bus stations don't interest my readers. I kept an eye on all three of them, figuring if you showed up, you'd want to know where Cherie was headed. I saw the kid call. Otherwise I would've phoned the ranch."

Jackson's mouth twitched in what might have been a smile "I guess I owe you, Digby. Didn't think I'd ever be saying that."

"Yeah, well, you caught me on one of my more noble days. I'll collect. Never fear. I like having people like you owe me favors. I gotta run to catch my bus, so good luck. I'm counting my blessings that I don't have a teenage daughter. Just sons."

Rachel was all smiles when she came back leading Sam by the hand. And Sam looked very proud of himself. "I stowed away in the back of the truck," he told Jackson. "Like a spy, you know? And I had to bum a quarter off an old lady so I could call on the phone." A shadow of uncertainty crossed his face. "I didn't wanna be a tattletale, but I was afraid that Cherie was gonna get in trouble. She thinks that she's really tough, but she's really just a kid."

Jackson squatted down to Sam's level and put his hands on the boy's shoulders. "Truer words were never spoken, Sam. I'm really thankful that you were looking out for her. But you've got to look out for yourself as well, pardner."

Sam glowed. Jackson experienced a rush of warmth as he realized that Rachel wasn't the only person at the Lazy M whom he loved.

But before he could get all warm and fuzzy, he had to deal with Cherie and Toby. "And speaking of the little devil . . ." he muttered as Cherie came out of the snack bar. Any hint of warm fuzzies dissolved in a flood of paternal indignation.

Rachel got his attention with a hand laid gently on his arm. "Let me fetch her, Jackson. You look like a short fuse burning down to a stick of dynamite. Besides, she just went into the ladies' room, and you are not going to scare the women in there by having "Devil Dog" Davis crash in on them while they're sitting on the pot."

That made him smile. "You *do* go to my movies."

She gave him a superior look. "Sam is the one who thinks Agent Davis is cool." But she grinned all the same. Bless her.

"Go get her. I'll deal with Toby."

"Leave him in one piece, please. He's just a kid himself."

Rachel sent Sam off with Jackson. Then she girded herself, metaphorically speaking, to face Jackson's daughter. Rachel herself had been a goody-two-shoes growing up, but she could relate to Cherie's need to rebel. Cherie at least had taken action, and if that action was ill-considered, at least it showed a certain amount of courage. Perhaps Cherie could teach Rachel a thing or two about taking chances, just as Rachel might teach her something of common sense and moderation.

Cherie was in front of the dirty mirror applying more eyeliner—as if she needed more!—when Rachel walked in. When the girl spotted Rachel in the mirror, her eyeliner took off across the side of her face and her mouth stretched in a quiet "Eeeeek!"

"Jig's up," Rachel told her.

"Oh, man! How did you find me?"

"Sam stowed away in the back of Toby's truck. He phoned home."

"I'm going to throttle the little dweeb!"

"You'll have to survive your father first."

Cherie's face fell "He's gonna kill me. I'm gonna be locked in my room wearing a chastity belt until I'm thirty!" She drooped against the sink.

"Tell me you weren't running off with Toby."

The girl rolled her eyes. "Oh, like I would get serious with Toby Whitman! I mean, he's an okay guy, but really not my type for any serious stuff. God! I just tapped him for a ride to the bus station, you know?" She gave Rachel a worried look. "I hope my dad's not killing the poor guy, because this was totally me, not Toby. I'm hard to resist when I turn on the charm, you know."

So was her father, Rachel mused. She did appreciate the fact that Cherie was concerned for Toby when she herself faced a truckload of trouble. Likely the girl was redeemable.

"I wasn't, like, running away or anything. I just wanted to go home, and then I'd go to Europe with Deanna and be out of everyone's hair. I screwed everything up, and I knew my dad would, like, ground me forever. I figured he and my mom would be glad enough to be rid of me for a while."

"Cherie, your dad loves you."

"Right."

"He's trying to protect you."

"I don't need protection!"

"Sweetie, we all need protection. I know it sounds corny, but you should be thankful that you have someone who cares enough to worry about you."

Her face crumpled. Tears threatened the black mascara.

"And your mom loves you, too, you know. She just has a really different way of showing it."

"Yeah. She is from a totally different planet!"

Rachel laughed and put an arm around the girl. "I've got news for you, kid. With all the people who care about you, you're not going to see any real freedom until we're all in our graves."

"Probably not even then," Cherie grumbled "One of mom's best friends is a hot-shot medium. She'll bring you all back from the Other Side to lecture me."

Tears streaked Cherie's face, but she gave Rachel a wry smile, then hit her with a change of subject. "So . . . are you going to marry my dad or not?"

"So . . . are you going to marry me or not?"

Jackson and Rachel sat on the ranch house porch nursing two glasses of lemonade diluted with vodka.

Rachel smiled into the dark. The half-moon had set, and the night was dark as only a country night could be. "When did I give you any indication that I'd changed my mind?"

"Crisis situations are always supposed to bring the stubborn, recalcitrant, unreasonable woman to her senses."

"Is that so?"

"Almost every script I've ever read."

The dark worked against her. His face wasn't even a blur in the night, so she couldn't read Jackson's expression. Was he teasing or serious? "Scripts," she scoffed. "Movies. You still live in the land of fiction."

"Oh, I don't know. Sometimes real life should have a happy ending, don't you think? A real happily ever after?"

Rachel smiled and took a sip of her drink. She had learned several lessons today—that she didn't want to face life without this man to help her through it; that everything in her world could change in a minute, without warning; that she couldn't hug peace, serenity, and familiar routine to herself like a child's comforting blanket. No risks taken meant no prizes won. And the man sitting beside her was surely a prize as well as a risk.

Her own child had hit the nail on the head in reminding her that anything worth having required hard work.

"Marriage is a big step," she temporized.

Jackson moved closer to her on the porch swing and snaked an arm around her. "Well, now, that's true. Marriage is a big commitment. Probably a period of temporary indenture could be arranged."

Rachel smirked. "I like the sound of that. There's still plenty around here you could do, starting with painting the guest cabins."

"Ha! Considering the trouble Cherie and I have taken to save your ranch from hordes of invading reporters and a takeover by the Queen of New Age, I think services owed might be from you to me. I have a half-built sailboat in L.A. that needs sanding. Good, gritty work—right up your alley."

She snuggled into the circle of his arm. "You are so out in left field."

"I'm perfectly reasonable."

"Total bullshit." His hand slipped inside the waistband of her jeans and idly caressed the small of her back. Thinking became almost impossible. Rachel sighed. Right then life was almost perfect. Cherie was glumly contemplating her misdeeds in her cabin, but she had shared secret smiles with Rachel on the way back from Springerville. Toby had survived his encounter with Jackson and conceived a sudden urge to find work in New Mexico. Sam was safely tucked in bed with Chesty curled at his feet, the Lazy M was once again a haven of peace and sanity, and a whole world of adventures—far from peace and sanity—awaited her.

She allowed her finger to trace lazy, sensual circles on his chest. "You'll have to learn to ride a horse. I mean, really ride a horse. I can't be with a man who rides like a city slicker."

"Since you'll have to put up with L.A. now and then, I guess that's fair."

"And you have to let me be a mom to Cherie—as much as she'll let me."

"It's your funeral."

"And we have to be nice to Mel. I like Mel, really. And Cherie needs her."

Jackson chuckled. "Any more conditions, Ms. Marsh?"

"Yes. Kiss me."

"I like that one."

The kiss was tender and demanding at the same time. If

America's women only knew—Jackson Stone kissed even sexier in real life than on the screen.

Huskily, he suggested against her ear, "There's a perfectly empty RV over there with a nice queen-size bed."

"What a waste."

"I'd carry you over the threshold, but I'd probably drop you going up the steps."

She laughed and batted at him. "You just lost your title as America's heartthrob."

"Then I'll just have to work that much harder to win it back."

Laughing, hand in hand, they walked toward the privacy of the motor home.

EPILOGUE

♡

Excerpt from *Jackson Stone: An Unauthorized Biography* by Joshua Digby. Paparazzi Press, 2012.

Professional cynics give little credit to celebrity marriages, and Jackson's first marriage to Melanie Carr (see Chapter 2—Witches, Wizards, and Mediums) was certainly a classic Hollywood failure, sensationalized by the press hoopla that attends such failures. The difficulty of a stable relationship in the entertainment industry is understandable. Hollywood is a culture of fantasy, not reality. Romance, not true love. Spectacle, not stability. Marriage in the rarified atmosphere of fame and wealth are mere temporary romantic stopovers. Fragile wedding vows with only romance as their backbone crumple easily when a new romance comes along, and in an industry that caters to the young, the beautiful, and the egocentric, romantic opportunities abound.

But in his second marriage to Hollywood outsider Rachel Marsh, our boy struck marital gold.

Few members of the press were invited to the Stone/Marsh wedding. The author of this book was fortunate enough to be one of them. The two were married in the springtime, just months after Stone made a total fool of himself trying to cowboy on the Marsh ranch, a resort that provided Old West offerings of real horses, cattle, and a few extraordinarily obnoxious sheep (see Chapter 6—The Perils of Stalking a Star). The outdoor wedding was a strange mixture of Hollywood and Down Home, with locals such as the eighty-something postmistress and a number of jeans-clad, slicked-up cowboys mingling with the likes of Mel Gibson, Clint Eastwood, John Travolta, Robin Williams, and Meg Ryan. Melanie Carr attended the wedding of her ex in bouncing good spirits. She blessed the couple with an ancient Egyptian ritual insuring long life and fertility. Steven Spielberg acted as Best Man, and Maid of Honor was a local restaurant owner who ended up heading for Las Vegas after the ceremony with one of the groomsmen—stuntman Barry Rafner.

Country-western star Clint Black entertained at the reception, but the singer was upstaged by Spielberg's Welsh corgi, who sneaked in with the ranch's sheep and nearly ran the creatures ragged before being chased from the pen by an irate border collie belonging to the bride's son. The cowboys had a fine time taking bets on who would win. No one took odds on the sheep.

Funky wedding aside, the Stones have built a surprisingly stable marriage, producing together two children, a boy born two years after the wedding and a girl born three years later. Rachel's older son, Samuel, attends Colorado State University as a pre-vet student, and Jackson's daughter Cherie, at twenty-three, has a budding film career of her own. Jackson Stone purposefully cut back on film projects after his marriage, yet his career expanded and blossomed. In 2005 he was nominated for the Golden Globe's Best Actor for his role in *Three Witches* and in 2010 he won the Best Director Oscar for *Year of the Stallion*.

Perhaps what makes the Stone marriage so strong is a continuation of the odd mix present at their wedding, the dilution of rarified film culture with an almost nineteenth-century flavor that still exists in pockets of rural America. Rachel Stone's Lazy M is a working ranch to this very day, and the Stones spend much of their time there. The guest-ranch part of the operation has been transformed to a summer camp for disadvantaged children.

In addition, the Stones invest heavily in the local area. Jackson Stone is a regular as grand marshal of the Greer Days parade and occasionally participates in the local rodeo. Much to the delight of the local population, he and wife Rachel entered the rodeo's "rescue race" the summer after their wedding. The exact purpose of the event eludes me, but it involves one person galloping a horse like mad the length of the arena to pull aboard a person who waits to be "rescued." Then they race madly back to the start line riding double. The Stones didn't win the race. In fact, I believe Jackson ended up in the dust. But the spectators wildly approved.

Perhaps the lesson taken from the Stone family is that Hollywood marriages that survive don't stay in Hollywood. Cherie Stone, who claims partial credit for her father's second marriage, once told me that her stepmother was Jackson's perfect match. "My dad's like an ornery stud horse," she comments. "He needs to be snubbed down good every once in a while, and Rachel's just the cowgirl to do it. She's not afraid of a grumpy bear or a mean-ass horse, and for sure she's not taking any guff off the worst cowboy who ever worked her ranch."

I think she was pulling my leg, but maybe not.

About the Author

EMILY CARMICHAEL, award-winning author of twenty-one novels and novellas, has won praise for both her historical and contemporary romances. She currently lives in her native state of Arizona with her husband and a houseful of dogs.